CREDO OF A NAZI

"How long have I been in the fucking Army? Nine years! And in all that time I've never been captured—and you know why? Because I'm a damn good soldier, better'n the rest of you could be in a million years . . . I go according to regulations, right? I got a crease in my trousers, just like the book says, right? I got a proper knot in my tie, I got a part in my hair . . . There's not one single thing about me or my uniform that doesn't go along with the rule book. Go on, laugh, but if you don't start right, you'll never make a good soldier. And when I decided to join the Army, I decided to do it proper. And I have, right from the start. And I don't give a damn about what we're supposed to be fighting for, I just do what I'm told—I'd kill my own fucking grandmother if I was ordered to. I'm a soldier because I *like* being a soldier, and what I like doing I like to be good at."

GESTAPO

SVEN HASSEL

A NATIONAL GENERAL COMPANY

GESTAPO

A Bantam Book / published March 1972

2nd printing
3rd printing

Bantam Books are published by Bantam Books, Inc., a National
General company. Its trade-mark, consisting of the words "Bantam
Books" and the portrayal of a bantam, is registered in the United
States Patent Office and in other countries. Marca Registrada.
Bantam Books, Inc., 666 Fifth Avenue, New York, N.Y. 10019.

PRINTED IN THE UNITED STATES OF AMERICA

CONTENTS

	PROLOGUE	1
I	THE INFORMER	5
II	SPECIAL MISSION	35
III	HAMBURG	76
IV	ON GUARD AT THE GESTAPO	99
V	PORTA AND THE SS	141
VI	PREVENTIVE DETENTION	162
VII	PRISON DISCIPLINE	220
VIII	EXECUTION	249
IX	A BIRTHDAY PARTY	287
X	DEPARTURE FOR THE FRONT	301

PROLOGUE

From somewhere behind us came the sounds of men shouting and of a general uproar. Tiny and the Legionnaire had stayed to guard the rear, while the rest of us pressed on. They were lying in wait amongst the thick undergrowth of the copse.

Four Russian soldiers appeared, hurrying through the trees. They wore the green insignia of the NKVD. They were still very young, very keen; still eager to chase and to kill.

They came charging round the bend in the path. The Legionnaire silently turned down a thumb, and Tiny grinned in anticipation. Their submachine guns cracked into the silence almost simultaneously.

Tiny had jumped to his feet and was firing from a standing position, the gun jammed hard against his hip. The whole of his massive frame shook under the recoil.

The Legionnaire, calm and collected as always in moments of action, was gently singing one of his interminable songs of death.

The Russians plunged forward, head first, onto the damp

earth. Only two of them still showed signs of life by the time the bombardment had ceased, and Tiny stepped forward to put the finishing touches to their handiwork. It was a necessary precaution, in these days of war; never mind about not hitting a man when he was down, even the mortally wounded are capable of picking up a gun and firing it.

"Sorry, pal!" Tiny looked down dispassionately at the dead soldiers. "We just can't take any chances, however much we love you!"

"Damn right," muttered the Legionnaire. "They'd put a bullet through our backsides as soon as look at us."

The platoon had been taken by surprise in the midst of a drunken debauch—celebrating Porta's birthday in the only way we knew how. We had been in no fit state to welcome the Russian patrol which had burst so unexpectedly upon us. The first we knew about it was when the windows blew open in our faces and we found ourselves staring into the gaping black mouths of four powerful PMs. Our instinctive reaction was to hurl ourselves to the floor and cover our heads. The Legionnaire and Porta had retained sufficient presence of mind to lob a series of hand grenades through the shattered windows, but how we escaped with our lives I'll never know. We were still reeling and weak-kneed from the shock.

We met up again at the far end of the wood. Eight men were missing.

"I saw two of 'em go down," volunteered Porta.

We wondered briefly what had happened to the others.

When Tiny reappeared, he was dragging with him an unwilling Russian lieutenant. The Old Man said firmly that we should have to take him along as a prisoner.

Shortly before we reached the minefield, we heard the lieutenant give a cry. We heard Tiny laugh, and the Old Man swore violently. Seconds later, Tiny emerged from the bushes—alone.

"Shit tried to get away from me," he explained cheerfully. "He asked for it, didn't he?"

We remained silent. We could see, hanging from Tiny's pocket, the length of steel wire that had come in so useful on so many occasions; whenever a quick, silent death was required . . .

"Did you strangle the poor bastard?" asked the Old Man disbelievingly.

Tiny shrugged. "I told you," he muttered, "he tried to get away . . ."

"In other words, you murdered him," said Stege.

I

THE INFORMER

All of us that remained of the Fifth Company were stretched out on our bellies beneath the apple trees, watching dispassionately as the reserve troops came up. We had been waiting for those troops for the last four days, and by now we were past caring whether they sent them or not. They arrived in trucks, moving slowly up the road in a double column. Their uniforms and their arms were still brand-new, smart and shining and almost unbelievably virginal.

We watched them with jaded eyes. No comments had been passed, and none were necessary; the approaching troops spoke for themselves. It was obvious to us that we could have nothing in common. We were soldiers, while they were only dilettantes. It showed in the careful way they carried their equipment; it showed in their stiff and shining boots. So beautifully polished and so utterly useless! No one could march very far in boots of such uncompromising newness. They had yet to be rubbed with their baptismal urine, which was the best treatment we knew for softening up and at the same time preserving the leather. Take Porta's boots, for an ideal example of a soldier's footwear; so supple that you could see every move-

5

ment of his toes inside them. And if they gave off an almost overpowering stench of urine, that seemed a small
price to pay for comfort.

"You stink like a thousand pisshouses!" Porta was once
told, rather sharply, during the course of a parade.

That was our colonel, sometimes irreverently known as
Wall Eye, on account of the black patch he wore over
one empty socket. It seemed to me significant that in spite
of his testy observation on the subject of urine, he never
put a stop to our habit of pissing on our boots. He'd been
in the Army long enough to know that it's the feet that
make the soldier. Get bad feet and you're worse than useless.

Tiny, still watching the arrival of the reserve force, suddenly nudged the Legionnaire in the ribs. "Where d'you
reckon they dug that lot up from? Jesus Christ, it's enough
to make a cat laugh! The Russkies'll mop 'em up before
they've even found out what they're supposed to be doing
here—" He nodded importantly at the Legionnaire. "If it
weren't for people like you and me, pal, we'd have lost
this war years ago."

The Old Man laughed. He was trying to shelter from
the pouring rain beneath a rather pathetic bush. "High time
they gave you the Knight's Cross—a hero like you!"

Tiny turned and spat. "Knight's Cross! You know where
they can stick that, don't you? Right up their asses—I
wouldn't give you a shit for it!"

There were sounds of cries and curses from the officers
at the front of the approaching column. One of the privates,
a little frail creature who looked older than God, had
lost his tin helmet. It had rolled to the side of the road with
a noise like a hundred tin cans collapsing, and he had instinctively scrambled off the truck and gone toddling after
it.

"Get back into line!" roared an Oberfeldwebel, outraged.
"What the hell do you think you're playing at?"

The old boy hesitated, looking from his precious helmet
to the apoplectic Oberfeldwebel. He scuttled back into the
ranks and marched on, and the Oberfeldwebel nodded grimly and remained where he was, blowing his whistle and
every so often shouting his lungs out, intent on hustling
these raw amateurs on their way to certain death.

As I watched the column advancing, I could see that the
frail old man was already near to breaking point; both

physically and mentally, I guessed. The loss of his tin helmet had probably been the final straw.

Lieutenant Ohlsen, our company commander, was standing to one side chatting to his counterpart, the lieutenant who had led the reserve troops up here. Neither of them had noticed the incident, neither of them had noticed that one of their men was on the point of cracking. And even if they did, what could they do about it? At this stage of the war it was a commonplace occurrence.

The old man suddenly fell to his knees, began crawling down the hill on all fours. His fellow soldiers looked at him nervously.

The Oberfeldwebel came running up, bellowing, "Stand up, that man there! What do you think this is, a goddamn tea party?"

But the poor little guy never moved. Just lay on the ground, sobbing fit to break your heart. He wouldn't have moved if he'd been threatened with a court-martial; he couldn't have. He didn't have the strength left, and he didn't have the will any more, either. The Oberfeldwebel walked up to him, stood over him chewing at his lower lip.

"All right—all right, if that's the way you want to play it, I'll go along with you. You've got to learn a thing or two, I can see that. You think you're exhausted, eh? Well, just you wait till you've got a load of screaming Russkies coming at you, you'll move fast enough!" He suddenly stepped back and rapped out an order. "Pick up that spade and get digging! On the double, if you don't want to get mown down!"

Obediently, the old dodderer groped for his spade, which had fallen from his pack. He began trying to dig. It was comical and pathetic. The rate he was going, it would take him the next thousand years to dig a hole for himself. According to regulations, it should take a man no more than 11½ minutes from the time he got the spade in his hand. And God help anyone who took a second longer! Of course, when you'd been in the front line as long as we had, you learned to do it in even less time—you had to, if you wanted to survive. And we'd had enough practice to put us in the champion class. The holes we'd dug stretched in a practically unbroken line from the Spanish frontier to the summit of Elbroux in the Caucasus. And we'd dug them in every conceivable sort of terrain. Sand, snow, clay, mud, ice—you name it, we'd dug holes in it. Tiny was particularly gifted at it. He could provide himself with a dugout in 6 minutes 15 seconds flat, and he boasted that he could do it even quicker if he really put himself out. He probably could have, only he was never put to the test because no one ever set up a new record for him to aim at.

The Oberfeldwebel stretched out a foot and pushed at his victim. "Come on, grandpa, you're not building sand-castles! At this rate we'll all be dead and buried before you've even scraped away the first layer!"

Grandpa suddenly expired. Just lay down and died, just like that, without even asking permission. The Oberfeld-webel seemed genuinely astonished. It was a good few sec-onds before he turned round and bellowed at the two near-est men to come and pick up the body.

"Call themselves bloody soldiers," he muttered. "God help Germany if this is what's being used to protect her. But just you wait, you innocent bastards! I'll get you licked into shape before you're very much older!"

Oberfeldwebel Huhn, the scourge of Bielefeldt, rubbed his hands together in anticipation. There weren't many men he couldn't lick into shape, once he set his mind to it.

And perhaps, after all, his treatment of the old man had had its effect; certainly none of the others dared to col-lapse.

"Callous bastard," said Porta carelessly; and he stuffed his mouth with a mutton sausage rifled from a dead Russian artilleryman.

We were all eating mutton sausages. They were stale and salty and hard as stone, yet they tasted pretty good for all that. I looked at my half-eaten sausage, and I re-membered the occasion when we had acquired them; only five days ago, and it seemed five months.

It was on our way back through a vast tract of thickly wooded land that we had stumbled upon the Russian field battery. As usual, it was the Legionnaire who first spotted them. We attacked with more speed and stealth than even Fenimore Cooper's Indian braves, cutting them down si-lently with our *kandras*.* By the time we'd finished it looked as if a heavy shell had exploded in their midst. We had come upon them right out of the blue. They had been ly-ing in a clearing, sleeping, sunbathing, relaxing, totally un-prepared for any sort of attack. Their chief had been drawn

---

*Siberian knives with a double-edged blade.

out of his hut by the sounds of the struggle. We heard him calling out to a lieutenant, his second-in-command, just before he appeared.

"Drunken bloody swine! They've been at the vodka again!"

Those were his last words. As he appeared at the entrance of the hut, his head was severed from his shoulders by one well-aimed blow, and two spouts of hot blood burst from his body like geysers. The lieutenant, who was behind him, didn't stop to inquire what was going on. He turned and plunged into the undergrowth, but Heide was on him almost immediately with his *kandra*. The lieutenant fell like a stone.

We were a horrible sight by the time the massacre was over. And the scene of the carnage was like some slaughterhouse nightmare. Several of us threw up as we surveyed it. The spilled blood and the trailing intestines smelled disgusting, and there were thick black knots of flies already settled on every juicy morsel. I don't think any of us really liked the *kandra*—it was too primitive, too messy—but it was an excellent weapon in certain circumstances. The Legionnaire and Barcelona had taught us how to use it.

We sat down on the ammunition boxes and the shells, with our backs to the corpses. We were not so squeamish that we denied ourselves the pleasure of eating Russian sausages and drinking Russian vodka. Only Hugo Stege seemed to have no appetite. We all used to make fun of Stege because he'd had a good education and was reputed to be brainy. Something of an intellectual. And also because no one had ever heard him swear. That in itself seemed abnormal enough, but even more incredible behavior came to light when Tiny discovered that Stege always, and assiduously, washed his hands before eating!

The Old Man was looking at the store of sausages and the crate of vodka. "Might as well take them with us," he decided. "Those poor devils won't be needing them any more."

"They had an easier death than some," remarked the Legionnaire. "They never really knew what hit them." He ran a finger down the razor-sharp edges of his *kandra*. "Nothing brings death as quickly as one of these."

"I find them disgusting," said Stege, and threw up for about the third time.

"Look, they asked for it," argued Porta fiercely. "Lazing about with their thumbs up their asses and their brains in neutral—there's a war on, in case you've forgotten! It could just as easy be us lying down there with our heads hacked off."

"That doesn't make it any better," muttered Stege.

"So what are we supposed to do about it?" Porta turned on him, furious. "You think I enjoy ripping people's guts out? You think I *like* this sort of life? Did anyone ever bother to ask you, when they dragged you into the fucking Army—anybody ever bother to ask you if you wanted to go round killing people?"

Stege shook his head wearily. "Spare us your homespun philosophies," he begged.

"Why?" said the Legionnaire, rolling his cigarette from one side of his mouth to the other. "It may be simple, but that doesn't make it less true—we're here to kill, like it or not. It's the job we've been given and it's the job we're expected to do."

"Besides," added Porta, beating wildly at a buzz of flies that were trying to get up his nose, "I don't remember you being particularly backward when it came to clobbering people. And what about when you took the thing in the first place?" He jerked a thumb at Stege's *kandra*. "What about when you swiped it off that dead Russky? What was the point of taking it if you didn't intend to use it? You didn't want it for cleaning your nails, did you? You took it in case you needed it to stick in somebody, just like the rest of us."

At this point the Old Man dragged himself to his feet and jerked his head impatiently.

"Come on. Time we were moving."

Unwilling and protesting, we nevertheless picked ourselves up and formed a column, single file, behind the Old Man. We moved off through the trees, to be joined shortly afterward by Tiny and Porta who, following their usual practice, had stayed behind to do a bit of looting. From the state of their faces, there seemed to have been some disagreement between them, and it looked as if Porta had been the victor; he was proudly displaying two gold teeth, while Tiny had only one.

As always, the Old Man raved at them without it having the least effect. "One of these days I'm going to shoot the pair of you. It makes me sick! Yanking the teeth out of the mouths of dead men!"

"Don't see why, if they're already dead," retorted Porta

cockily. "You wouldn't leave a gold ring to rot, would you? Or set fire to a bank note? So what's the difference between them and teeth?"

The Old Man simply glowered. He knew, as well as the rest of us, that in every company you always had your "dentists" who went round the corpses with a pair of pincers. There was little, if anything, that could be done about it.

And now, five days later, we were sitting beneath the fruit trees, watching the reserves come up and stuffing ourselves with mutton sausages. The rain was slashing down, and we pulled our slickers higher over our shoulders. These slickers served a variety of purposes, being used, as circumstances demanded, as capes, tents, camouflage, bedding, hammocks, shrouds, or simple sacks for carrying equipment. A slicker was the first item to be handed to us when we went to collect our gear, and was the one we valued above all others.

Porta screwed his head around and squinted up into the wet sky. "Bloody rain," he muttered. "Bloody mountains—worst goddamn sort of country you can get." He screwed his head back again and glanced at his neighbor. "Remember France?" he said longingly. "Jesus, that was something! Just sitting on your ass in the sun, drinking wine till the cows came home—that was something, eh? That was quite something!"

Heide was still staring moodily down at the approaching column of men. He pointed with his mutton sausage toward Huhn, who had tortured the beat old man with the tin helmet. "Going to have trouble with that one," he said sagely. "Feel it in my bones."

"No bastard gives us any trouble and gets away with it!" Tiny blustered. He glared in the direction of Heide's pointing finger. "Let him just try and he'll get what's coming to him. One thing I am good at, it's exterminating rats like him."

"That's all any of us are likely to be good at by the time the war's over," said Stege bitterly. "Killing people—that's all it's taught us."

"At least it's something useful," jeered Tiny. "Even in peacetime there's always a use for professional killers—right?"

He jabbed at the Legionnaire for confirmation. The Legionnaire solemnly nodded. Stege merely turned away in disgust.

The lieutenant who had brought up the reserve troops

now began to assemble them in ranks, preparatory to his own departure. He had delivered them as ordered and was now suddenly anxious to be gone, prompted perhaps by some instinct warning him that it might not be wise to hang around too long. The area was not a healthy one.

With the men ranged before him, he delivered his parting speech. They heard him out with an air of total indifference.

"Well, men, you're at the front now, and pretty soon you'll be called upon to fight against the enemies of the Reich. Remember that this is your chance to win back your good names, to become honorable citizens of the Fatherland and earn the right to live among us once again as free men. If you acquit yourselves well, all marks against you will be expunged from the records. It's entirely up to you." He scraped his throat self-consciously and fixed them with a stern eye. "Comrades, the Führer is a great man!"

There was complete and uncompromising silence following this observation. And then Porta's evil laugh rang out, and I'm pretty sure I caught a muttered "Balls!" The lieutenant swung round in our direction, the blood rushing up his neck and staining his cheeks. He stiffened, and his hand went automatically to his holster. Then he turned back to his own band of villains.

"Let there be no doubt in your minds! All your actions will be noted and recorded!" He paused significantly to let this sink in. "Do not disappoint the Führer! It is up to you to take this opportunity of making amends for the crimes you have committed against Adolf Hitler and against the Reich." He breathed deeply and glanced once more toward the twelve of us sheltering beneath the apple trees. He met the defiant stares of Tiny and Porta, the one looking a complete half-wit, the other with a face as low and cunning as that of a fox. He blenched slightly, but nevertheless pressed on. "You will find yourselves fighting side by side with some of the bravest and best of Germany's sons— and woe be to any one of you who shows himself a coward!"

His voice went droning on. The Old Man nodded appreciatively. "I like that," he said. "The bravest and best of Germany's sons—Tiny and Porta! That's a laugh!"

Tiny sat up indignantly. "What's so funny about it? I'm certainly the bravest and best of *my* mother's sons . . ."

"God help us!" Heide shuddered. "I bet you're the only one!"

"I am now," said Tiny.

"What happened to the others?" Porta challenged him. "They get killed or something?"

"I'll tell you. The first one, dope that he was, went off voluntarily to the Gestapo—*voluntarily*, I ask you! Bloody fool—Stadthausbrücke No. 8," recited Tiny, as if it were engraved forever on his memory. "They wanted him for questioning about something or other—I forget what exactly. Something to do with painting slogans on a wall—he was a great one for painting slogans on walls. Anyway, he went off one fine day and wasn't never seen again. And as for the next one—as for Gert—" He shook his head contemptuously. "You know what he went and done?"

We all wonderingly assured him that we didn't. Tiny made a gesture of disgust. "Only went and volunteered for the fucking Navy. Ended up in a U-boat."

"What happened to him?" I asked.

Tiny spat. Heroes were evidently not in his line. "Went down with the fucking boat, beginning of '40. We had a postcard from Admiral Doenitz about it. Lovely, it was. It said, *'Der Führer dankt Ihnen.'** And it had a lovely black border and all." He suddenly gave a short bark of laughter. "Bet you can't guess how that ended up!"

We could, knowing Tiny, but we didn't want to ruin his story.

"My old lady used it to wipe her ass on. Went to the shithouse one day, discovered she didn't have no paper in there, so she calls out to me to bring her some what's nice and soft. Well, I couldn't see no newspaper or nothing, so I grabbed up the admiral's postcard and shoved that through the door to her. She was calling him all the silly bastards under the sun afterward. Scraped her ass to bits it did. Hard and rough, she said it was. Hard and fucking rough."

We roared our appreciation, with Tiny roaring louder than any of us.

"So now you're the only one left?" I said, when the laughter had died down.

"That's it," agreed Tiny proudly. "Eleven down, one to go. The Gestapo nabbed some of 'em. Three got drowned at sea. The two youngest kids, they was burned alive in an RAF raid. Their own stupid fault, mind you. Refused

---

*The Führer thanks you.

to go into the shelter. Wanted to stay up top and see the fucking planes go by—well, they saw 'em all right!" He nodded owlishly. "So anyway, there's only me and the old lady left now. Some going, eh?" He looked round at the rest of us, studying each in turn. "I bet there ain't many as have sacrificed what we have. Eleven at a blow, and all for Adolf—" He gnawed hungrily at his sausage and took a turn at the vodka bottle. "Screw the lot of 'em!" he let out defiantly. "So long as I get out of it alive, I don't care no more—and something tells me that I'm still going to be here at the end."

"That wouldn't surprise me in the least," murmured the Old Man.

The Legionnaire was crouched over a stew pot, absorbed in stirring the contents. Porta craned over his shoulder and stuffed one or two fairly dry logs into the fire. The thick, globulous mass in the pot heaved itself up in a series of miniature geysers, which exploded and left craters behind them. It smelled rather strong, but that was hardly surprising; we had carted that mess everywhere with us for days past, each of us transporting a share in his canteen.

"It has to ferment," explained Barcelona when some of us began to show signs of rebelling.

It had now, it appeared, duly fermented and was ready for distilling. The Legionnaire fixed a tight lid over the stew pot and Porta set up the distilling apparatus. We sat round in a circle, waiting breathlessly for something to happen.

Our meditations were interrupted by some halfhearted cries of "*Sieg heil!*" coming from the assembled ranks of the reserve troops.

The visiting lieutenant drove away in an amphibious VW, and Lieutenant Ohlsen, losing no time, took the newcomers in hand and delivered one of his special pep talks. When at last they were told to fall out, they did so almost literally, collapsing on the ground, huddling together beneath the trees in wet, miserable groups. They threw down their equipment and some of them even stretched full length on the soaking grass. I noticed they kept a respectful distance from the rest of us. It was plain that we intimidated them in some way.

Oberfeldwebel Huhn made for our group and cut straight through the center of it, his step heavy and confident. As he passed by the stewpot, he caught it with the side of his boot and the whole thing rocked. The Legionnaire managed to set it upright, but not before a few precious drops of liquid had spilled over the side. Huhn glanced down and went on his way without a word of apology. We smelled the newness of his equipment, heard the creaking of his unbroken leather boots as he passed.

The Legionnaire pursed his lips. He gazed thoughtfully after the retreating Huhn for a few seconds, then turned toward Tiny. Not a word passed between them. But the Legionnaire turned down a thumb, and Tiny nodded. With his sausage still in his hand, he heaved himself to his feet and marched purposefully after the Oberfeldwebel. His slicker billowed out behind him, so that he looked rather like a walking barrage balloon. "Hey, you!" he called. "You spilled some of our schnaps!"

At the first cry of "Hey, you!" Huhn had gone on walking—evidently never dreaming that anyone of lower rank could dare to address an Oberfeldwebel as "Hey, you." But at the mention of the word schnaps, he must have realized that it was, indeed, himself that Tiny was accusing. He turned, slowly and incredulously. At the sight of Tiny his jaw sagged and his eyeballs strained at their sockets. "What's got into you?" he roared. "Didn't anyone ever teach you the right way to address your superiors?"

"Sure, sure," said Tiny impatiently. "I know all that crap. But that's not what I wanted to talk to you about."

Huhn's cheeks slowly grew mottled. "Have you gone stark raving mad?" he demanded. "Do you want me to put you under arrest? Because if not, I advise you to watch your goddamn language! And just try to remember, in the future, what it says about it in the HDV."[*]

"I know what it says in the HDV," retorted Tiny imperturbably. "I told you once, that's not what I want to talk about. We can discuss that later if it really interests you. But right now I want to talk about our schnaps you knocked over."

Huhn breathed deeply and carefully, right down to the bottom of his lungs. And then he breathed out again, with a prolonged whistling sound. Doubtless, in all his seven years of Army service, he had never had a parallel experience. We knew that he had just come from the harsh military camp of Heuberg. If anyone there had dared to ad-

---

[*]Heeresdienstvorschrift (Army Service Regulations).

dress him as Tiny had just done, he would have shot him
out of hand. From the way he kept twitching at his holster,
I guessed that he had half a mind to shoot Tiny out of
hand. But it was not so easy to get away with it, with all
those witnesses around. We were all leaning forward, watching.

Tiny stood his ground, the sausage still absurdly clenched
in his huge paw. "You knocked over our schnaps," he repeated obstinately. "The least you could have done was
apologize, I should've thought."

Huhn opened his mouth. It remained open for several
seconds. Then his Adam's apple bobbed up and down a
few times and he closed it again without a word. The
whole scene was quite ludicrous. Even if he hauled Tiny
before a court-martial, they would almost certainly never
believe a word of the indictment. Yet something had to
be done. An Oberfeldwebel couldn't allow a cretinous great
oaf of a Stabsgefreiter to stand there insulting him and
get away with it.

Tiny jabbed his sausage into Huhn's chest. "Look at it
this way," he suggested. "We've been carting that stuff
around with us for days now. It's been everywhere with
us. And not a drop wasted, until you came along with
your big clumsy boots and went bashing into it. And not
so much as a word of apology!" He shook his head. "I
don't know what *you're* complaining about, I'm sure. Seems
to me it's us what ought to be complaining, not you. Here
we are, minding our own business, brewing up our
schnaps . . ."

Huhn brushed the sausage to one side and took a step
toward Tiny, his hand clutching the butt of his automatic.
"All right, that'll do! That's quite enough of that! I'm a patient man, but I've had as much as I can take. What's
your name? You've asked for trouble, and believe me I'm
going to see that you get it!" He pulled out a notebook
and pencil and waited expectantly.

Tiny just raised two fingers in an unmistakable sign.
"Screw you! Your threats don't mean a damn thing out here.
You're at the front now, remember? And we're the boys
that have survived. And you know why we've survived?
Because we know how to look after ourselves, that's why.
And I'm not at all sure that I can say the same for you.
In fact, I got a very funny feeling that you ain't going
to see out this particular spell of duty. You need a very

strong head to survive out here, and I just don't think you got it . . ."

God knows what would have happened next if Lieutenant Ohlsen hadn't intervened and spoiled the fun. It was just getting to the really interesting part, when he walked up to Tiny and jerked his thumb over his shoulder. "Get lost, Creutzfeldt. On the double, if you don't want to end up under arrest."

"Yes, sir!" Tiny gave a quick salute, smacked his heels sharply together and left the scene of combat. He came slowly back to the rest of us. "I'm going to get that bastard one of these days!"

"I told you," said Heide. "I told you we'd have trouble with him."

"Don't you worry." Tiny nodded significantly and closed one eye. "I got his number. It's only a matter of time . . ."

"For God's sake!" burst out the Old Man. "You're going to find yourself in real trouble one of these days if you keep bumping off every NCO you take a dislike to."

Tiny opened his mouth to reply, but before he could do so there was a wild cry of triumph from the Legionnaire. "She blows! Quick, give me the connection! Get a bottle!"

We were at once thrown into hectic activity. I thrust the rubber tube into the Legionnaire's outstretched hand, Porta shoved a bottle next to the stewpot. The apparatus was connected and we watched breathlessly, like children, for the first miraculous signs of distillation. The vapor was already turning into precious drops of liquid.

"She's coming!" yelled Porta.

The excitement was almost unbearable. I felt the saliva collect in my mouth; I suddenly knew a thirst such as I had never known before. Heide ran his tongue round his lips. Tiny swallowed convulsively. Slowly the bottle began to fill.

All night long we maintained our watch. Bottle after bottle was taken away full of home-brewed schnaps. We forgot all desire for sleep. Lieutenant Ohlsen watched us for a while, his expression decidedly skeptical. "You must be nuts," he declared at last. "You're surely never going to try drinking the vile-looking muck?"

"Why not?" demanded Tiny belligerently.

The lieutenant just looked at him and shook his head. Lieutenant Spät also took a fatherly interest in our brewing activities. "Aren't you going to filter it?" he asked anxiously.

"Not worth the trouble," said the Legionnaire.

"But, my God, you drink it in that state and you'll be bowling about the ground in hoops!"

"So long as it's alcoholic," said the Legionnaire calmly. "That's all that matters."

Lieutenant Ohlsen shook his head again and retired with Spät. Clearly they did not give much for our chances.

The following day found us still at peace beneath the apple trees. For the moment, the war seemed to have passed us by. We continued our brewing, except that by now we had outworn our first mad rapture and had split ourselves up into groups to spread the work load.

All day long and well into the evening we tended our schnaps. Shortly after midnight we heard the sound of a vehicle screaming down the mountain road toward us. It came to a halt nearby and an NCO jumped out, covered in mud and in one hell of a sweat. "Where's your commanding officer?" he shouted.

Lieutenant Ohlsen was woken up. He took the message and the man went chasing off again at full speed. We watched with foreboding.

"Son of a bitch," muttered the Legionnaire. "That kills it!" He went off to see how the brewing operation was progressing. "Step it up," he ordered. "If we're quick about it, we'll manage to get another bottle or so before we're moved on."

"We already got thirty-one," announced Porta triumphantly. "I been counting 'em!"

Tiny seemed agitated about something. "What I want to know is, when are we going to get stuck into it?"

"When I say so, and not before." The Legionnaire glared at him. "I find anyone dipping his fingers in before I give the okay and there's going to be trouble!"

Tiny shrugged a sullen shoulder and walked off, muttering to himself. At that moment Lieutenant Ohlsen's whistle blasted shrilly through the darkness. It was a most unwelcome sound.

"Fifth Company, get ready to move! And don't take all night about it!"

Reluctantly we set about dismantling our still. While we were at work, Oberfeldwebel Huhn came busying up to us, shouting as usual at the top of his voice. "Get cracking, you lazy bastards! Get a move on! What's wrong with you? You deaf or something?"

"You'll be deaf in a minute," muttered the Legionnaire threateningly.

Huhn swung round on him, but at that point the Old Man rather surprisingly stepped in. He walked up to Huhn, standing so close to him that their steel helmets were almost touching.

"Oberfeldwebel Huhn," he began calmly, respectfully, but with menacing overtones, "there is something I have to say to you. Something I feel you ought to know. I am in command of this section, these are my men and it's up to me to see that they carry out orders. I don't quite remember what the procedure is back home in the barracks, but I do know what it is at the front—which apparently you have yet to learn. And all I'm saying is, either you keep your nose out of my territory or I shall give my men full permission to go ahead and teach you a thing or two. And they could, believe you me!"

Porta gave a loud bray of laughter. "Might as well talk to a dumb ox for all the good that'll do!"

Huhn took a step toward him, then stopped sharp at a look from the Old Man. He contented himself with a tight-throated "You needn't think you'll get away with this!" flung over his shoulder as he went running off to complain.

We saw him buttonhole Lieutenant Spät, who listened with half an ear for the first few minutes and then walked off leaving him in full flood.

Lieutenant Ohlsen called impatiently from the road. Porta and Tiny picked up the heavy stewpot between them and took their place in the column a short way ahead of the lieutenant, who pretended not to have seen their extra item of equipment.

The new troops came up at a panic-stricken run, disorganized and uncertain. One of them banged into Porta and sprang back, terrified.

"You do that again and you'll get your teeth rammed right down the back of your goddamn throat!"

The man went white, but sensibly kept quiet.

"Goddamn amateurs," growled Tiny.

Lieutenant Ohlsen shouted a command and we came smartly to attention. Section leaders relayed his orders as we did a half-turn to the right.

"Porta, where's your frigging helmet, for Christ's sake?"

The lieutenant pounced on him irritably. "What the hell is that monstrosity you've got on your head?"

Porta reached up a hand to his old yellow hat.

"I haven't got one to wear, sir. The Russkies swiped it."

Lieutenant Ohlsen exchanged a despairing glance with Lieutenant Spät. They always gave up when it came to dealing with Porta.

"All right," said Ohlsen wearily. "Put it back on again—whatever it is! You can't march bareheaded."

"Yes, sir."

The unsightly yellow hat was once more crammed onto Porta's head. The column moved off in the inevitable rain, which was blowing straight at us and stinging our faces. A moment of excitement was caused by a hare suddenly running across our path, almost upsetting the precious stew-pot as Porta, always on the lookout for food, made an involuntarily swipe as the creature shot by.

"What the hell are you doing?" shouted Tiny.

"We could have skinned it and ate it," said Porta regretfully. "We could have put it in the pot along with the booze."

Tiny stared at him. "Who'd want to ruin good booze with a lousy hare?"

"They do in high-class restaurants," said Heide, who always knew everything. "They're regarded as a great delicacy, hare done in wine—jugged, they call it."

"Fuck the hare," Tiny brushed him off. "I'd sooner have a bird—" His demonstrating hand left no doubt as to what kind of bird he had in mind. "I've almost forgotten what they look like, screw me if I haven't. Remember that Russian, him that had it with a goose? Got hard up for a bit of the other so had to make do with a goose. Not sure I couldn't do with a goose myself, come to think of it . . ."

"Crap," said Heide. "You couldn't do anything if it was handed to you on a plate. Not in this weather you couldn't."

"Who are you kidding?" jeered Tiny. "The way I feel right now, I could do it stark naked at the North Pole. What about that time at the Turkish frontier—you forgotten that, have you? Snow was inches deep on the ground . . ."

"That's different. You could do it in snow, but you certainly couldn't do it stark naked at the North Pole," objected Steiner earnestly.

Steiner was a driver who had been sent to us as punishment for selling an army wagon to an Italian in Milan.

He tended to have a very literal mind. "Nobody could do it at that temperature," he insisted. "It'd be a physical impossibility."

"Speak for yourself!" Tiny bristled, insulted. "It's the temperature inside you what counts—just depends how much you want it, right?"

"That's just not true," said Steiner obstinately. "I mean, for a start, you couldn't even get the thing *in*—not in that weather you couldn't."

"Who says?" Tiny swung round on him so violently that the contents of the stewpot slopped over the rim. "You might not be able to, but I bloody well know I could! Why, I can still remember . . ."

"Keep your voices down!" snapped Lieutenant Ohlsen, a few paces behind us. "We're not far from the enemy, we don't have to advertise ourselves."

We turned off the main road and began toiling up toward the mountains. We were walking on grass now; thick, springy stuff that muffled the sound of our footsteps. Somewhere nearby, in the shadows, a cow blew contentedly through its nostrils and we could smell its warm milky smell. All orders were given in a low voice.

"Single file from this point on."

Oberfeldwebel Huhn lit a cigarette. Lieutenant Spät caught the flicker of the match and strode up in a fury. "What the hell do you think you're playing at, for Christ's sake! Put that thing out and get down to the rear of the column and stay there!"

Huhn disappeared without a word.

Suddenly, through the misty gloom, we were able to make out the shape of a building. It was a farmhouse, with a faint light coming from one of its windows. Lieutenant Ohlsen held up a warning hand and we shuffled to a halt. We had had experience with farmhouses before. They sometimes contained innocent farmers and their families, but one could never be sure; they had been known to hide a platoon of enemy troops and a nest of machine guns.

Ohlsen turned and beckoned to us. "Heide—Sven—Barcelona—Porta—" He picked us out one by one and we crept forward. "Go and get the place cleaned up. And watch your step; if the Russkies are there, they'll have set up a guard for sure. Don't shoot unless you have to. Use your *kandras*."

We pulled them out and slipped silently forward through

the shadows. As always on these occasions, my whole body was taut and trembling.

We had covered only a few yards when I became aware that Tiny had joined us. He had a knife clenched between his teeth and his length of steel wire in one hand. He laughed delightedly at our expressions and put his mouth close to Porta's ear. "Any gold teeth going, I claim half of 'em!"

Porta shook his head and said nothing. He was the first of us to reach the objective. Silent and supple as a cat, he hauled himself up to the window ledge and was inside the farmhouse before the rest of us had even arrived. We followed him in and stood shivering in the dark. Somewhere in the house, a door creaked. Heide jumped visibly and pulled out a hand grenade. Barcelona closed his fingers over his wrist. "Don't be a bloody fool!"

Tiny, the knife still between his teeth, flexed his length of wire. Porta turned and spat over his left shoulder; he said it brought him luck.

We waited a moment, listening, and then Tiny suddenly plunged off into the blackness. After a while we heard a faint sound; a faint gurgle, a faint choke. Then silence again.

Tiny returned, with a dead cat in the wire noose. "Poor pussy!" He dangled it before Heide's face, and we breathed again.

"It could have been the Reds," muttered Heide defensively, but he put the hand grenade away again.

Tiny laughed and tossed the dead cat into a corner.

Having disposed of the enemy, we began to make free of the place, opening all the drawers and closets to see what took our fancy. Tiny found a pot of jam. He took it away to a corner, sat down cross-legged on the floor and happily dug into it with his fingers. Porta picked up a bottle, look it at the label in the dim light and came to the conclusion that it was brandy. He took a large swig, then shook his head and held out the bottle to Heide. "Funny sort of brandy," he remarked, plainly puzzled.

Heide sniffed at it, took a cautious mouthful, swilled it round a bit, then spat it out in disgust. He kicked the bottle angrily across the room. "Some brandy! That was more like tetrachloride, you stupid jerk!"

Tiny cackled contentedly. "Ought to stick to jam—know where you are with jam!"

"Fuck off!" said Porta furiously.

Again there was the creak of a door. We froze on the spot. A moment's silence, then Tiny and Barcelona dived behind a couch. The pot of jam rolled across the room and the contents spilled over the carpet. Porta charged across to the door and kicked it open. "Whoever you are, we've got you covered!"

Silence.

I stood nervously fingering the hand grenade that I had pulled out. There certainly had been someone there. We could all feel it, and we crouched like wild beasts waiting to spring. We were in the mood where killing would be partly a necessity, an act of sheer self-preservation, and partly a positive animal pleasure, a release of tension and a source of deep satisfaction.

We listened.

"We ought to call up the company," muttered Barcelona.

"Sooner set fire to the place," suggested Tiny. "Then we could pick 'em off like flies as they come out. Nothing like a nice bit of fire for flushing a place out."

"Use your dimwit head!" snapped Porta. "Light up the whole damn neighborhood for miles around?"

Again there came that creaking, as of a door or floor-boards. Unable to bear the tension any longer, Porta switched on his flashlight and went charging out through the door at the far end of the room. We saw him, with scant regard for the possible consequences, flashing the beam into the shadows. He struck lucky. Pressed against a wall, obviously trying to merge into the darkness, was a young girl. She had a large club gripped in one hand, and she was clearly terrified.

We stared at her disbelievingly. Heide was the first to recover. He turned to Tiny with a suggestive smile. "There's your bird," he said simply.

Tiny walked across to her, chucked her somewhat brutally under the chin and tickled her behind the ear with the tip of his lethal steel wire. "You speak German?"

She stared up at him out of wide-open eyes.

"I'm afraid I had to strangle your cat," said Tiny gracelessly. "But I can always get you another, if you're nice to me . . ."

The girl licked her lips with the tip of her tongue. "I —I not partisan," she stammered. "*Nyet, nyet!* I not Communist bastard. I like very much soldiers germanski—*poni-maite?"*

"Sure we understand," said Porta with a leer. "You not partisan, you not Commie bastard, you love German soldier —so what's the idea of putting tetrabloodychloride in a brandy bottle, eh?"

She shook her head. "*Nyet* understand."

"No one ever does understand when they're being accused of something nasty," sneered Heide.

Tiny gestured toward the girl's club. "What's that great lump of wood for? Bit heavy for you to lug about, ain't it? Here, give it to me. I'll look after it for you." He snatched the club away from the terrified girl, who shrank farther back into the angle of the wall.

"I not beat soldier germanski," she said imploringly. "I beat only Russki—Russki wicked men. Germanski good, good men!"

"More than that, sweetheart, we're bloody angels!"

Heide laughed sarcastically. Barcelona moved closer to the door. "Are you alone?" he asked, in Russian.

The girl looked up at him wonderingly. "Are you an officer?"

"Of course," Barcelona lied with his usual aplomb. "I'm a general."

"Well—" She hesitated a moment, then abruptly seemed to make up her mind. "The others are down in the cellar. There's a trapdoor beneath the carpet."

She waved a hand toward a corner of the room, and rolling back the rug, we discovered that there was indeed a trapdoor sunk into the floor. It was well camouflaged and I doubt if we should ever have noticed it by ourselves.

"Russian soldiers?" asked Barcelona.

"*Nyet, nyet!*" The girl shook her head vehemently. "Only family and friends. Not Communists. All Fascists. Good Fascists."

Heide laughed and rubbed his hands together.

"That'll be the day!"

There were sudden movements in the room next door. We swiveled round, gripping our *kandras*. The girl whimpered and made a sudden dash for the door, but Barce-

---

*Understand.

Iona grabbed her by the arm and dragged her back. "You stay where you are. We like you here with us."

At that moment Lieutenant Ohlsen appeared, followed by the rest of the section. "What's going on?" he demanded. His gaze swept round the room, taking in the empty jam jar, the deceptive bottle of brandy, and the girl. He glared at us. "Have you taken leave of your senses? There's a whole company waiting out there, while you sit on your asses and stuff yourselves with jam and brandy!"

Porta put a finger to his lips. "Not so loud, sir." He nodded toward the trapdoor. "There's a whole battalion of Russian Fascists stashed away down there. And as for the brandy," he kicked disdainfully at the bottle, "that was a lousy trick, if you like. It's full of tetrachloride. Could have poisoned ourselves."

Lieutenant Ohlsen frowned, walked across to the trapdoor and squatted down to examine it. The Legionnaire and the Old Man came into the room after him, both of them preparing Molotov cocktails.

"They're down there?" said Ohlsen. "In the cellars?" He turned to Tiny. "All right, get it open."

"What, me?" Tiny gasped indignantly, and took a step backward. "No, sir! I may look simple, but I'm not that stupid! Anyone opens that up gets a bundle of firecrackers slapped in his face!"

"Oh, for Christ's sake!" snapped the Legionnaire. He joined Ohlsen, bent down and seized the ring that opened the trapdoor. "Okay, here goes! Watch out, you bastards!"

Before he had a chance to pull on the ring, the girl hurled herself at him, screaming and knocking him off balance. "*Nyet, nyet!* Small child in there!"

The Legionnaire thrust her impatiently away. Porta picked her up and pushed her to the far side of the room. "Come off it," he said to the Legionnaire. "You ain't going to kill a kid, are you? I thought the goddamn Frogs were supposed to be gentlemen; not child murderers!"

"Have you finished?" asked the Legionnaire coldly.

"No, I haven't," said Porta. "Not by a long way I haven't. I . . ."

Lieutenant Ohlsen got to his feet, white with anger. "Shut up, you two, we haven't got all day to hang around while you sit down and argue ethics! It's either them or us, and it's my job to make damn sure it's not us!"

Tiny, seating himself on the edge of the table and swinging his legs, began thoughtfully to rub his length of steel wire up and down his thigh. "Sir," he said hopefully, "I ought to report that I strangled a Russian cat just before you came. I could strangle the rest of 'em easy as pie if they'd only come up here and let me . . ."

"I'm not interested in cats, Russian or whatever!" Ohlsen turned and jerked his head at the rest of the section. "Get the trap covered with light machine guns and PMs. The first man out of there with any sort of firearm and he gets what's coming to him. And any monkey business out of any one of 'em and they'll find themselves blown to hell and back." With a quick, determined gesture he whipped open the trap and called down into the cellars, "All right, you can come out of there. One at a time with your hands above your heads. I'll give you five minutes, and then you can expect trouble . . ."

We stood around, waiting. The first to emerge was a little old hag, her sticklike arms held trembling above her skull-like head. After her came five other women. One was carrying a small baby in her arms. A pause, and then the men arrived. There were several of them, most of them young. Heide and Barcelona searched each and every one of them, and Tiny demanded plaintively that he be allowed to search the women, which only provoked a fresh outburst of rage from Lieutenant Ohlsen, whose temper was never at its sweetest when Tiny was around.

"You lay so much as a finger on any one of them and I'll shoot you, you great slob, so help me God I will. Are there any more of 'em down there?"

The Russians all solemnly shook their heads. We stared at them, not sure whether to believe them. Porta jabbed Tiny in the ribs. "Why don't you try your strangling trick on one of 'em? We can at least be sure of getting at the truth that way."

Tiny, of course, was only too happy to oblige. He stepped up to the nearest Russian and adroitly twisted the wire round his neck. He tightened his grip a moment, then relaxed it. Porta smiled.

"All right, tovarich. Now you know what's coming to you if you're telling a whopper, don't you? Have you left anyone else down there or haven't you?"

The man shook his head, eyes bulging and Adam's apple working frenziedly.

"Let him go!" snapped Lieutenant Ohlsen. "How many more times do I have to tell you two that I will not stand for this sort of thing? We're supposed to be soldiers, for God's sake, not Gestapo gangsters!" He turned back to the prisoners. "All right, now let's have the truth out of you. Is there, or is there not, anyone else left in the cellars?"

A row of heads silently replied in the negative.

"Okay. Kalb, toss a couple of Molotovs down there!"

The Legionnaire shrugged a shoulder and prepared to do so. Immediately, one of the women gave a harsh cry. "*Nyet, nyet!*"

The legionnaire cocked an eyebrow at her. "What's the matter, old woman? Any objections to our blowing up an empty cellar?"

Lieutenant Ohlsen bent down to the trap. "All right, we know you're down there—you might just as well come up in one piece as be blown to bits."

Two young men came slowly up the steps. The Legionnaire looked at them and nodded. "Another three seconds," he said grimly. "That's all it needed."

Heide and Barcelona ran their hands over the two men, searching for weapons, and Lieutenant Ohlsen looked sternly at the Russians. "I hope that really is the lot this time."

It was the Legionnaire and I who went down into the cellar. We crouched for a moment behind some barrels, and hearing no sound, we crept forward. We explored the cellar thoroughly. It was a vast place, running the whole width of the house, and there were a dozen places where a man could hide, but we found no one. As we were about to turn back, a sudden noise made us spin round, our fingers twitching neurotically on our triggers.

It was Tiny, beaming all over his large moronic face.

"Only came to see if there was any more broads down here," he explained when the Legionnaire and I had run out of abuse. "Thought I'd help you look for 'em."

"Well, we don't need your fucking help," hissed the Legionnaire. "And in any case you've missed your chance, the place is empty."

Pushing Tiny before us up the steps, we rejoined the others. Porta had uncovered a fresh cache of bottles, and was cautiously tasting the contents of each one in turn. "Vodka?" he asked the Russians. "Nix vodka?"

They stared at him, silent and unsmiling.

"You search the whole place?" asked the lieutenant. "Okay, let's get going."

He went outside with the rest of the section, leaving us

behind with the Russians. I noticed that Heide was staring at the two young men, the last to emerge from the cellar, with narrowed eyes. Barcelona and Porta, too, seemed to be fascinated by them.

"What's up?" I asked.

"That couple there——" Barcelona looked over at them. "They're not babes in arms. They're professionals, or I'll eat my hat."

I looked at them in turn. "Deserters?" I queried.

"Deserters, my ass!" Barcelona spat contemptuously. "I know their type. I've seen too many of 'em before. Only two places you find rats like that: the NKVD or the SS. And people don't desert from either of them."

"So what would they be doing here?"

"That's what I'd like to know."

Tiny bustled up with his steel wire. "Shall I finish 'em off?" he asked with his usual eagerness.

Lieutenant Ohlsen came back at this point. He eyed Tiny sourly. "What's going on here?"

Barcelona turned to Porta. "Try them in Russian," he suggested. "You speak the lingo better than I do."

"Feldwebel Blom!" The lieutenant strode over to us. "Who is in command here? You or me? If there's any interrogating to be done, *I* shall give the orders for it. Until that time, perhaps you'll be good enough to leave these men alone."

"Yes, sir," said Barcelona between his teeth.

Porta shrugged in disgust, picked up his tommy gun and followed us from the room. At the door he turned to look threateningly at the two boys. "You've got away with it this time, pals, but don't try chancing your arm again—at any rate, not when I'm around, see?" They stared at him, unblinking. Porta suddenly laughed. "I'll tell you what," he said. "You can thank your lucky stars we'd got an officer with us. I don't reckon he understands too well what this here war's all about—but we understand, you and me. *Ponimaite,* tovarich?"

Outside we fell into line, single file, behind Lieutenant Ohlsen.

"Where the hell's Tiny got to?" demanded the Old Man as we moved off. "And the Legionnaire? Where the hell are they?"

No one knew. The last time we had seen them, they had still been in the farmhouse. With foreboding, the Old Man made his report to Ohlsen, who swore long and loud in

language totally unbecoming an officer. "For Christ's sake!
Don't you have any control at all over your section, Beier?
Take some men and go back and find them. And don't
take all day about it, we've wasted enough time as it is.
I don't intend to wait for you, so you'll just have to try
and catch up with us."

The Old Man led us back to the farmhouse.

"They'll be down in the cellar, pissed to the eyeballs,"
said Heide bitterly.

"If they've discovered a secret horde of schnaps and
haven't told me about it, they'll damn well pay for it!" Porta
threatened.

Just before we reached the farmhouse we were brought
to a halt by a low, warning whistle. The Legionnaire appeared out of the shadows.

"Where the hell have you been?" snapped the Old Man.
"Where's the other stupid jerk got to?"

"Out hunting," the Legionnaire told him with a grin.
"Our two comrades back there thought they'd pull a fast
one on us, so we've been keeping an eye on them."

"Out hunting?" repeated the Old Man testily. "Hunting
what, goddamnit? If he lays a hand on any of those
women . . ."

He pushed past the Legionnaire toward the farmhouse, but
the Legionnaire hauled him back. "I shouldn't, if I were
you. It's liable to get pretty hot around here in a minute."

The words were scarcely out of his mouth before an object came flying through the air straight at us. Barcelona
acted promptly, caught it as it fell and hurled it right back.

There was the sound of an explosion, then a flash of
light.

"Amateurs," said Barcelona coolly. "Can't even throw a
hand grenade!"

The unmistakable, trumpeting voice of Tiny came to our
ears. From somewhere nearby, in the darkness of the undergrowth, there were the sounds of a violent struggle. Loud
oaths in German and Russian. The noise of snapping twigs,
and of steel clashing against steel. Someone choked and
gurgled. Then silence. We stood waiting.

"That's one dealt with," said Tiny, making a brief appearance before joyously plunging off again.

Next came the sound of running footsteps, and then a
shot.

"What's going on around here?" demanded Heide furiously.

"Better go and take a look—spread out and watch your step," commanded the Old Man.

In the bushes we tripped over a corpse. Porta knelt down to inspect it. "Strangled," he said briefly.

It was one of the two young Russians. By his side we found a pouch of grenades. Enough to wipe out an entire company.

"Meant for us, presumably—just as well you did stay behind," conceded the Old Man. "Though mind you," he added, "that still doesn't in any way excuse your behavior. The lieutenant's hopping mad, and I don't blame him."

The Legionnaire gave a superior smile. "Lieutenants! As if they had all the answers! If I'd relied on lieutenants all my life, I doubt if I'd still be here to tell the tale."

"Anyway," I said to Barcelona, "it looks as if you were right about those kids being NKVD."

"Sure I was right," he said scornfully. "I've been around. I know a thing or two."

"And like he says," added Porta, jerking a thumb at the Legionnaire, "lieutenants don't have all the answers. Not by a goddamn long shot they don't."

We stood in silence a while, straining our ears in the darkness but hearing no further sound from the direction in which Tiny had disappeared, and then the Old Man turned to the Legionnaire with a question which had obviously been troubling him for some time. "How did you find out what they had in mind?"

"Who? The NKVD squirts?" The Legionnaire shrugged. "The girl told us. Just before we left."

The Old Man narrowed his eyes. "She told you?"

"That's what I said—she told us."

"Why? What she do that for? Why'd she want to go and sell out her own countrymen?"

The Legionnaire raised a cold eyebrow in the face of the Old Man's obvious suspicions. "D'you know, I didn't stop to ask her—I can only assume she didn't like the look of them. They weren't all that pretty."

Porta laughed cynically. "More likely you held a gun at her head!"

"Could be," agreed the Legionnaire smoothly. "Only in this case it happened not to be necessary. She volunteered the information."

"She must be nuts," I said. "Any of her buddies find out and she'll have had it."

"That's her problem," said the Legionnaire indifferently.

There was the sound of heavy footsteps and of deep breathing somewhere behind us, and we instantly held our rifles at the ready, peering through the darkness and expecting God knows what to burst upon us—a herd of wild animals or an enemy platoon at the very least—but it was only Tiny.

"Shit got away from me! These fucking fir trees could hide a whole fucking regiment and you'd never be able to find 'em. Anyway, I got his gun off of him. I'm pretty sure I hit him, but he still managed to give me the slip."

The Old Man took the heavy gun from Tiny and weighed it throughtfully in his hand. "A Nagan, eh? Well, that looks like the NKVD if anything does."

"Just like we said right at the start," said Porta in disgust. "If the brass only listened to us a bit more than what it does, this fucking war might be over by now."

The Old Man handed the Nagan back to Tiny and we set off warily through the night to rejoin the rest of the company. Barcelona was carrying on about the girl. She obviously worried him; at that stage, I don't think that any of us were inclined to believe the Legionnaire's story of her having volunteered the information. It sounded altogether unlikely; for my own part I was pretty certain that Tiny had been at her with his lethal steel wire.

"Why didn't you bring her along with you?" demanded Barcelona. "You know damn well what those bastards are likely to do when they find out. You've seen the way they treat people."

"There's no concern of ours," said the Old Man. "We're just here to fight the war, not play nursemaid to traitors."

"I disagree," said Barcelona hotly. "Paid traitors are one thing. People who are forced to be traitors are something else again. You put a gun to someone's head and . . ."

"Lay off it," said the Legionnaire. "For the last time, nobody forced that bitch to talk. She chose to. Of her own free will. That howling brat they had back there—that was hers. And you know who the father was? A captain in the bloody SS! That's the sort of whore *she* was!"

"He probably raped her," said Barcelona.

"I don't give a damn what he did to her," said the Legionnaire coldly. "All I know is that on her own admission she's been busy betraying her own people right, left and bloody center whenever she's had the opportunity. She told us so herself. Seems to think it's her mission in life. And in my book that's treachery, and any traitor can go screw himself for all I care, whichever side he's on."

"She," said Barcelona.

"She, he, or fucking it," said the Legionnaire. "It's all one to me."

"She probably thinks she's in love with the bastard."

"Christ almighty, a second ago you were saying he raped her!"

"Anyway, she was a bitch," said Tiny conclusively, "and I don't give two shits what happens to her. She squealed on her own mother, she told us so. Got her sent off to Siberia, all for stealing a leg of pork. I'd have done her in on the spot, except we had more important things to think about."

It seemed obvious now that the girl had indeed volunteered the information. Tiny would have been the last to conceal another victory for his steel wire, and the Legionnaire would have seen no reason to conceal it if the truth had been dragged from her by force. He was never wantonly vicious, but he could be ruthless when necessary and never made any secret of it. On the whole, then, I was now inclined to believe his story, and to feel little concern for what happened to the girl. Barcelona continued to harp on it purely, I think, as a matter of principle.

"She doesn't stand a chance," he said. "They'll polish her off in no time. You ever seen what they do to traitors in this part of the world? They're only half civilized, these people. They're . . ."

"Spare us the details," said the Old Man. "Do you mind?"

Stege suddenly laughed; bitter and reflective. "'The enemy values treachery yet scorns the traitor.' Schiller was quite right apparently."

"Schiller?" said Porta blankly. "What the hell's he got to do with anything? He's dead, ain't he?"

"Oh, long since," said Stege. "Before you were born . . ."

"You should have seen the way his tongue came out of his mouth," said Tiny boastfully.

We turned to stare at him, digesting this altogether astonishing reference to Schiller. It wasn't, of course; Tiny was merely reliving his latest moment of glory with the steel wire, when he had strangled the NKVD man.

"He had his hands round my neck, but I was too strong

for him. He never said a word. Just choked and gurgled and made odd noises. They do that, when you really put the pressure on. They . . ."

"Jesus Christ!" said Heide. "That's all you seem to live for—sex and strangulation!"

"Each to his own," said Tiny pompously. "We're here to kill, so I do it the way I like best. Let's face it," he said in eminently reasonable tones that forestalled all attempts at argument, "everyone's got their favorite way of doing it."

It was true, I suppose. We each had our own preferred methods. The Legionnaire was a devotee of the knife, while Porta was a crack shot with a rifle. Heide liked playing about with flamethrowers, while I myself was accounted pretty slick with a hand grenade. Tiny just happened to enjoy strangling people . . .

The crows objected most strongly when we came along and disturbed their feast. They had settled in a great black cloud on the corpses, and as Porta fired into their midst they rose up annoyed, circled round our heads in a brief moment of panic and then flew off to the nearest trees, where they set up a harsh chatter of protest. Only one remained behind; it was entangled in a mess of intestines and was unable to free itself. Heide promptly shot it. We dragged the bodies inside and piled them up in heaps. Lieutenant Ohlsen came to look at our handiwork and began swearing at us. He insisted that we lay them out decently, in neat lines, one next to another.

"Some people," observed Heide to Barcelona, "are a bit fussy about these things."

Grumbling, we nevertheless rearranged the bodies as the lieutenant wished. As for the officers who had been murdered in their beds, sprawled over the side in their silk pajamas with their throats cut, we left them to rot where they were. Dark patches of blood stained the floor, and the flies were already thick on the ground. In one room a radio was still turned on. A persuasive voice was crooning, "*Liebling, sollen wir traurig oder glücklich sein?*" ("Darling, shall we be sad or gay?")

We sprinkled gasoline over the entire garrison and retreated. Once outside and at a safe distance, Barcelona and I tossed half a dozen hand grenades through the windows.

From the other side of the hills, we heard the drunken singing of jubilant Russian troops:

Esli zavtra voyna, esli zavtra pokhod,
Esli zavtra sila nagryanet,
Kak odin chelovek vec sovietsky narod
Liubimuyu rodinu vstanet.

(If war comes tomorrow, if tomorrow we march,
If hostile might besets us,
As one [man] the Soviet people will rise
To defend their beloved motherland.)

The Old Man looked in their direction, away across the hills in the misty distance, and then back at the burning garrison with its murdered men.

"Well, there it is," he said. "That's their war, that they seem so happy about."

II

SPECIAL MISSION

We caught up with the rest of the company in a pine-wood. Lieutenant Ohlsen was not, on the whole, exactly pleased with our prolonged absence, and it was some time before he was able to express himself in language that did not bring a blush of modest shame to our cheeks.

During the next few days we had several skirmishes with parties of marauding Russians, and lost perhaps a dozen men in all. By now we were becoming fairly expert in the art of guerrilla warfare.

We had with us six prisoners, a lieutenant and five in-fantrymen. The lieutenant spoke fluent German, and he marched with Lieutenant Ohlsen at the head of the com-pany, all differences temporarily forgotten.

To compensate ourselves for having to drag prisoners along with us, we made two of the infantrymen carry the stewpot containing our fermented alcohol.

It was early in the morning—with the sun shining, by way of a change—when we spotted the chalet, a moun-tain hut with a balcony running round it, two German in-fantrymen standing guard at the entrance. As we approached it, two officers came out and stood waiting for us. One of them, the more senior, was a lieutenant colonel, wearing a ridiculous monocle that kept flashing in the sun. He raised a hand in patronizing salute to Lieutenant Ohlsen, and as we moved up, he looked us over with a condescending stare.

"So you've arrived at last—I expected you some time ago. I don't ask for reinforcements unless I have need of them—and when I do have need of them, I expect them straightaway." His monocle roved up and down our ranks, glinting contemptuously. "Well, your men look to be quite an experienced band—one hopes that one's confidence does not turn out to be misplaced." He removed his monocle, breathed on it, polished it, screwed it back in again and addressed himself to us over Lieutenant Ohlsen's shoulder. "Just for the record, I should like to make it clear from the start that we're rather hot on discipline in this neck of the woods. I don't know what you men have been used to out there, but now that you're here you can start flexing your muscles. Hm!" He nodded, apparently satisfied that he had made some kind of point, and turned back to Ohlsen. "Allow me to introduce myself: Lieutenant Colonel von Vergil. I'm in command here." Lieutenant Ohlsen saluted. "I sent for reinforcements some days ago. I expected you long before this. However, now that you've arrived, I can certainly use you. Over that way, on the edge of the woods. Hill 738. Enemy's been rather busy there lately. You'll find the left flank of my battalion nearby. Make sure you maintain good lines of communication."

"Sir." Lieutenant Ohlsen saluted again, with two fingers to his helmet.

The colonel opened his eye and dropped his monocle. "Do you call that a regulation salute, Lieutenant?"

Ohlsen stood to attention. He clicked his heels together and brought one hand up very smartly.

The colonel nodded grudging approval. "That's better. We don't tolerate slapdash ways here, you know. This is a Prussian infantry battalion. We know what's what, and we maintain the highest standards. So long as you are under my command, I shall expect that you do the same." He placed his hands behind his back and leaned slightly forward, frowning. "What's this foreign scum you've brought along with you?"

"Russian prisoners, sir. One lieutenant and five privates."

"Hang them. We don't keep that sort of trash around here."

There was a moment's pause. I could see Lieutenant Ohlsen swallowing rather hard.

"Did you say—*hang* them, sir?"

"Of course I said hang them! What's the matter with you, man? Are you slow-witted or something?"

The colonel turned on his heel and stalked back into the chalet. Lieutenant Ohlsen followed him with his eyes, his expression grim. We all knew the colonel's type: an Iron Cross maniac, with not a thought in his head beyond that of personal glory and gratification.

The Russian lieutenant raised an eyebrow at Ohlsen. "So what happens?" he murmured. "Do we hang?"

"Not if I can help it!" snapped Ohlsen. "I'd sooner stand by and watch that buffoon strung up!"

A window on the first floor was flung violently open by an NCO, and the buffoon himself looked out.

"By the way, Lieutenant, one word of warning before you take up your positions: when I give an order, I expect it to be carried out immediately. I trust I make myself clear?"

"Son of a bitch," muttered Porta. "That's all we needed. A goddamn Prussian nut . . ."

Lieutenant Ohlsen rounded on him sharply. "Do you mind? There's no need to make the situation worse than it already is."

The colonel's adjutant, a young pink-faced lieutenant, appeared at the door with orders from the colonel that we were to take up our positions immediately—and to do so strictly according to the rule book. Whatever that may have meant. After years of fighting at the front, you pretty well make up your own rule book.

We reached Hill 738 and set about digging ourselves in. The earth was hard, but we'd come across harder, and it was better than endless footslogging across enemy-infested countryside. Tiny and Porta sang as they worked. They seemed exaggeratedly happy.

"They've been at that bloody schnaps," said Heide suspiciously.

Lieutenants Ohlsen and Spät were sitting in a dugout with the Russian officer, talking together in low, urgent voices. Barcelona laughed. "I bet they're giving Ivan the times of the local trains!"

"So what?" demanded Stege fiercely. "Ohlsen's not the type to go round hanging prisoners just because some pathological Prussian tells him to. He'll see they get out all right."

"Jesus Christ!" said Heide incredulously. "He's not going to let the bastards go?"

"What else can he do?" said Barcelona. "If they're still here this time tomorrow, old Batty Bill's likely to string 'em up himself—and the lieutenant along with them."

"Serve him right," decreed Heide self-importantly. "He ought to obey the orders of a superior officer. That's what he's here for. In any case, I don't go along with all this balls of taking prisoners. What's the point of it, unless you want something out of 'em? And when you've got it, shoot the bastards. Prisoners are nothing but a frigging nuisance. You may have noticed," he added, smugly, "that *I* never take any."

"Sounds fine when you're sitting here in your own trenches," allowed Barcelona, "but you can bet your sweet life you'd sing another tune if you were in the hands of the Russians."

"If ever I were," said Heide with dignity, "I should take what was coming to me. And if they kept me prisoner instead of shooting me, I should think they had rocks in their heads. Only thing is, I don't ever aim to *be* in the hands of the Russians."

"Big talk!" jeered Barcelona.

"See here," Heide turned on him angrily. "How long have I been in the fucking Army? Nine years! And in all that time I've never been captured—and you know why? Because I'm a damn good soldier, better'n the rest of you could be in a million years!" He faced them challengingly. "I go according to regulations, right? I got a crease in my trousers, just like the book says, right? I got a proper knot in my tie, I got a part in my hair—" So help me, he even snatched off his helmet to display it! "There's not one single thing about me or my uniform that doesn't go along with the rule book. Go on, laugh, but if you don't start right, you'll never make a good soldier. And when I decided to join the Army, I decided to do it proper. And I have, right from the start. And I don't give a damn about what we're supposed to be fighting for, I just do what I'm told—I'd kill my own fucking grandmother if I was ordered to. I'm a soldier because I *like* being a soldier, and what I like doing I like to be good at."

There was a moment's pause.

"I don't really see what all that has to do with taking prisoners," commented Stege.

"Jesus, how dumb can you get?" demanded Heide in disgust. "And you a student! Listen," he leaned forward, "I never went on to secondary school. Nothing like that, see? But take it from me, I know what I'm doing and I know where I'm going. And one thing I know for sure is, never take prisoners. How do you think I've managed to survive this long? Why is it that I was made an NCO after only five months, while you're still only a buck private after four years? Why is it that hardly any students get to be officers—whereas I'm going to become an officer in record time just as soon as the war's over and I can start training? Why is it . . ."

"Oh, I don't know," said Stege, growing bored. "I daresay you're quite right."

"You're damn right I am! I don't need a kid like you to tell me I'm right." Heide sat back, satisfied. "I'm not letting those Russian bastards get out of here alive, that's for sure."

Stege jerked his head up again. "You touch them and I'll go straight to Lieutenant Ohlsen!"

"Try it! Just try it, and see where it gets you!" jeered Heide. "He can't afford to lay a finger on me!"

Stege looked at him contemptuously. "I can only say thank God *I'm* not a model soldier."

"Oh, shove it!" Heide turned away.

We had just finished digging when the first shell came over. We heard the familiar whistling sound as it went to earth somewhere nearby, then the shrill screams of a man in agony, and one of the new recruits leaped out of his hole and fell sprawling on the ground.

"I've been hit!" he yelled at the top of his voice.

Two of his comrades came out after him. They took him up between them and ran off with him, back behind the lines, away from danger. Barcelona pulled a face as he watched them.

"Don't you worry, bud, they'll get you out of here just as fast as their legs can carry 'em—thousands of miles away, to the farthest hospital they can find . . ."

"Beginner's luck," muttered Heide sourly. "Not a clue about what to do with a machine gun, but give 'em a wounded man to carry and they're off like greased lightning. Didn't take 'em long to learn that, did it?"

At the bottom of a dugout we had installed our stewpot, the lid held tight by a pile of stones so that nothing short of a direct hit could possibly upset our precious liquid.

By now it was almost night. The moon was hidden by a carpet of cloud and the sky was a thick velvety black.

"God, it's so quiet," murmured the Old Man. "If I hadn't been at the game so long, I'd almost feel tempted to go for a stroll up top and see what's happening."

In the distance we heard a dog bark.

"Where the hell *are* the Russians anyway?" demanded Barcelona.

The Old Man pointed toward the pine trees, standing stiff and straight like sentinels. "Out there in their dugouts—wondering why it's so quiet and what the hell we're up to."

"Well, I wish they'd come out and fight," grumbled Heide. "There's nothing like silence for driving you crazy."

A spine-chilling laugh suddenly cut through the night, but it was only Porta, cheating at craps with Tiny a few dugouts away. Somewhere on the other side a machine gun began barking. One of ours replied with a few melancholy salvos. As we watched, over beyond the pine trees, an ocean of flames rolled forward, leaping skyward wave upon wave, each wave preceded by a gigantic explosion. It seemed as if the very mountains were trembling.

"Rocket batteries," observed the Old Man. "So long as they don't come any closer . . ."

Again we heard the guard-dog barking of the machine guns. In the dark night, somewhere to the north, a series of luminous flashes tore open the sky.

In the midst of it all, a messenger arrived from the colonel. He was going at top speed, red in the face and screaming aloud like a madman, "Message for the Fifth Company! Message for the Fifth Company!"

Lieutenant Ohlsen strode up to him in a fury. "Keep your voice down, you lunatic! The whole front's liable to go up in a sheet of flame with you carrying on like that!"

"Yes, sir. Sorry, sir. But it's a very important message, sir. The colonel wants to see you immediately to have your report and give you some new orders."

"For crying out loud . . . !"

The lieutenant turned away, muttering. The messenger stood a moment, bewildered. He had a smooth, scrubbed face, a spotless uniform and an air of curious innocence.

Porta looked him up and down a few times. "Where's your outfit come from?"

"Breslau," was the proud reply. "Forty-Ninth Infantry." And the pink face looked down wonderingly at Porta in his dugout.

Porta gave one of his satanic laughs. "You're another of the medal boys, eh? Well, run off and get your Iron Cross, you're welcome to it—you'll find it lying in a pile of shit somewhere!"

Startled—as well he might be, not knowing Porta—the messenger turned and ran back to the colonel.

The mountains trembled again, as if shaken by some deep internal agony. Streaks of red and blue fire shot across the sky. The countryside for miles around seemed bathed in a sea of perpetual fire, and we screwed up our eyes against the glare and cowered deep into our dugouts. For the moment it was the Russians who were bearing the brunt of it, but we ourselves weren't exactly in clover.

"Jesus Christ!" whined Heide, wiping the back of a trembling hand across his forehead. "I don't know what those frigging Do batteries do to the Russians, but they sure put the shits up me all right. Half the time the silly bastards don't seem to know which way they're aiming the pissing things . . ."

"Watch out!" yelled Steiner. "The Russkies are joining in!"

Almost before he had finished speaking, the ground began to heave and shake as the heavy Russian guns joined in the bombardment. We curled up in our holes, nose to tail like dogs left out on a winter's night, our hands clasped protectively over our helmets. Through half-open eyes I saw the wall of fire rise up behind us as the 12-cm. shells landed from the Russian lines and the hot blast of air washed over me.

Then suddenly—so suddenly that I knew a sense of shock —there came a lull. The barrage stopped and not a sound could be heard.

Those of us who had been through it all before stayed crouched in our holes, but several of the newcomers incautiously raised their heads to see what was going on. Lieutenant Spät shouted from his dugout, "Keep your heads down, you damn fools!"

It was too late for some of them, for as suddenly as the silence had fallen, a new series of explosions rained down on us. Disconcertingly closer than the previous lot—right outside our front door, as it were.

"Third time lucky," I heard Barcelona mutter. "It'll be smack on next time."

I felt he was probably right. They couldn't go on missing us for ever. The luck was bound to change.

"They've got a sniper up in those pine trees somewhere," said Steiner.

During a second lull, he risked sticking his head out a few inches and yelling to Porta, "Hey, Porta! Pick that bastard off, can't you, and then perhaps we'll get a bit of peace."

"I'll have a go," said Porta. "Anything for a quiet life— if only I can spot the jerk."

He crawled out of his hole and wriggled forward, lying full length on the ground and scanning the pine forest with the infrared sights on his rifle.

"I could have a go at him," said Tiny, pulling his length of steel wire from his pocket and starting out of his dugout. "I could reach him, I bet. Just let me get this round his neck and we'll . . ."

"Get back!" hissed Lieutenant Spät.

Just in time. As Tiny dropped back into his hole, a new salvo was fired. It landed among the trenches, and from farther along the line we heard the usual cacophony of shrieks and screams coming from hideously injured men.

"That's it," said Barcelona. "Some poor bastards have copped a packet—maybe now they'll leave us alone for a bit."

"Sure, until we start up again with that stinking Do!" said Heide bitterly.

The Legionnaire had wriggled out to join Porta. With his sharp eyes he had spotted a movement among the pine trees, and he reached across and jabbed Porta in the ribs. "There he is—just on his way down—do you see him? To the right of that bloody great tree over there. Look sharp or you'll miss him!"

Porta settled his rifle into his shoulder and glared despairingly through the sights. "Where, for Christ's sake? I can't see him . . ."

"Look—you got that big tree over there? Head and shoulders above all the other trees? Three fingers away to the right . . ."

"Got him!" Porta jubilantly stuck up a thumb. "Yeah, I

can see the bastard all right now—just working his way down—not suspecting a thing—the poor creep's got the Order of Stalin pinned on his chest! Would you believe that? The Order of frigging Stalin . . ."

"Goddamn it, stop babbling and get on with the job!" hissed the Legionnaire between his teeth.

"All right, all right, don't panic," said Porta equably. "Plenty of time yet. Just one step more . . ."

As he spoke, he curled his finger round the trigger. There was one short, sharp crack and the unsuspecting sniper crashed down into the forest with half his head blown away. The Legionnaire nodded. "Good. Let's have your book and I'll mark it up."

Porta handed over one of the little yellow notebooks that were carried by all the crack shots in the Army for the purpose of recording their scores. The Legionnaire marked up Porta's latest success and flipped back through the preceding pages. "Not bad," he commented.

"I've got just as many with my steel wire," said Tiny jealously. "And that takes a helluva sight more guts, let me tell you. No sitting about on your ass with your eye glued to field glasses—you got to be right out there in the thick of it, right up close—" He nodded aggressively at the Legionnaire, and then, struck by a sudden thought, turned back to Porta. "Hey, what about his teeth?"

"Never saw 'em," said Porta regretfully. "The bastard never smiled. Why don't we go take a look at him? Fifty-fifty?"

Tiny needed no second invitation. They went crawling off into the pinewoods, risking their necks for the chance of some gold fillings.

Lieutenant Ohlsen was also taking the opportunity to stretch his legs.

"Take over for a bit, will you?" he said to Spät. "I'd better go and see what that old woman of a colonel wants. Shan't be away long."

He set off at a run away from the trenches, making for the comparative safety of the wooded area where the colonel had his headquarters. A machine gun began spitting out a steady stream of luminous projectiles, but the gunner was obviously no expert and they fell short, landing harmlessly some way off.

That was all for the time being. The rest wasn't to filter

through to us in bits and pieces until later—well after
Lieutenant Ohlsen's return.

It appears that when he arrived panting at the chalet,
the colonel showed some reluctance to be disturbed, but
eventually condescended to hear Ohlsen's report, which he
himself had been demanding as a matter of urgency only
a short time since. The seven officers with him listened with
an equal lack of interest.

They were seated around a table, laid with a thick
cloth and supporting a rich spread of food and wine. Ohlsen, thinking that he must be in some kind of wonderland,
took in all the details as he talked: cut glass vases full
of flowers; a shining crystal chandelier; blue porcelain crockery; batmen in white coats hovering respectfully at every
elbow. For a moment his voice faltered; it seemed hardly
possible that vicious slaughter and luxurious dinner party
could be taking place simultaneously, only yards away from
each other.

As he faltered, Colonel von Vergil adjusted his monocle
and took stock of this insolent lieutenant who had come hot-
foot from the fighting to interrupt his meal. He looked first
at the thick crust of mud on his boots, then let his gaze move
slowly up the filthy black uniform, creased and torn, and
stiff with the accumulated dirt of several months' hard wear
in the front line. The death's head insignia of the Hussars,
yellowing and rusted, grinned mockingly at him, proclaim-
ing without shame that it was a long, long time since it had
been polished to the looking-glass shine laid down in regulations. The soiled red ribbon of the Iron Cross ended not
in a medal but in a tattered fringe. The Iron Cross itself
had been lost some time back when the lieutenant's tank
had gone up in flames. The left sleeve of his greatcoat was
hanging by a few threads. The leather flap on his holster
had been wrenched off. In place of an officer's belt, he
was wearing one that rightly belonged to a private. His right
hand was black with congealed blood.

The colonel let fall his monocle and turned away in
distaste. Just as he had always suspected—these officers one
found at the front had no sense of style, of rank; not the
sort of people one would care to know socially—obviously,
or they would not have been at the front in the first place.
The colonel himself was there only through the grossest of
mistakes and the most ludicrous bungling by some cretin
in the Bendlerstrasse.

His regiment, the 49th Infantry, was both rich and aristocratic, and until now it had seen no frontline action except for the occupation of Denmark and two days in France before the armistice. Life was easy, and life was opulent.

And then came the fatal day when the blundering idiot in the Bendlerstrasse had chosen to promote the regiment's commanding officer, Colonel von der Graz, to the rank of brigade general, and had sent him off with an infantry division to the Balkans. That was only the start of it. The full tragedy of the situation had not at once come home to the bereaved 49th, then happily installed at Breslau. For some time they had lived in the belief and hope that the colonel's successor would be chosen from among their own elite. They had two lieutenant colonels who were due for promotion to full colonel, and the more venerable of these, whose connections were unimpeachable, had even gone so far as to announce in advance the changes he intended to make when he was in charge of the regiment.

The dream had been shattered one unforgettable Friday morning, at twenty minutes to nine—a time and date that were imprinted on the memory of every officer in the regiment, for at twenty minutes to nine their new colonel had arrived to take over. A colonel whom nobody knew and nobody wanted. He had come straight from active service in Demjamsk. There was none of the dilettante about him; he was tall and craggy, and tough and outspoken, and he wore a patch over one eye.

Throughout that fateful Friday he roamed about the barracks with a black frown of displeasure gathered on his lined forehead, and his nose to the ground like a dog on the scent of trouble. One of the orderly room officers, seeking to ingratiate himself, struck on the bright idea of introducing the new colonel to the regiment's wine cellar, which was famed for miles around, and which was stocked with sufficient delights to gladden the heart of any connoisseur. Perhaps the colonel was not a connoisseur. At any rate, he merely picked up one or two of the dusty bottles, read the labels, raised a cold eyebrow at the officer and marched out without a word. It was that eyebrow, together with the total lack of comment, which really rattled the officer. An hour later he packed his bags and departed, anticipating what he felt to be a certainty.

It was late in the day before the colonel ceased his wanderings and seated himself in his predecessor's chair, behind the large acajou desk. The majority of the officers were already in the casino, bravely attempting to carry on as usual, but the champagne tasted somehow different and the charms of gambling seemed suddenly to have vanished. The storm clouds were gathering about their heads, and they felt menace in the air.

And then the blow fell: the colonel called his officers back to barracks. Most of them, in fact, had gone off for the weekend on a forty-eight-hour pass extending from Thursday evening to anytime on Monday. It was, perhaps, stretching things a bit, but it had long since been accepted as normal procedure in the 49th.

Having recalled as many of his officers as could be found, the colonel then demanded to be told the exact total strength of the regiment. This should have been kept daily up to date by reports from company commanders, but through some oversight—ascribed by the officers concerned to slackness on the part of the Hauptfeldwebels— it was many weeks since anyone had taken the trouble.

The adjutant languidly called the various companies to see what the position was. His interest in the result was purely academic; he had an uncle who was a high-ranking staff officer in that part of the Army which still remained on German soil, and as far as he was concerned, the new colonel was no more of a nuisance than the buzz of a bee. Noisy, perhaps, but easily brushed aside.

With a slight smile on his lips, he reported back to the colonel. "I regret to say, sir, that the exact strength of the regiment cannot at this moment be ascertained; the Hauptfeldwebels are all on forty-eight-hour leave."

The colonel ran a thoughtful finger beneath the rim of his black eye patch. "Where is the ordnance officer?" he asked.

The youngest lieutenant in the regiment came up at a gallop. He saluted breathlessly. "Lieutenant Hanns, Baron von Krupp, Ordnance Officer, sir."

The colonel looked at him a moment, then nodded slowly; the way he nodded was rather sad and rather contemptuous.

"So that exists here, too, does it?" He grunted. "Well, Baron von Krupp, perhaps you wouldn't mind checking that at least we have a guard mounted—or are all the sentries also on leave?"

Lieutenant Hanns saluted again and turned to go, but as

he opened the door, the colonel called him back and dropped another bombshell. "I want an accurate figure for the number of men at present in barracks—and I'll give you quarter of an hour to get it."

The adjutant smiled again in his superior manner. He was pretty sure that the figure would prove to be only thirty percent of that laid down by regulations. It was many months since anyone had troubled about such trifling matters. Breslau, after all, was not Berlin; no one ever came to Breslau.

Left with his officers, the new colonel commented—politely enough, but not concealing his astonishment—on the fact that not one of them had a decoration from the front.

"Oh, no, sir!" said Captain Dose, rather shocked. "We've never been sent to the *front,* sir."

"Have you not, indeed?" The colonel slowly smiled, a smile which chilled the hearts of his assembled officers. "Well, rest assured that that shall be remedied. You shall have your chance the same as everyone else. The war is not yet over. Before the night is out, I shall expect to receive from each one of you a request for transfer to active duty at the front." He turned to the adjutant, who was still smiling suavely. "I want you to send telegrams to every man on a forty-eight-hour pass. All leave is canceled forthwith. They are to report back to barracks immediately. And you can sign it in my name. I imagine you know where these men can be found?"

The adjutant just perceptibly hunched a shoulder. In point of fact he had no idea where any of them might be. The best he could do would be to send out men in search of them, which meant combing every bar and brothel in the town—a long and distinctly speculative operation. He looked across at Captain Dose and decided to indulge in some buck-passing. Dose was known to be something of a fool.

"I think that's your pigeon?" he said pleasantly, and picking up a sheaf of telegram forms, he thrust them at the astonished captain. "Here. Send one to every man on leave. I assume you have their names and addresses?"

Too stunned to speak, Dose staggered from the room. He spent the rest of the night alternately looking up nonexistent or out-of-date addresses in an address book and praying feverishly for a passing airplane to drop a bomb on top of the colonel's quarters.

Despite all his efforts, he succeeded in rounding up only nine of the 1,800 men who had left the barracks.

On Monday, the remaining 1,791 rolled up as was their habit, at whatever time of the day took their fancy, looking forward to a few hours of peace and quiet in which to recover from the weekend debauches. And for each man, a shock was in store: the entire barracks had been changed overnight from a free and easy and relatively luxury hotel to a disciplined military establishment. On every officer's desk was a terse note to the effect that the colonel wished to see him straightaway.

The youngest and least experienced dropped everything and ran. The more prudent put in a few telephone calls to feel out the lay of the land, whereupon several of them at once fell gravely ill and were taken away by ambulance.

Among the former was Captain (Baron) von Vergil. Three hours after reporting back to barracks he found himself with orders to proceed to the Russian front. Promoted, it is true, to the rank of lieutenant colonel, but that was small compensation when he considered the probable horrors of frontline warfare. Not the danger so much, but the discomfort. He thought of lice and mud and stinking bodies and rotting feet, and it was almost too much for a civilized man to bear. He could have cried then and there, had there been anyone likely to sympathize with him.

Eight days after the arrival of Colonel Bahnwitz, the 49th Infantry Regiment had disappeared, along with its famous wine cellar. Each officer had carried away his share of the booty. No one had left with less than two truckloads of wine, and the Baron had taken three.

And now here he was on the Eastern front, experiencing the harsh facts of warfare. In what must almost certainly have been record time, he had succeeded in getting himself and his men hemmed in by the Russians. He had at once sent out hysterical appeals for help, and had been soothed and reassured; help was on its way. And now help had arrived, and what help it was! A tank company without a tank to its name; a band of ruffians and scoundrels wearing filthy rags and stinking to high heaven. It was little better than an insult. Colonel von Vergil, after all, could not be expected to know that this band of ruffians, led by two tough and experienced officers, was a gift from the gods and probably his one chance of getting out alive. This one company, in fact, was worth an entire regiment of sweetly smelling, freshly laundered troops from a barracks at Breslau.

Colonel von Vergil sipped his wine and stared over his glass at the white ribbon attached to Lieutenant Ohlsen's left sleeve. On the ribbon were the words "Disciplinary Regiment," ringed with two mutilated death's heads. The colonel twitched his nostrils; the lieutenant smelled of blood and sweat and looked as if he had not seen a bar of soap since the start of the war. The colonel put down his wine and took out a cigarette to drown the stench of unwashed body.

"Thank you for your report, Lieutenant."

He paused a moment, lit the cigarette with a gold lighter and leaned back in his chair.

"You are aware, of course, that according to regulations, each soldier—" and here he leaned rather heavily and deliberately on the word, "each soldier is obliged to clean his equipment and see to his uniform immediately after combat. In this way, it will not deteriorate and should remain in much the same condition—allowing, naturally, for normal wear and tear—as when it was first issued. Now, Lieutenant, I think you'll agree with me that one quick glance at your uniform is all that is required to convince anyone but a blind man that you have been almost criminally negligent in this respect. I am not at all sure that it could not even be classed as active sabotage. However—" He smiled and blew out a cloud of smoke, "in your case, I am prepared for the moment to be lenient; to take the view that it is more a question of fear and of personal cowardice that has led to this negligence on your part rather than any deliberate attempt at sabotage. When a man's nerve is gone, so I am told, he may well act in curious ways."

Lieutenant Ohlsen's face grew slowly scarlet—with rage, not shame. His fists clenched at his sides and his eyes glittered with a moment of fury. But he was too experienced a soldier not to have learned self-control. One word from this clown Vergil and Lieutenant Ohlsen could well find himself a dead man, and while dying for one's country might still have a certain glory clinging to it, dying for a fool like Vergil was just plain lunacy.

"I'm sorry about my uniform, sir." The lieutenant spoke stiffly, through half-closed lips. "The company was sent out on a special mission three and a half months ago. We've been in continuous action ever since. Only twelve men survived from the original company so I think you'll appreciate, sir, that in the circumstances none of us has so far had much of a chance to sit down and polish our equipment or mend our uniforms."

The colonel took another sip of wine and patted his lips with his white starched napkin.

"Excuses are totally irrelevant, Lieutenant. Furthermore, I would remind you that when being interrogated you do not speak unless a question is put to you. I did not put a question to you. Should you wish to make any sort of observation, you should request permission to speak in the usual way."

"Very well, sir. In that case I wish to request permission to speak."

"Certainly not!" snapped the colonel. "Nothing you say can possibly alter the facts. Get back to your company and never let me see either you or your men in that deplorable state again." He paused, looking across at Ohlsen with a triumphant gleam in his eye. "I shall give you until ten A.M. tomorrow, Lieutenant, by which time I shall expect the matter to have been attended to. I shall come round personally to inspect you at that hour. And, incidentally, that reminds me of another matter that should have had your attention by now. Those Russian prisoners you had with you—have you got rid of them yet?"

Lieutenant Ohlsen swallowed hard. He looked the colonel straight in the eye. "Not yet, sir. No."

The colonel raised an eyebrow. He sat for a moment, tapping the ash from his cigarette and gravely staring into the ashtray.

"Sabotage," he said at last, in a low, intense voice. "Sabotage and insubordination. But after all, we are human, Lieutenant; we give you once more the benefit of the doubt. Possibly we did not make ourselves sufficiently clear in the first instance. Ten o'clock tomorrow morning, Lieutenant. That is an order. I shall expect the prisoners to have been hanged by then. I look forward to receiving your report in confirmation."

Lieutenant Ohlsen licked his lips. "Excuse me, sir, but— I can't just hang them—not just like that, in cold blood. They're prisoners of war . . ."

"Is that so?" The colonel seemed amused. "Whatever they are, Lieutenant, I believe that your first duty is to carry out the orders of your superior officers—not to question either the validity or the wisdom of those orders. I trust, for your own sake, that all is as it should be to-morrow morning." He waved his napkin as a sign of dis-missal, turned back to the dinner table and picked up his glass. "Your health, gentlemen."

The seven elegant officers raised their glasses. Lieutenant Ohlsen turned abruptly and left the room. As he made his way back to the company through the dangerous dark-ness, he prayed aloud to the Russians to drop a few shells in a few selected places.

"Just a few—just a few very little ones—just enough to blow that load of pie-faced nincompoops sky-high off their great fat asses—dear Ivan, that's all I ask!"

But the night remained dark and the silence unbroken. Ivan was evidently not listening to his prayers.

Lieutenant Ohlsen regained the Fifth Company and jumped down into the trenches, where he sat a moment with clenched fists, trembling with rage against the colonel.

"What's up?" asked Spät, looking sagely at his brother officer as he ground out the butt of a cigarette.

"That fucking man—that fucking man!"

For a moment it seemed that this was all he could say. He spat it out viciously while we watched him sympathet-ically and at the same time waited hopefully for more. And at last it came, in language that we could understand and appreciate. The invective rolled out of him in a fine unbroken flow of obscenity, and the Old Man shook his head and regarded the lieutenant with an air of grave paternal anxiety. "What's he done now?" he asked, when at last he could get a word in.

Lieutenant Ohlsen looked at him wildly. "I'll tell you what he's done! He's arranged an inspection for ten o'clock to-morrow morning! Make sure we're all neat and clean and polished in accordance with regulations! Take time off to polish our rifles and sew on our buttons!"

"Do what?" said Porta, startled.

The lieutenant turned on him. "You heard!" he snapped irritably.

Porta gave a great cackle of delighted laughter. He turned and shouted into the darkness, "Hey, Tiny! You catch that? We got to change our ways, you and me. Got to wash our faces and brush our uniforms. Got to get our holes swept out by ten o'clock tomorrow morning, make sure we're liv-

ing nice and clean and tidy like, without no crumbs on the
floor!"

The answer came roaring back down the trench. "What
holes you on about? Assholes?"

Our laughter must have been heard for miles around.

"For Christ's sake," implored Lieutenant Ohlsen, who had
had a trying enough time already, poor man, "don't make
so much bloody noise."

"Sh!" hissed Porta, laying a great grimy finger on his lips.
"We'll wake the Russkies up!"

"Yes, and that won't be as damn funny as it sounds!"
snarled Ohlsen.

We subsided into silence. The tops of the mountains
were lost in swirling cloud, and the moon had disappeared
behind a thick blanket. The night was black but peaceful.

Lieutenant Ohlsen settled down in the trench between
Spät and the Old Man and beckoned them to come closer.
He began speaking in low, urgent tones.

"Look, I'm in a bit of a jam," he said frankly. "If you've
any suggestions, I shall be only too glad to hear them.
That stupid cunt of a colonel up there insists that we dispose of our prisoners by ten o'clock tomorrow morning.
He's coming round for a personal inspection to make sure
the job's been done properly—so what I want to know is,
what the hell are we going to do about it? How do we
arrange it so that they keep their heads on their shoulders
and that jackass is satisfied we've done the job?"

There was a silence, while Spät frowned into the darkness and the Old Man pulled deeply on his pipe.

"That's a pretty tall order," he said at length. "Means
hiding the six prisoners and finding six dead bodies to
show the colonel—not so easy."

"Suppose," suggested Spät, "we just closed our eyes and
let them escape?"

"You heard what Boris said," objected Ohlsen. "They'd
be shot the minute they got back to their own lines."

"What—just for having been taken prisoner?" Spät shook
his head. "He must be exaggerating. I find that very difficult to believe."

"Well, all right, let's ask him. See if he's got any ideas.
Damn it all, it's his head I'm trying to save."

Spät sent off for the prisoner, and a few moments later
the young Russian lieutenant jumped down into the trench.
Ohlsen briefly explained the position to him.

"So that's how things stand," he ended up. "And, frankly, there's not a damn thing I can do about it unless you've got any bright ideas."

The Russian smiled rather grimly and shook his head.

"I only wish I had. Unfortunately, they're no more civilized on our side of the line than yours. We've only got to show our faces back there and we'd be shot immediately as traitors." He caught the skeptical expression on Spät's face and nodded sadly at him. "Oh, yes. It's quite true, my friend, I can assure you of that. A soldier in the Red Army is supposed to die for his country sooner than let himself be taken prisoner—words of Uncle Joe!"

"How about the partisans on our side of the line?" the Old Man wanted to know. "Couldn't they be any help?"

"It is a possibility," allowed the Russian, but he didn't sound too enthusiastic. "Only trouble is, each group of partisans is in direct communication with headquarters, and while a local group might not see any discrepancy in our story, you can bet your sweet life that the boys at HQ would know damn well that our detachment is nowhere near this section of the front. Obviously we can't tell them we're escaped prisoners, they wouldn't take at all kindly to it. All we could hope to do is string them a line about having been cut off during an attack and say we've been in hiding ever since and, frankly, I doubt if they'd swallow it. Probably wouldn't even bother to hear us out. Shoot first and see who you've shot afterward, that's their motto —and believe you me, they stick to it. I've never known such a trigger-happy mob."

Lieutenant Spät lit a cigarette, crouching over it and shielding the glow with a cupped hand.

"If the worst comes to the worst," he suggested, "I suppose we could always organize a sort of perpetual hide and seek—get hold of some German uniforms for you and push you in among the men. Sooner or later you'd presumably get your chance to push off somewhere . . ."

"If we hadn't already been shot as spies first!" retorted the Russian. "My men can't speak German, remember? I know you're doing your best to be helpful, and don't for God's sake think I'm not grateful, but, frankly, I don't fancy the idea of dressing up in enemy uniform and sitting back to wait for the ax to fall."

Spät shrugged his shoulders. "I can't say I blame you." There was a long, troubled silence, broken eventually by Lieutenant Ohlsen. "We don't seem to be getting anywhere, do we?" He turned to the Russian. "Have you no ideas at all?"

"Not so much as a single germ," confessed the prisoner with a faint, fatalistic smile. "And considering you're putting your own lives in danger, I'm only surprised that you're bothering your heads over us—it's really only a question, when it comes down to it, of which side hangs us, yours or ours."

"Why don't we try asking Porta?" said the Old Man suddenly.

Lieutenant Ohlsen looked at him a moment, then laughed.

"Three officers and a Feldwebel and we can't produce a single sound idea among us! We have to turn round and ask a semiliterate rogue of an Obergefreiter!"

Spät smiled, and the Old Man hunched a shoulder.

"It's a totally ludicrous suggestion, and well you know it—but it's certainly far and away the best we've had yet," conceded Ohlsen with a grin. "Call the loudmouth over here and let's see what he's got to say. Knowing Porta, it wouldn't surprise me in the slightest if he came up with something."

Porta wriggled into the trench on his stomach, heaved himself into a comfortable position and leered round at the assembled company.

"What's up now?" he demanded cheerfully. "Dirty work at the crossroads, I bet, or you wouldn't want me here!" Spät offered him a cigarette, and he clawed one out of the packet and stuck it behind his ear. "Thanks. Don't mind if I do. Never refuse a smoke, that's the only motto worth having around this dump."

He glanced expectantly at Lieutenant Ohlsen, who came straight to the point. "Porta, we need your help. We've got to do something to keep our prisoners' heads on their shoulders, and we've got to do it quick. Any bright ideas?"

"Ah, now you're asking," said Porta maddeningly. "The fellas have all been discussing it, ever since you come back from seeing the colonel!"

"How did they know about it?" demanded Lieutenant Ohlsen indignantly.

Porta laid a finger along the side of his nose. "We got our ways."

"And what conclusions have you come to?"

"Well, Heide, for a start; he don't want nothing to do

with any of it. Letting 'em go, I mean. He swears blind
that you let 'em go and he'll shoot the lot of 'em as they're
crossing the line. Could be that's probably the best idea. Save
you a lot of trouble, that's for sure."

The Old Man took his pipe from his mouth and clicked
his tongue impatiently. "Come on, Porta, wake up! You can
do better than that, don't let me down. If that was the way
the lieutenant felt about it, he'd go ahead and shoot the
prisoners himself. We're trying to find a way of saving
them, not of murdering them—and we haven't got all night
to do it in either!"

"Okay, okay, take it easy and have a bit of patience—
as the spinster remarked when she tried it out on herself
with an overripe banana."

"Christ almighty!" said Spät, swallowing a burst of laughter
and half choking himself as a result.

"Never mind the jokes, people's lives are at stake!" snapped
the Old Man.

"I get you!" said Porta scornfully.

Lieutenant Ohlsen reached across and tapped him on the
shoulder. "Porta, please—I've told you, we desperately need
your help. I know you're resourceful, so if you've any useful ideas, don't hesitate to trot them out."

Porta looked at him reflectively. "Well, I did have a sort
of idea—dunno whether you'll go for it though."

"Let's hear it."

"It's kind of complicated to explain, but what I thought
was, if we could get hold of six bodies—well, we've got
three already, we picked off some of their snipers, and we
can easy get another three from somewhere, that's no problem . . ."

"So?"

"So then, well—me and Tiny and one of the fellas, the
Legionnaire perhaps, we go up and take a few potshots
at the enemy, see? Make sure they're all bedded down for
the night, then a few quick bursts of the old machine gun
fire up and down the trenches—" Porta demonstrated, spraying the three officers with imaginary bullets. "They'll soon
get the wind up. Make 'em think a whole bloody battalion's about to burst in on 'em. Soon as we've woken 'em
up, we get the hell out and head back home again. Like this
—see?"

With the point of his bayonet, Porta sketched out the
proposed movements. The Old Man and the three officers

nodded, doubtful, but vaguely beginning to follow the tortuous drift of his idea.

"So then, of course, everything starts up for real," continued Porta. "We get Barcelona standing by with a flame thrower, and as soon as I give the go ahead, he lets 'em have it good and proper in the outposts. Then you come in with the big shells. And by that time, nobody but us knows what the hell's going on—but it's a safe bet those silly bastards over there on the rocket battery'll start shitting green. Only a matter of seconds before they join in the fun, and once that happens, the enemy's bound to think a whole frigging army's attacking 'em, and they'll throw in everything they've got. And that'll wake up the colonel and his glory boys over there—" He jerked a contemptuous thumb in the direction of Colonel von Vergil's troops on our flank. "Soon as they know what's going on, you can bet your sweet life they'll beat it. They won't stick around to see what's going to happen next, not that bunch of queens. I bet we'll be shut of the whole damn lot of them before you can say knife."

Lieutenant Ohlsen made a faint sound of approval. "And how about our Russian friends here?"

"Yeah, well—soon as the show gets going, they scram, see? They scamper back to their own lines. Mind you—" Porta turned to the Russian officer, "I'm afraid we'll have to rough you up a bit." He sounded none too regretful. "Make it look like you've been in the wars and all that—still, Tiny can take care of that. I've got it all worked out, see? Your story is, you was cut off in your own sector and fell in with some partisans what took you off to a farm with 'em—same one we flushed out farther back, right? Tell you about it later. So anyway, one of the partisans gets killed, the other escapes. Just like actually happened. You and your men manage to get out, don't know where you are, but land here, see?—behind the enemy lines. Can't think how to get back to your own side, so you do the only thing possible and start shooting—you with me?"

The Russian officer grinned. "You mean, it's us that's supposed to have set the whole thing off and forced your troops over there to abandon their trenches?"

"Well, why not?" said Porta reasonably. "Wouldn't take more'n one man with a couple of hand grenades to send that lot running."

"But what about your own company?" asked the Russian. "The minute we get back to our own side and tell them the position, they'll know that some of your troops have pulled out. They're not going to sit around on their cans. They'll start moving in to occupy the abandoned trenches."

"Tell you something." Porta leaned forward. "That lot over there," he nodded scornfully toward the Russian lines, "are just about as useless as that lot over there," his thumb jerked as scornfully in the direction of the colonel's troops. "You think Tiny and me could've gone out and picked up three corpses just like that? Not on your life! Not if they'd been soldiers worth their salt we couldn't. I tell you, the way they carry on over there, you'd think they was out for a Sunday afternoon stroll in Moscow, not fighting a fucking war!"

"May I ask," said Lieutenant Ohlsen, "when you and Tiny were thinking of getting the ball rolling?"

"Three o'clock, say?" suggested Porta. "Seems like a good sort of time. What I pictured was, me and Tiny and the Legionnaire, say, we'd set off about two-thirty, and at three o'clock sharp—wham!"

"Why three o'clock?" Spät wanted to know.

"Well, for one thing, nobody expects an attack to come at three o'clock in the morning. I mean, you wouldn't your-self, would you? Because it's a stupid sort of time to get into a fight, if you know what I mean—most of the silly bastards'll be asleep anyway. Theirs and ours. Won't even know what hit 'em. Even so," he turned to the Russian," "you'll have to move pretty fast when the time comes. I'll show you the best way to go."

The Russian nodded gravely. "Thank you. I must say . . ."

"One other thing," interrupted Porta. "Keep out of Tiny's way. He's a big guy with a bit of steel wire what he's sort of got into the habit of knotting round people's necks when they're not looking. He's kind of overenthusiastic about it just at the moment. You bump into him and I won't answer for the consequences. He tends to get a bit excited, if you know what I mean. Then there's Heide. He's just a murdering bastard, pure and simple. If he can pick you off, he will, but there's nothing I can do about that. As for the new boys, I dunno what they're like but I don't reckon they're up to much. Anyway, you come with me and I'll show you the way you'll have to go. And keep your head down if you don't want it blown off. Your little red brothers have a lot of snipers in this part of the world."

They pulled themselves out of the trench and crept toward the barbed wire, on the other side of which lay no-man's-land. They were soon swallowed up in the darkness.

They returned fifteen minutes later. Judging from the continued silence of the night, they had not been spotted.

"Okay," said Porta. "That's settled, then."

"It would seem so," murmured Lieutenant Ohlsen, if somewhat ruefully.

They synchronized their watches. The time was then 2205 hours. Porta crept back to his own dugout, which he shared with Tiny. We heard some muffled talk between them, then a great shout of laughter from Tiny. The Legionnaire swore at them, a stray bullet passed overhead, and then all was silent again.

Shortly after midnight, the two officers left the trenches for a tour of inspection.

"I wonder why silence is always so damned unnerving?" muttered Lieutenant Spät, staring up at the dark, cloud-covered sky.

They moved slowly up the hill, placing their feet with care, making as much use as possible of trees and bushes, melting from one shadow to another. They had gone only a few yards when a disturbing sound came softly to their ears. It was deep and regular, something of a cross between the growling of a dog and the grunting of a pig. They stood still and listened, guns at the ready.

"What the hell is it?" hissed Ohlsen.

They went on listening, then an incredulous grin spread over Spät's face. "It's some silly bastard snoring!"

Cautiously they moved forward, walking across the wet, spongy grass, and almost fell into a deep hole, at the bottom of which, curled up nose to tail, was an NCO. His submachine gun was lying carelessly by his side and he was snoring fit to wake the dead.

Lieutenant Spät bent down, closed his fingers over the gun and brought it slowly out into the open. He then pointed it into the man's chest and woke him with a smart tap on the side of his head.

"What's going on?" The man instinctively moved to sit up, but found himself thrust down again by the mouth of his own gun.

"That's what I should like to know," said Ohlsen grimly. "Just what the hell *is* going on? You'd have looked pretty goddamn sick if we'd been a couple of Russians, wouldn't you?"

"I've set all the guards . . ."

"I'm sure you have! And the chances are they're all having a nice cozy snooze as well—a fine example *you* set them, don't you? You deserve to be shot on the spot."

The man sank back, cowering. Ohlsen gave him a contemptuous look, then jerked his head at Spät and they continued on their way. A little farther on they heard Tiny's jubilant laugh ring out. Dimly, they discerned Porta's grotesque yellow hat in the darkness and heard the rattle of dice.

"Christ almighty!" said Spät with a certain grudging admiration. "Don't they ever give up? How can they even see the spots in this light?"

Ohlsen shrugged.

"They probably can't. They probably prefer it that way—gives them more scope for screwing each other!"

The two officers completed their tour of inspection and returned to their dugout just as the field telephone rang.

"Emil 27," said Heide in a low voice. He listened a moment, then passed the headset to Lieutenant Ohlsen. "It's the colonel for you, sir."

Ohlsen pulled a face. "If I must—" He took the headset. "Lieutenant Ohlsen here, sir . . . Yes . . . Yes, I see . . . Of course, sir. Whatever you say." He thrust the headset back at Heide and turned to the Old Man. "That, as you may have gathered, was the colonel. He wants the first section up there at ten A.M. sharp tomorrow, all nicely brushed and polished and ready for inspection. The second section to follow at eleven, the next at twelve, and so on."

"Delightful," murmured Spät.

"I could think of another word," said Ohlsen dryly. "He also wants to see six corpses produced along with the first section."

They looked at each other, shrugged their shoulders and retired into their blankets for a couple of hours' sleep.

As for the rest of us, all we could do now was catnap. At half-past two we watched Porta, Tiny and the Legionnaire move out of the trenches. We watched them crawl under the barbed wire and saw them swallowed up in the darkness. The Old Man and Barcelona alerted us for action. Three groups of mortar batteries were already standing by.

Barcelona was hugging the heavy flamethrower against

himself. For the umpteenth time he was checking the mechanism.

"If I could only change this blasted valve," he muttered. "I know the damn thing's going to give way sooner or later. I had to mend it with chewing gum last time, and I haven't been able to get hold of a new one yet."

"No good worrying about it now," said Ohlsen. "We've only got four minutes to go."

Heide turned threateningly from his position behind the heavy machine gun and addressed a group of the new arrivals. "Any one of you doesn't move when I move and he gets a personal bullet from me right up his backside—understand?"

The youngest of the recruits, a boy who could not have been more than seventeen, promptly burst into loud sobs. Heide moved away from the gun and slapped him sharply two or three times across the face.

"Stop that fucking racket! Nothing's liable to happen to you that won't happen to anyone else. We all stand to get our heads blown off, you're not the only one."

The boy seemed transfixed by terror. He opened his mouth and screamed; a long, tearing, uncontrollable scream. The other recruits looked at him nervously, looked away again. Heide took hold of him and shook him, slapping him back and forth across the face as he did so.

"Stop that whining! You want me to finish you off before the enemy has a chance to get at you?"

Lieutenant Ohlsen and the Russian officer stood side by side, watching the scene in grave silence. Heide's actions were brutal but necessary. The new recruits were scared enough as it was, and if the boy hadn't been taken in hand, his panic might well have spread like wildfire throughout the entire company. From now on, Heide's section would at least be kept at their posts through a common fear of Heide himself, probably transcending even their fear of the enemy.

"That's a good man you've got there," remarked the Russian.

"He's all right," agreed Ohlsen shortly. "So long as we're at war, I suppose we have to have men like him."

Seconds after he had finished speaking, an explosion shook the ground beneath us, to reverberate with the crash of a gigantic thunderclap. It was followed by the long, harsh cry of someone in agony. And then, silhouetted against the dark sky, lit up by the sudden burst of flames, Tiny's familiar shape surged into view near the enemy trenches. His submachine gun was jammed into his hip, and we saw the endless stream of bullets ploughing up the earth, a flashing series of brilliant red dots moving through the night as he sprayed the gun along the front line of trenches. Simultaneously we saw the fugitive figures of men running panic-stricken away in every which direction from this unexpected attack.

As he watched, the Russian lieutenant pursed his lips and gave an admiring whistle. "Some troops you got there!"

Lieutenant Ohlsen turned and shouted to Barcelona, who came up at a run with the flamethrower. The chewing gum held, the valve did its work, and now the scene was lighted by a sea of fire. Black smoke curled upward, and across the stage ran screaming human torches, men demented by pain and terror.

Ohlsen held up a hand—and dropped it. It was our signal to join in. Heide howled like a demon as he sent across salvo after salvo from the heavy guns. His men worked with him, hardly aware of what they were doing but too scared to stop.

"Mortars—fire!"

As Lieutenant Spät gave the command, the mortars went into action. Shells were sent across to add to the general confusion, curving across the sky and landing on the far side of the Russian trenches.

I folded up the tripod of the heavy M.G., ran forward and installed myself in a shell hole in the middle of no-man's-land, my loader following with the ammunition. From the trench in front of me a group of men began scrambling up, running blindly toward me. I lay flat on my belly, hugging the butt against my shoulder, taking my time, taking aim, just as if I were back on the practice range in camp.

As I fired, the noise of the gun was lost in a new series of explosions. The Russians had had time to collect their scattered wits and had opened up with their rocket batteries. The shells were whizzing over and exploding behind us, and the whole sky was alight with screaming missiles.

I scuttled back from my exposed position, throwing myself down near Lieutenant Ohlsen, gripping the machine gun and waiting for the storm to subside. The Russian lieutenant took his opportunity and struck out toward his own lines, followed by his men. I was too concerned at that moment for my own safety to care very much what happened to any of them.

The colonel's battalion reacted exactly as Porta had foretold; they took to their heels and ran. What was more surprising was that the Russians did not at once move forward into the attack; only subsequently did we discover the reason: most of their troops had, also, decided not to stay around for the battle!

It was seven hours before the sector calmed down to something like normal. Even then there was a continuous if half-hearted exchange of gunfire.

Toward the end of the afternoon we were able to reestablish contact with the battalion. It seems that the colonel had temporarily lost interest in our forthcoming inspection and had canceled it in favor of more pressing business.

There was a great scurrying to and fro of men, frantic exchanges of messages, and urgent repairs carried out to severed telephone wires, with demands from HQ as to what was going on. Lieutenant Ohlsen was able to report that a surprise infantry attack had taken place and a detachment had been sent over to try to capture our trenches. Fortunately the neighboring company gave roughly the same garbled explanation and it was never queried.

As soon as the lull came, we went on a scavenging expedition and returned with the bodies of six Russian soldiers, which we solemnly strung up on trees for the benefit of Colonel von Vergil. Lieutenant Ohlsen sent in a written report confirming that he had carried out his orders.

The following day, the colonel sent along his adjutant to verify the truth of this statement. Having gone to all that trouble, we were eager to show off our handiwork, but the adjutant must have had a weak stomach or something; he didn't want to see the dead bodies hanging from the trees.

"I'll take your word for it, Lieutenant—just a matter of form, you know."

And nothing would persuade him otherwise. Lieutenant Ohlsen watched him walk off with a handkerchief to his nose and shook his head in disgust. "All that killing to no purpose whatsoever . . ."

Later that evening we received an order to send out a reconnaissance patrol behind the Russian lines to assess the strength of their artillery and find out whether they had any tanks.

Of course, it was our section that was sent. It had to be. None of the new recruits would have lived beyond the first dozen yards.

One after another we left the trenches and stole across toward the Russian lines. Tiny was actually running, gripping his steel wire in one hand.

"Half and half!" he hissed as he shot past Porta; we didn't need to be told what he meant.

"Don't blame me," grumbled the Old Man. "Don't blame me when they have you up before the firing squad—Jesus Christ, the times I've warned you! It's not only the moral issue, it's you're breaking regulations. Two regulations, in fact."

"Jeez!" said Porta wonderingly. "You don't say!"

"Stealing things off corpses—that's against the law the world over. Second, all that stuff you pinch—gold teeth, rings, watches—you know as well as me it belongs to the state and should be handed over to the nearest SS bureau; that's the law in Germany, if nowhere else. Just as you know the death penalty is what you get for breaking it."

"Old Man, you're nothing but a goddamn pessimist!" declared Porta.

"I'm not handing mine over," said Tiny, who had slowed down to a walk to listen. "I'm keeping mine till the end of the war. Know what I'm going to do then? I'm going to buy me a pork butcher shop and a brothel."

"With other people's gold teeth!" muttered the Old Man.

"And why not?" demanded Tiny hotly. "I've heard that in the concentration camps they yank 'em out while people are still alive and kicking and might need 'em—we at least have the decency to wait until they're dead."

"Decency!" said Stege. "Don't make me laugh!"

Porta at once rounded on him. "You keep it out of it, pansy face! Get back to your books and mind your own damn business!"

Stege merely shrugged an indifferent shoulder and turned away. He was accustomed to Porta's constant stream of abuse.

We were a considerable way behind the Russian lines when the Old Man suddenly brought us to a halt and stood pointing into a ravine at the side of the road. "Something down there," he said tersely.

Tiny and the Legionnaire pushed their way through the bushes and lay flat on their bellies, staring down over the edge of the ravine. Then the Legionnaire turned and waved. "It's okay—they're buddies of ours! Come and take a look!"

We all moved forward through the bushes, staring over in our turn.

"Buddies?" queried the Old Man, gravely looking down at the five corpses.

"Yeah, and they didn't fall and they weren't pushed," said Porta. "Shot in the back of the neck, that's what they were, poor jerks."

"What's that pinned on 'em?" demanded Tiny. "There's a bit of paper stuck on their chests."

Porta scrambled down the side of the ravine and came back clutching one of the pieces of paper. On it was written in Russian: "Traitor to his country."

"All that hard work for nothing," muttered Barcelona regretfully. Makes you wonder if it was worth it, doesn't it?"

"The lieutenant's not there," said the Old Man. "Maybe he got away . . ."

"More likely reserving VIP treatment for him, seeing he's an officer."

"Poor bastard . . ."

"Jesus Christ!" said Heide. "Why waste your tears on that lousy bunch of scum? If I'd known what was going on I'd have shot 'em all myself; I've said that right from the start."

Barcelona looked at him through narrowed eyes. "Bastards like you," he said contemptuously, "always lose out in the end. You know that? Every time. You're not the first I've met. When I was in Spain there were several of 'em. Great loudmouthed cunts that never knew when to stop." He shook his head. "They're all underground now. Where they belong. They asked for it and they got it. And so will you, in the end."

"Only you won't be here to see it!" snarled Heide.

It was almost daylight when we arrived back at our own lines. Everything was quiet, and we settled down comfortably in our trench for what rest we could get. We kept an eye open for surprise attacks by the Russians, who were fond of that sort of thing, but they showed no signs of aggression.

"If you're all sitting snug," said Lieutenant Ohlsen in a friendly, "once-upon-a-time" sort of voice, "I'll tell you a story." We looked at him suspiciously. "I've kept it until now as a nice surprise for you—you'll be pleased to hear that the colonel has overcome his stage fright and has renewed his invitation to the company to present itself for inspection tomorrow morning—" Our faces fell. We looked down at our black hands and our filthy uniforms, and Lieutenant Ohlsen beamed around at us. "There. I knew you'd be overjoyed. I said to Lieutenant Spät at the time, I can hardly wait to tell them. I can hardly wait to see their little faces light up and the tears of gratitude come into their eyes . . ."

"Like fuck!" said Porta. He spat out a mouthful of sunflower seeds that he was chewing. "Jesus Christ almighty, where do they dig up these cretins, for God's sake?"

Lieutenant Ohlsen shook his head, looking suddenly weary. He pursed his lips and there was a hard streak in his eyes and bitter lines around his mouth. Despite the bantering tone he had used to us, you could tell that the colonel and his autocratic stupidity had brought him almost to breaking point.

Porta, meanwhile, went raving on. He was a great talker when once he got started, and although his choice of adjectives tended to be limited, he delivered them with such vehemence that we never tired of hearing them. Having told us all very forcibly exactly what he thought of the colonel, and of the colonel's parents and the colonel's grandparents, and having gone on to suggest in graphic detail several alternative courses of action open to the colonel (suggestions which ranged from the mildly indecent to the grossly obscene), he then switched abruptly to a better humor and fell to hectoring Tiny, always the butt of Porta's heavy-handed wit.

"Look at you!" he roared. "Call yourself a soldier! You're nothing but a frigging disgrace! Look at that uniform— in fine shape it was when they first give it to you. Look at it now—ruined! Completely bloody ruined! Half the buttons off of it, covered in shit, all tattered and torn—how the hell have you got it in that state anyway? You been fighting again, have you? You ought to be ashamed of yourself, getting into that horrible state. And what about your tin helmet, eh? Where's that gone? And what about that nice gas mask they give you? You've gone and lost it, haven't you?" He made a gesture of disgust. "What's the use, eh? I ask you, what *is* the use of giving people like him lovely new uniforms, when all they does is go and mess 'em up? Is it any wonder the poor colonel has to go and disturb himself giving us the once-over when we got people like you stinking the place out?"

He leaned closer to the startled Tiny.

"When did you last wash your ass, that's what I'd like to know. I bet if you took your pants down and had a look, you'd find it full of bloody great clinkers—and we have to live with it! Us, what's managed to keep ourselves clean and decent and not smelling like a million assholes!"

He stared round at the rest of us; stinking, louse-ridden, dirt-encrusted.

"We're decent enough guys," he said virtuously. "We're used to certain standards of hygiene. Like the colonel. That's why he has to call inspections in the middle of the war and make sure we've not got ingrowing toenails or fungus in our belly buttons." He stared very hard at Tiny. "These things are important, you know. You might think it's more important to stay down here in the trenches and keep an eye on them Russkies over there. In case they take advantage of our absence, get me? But that's where you'd be wrong, see? 'Cause unless you're a nice clean soldier what brushes out his pubic hairs now and again and stops to polish up his buttons before he goes into an attack, you won't be *fit* to fight the fucking Russkies! How do you think a Russian's going to feel if he sees a scarecrow like you coming at him with a bayonet? He won't be able to take you serious, will he? I mean, he can't be expected to, can he? I mean, let's be reasonable about it. A dirty great lout like you, what can be smelt stinking for miles around—he'd laugh his bloody balls off!"

"No he wouldn't," objected Tiny, who as usual had followed the whole of Porta's argument with the utmost seriousness.

"What you mean, he wouldn't? 'Course he would! Anyone would!"

"Well, they damn well wouldn't, so that's just where you're wrong!" Tiny pointed triumphantly at Porta. " 'Cause I'd have stuck the bayonet in 'em before they had a chance, see?"

Porta turned to the rest of us with a wide gesture of despair, and we looked at Tiny's face, puckered with bewilderment, even now not too sure whether he had scored a point, and we fell about laughing. Even Lieutenant Spät was grinning. Lieutenant Ohlsen was the only one to keep a straight face. I was not even sure that he had been listening. He was staring along the lines, watching men who were dog-tired, who had been under constant pressure and without sleep for days on end, painfully scrubbing themselves with icy water. There were no towels for drying. There was no soap, there were no razors. Uniforms that were beyond all hope of cleaning or repair were being sponged down in pathetic attempts to make them fit for the colonel's inspection. Equipment was being polished on pieces of filthy rag.

As our laughter died away, we followed Lieutenant Ohlsen's gaze, reflecting bitterly that soon we ourselves would have to put our protesting bodies to work and begin on our own spit and polish. I looked across at the lieutenant and saw a muscle twitch in his face.

"Great screaming queen," he suddenly muttered through clenched teeth. "Stupid fucking pigheaded, birdbrained bastard!"

A sudden shocked silence came upon us. We stared at the lieutenant, stunned. It was not so much what he said that startled us—compared with Porta's more choice expressions his language was mild indeed—but the way he said it. We had known the lieutenant in moments of anger and exasperation, we had known him impatient, we had known him sarcastic, but this was the cold, grim, almost desperate bitterness of a man who has taken just about as much as he can stand, and even Porta was moved to silence.

Ohlsen turned slowly to look at us. He shrugged his shoulders apologetically and rubbed a hand across his brow.

"Sorry," he said abruptly. "It gets you down at times."

"They treat you like machines," muttered Spät. "Only you're not machines, you're human beings. And when something comes along to remind you of it, it makes you feel so damned sick of it all . . ."

The inspection took place the following morning, as planned. We lined up like a bunch of renovated scarecrows. Any officer who had been at the front as long as we had would have been agreeably surprised by our appearance. We had indeed wrought miracles. At the risk of catching pneumonia, we had bathed in pools of icy water. A certain amount of dirt was still engrimed, but the top layer at least had been removed. Our uniforms were still damp and creased, but the few buttons that remained were highly polished and gleamed quite indecently bright in the pale morning sunshine. Altogether it was a brave show, and we felt that we deserved commendation.

Unfortunately, Colonel von Vergil, being fresh out from a home base, set far higher standards than any field officer. He raged over torn uniforms, he fumed over missing buttons, and he became almost apoplectic over the state of our boots. His own were shining like any looking glass, but when Lieutenant Ohlsen asked him whether we were supposed to carry tins of polish into the trenches with us in preference to boxes of ammunition, he dismissed the question as being both irrelevant and insubordinate.

Another inspection was called for the following day, and when that also failed to satisfy him, we were hauled back the next day, and the next day, and the next. It was a wearisome farce that exhausted everyone to no purpose and cost the life of at least one man, who collapsed with a hemorrhage as his section was being forced to crawl five miles on their stomachs, dragging gas masks and full equipment with them. Lieutenant Ohlsen was almost out of his mind, but the colonel had the immovable obsession of the insane and there was nothing Ohlsen could do. He tried on several occasions to contact our regiment, but without success; the entire front was in a state of confusion and most of the lines of communication had been cut.

When the idea of constant inspections began to lose its appeal, the colonel hit on the notion of sending us out on endless and increasingly pointless patrols. And never a day passed but Lieutenant Ohlsen had to make the hazardous journey from the trenches to the colonel's headquarters to answer a string of meaningless questions.

It was fortunate that during this period the Russians were apathetic and for the most part left us alone. We had regular exchanges of sniper fire, but these, I think, were conducted on both sides more for show than anything else. Farther away toward the north, we knew that there must be very heavy fighting. We heard the sounds of gunfire and explosions both by day and by night, and the sky was almost always a blaze of fire on the horizon.

"It's got to come our way soon," muttered Heide pessimistically. "We've had it easy long enough."

"Easy?" Porta gave a derisive laugh. "You call it easy, living with that nut breathing down your neck the whole time? I'd rather have a skirmish with the Russians and be done with it!"

"Don't worry," said Tiny confidently. "I bet the war'll be over pretty soon. You and me'll be back home within a couple of months."

The little Legionnaire opened one eye and raised a sardonic eyebrow. "Don't you kid yourself—this war's going on a lot longer than a couple of months."

There was a wild shout as Barcelona came running up.

"They've broken through on the left flank! It's started up again!"

The Old Man sighed. He calmly knocked out his pipe and stood up. "Ah well, we knew it had to happen. Silence is only made to be broken."

Lieutenant Ohlsen was already shouting orders. The scene was already breaking up into that confusion which leads eventually to a strict pattern in which every man has his place and knows what he must do. We picked up our weapons, began checking them, cramming our helmets on our heads, preparing once more for action. Those sections which had been resting were brutally woken and came up at a run, stumbling and yawning and still not too sure what it was all about. Behind us we could hear the crack of rifles and the explosions of mines and hand grenades.

Lieutenant Ohlsen turned to Spät. "Stay here with the first section and keep the road clear. We'll need you to cover us on the way back. The rest of the company, come with me."

We fell in behind him, single file. As we moved forward, we stumbled on two men of the colonel's battalion, hiding behind some rocks and half dead with terror.

"Come on, come on, get over here!" Lieutenant Ohlsen nagged them to their feet and pushed impatiently at them with the butt of his PM as they stood there shivering and incoherent. "What happened? Where are the rest of your section?"

"Gone." They shook their heads, still dumb with fright.

"Gone where? You mean they're dead or they've run off or what?"

"The Russians came at us—suddenly—out of nowhere . . ."

They babbled to a halt. Only by dint of much coaxing and bullying did Lieutenant Ohlsen prize the story out of them.

It appeared that despite persistent warnings from one or two frontline veterans, Colonel von Vergil had seen no necessity for having more than a couple of men on guard.

The experienced soldiers had been contemptuously dismissed as cowards and old women, and the colonel had given it as his opinion that the Russians were on the point of packing up and going home after their last abortive attack and the comparative silence of the past few days. Only yesterday he had been overheard telling the adjutant that in fact there was far more danger back home in Germany, from RAF bombing raids, than he had yet to meet at the front. The result was that when the Russians ultimately launched the attack that we (but not the colonel) had been expecting, they met with virtually no resistance. The two men on guard had apparently been taken by surprise, since they had not sounded the alarm, and according to the two babbling survivors—who frankly confessed they were still alive only because they had taken to their heels—the whole attack had been incredibly rapid and incredibly silent. No guns or grenades had been used, only bayonets and *kandras*.

"In other words, it was a massacre," Lieutenant Ohlsen put it to them grimly.

"Yes, yes!" they nodded simultaneously, eager to impress on us the horror of the experience; although one of them, perhaps wishing to show that they had not given in altogether without a struggle, did add that Lieutenant Kalb had managed to throw one hand grenade before being run through with a bayonet.

"I see." Lieutenant Ohlsen stared up the path that led to the colonel's chalet. He turned back to the survivors. "And —ah—how about the colonel?" he asked casually.

They didn't know; they hadn't seen the colonel.

"Let's hope they stuck a bayonet up his backside," muttered Porta.

"Perhaps," suggested Tiny, "we ought to hang around down here until they've finished the job? Make damn sure of it!"

"Creutzfeldt, keep your voice down!" snapped the lieutenant. He waved his arm at the column of men and pointed up toward the chalet. "Follow me, we're going up there."

We heard the Russians long before we reached the chalet. The sounds they made were familiar to us. They were the joyous sounds of men carousing.

"Pissed to the eyeballs," murmured Barcelona with a smile. "They'll have found the colonel's wine."

"Jesus Christ!" said Tiny nervously. "Let's get up there quick before the bastards drink it all!"

As we came in sight of the chalet, we could see, as well as hear evidence of Russian occupation. The windows were open, and through them came snatches of drunken song and a continuous hail of paper, boxes, crockery and German uniforms.

"Look at 'em," sneered Porta with more than a touch of envy. "Call that war? Looks more like a fucking debauch to me."

Heide ran a hand caressingly along his rifle. "You wait till we get stuck in there among 'em—won't know what's hit 'em till it's all over!"

"Especially," added the little Legionnaire with a grin, "when they discover we're not the same papier-mâché soldiers as the last lot they had to deal with . . ."

Lieutenant Ohlsen gave the order to fix bayonets, and we charged. I found myself hurtling up the hill toward the chalet with the Old Man and the Legionnaire by my side, the lieutenant just ahead of us, Porta and Tiny screaming like savages just behind. I saw one or two round Russian faces staring openmouthed in horror as we launched ourselves upon them. They didn't stand a chance, that first lot. We cut straight through them and surged on to engage in some vicious hand-to-hand combat which soon became a tangled nightmare of interlocked men, slashing and cutting amid the corpses of their comrades, slipping and squelching in pools of spilled blood, crushing underfoot the writhing bodies of the wounded.

I looked up suddenly to find an enormous Russian lieutenant bearing down on me. He was wielding his machine gun like a club, and I was able to sidestep the lethal blow just in time. As a purely reflex action, I brought up my bayonet and thrust it blindly at the man. There was a moment of resistance, then the blade slid smoothly into the soft flesh of his groin. He fell backward with a scream, taking my rifle with him. In my terror and my haste to retrieve the weapon, I leaped forward with both feet planted squarely on the face of a wounded man. Whether he was one of ours or one of theirs, I didn't stop to see. I snatched up my rifle and plunged on, with his agonized shrieks ringing in my ears.

Now and again, in the hideous confusion, I caught a brief glimpse of one of my own outfit. At one point I was dimply aware that Porta was by my side, but then he was swallowed up in the vicious scrimmage of bodies and disappeared. I fought my way out into the courtyard and saw Tiny. He had lost his gun and a couple of Russians were heading straight for him. I gave a loud yell, but Tiny had already swung round to meet them. With two enormous fists he caught them each by the throat and their heads went crashing together. As they fell, he snatched up one of their guns and began spraying bullets in all directions. We had reached that stage of desperation where it was every man for himself and if you mowed down some of your own side, then it was just their tough luck.

I saw a Russian crouching behind a pillar, taking aim with a pistol. Before he had time to fire it, I had blown off half his head, and I watched dispassionately as he crumpled up in a bloody heap.

I turned and saw Porta charging with his bayonet, plunging it deep into the back of a young Russian who was attempting to run away.

I saw Heide trampling savagely on the face of a dying man, who even in his last moments of agony was still clutching his gun to his chest.

How many men had been killed, and how long the slaughter had continued, I had no idea. Was it minutes or was it hours before we reassembled, victorious, in the courtyard behind the chalet? At that point we neither knew nor cared. For the moment it was enough that we had survived.

We threw ourselves to the ground, panting, exhausted, covered in mud and blood, our uniforms torn, our helmets and our weapons tossed wearily to one side. Some of the youngest of the new recruits had tears rolling down their cheeks, making channels in the grime. As for the rest of us, once the first shock of being still alive had worn off, we began searching with bloodshot eyes for our friends. Were they still with us? Or were they lying inside in the charnel house with their guts ripped out or their heads blown off?

I saw Barcelona a few yards away, stretched out full length, his uniform in ribbons. The Old Man was leaning against a tree trunk, smoking his inevitable pipe. Tiny and Heide were still there, Heide with his eyes closed, Tiny an indescribable mess, looking as if he had dipped his head in a bucket of blood. My gaze roamed farther afield and

I saw Stege, lying on his back and staring bleakly up at the clouds overhead. And there was the Legionnaire, sitting on some steps smoking a cigarette and already hard at work stripping down his gun ready for the next action. The Legionnaire was a professional soldier. He had been fighting for fifteen years and his first thought was always for his weapons. Farther off were Porta and Steiner, sharing a bottle of liquor they had found somewhere. Steiner looked to be already half drunk.

They were all there. All the old hands, the ones who had lived through it before and were still here in one piece. But over a third of the new recruits had gone. Their bodies lay where they had fallen, sad islands of death among the survivors. Someone suggested tentatively that we bury them, but we took no notice. Why tax our strength any further, digging holes for corpses? We were alive and exhausted, while they were dead and could feel no more.

Lieutenant Ohlsen came out of the chalet. He had lost his helmet and had a deep gash running from the corner of his eye to his mouth. He sank to the ground and we looked at him expectantly. He hunched a shoulder. "They were all dead before we got here."

Porta gave him a cigarette. "How about the colonel, sir?"

"Him as well—his throat was slit from ear to ear."

There was a silence, then a malicious grin spread itself across Porta's lips. "Maybe there is a God after all," he muttered.

The lieutenant frowned and turned to Heide. "Take two or three men and go and collect all the dog tags."

"What, Russians as well?" demanded Heide.

"Of course. You ought to know that without being told."

As soon as Heide had completed his task, we set fire to the chalet and made our way back to the road, losing more men as we did so, thanks to the Russians waking up again and pounding us with mortars.

"Always us," grumbled Porta, running for cover. "Anything goes wrong, and it's always us that gets caught up in it."

Tiny and the Legionnaire were already setting up the heavy machine gun. Lieutenant Ohlsen turned back to wave an impatient hand at the new recruits, who were lagging behind, uncertain whether to follow the rest of us up the road or dive into the nearest shell hole.

"Stop dithering and get a move on, for God's sake! This is no time to hang around admiring the bloody scenery!"

They shambled forward like a bunch of terrified sheep. One of them suddenly gave a shrill howl of pain and began running in circles, both hands pressed to his belly. Our platoon medic, Berg, at once turned back for him. He dragged the boy to the side of the road and tore open his uniform, but he was too late, he was already dead.

We watched as Berg slung his Red Cross bag over his shoulder and ran forward to rejoin us. Shells landed before and behind him. His helmet was blown off and he staggered from the blast, but somehow he made it. A loud cheer went up. Berg was deservedly popular. We had watched him risk his life many times to help an injured man, caught in enemy fire as he lay wounded in the middle of a minefield or tangled on some barbed wire. I remembered at Sebastopol, when Berg had deliberately gone back into a burning building and stumbled through the inferno with an unconscious Lieutenant Hinka slung over his shoulders. He had been recommended for the Iron Cross for that particular exploit, but had politely refused it, saying that he had no interest in collecting scrap iron. Two years later his uniform was still bare of any form of decoration save his Red Cross insignia.

The company eventually straggled to relative safety in a thickly forested area which projected beyond the mountains like a wooded fjord. We were on our own once again; the battalion from Breslau had been completely wiped out.

We had been on the same train for several days, ever since leaving the front, and we had stopped at many stations. Frequently we had been shunted into sidings and left there for hours on end to make way for trains carrying more important cargos—arms or ammunition probably. We were only soldiers returning home, and therefore fairly far down on the list of priorities.

Now, on the seventh day of our journey, we had come to yet another stop. The train shuddered to a halt and for several minutes we stayed where we were, sitting on the straw in our cattle truck, too lethargic even to open our eyes. After a while Porta stirred himself sufficiently to pull open the sliding door and have a look outside.

"Hamburg!" He turned back to the rest of us. "We're in Hamburg!"

"Hamburg?"

We cheered up slightly. The Legionnaire stretched luxuriously and the Old Man was moved to pull out his pipe and stick it in his mouth.

"It's Whitsun," he told us suddenly.

We all looked at him.

"So what?" said Heide. "What's Whitsun got to do with anything?"

The Old Man shrugged his shoulders. "I don't know— it just occurred to me . . ."

"This time last year," said Porta, "we were at Demjamsk."

"And the year before that," added Tiny, "it was Brest-Litovsk. Do you remember Brest-Litovsk? Do you remember . . ."

"Shove it!" said the Legionnaire irritably. "I wish you wouldn't keep looking backward all the time, it's morbid and unnecessary. Why can't you try looking forward for a change?"

"All right, if that's what you want—" Porta closed his eyes a moment, and a smile of beatific lechery appeared on his lips. "First thing I do tonight, when they let us out of here, is find me a whorehouse—how about that? That appeal to you?"

From the cheers that went up from the assembled company, it seemed that it did!

III

HAMBURG

We were sitting in the canteen, waiting for Barcelona. We had been sitting there for some time, and one or two of us—notably Porta and Tiny—were well on the way to becoming exceedingly, gloriously drunk.

The place smelled of stale beer and frying, and the air was thick and heavy with cigarette smoke. The serving women, rushed off their feet and in no very good mood, were deliberately making as much noise as possible, throwing piles of knives and forks into the sink and clattering the crockery on the draining board. They grumbled incessantly as they worked.

Porta, prompted by God knows what drunken whim, suddenly leaned across the table and pointed an accusing finger at a Dutch SS man, who had been sitting in a peaceful coma, minding his own business, ever since we had been there.

"Look at the ugly great swine," he said, his voice slightly blurred by drink. He turned to the rest of us, and with a gesture invited us to inspect the unfortunate man. "Look at those great ears! If there's one thing I can't stand, it's ears that look as if they're about to take off."

I stared with interest at the man's ears. They certainly had a tendency to stand out at right angles from his head, but perhaps I hadn't yet drunk enough to see this as sufficient reason for pitching into him.

A girl came up with a tray of beer mugs. She slapped them down in front of us, and the beer frothed over the edge and made a great stinking lake over the table. Porta planted both elbows in it and turned his attention to more likely prey, a young soldier wearing the silver insignia of the SD* on his collar. The Dutch SS man had remained totally unmoved by the reference to his ears, and was probably even more drunk than Porta, but the young soldier was already looking nervous.

"Listen, you bastard—" Porta blew his nose loudly between finger and thumb and wiped it across his sleeve, "I got a knife here. We all got knives. Me and my friends, we all got knives—you know what for? You know what we use 'em for?"

The SD man turned away and wisely kept his mouth shut, but Porta was out to annoy someone and he dragged the man round to face him again. "You want me to show you?" he asked with a revolting leer. "We use 'em for cutting things off. You want me to show you what it is we cut off?" He made an obscene gesture in the air, and Tiny obligingly guffawed.

"Really, I'm not in the least interested in your wretched knives," said the man, and he yawned and turned away again.

His attempt to assume an air of lofty disdain merely provoked Porta into a drunken fury. He brought his fist crashing down onto the table. All the beer mugs jumped and rattled and a fresh wave of beer came slopping over the edge.

"Why don't you fuck off and leave us alone?" shouted Porta. "What right have you got to sit here at our table, you filthy swine? Get out of it before I throw you out!"

I picked up my half-empty beer mug and looked on with a fuddled, and consequently somewhat dispassionate interest. The Legionnaire leaned back and crossed his legs at the ankle, sliding half out of his chair. The Old Man was staring mournfully into his beer mug. Tiny seemed the only other person to be really very much interested.

---

*Sicherheitsdienst (Security Service).

The SD man voiced what seemed to me, in the circumstances, a mild and reasonable objection to Porta's rude hectoring. "I was here first, you know—and I really don't think it's up to you to give the orders."

Porta snorted and spat. "So what if you've been here since the first day of the war? I'm telling you, now, to get the hell out of it!"

"And I'm telling you," retorted the SD man, growing pardonably exasperated, "that I shall do no such thing!"

Porta looked round wildly at Tiny for support. "Insubordination! You heard that, did you? Refusing to obey the orders of a Stabsgefreiter!" He staggered to his feet, thrust out an arm and pushed it under the man's nose. "You see that?" He jabbed a finger at his stripes. "You know what that means, I suppose?"

The SD merely took hold of the arm between finger and thumb and delicately swung it back toward Porta, screwing up his nose as if he could smell a bad smell—which he most likely could.

"Well, so help me!" cried Porta, growing ever more excited. "If that don't beat all! You see that, did you?" He turned again to Tiny, who nodded eagerly and pushed back his chair. "Make a note of it! Take his name and number! He used violence on a Stabsgefreiter—go on, get it wrote down!"

"Fuck off," said Tiny sullenly. "You know I can't write."

"Then take him outside and beat the living daylights out of him!"

"Look here, you uncouth bastard . . ."

The SD man rose to his feet, and Tiny rose with him. They faced each other across the table. Tiny scratched his enormous chest, hitched up his trousers, reached out a hand and closed it over the man's collar. "Come on, little one— let's go talk outside."

The SD man opened his mouth to shout, but such was the pressure of Tiny's vast paw that all that came out was a strangulated squawk. Tiny frog-marched him to the door and Porta sat down again, red in the face and still angry.

The Dutch SS man was now lying across the table with his head in a pool of beer.

"Look at that," I said to the Legionnaire. "He's passed out."

And I laughed hilariously, as if it was the funniest thing

in the whole world. The Legionnaire, who rarely if ever lost control, merely smiled pityingly at me.

A few moments later Tiny reappeared—alone.

"Where's he gone?" I said.

"Lying in the gutter," said Tiny. He sent his fist crashing into the palm of his hand and winked at me. "Out like a light first go. Hey—" He looked round at the Legionnaire. "You remember the day you and me first met?"

"I remember," said the Legionnaire.

"What happened?" I asked, just sufficiently drunk to be obliging and give Tiny the chance to show off.

By way of reply, he grabbed my hand as if to shake it in normal greeting and slowly began crushing it until I gave a loud yell of pain. "That's what happened," said Tiny proudly.

"Very amusing," I said, shaking my hand up and down. "What's the point of it?"

"Ah," said Tiny, winking. "That'd be telling, wouldn't it?"

The Legionnaire gave one of his patronizing smiles and shook his head at me. "Allow him his little moment of glory," he murmured.

"Well, that's what happened!" protested Tiny.

"Of course it is," agreed the Legionnaire smoothly. "But never again, my friend! I don't get caught twice the same way!"

"Nor me," I grumbled, tucking my injured hand beneath my armpit.

Porta was banging on the table again, calling loudly and lewdly for more beer. The girls just sniffed and turned their backs on him, but Big Helga, the superintendent, left her place behind the counter and came storming over to our table. She placed herself before Porta, legs apart and arms akimbo, her vast body a mass of indignant ripples.

"How dare you call my girls by such names? What do you think this is, a brothel?"

"Brothel, my ass!" retorted Porta. "With a scabby crew like that? Times might be hard, sweetheart, but nobody's that desperate!"

"I shall report you," said Big Helga, as she said many times a day to many a different soldier. "We do a good job here, and I'd like to know where you guys would be without us."

"I could tell you," said Porta.

Big Helga took a step away from him. "They're all good girls here, and Gertrude, let me tell you, has a boyfriend in the SD. If there's any more lip from you people, I shall have her report you."

"Aw, stop bellyaching!" said Tiny. "You know you love us, really."

"All we want is some more beer," I put in. "Anyone'd think we'd asked for six whores, the way she's carrying on."

Big Helga simply sniffed and went back to the counter. She picked out Gerda, the least attractive of a rather poor bunch, and grudgingly sent her over to us with the order. Gerda wasn't a bad girl, but they didn't call her "Beanstick" for nothing. She was the nearest thing to an animated telegraph pole I ever saw.

"If you only had a bit more rump on you, I'd be almost tempted to take you to bed with me," murmured Tiny, regretfully sliding a hand up Gerda's skirt and trying to feel her nonexistent bottom.

Gerda showed what she thought of this invitation by slamming the tray hard down on Tiny's head and stalking away again.

At this point we were rejoined by Barcelona, who brought the unwelcome news that we were on guard duty as of that evening.

Barcelona was wearing an enormous bandage around his neck, which obliged him to hold his head stiff and straight. During our last days in the mountains he had been wounded in the throat by a stray hand grenade, and he was now temporarily exempt from active service. He could, and should, have stayed in the hospital, but thanks to Lieutenant Ohlsen pulling a few strings, he had been allowed to come back to the company and take up duty in the orderly room —not that he was very often to be found in the orderly room; he was more frequently in the canteen or the armory.

There were those who thought he was a fool for not having taken advantage of a few months' rest in the hospital, but Barcelona had been in the Army long enough to know that once in a hospital and separated from your comrades, almost anything was liable to happen to you on your discharge. The chances of being sent back to your own company were remote, and these days it was almost certain death to be the newcomer in an established group. All the worst and most dangerous tasks would automatically come your way, and death seemed to be a foregone conclusion.

"Jesus!" said Barcelona, looking at the table with its array of beer mugs. "You've been packing it away, haven't you?"

"Never mind that," said Porta. "What I want to know is, where we're supposed to be on guard duty—I wouldn't mind the local brothel . . ."

"No such luck." Barcelona shook his head and picked up someone's beer mug. "It's the fucking Gestapo."

"What fool thought that one up?" demanded the Legionnaire.

Barcelona hunched a shoulder and threw a sheet of paper onto the table. The Old Man rescued it from a pool of beer and looked at it indifferently. "Nineteen hundred hours—Karl Muck Platz, Hamburg." Gloomily he folded the paper and put it in his top pocket.

Steiner came suddenly to life and glared at Barcelona as if he personally had made the arrangements. "Bloody Gestapo!"

"Don't look at me," said Barcelona. "I'm not the clown who thought it up. Anyway, just thank your lucky stars it's nothing worse. The fourth section's on duty at Fuhlsbüttel— execution squad for the Wehrmacht."

"I wouldn't mind swopping," said Tiny, perverse as ever. "There's always the chance of picking up a bit extra on executions. We've done it before now, let's face it . . ."

"How?" demanded Stege suspiciously. "How have you done it?"

"Easy. You promise some guy his life and he's willing to give you anything you ask for."

"You mean you'd take money from a condemned man?" Stege sounded as if he could hardly believe his ears.

"Well, and why not?" said Tiny aggressively. "You'd be willing to pay someone for getting you off the hook, I bet."

"Any case," added Porta, "it ain't that easy. They find out what you're up to and you'd be for the high jump yourself."

Stege opened his mouth to protest, but before he could speak, Heide had woken from a deep sleep and found himself confronted by a solid wall of empty beer mugs. He swept them away angrily.

"We've drunk too much!" He belched and reached out

for the nearest full mug. "How did we get through all that lot?"

"Beside the point," said Tiny. "We did, and that's all that matters—apart from the fact that it's you what's going to pay for them. You're the only one with money."

"Me? I'm broke!" Heide objected.

"Like hell! You got a whole wad stuck down the side of your boot!"

Heide looked at him incredulously. "How do you know that?"

Tiny shrugged his shoulders. "I had a look, didn't I? I wanted some dough the other day, so I went through your locker. It's the only one with a faulty lock, you ought to get it looked at. Doesn't close right, you see."

"You mean you deliberately went through my things?"

"I suppose you could put it that way."

"So it was you swiped that hundred marks?"

"Now look," said Tiny, "just watch out. I never said I took nothing, did I?"

"But it's plain obvious you did!"

Tiny sneered. "Try and prove it!"

"I don't have to prove it! You've as good as admitted it— by God, you're not going to get away with this!" Heide's face was sheet-white with rage. "I'll see you busted if it's the last thing I ever do. I'll see you hang for this. I'll see you . . ."

"For Christ's sake," said the Legionnaire languidly, "does it really matter?"

"It does to me!" snarled Heide.

"Look here," said Porta, as if suddenly possessed of an idea that would solve the entire problem, "why don't we take a few bottles of booze on duty with us? Old Beanstick wouldn't mind slipping them to us under the counter."

"Yeah? And what do we do with 'em when we get to Karl Muck?"

"Stash 'em away somewhere safe. It's okay. I know one of the boys that's been on guard duty there just recently, he says it's a real dandy of a place. Right down in the cellars. Nobody ever bothers to come and take a look at what you're doing."

"What about the cells?" Steiner wanted to know.

"What about 'em? None of the prisoners ain't never there for more than one night. Most of 'em are got rid of the following morning. The ones the Gestapo want to pull about a bit, they take up top with 'em. More convenient. Saves 'em

running up and down the stairs every time they feel like
yanking a few fingernails out. You don't need to worry about
the cells—the prisoners won't bother us none."

"How about that statue of the Emperor on his horse?"
suggested Heide, suddenly forgetting his hundred marks and
taking an interest in Porta's idea. "The legs are hollow. I bet
you could stuff quite a few bottles up there and no one'd
notice."

"I already thought of that," claimed Tiny. "I was just
about to say it myself. I always think of good places for hiding things in—that's why I looked in your boots that time,"
he confided to Heide, who at once relapsed into fierce sulks.

"We'll get half a dozen large bottles," decided Porta.
"We'll have a mixture." He beckoned to Gerda, who peeled
herself away from the side of the counter and suspiciously
approached us. "Six bottles," he told her. "Dortmünder up to
there—" He demonstrated with fingers and thumb held
apart, "and the rest, slivovitz. That okay?"

She shrugged. "If you say so. I shouldn't fancy it myself,
but there's no accounting for some people's tastes, is there?"

She turned away with a sniff, and Porta rubbed his hands
together and looked toward the Legionnaire for confirmation. "That's right, ain't it? Put the beer in first, then the
slivovitz?"

The Legionnaire inclined his head, an expression of faint
amusement on his face, as if he were watching a crowd of
children.

Gerda came back with the first bottle, shaking it energetically to mix the two liquids. Porta snatched it from her, horrified. "What the hell are you trying to do? Blow us all up?"

"With any luck," she said sourly.

She brought the rest of the bottles, banged them noisily
onto the table and silently held out her hand for the money.
She stood there counting it and checking every bill to make
sure it wasn't a forgery. While she was doing so, Steiner
came out of the men's room. He stood by the table, belching
and doing up his fly, regardless of Gerda still counting her
money.

"Nothing more satisfying than a good pee," he informed
us with a sigh of contentment. "Specially when you've held
onto it a bit . . ."

He picked up his beer mug and emptied it in a few quick
gulps, his Adam's apple bounding vigorously up and down
his throat. He then belched again and wiped his lips along

the back of his sleeve. Gerda gave him a long, slow look of contempt, placed the money in a bag she wore beneath her apron, and marched away from us, her back held very straight.

"What's satisfying about it?" demanded Porta, who was in a mood to quarrel with anyone over anything, no matter how banal.

Steiner looked at him. "What d'you mean, what's satisfying? You've pissed often enough, haven't you? You should know what's satisfying about it."

"Well, I don't," said Porta. "What's the matter with you, anyway? You some kind of a pervert? You . . ."

"Aw, fuck off!" said Steiner, trying to sit down and discovering that Porta had spread himself out over half the bench.

Porta banged his beer mug onto the table and staggered to his feet. "Nobody tells me to fuck off and gets away with it!" he roared.

He swung an arm wildly in Steiner's direction. Steiner ducked and promptly retaliated, catching Porta a blow on the side of the head. Porta stepped backward, knocking over the bench, and Steiner followed him, his arms going like piston rods. For a few moments they fought each other in dedicated silence, merely tossing off the occasional oath to encourage themselves, and then Steiner, growing suddenly adventurous, picked up a beer mug and hurled it at Porta's head. Porta bent sideways and the missile flew past him and smashed into the far wall.

Immediately, Gerda was upon us, a large wooden truncheon clasped in her hand. "Who threw that beer mug?"

Enthusiastically we pointed at Steiner. Gerda, without a second's hesitation, brought her truncheon crashing down on his shoulder, and while Steiner was reeling from the blow, followed it up with a quick chop to the head.

Steiner promptly forgot his quarrel with Porta. Howling with pain and indignation, he turned on Gerda, who took to her heels and fled for the comparative safety of the counter. Steiner plunged after her, turning over tables and chairs as he galloped across the room. He caught up with her just before she reached the counter, and pushing her up against the wall, began thumping her head hard against the wall. Gerda fought like a tigress, biting, scratching and kicking, using her teeth, her nails, her knees, anything that was handy, and all the while howling at the top of her voice.

Suddenly the door behind the counter opened and Big Helga appeared. She took in the situation at a glance, calmly picked up a champagne bottle and sallied forth to join in the action.

Steiner was far too preoccupied to notice this new and highly dangerous attack on his right flank. Helga took careful aim and the champagne bottle caught Steiner neatly in the nape of the neck. He crumpled instantly into a sawdust heap, blood and champagne mingling together.

"Murderer!" screamed Helga, kicking him ruthlessly where he lay.

"Sex maniac!" screeched Gerda, snatching up the broken neck of the champagne bottle and attempting to carve open Steiner's face.

With surprising agility for one so enormous, Big Helga prized the broken glass away from her—not that she had any sympathy with Steiner, but a murder on the premises might not go down too well with the authorities. Gerda had to content herself with a stream of obscenities, the like of which I swear I had never heard before, accompanied by a furious kicking of Steiner's bloody and unconscious body.

The girl named Gertrude, who had a boyfriend in the SD, came staggering up the stairs with a crate of beer in her muscular arms. She had long, lank, tarnished fair hair and a perpetual pus-filled spot on the side of her nose.

Gerda immediately fell upon her, pointing excitedly at Steiner and shouting something about revenge. Gertrude dumped her case of beer and looked down at Steiner without much interest. "What am I supposed to do about it?"

"Tell your boyfriend in the SD!" urged Gerda, aiming another vindictive kick into the small of Steiner's back.

"À la bonne heure,"* replied Gertrude in French.

She had no idea what the expression meant, but it sounded good and she used it frequently. She had picked it up from a French sailor to whom she had once been engaged for eight days, the length of time his boat had been in Hamburg. She had been engaged to many another sailor since then, but she had never forgotten *à la bonne heure*. If you wanted any special favor from Gerda, you had only to remark, in tones of admiration and wonderment, "Oh, you speak French, do you?" and she would rise immediately to the bait. Unfortunately the favor was almost always accompanied by a

_____

*That's the spirit!

recital of her favorite fairy tale—of how she had been born into a rich French family and of how they had abandoned her at an early age and left her in a fashionable boarding school, the location of which was vague and could never quite be pinned down; but if you were prepared to hear her out, then she in return was willing to grant you all manner of small favors.

Porta and Tiny had once strung her along very successfully for a whole evening, eating half the food in the canteen and drinking themselves into a near paralytic stupor—all at Gerda's expense. Mind you, Tiny had paid for it later. On returning to barracks he had suddenly taken a notion into his head to demonstrate to Porta the regulation manner in which an infantryman—and in particular an infantryman belonging to the regiment in which he had himself begun his military career—should fall to the ground on all fours and crawl along on his stomach. As Porta stood watching him, he saw Tiny hurtle groundward, flat on his stomach, and crash his head straight into a piece of sharp stone. The stone made a hole the size of a pigeon's egg in Tiny's forehead, and the blood ran in rivers down his face, but he picked himself up and linked arms with Porta, and they rolled back to barracks singing at the tops of their voices: "*Soldaten sind keine Akrobaten!*" (Soldiers are not acrobats.)

The idea seemed to amuse them, and they were still trying unsuccessfully to turn cartwheels when they landed up outside the door of the infirmary and Tiny passed out.

Now, however, he was very much awake. Leaning forward over the beer-slopped table, he shouted across to Gerda, "Hey, Beanstick! You want someone to come and kick his face in for you? Stand me a couple of pints and I'll do it like a shot!"

"Watch it," growled the Old Man from the far end of the table.

The Legionnaire stretched out a steely hand and closed it round Tiny's wrist. He shook his head disapprovingly. "A joke's a joke, but we don't want a corpse on our hands, do we?"

"Don't we?" Tiny considered the matter. "Why not?"

"Because they're damn difficult things to get rid of," I suggested.

"Why? Why not take 'em down and dump 'em in the water?"

Barcelona gave a short crack of laughter. "You ever tried

marching down to the harbor with a corpse tucked under your arm? You'd have the cops down on you like a ton of bricks before you were even halfway there."

While Tiny was digesting this disagreeable possibility, Heide suddenly took his nose out of his beer mug to inform us that he was in no mood to stand guard duty that night and had half a mind to go to the brothel down the road to see their renowned whore in the green dress. We had all heard of the lady in question, though speaking for myself, I had never seen her in the flesh.

"Mark you, she's expensive," said Barcelona gravely.

"But worth it," said Heide.

"You know old Bernie the Boozer?" Porta leaned toward us, his eyes gleaming. "He told me that for a couple of thousand he'd spent a whole night and half the next day with her. According to him, he was on the job nonstop and did it sixty-seven times."

"Like hell!"

"It's true," insisted Heide. "I saw him the day after, he hardly had the strength to get out of bed."

"Ridiculous way to spend your money," said the Legionnaire.

"Oh, I don't know . . ."

With an obscene smile on his lips and his thoughts obviously far away, Porta pulled out a seagull's egg and cracked it into his beer. With the point of his bayonet he stirred the mixture dreamily round and round.

I watched him, fascinated. "Is it good?" I asked.

"Horrible," replied Porta, licking his bayonet clean.

"Tell us that story of the girl you asked to marry you," suggested the Old Man, leaning back in his chair and filling his pipe. He glanced at his watch. "We've just got time before we go on duty." And he hauled his feet up on the table, settling comfortably in his chair and preparing himself to listen to one of Porta's rambling excursions into storytelling— part truth, part invention, the more improbable passages being, to anyone knowing Porta, the ones most likely to have taken place.

The rest of us followed the Old Man's example and put our feet up on the table. Steiner was lying on the floor groaning, and we left him to it.

"Well, it was right back at the beginning of the war," Porta began, coaxing the remains of his egg yolk up the side of the glass with one finger and sliding it into his mouth.

"Before all the fighting broke out. I was with the 11th Regiment at Paderborn—don't know if you've ever been to Paderborn. Horrible, it was. Dead as a doornail, nothing to do from one day to the next except stand and stare at all the pie-faced hicks that lived there running off to church every five minutes. Not only that, but to tell you the honest truth I wasn't all that struck on the idea of fighting this war from the word go. Seemed pretty crazy to me; shells and bombs and Christ knows what—nothing to eat, nothing to drink—" He drew in a breath and shook his head. "Didn't do nothing for me at all. It's not for you, I says to myself. It's not for you at all, Porta, my boy—you got to get out of this as quick as you can. Well, as you know, I'm not one to sit around on my ass doing nothing. No sooner said than done, that's me. So the minute I'd made my mind up, I got this rather serious malady what threatened to do me in."

The Old Man laughed. "I'll never forget it—God knows what he didn't do to himself to try and get sick. The stuff he ate—Christ, it would've felled an elephant! But not this guy. Oh, no! The more he tried, the healthier he got."

"Yeah, I reckon I got so toughened up you could've bounced me all over a fucking minefield and I'd've come out in one piece." Porta sucked the egg off his fingers, picked up a leg and farted, then settled back to his story. He grinned at us knowingly. "I did it all right in the end, though. I was a bit green in them days, but I wangled my way into the infirmary all right."

"I remember the infirmary!" cried Tiny excitedly. "Stuck away round the back of the cathedral. They shoved me in there when my big toe swelled up. Enormous, it was. Almost had to take it off." He turned to Porta. "Here, you remember that sawbones they had in there? Him with the wooden leg? What was his name?"

"Brettschneider," said Porta.

"Yeah, Brettschneider, that was the bastard! I remember when I was in there . . ."

"What about my story?" said Porta coldly.

Tiny looked at him a moment, blinked, then said, "All right, go ahead."

"Thank you. Well, like I was saying, I got took off to the infirmary, where I saw this doctor you just mentioned. And he was a bastard, I'll grant you that. First day I was in there, he comes marching up to me with half the hospital trailing behind him. They screech to a halt at my bed, and he stands there, coughing in my face and asking me what I'm playing at and what I think's wrong with me. So I explains about how I'm paralyzed practically all over and can't feel a thing, and how unfortunate it is, on account of the war starting up, and how I wanted to do my bit and all that, and all the time he just goes on standing there and coughing—and me paralyzed all over," said Porta indignantly. "Paralyzed all over and couldn't even move out of the way. Might have had TB or the galloping clap for all I knew. So anyway, after a bit I gives a sort of groan, like—" Porta gurgled hideously in the back of his throat, "and he agrees with me about it being unfortunate, and then quite sudden like, he whips off all the bedclothes and leaves me lying there exposed with all these strangers looking on like I was some sort of specimen been tipped out of its bottle. So then he starts kind of prodding and poking and saying can I feel it and does it hurt, and me just lying there and making like I can't feel a damn thing, and all the time I'm thinking, you're not going to catch me, you bastard, you scum, you lousy stinking medico. Anyway, after a bit he straightens up and tells everyone how sad it is, this poor soldier going and getting paralyzed right at the start of the war. 'But never mind,' he says to me. 'I reckon we can put you right again. How did you say it come on?' he asks. 'Sort of sudden like? Just about the time when war was declared? Like a sort of shock?'" Porta looked round at us and closed one eye. "Stringing me along, see? Making like he was easy to con. So I thought I'd pile it on a bit, give it a few details. 'You're right,' I says. 'That was just how it come on, like a sort of shock, all through the body, like you said. I was standing in line with the others—we was being given our gear, see—and all of a sudden I come over bad. Real bad. Cold sweat and stars and everything turning round and this horrible kind of ringing in the ears. I managed to go another few yards and then I got this paralysis like, and I just blacked out—' Oh, I tell you," said Porta, "I really laid it on thick. Like I said, I was green in them days—I even forced a few tears out and carried on about how bad I felt, not being able to fight and earn medals and how proud my poor old mom and dad would've been if their son had been a hero. 'Tell me!' I cries, all ardent like, 'surely there's some way a man what's paralyzed can serve his country and his people and his Führer?' You know what the bastard said?"

We shook our heads obligingly, though some of us had

obviously heard it all before in one version or another. Porta spat.

" 'Oh, yes,' he says, 'you can get up and start walking again just like everyone else has to.' And with that, he bashes me real hard on the kneecap when I'm not ready for it, and my old leg shoots out and knocks his glasses off—Jesus, I don't know who was more mad, him or me! So anyway, when he's recovered a bit and they've picked his glasses up for him and stopped sniggering behind their hands, he takes some bloody great long thing off a tray and begins shoveling it down my lughole until I think it's going to come out the other side of my head—and when he's finished playing with that, he yanks my eyelids somewhere over the top of my head and has a good long look at my eyeballs, till after a bit—thinking maybe he's color-blind—I says, 'They're blue,' and he says, 'What?' and I says, 'Blue, fancy having a doctor what's color-blind,' and he just cusses me all over the bed and starts fishing down my throat looking for my tonsils. God, that bastard had a field day! He was in my mouth, down my ears, up my ass, everywhere he could possibly poke something he poked it . . ."

"So what happened in the end?" asked Stege, who was new to the story.

"Hang on a minute, I'm getting there!" said Porta irritably. He couldn't bear to be interrupted, or urged on to the conclusion before he was ready for it. "Next thing the bastard does, he stands back and says how sorry he feels for me. 'It's enough to break your heart,' he says, 'seeing this young man what's so gravely ill and asks nothing more but being able to serve his people and his country and his Führer. It might be better,' he says, 'to put you in an isolation ward—like maybe a military prison? But we'll see how you go,' he says. 'It wouldn't surprise me if you was to get better quite sudden. It's the way with these maladies like what you've got. They attack people sudden and they go sudden, especially at times like now, when the country's at war. You'd be surprised,' he says, 'how many other brave boys like you have been struck down in the prime of life this past week or so—and most of 'em,' he says, grinning with his dirty great teeth, 'most of 'em's already up and about and back with their units—just like you're going to be.' " Porta shook his head. "What a bastard! Next thing I know, he's trying to get me out of bed—trying to get me to walk, like some corny miracle in the Bible! He has four of 'em haul me out and set me upright, and of course as soon as they lets me go I just collapses on the floor and they has to put me back again. He doesn't like that. You can tell he doesn't. For two pins I bet he'd have given up and walked off and left me to it. Only he couldn't do that, on account of he was supposed to be curing me, so he sort of pulls his face together and starts telling the sister what sort of treatment she's got to give me. 'We'll start off gentle,' he says. 'Nothing too drastic—put him on a fluid diet,' he says, 'for a start. No solids. No meat. Right? And of course, no alcohol. Give him emetics every day,' he says, 'to make him vomit. Purge him every other day, clean his bowels out. If that doesn't work, try him on quinine—but nothing harsh, not just at the moment. We'll see if we can't cure him the easy way first.' And then he grins at me, the bastard, and he leans over the bed and he says, 'We'll have you out of here and serving at the front in record time, you see if we don't—we'll have you winning medals yet,' he says. 'You'll have your chance to be a hero.' Honest," said Porta, "it was more like a threat than a promise. So I thanks him very kindly with tears in my eyes, and all the time I'm swearing to God he's not going to get the better of me . . .'"

"And does he?" asked Stege. "I mean, did he?"

"'Course he did," said Porta scornfully. "With half the Army trying it on? He could spot them a mile off. Took him eleven days to get me back on my feet again. Eleven days of purgatory! He drove me out of that place, you know that? They get you to such a state you'd sooner walk through a fucking minefield than let them go on messing about with you. I remember there were four others in the same ward with me. One had rheumatism, one had kidney trouble, one had lost his memory and one was just a nut—at least, I thought he was. He acted like one all right. Old Brettschneider said he was as sane as anyone else. I dunno, though. We were all 'cured' at the same time and sent back together to the regiment. Well, we'd only been back a couple of days when this nut sticks a gun in his mouth and pulls the trigger. Leaves half his brains splattered about on the ceiling —I dunno whether you'd really call that sane . . ."

"It's all very well," said Stege, "but you can't blame the doctor. He was only doing his job. He never knows, when he sends a malingerer packing, whether he's going to crack up under the strain . . ."

"Balls!" said Porta.

"I remember that incident," put in Barcelona. "Wasn't it

that bastard of a sergeant—what was his name? Gerner, was it? Well, wasn't it him that drove the poor jerk to it?"

"Just like he drove many others," agreed Porta. "Were you there that time he had a go at Schnitius? You remember Schnitius? The one what ended up having his feet amputated? Well, he used to go round in fear and trembling of Gerner. Were you there that time he cracked down on him?"

"It rings a bell," said Barcelona. "Something to do with an ashtray, wasn't it?"

"Yeah. That's the one. Gerner come round on one of his inspections—you know what he was like about the place being spotless all the time? Well, he comes round one day and we're all standing to attention as neat as you please without a speck of dust to be seen anywhere, when old Schnitius suddenly discovers he's forgotten to empty his ashtray. Now Gerner doesn't smoke and he goes mad about ashtrays full of cigarette butts and so forth, so without stopping to think, Schnitius picks it up and shoves it under the bolster on his bunk. Anyway, it all goes okay until Gerner's just about to leave the room, when suddenly something makes him look round and he sees smoke rising up, like the bolster's on fire. So of course he rushes up, screaming like a maniac, and it's Schnitius' bed and old Schnitius is standing right by it, so he hasn't got much chance, really, and Gerner turns on him and says, 'Is that you what's left this shit lying round here?' And Schnitius can't very well deny it, so next thing we know, Gerner's making him eat up all the ash and the butts and the crap and lick out the ashtray into the bargain . . ."

"Jesus, yes!" cried Barcelona. "And shortly after that the poor devil spewed it all up all over the floor of the latrine . . ."

"Yeah, and Gerner comes along and catches him at it and tells him he can bloody well get down on his hands and knees and lick it all up again."

Steiner, who had been slowly and painfully recovering and had taken his seat in our midst, with a handkerchief pressed to his bleeding head, now quite suddenly transferred the handkerchief to his mouth and turned away, heaving.

I leaned forward eagerly to Porta. "Did he do it?" I asked. "Did he actually do it?"

"Sure he did it," said Porta. "He was scared stiff of that creep."

I sat back again. "I wouldn't have done it," I said.

Porta looked at me. "Schnitius wasn't full of booze like

you are. And he was new to the Army. Didn't know how to stick up for himself. Anyway, he was still down there on his hands and knees, throwing up again as fast as he cleared one patch up, when the CO comes along—Lieutenant Henning," he said to Barcelona. "He was all right, as officers go, but it used to make him mad when he had to deal with squabbles between the men. So he hauls Schnitius into his office and asks him what the devil he thinks he's doing, and Schnitius, like the stupid jerk he is, goes and shoots his mouth off about Gerner and the way he's been treating him. So then, of course, the lieutenant gets madder than ever and calls Hauptfeldwebel Edel into his office and tells him to tear strips off Gerner. And the result is that Gerner gets put in the brig for ten days and the rest of the NCOs gang up together and beat the hell out of Schnitius for what he done to Gerner. If the fool had had any sense, he'd never have mentioned Gerner in the first place. He'd've said he enjoyed eating spew, or he was just doing it for a lark, or something. Only like I said, we was all so green in those days . . ."

"Hang on a minute," interrupted the Old Man. "I thought you were going to tell us about this girl you asked to marry you?"

"Ah, yes," said Porta. "Yeah—well, it was after I'd been driven out of the infirmary. While I was in there I'd seen this broad several times and taken a bit of a fancy to her. She used to hang about after Brettschneider when he come round the wards with his little band of followers. I was really quite gone on her. When I got out, I started sending her postcards. First one I sent, I'll always remember that, it was one of them old ones they was bringing out, with some Feldwebel dressed up in old-fashioned gear choking the life out of a Polish dragoon or some such. And across the top, in large letters, it said 'Vengeance.' I remember wondering at the time whether she'd get the message."

"What message?" said Stege.

"Well—that I wanted to slip her a length, see?"

"And did she get it?" Stege asked, bewildered.

He had yet to learn that when listening to one of Porta's stories, you accepted it as it came, without troubling too much about the internal logic.

"No, I don't think she did at first. Any rate, I didn't hear nothing from her. So in the end I sent one with a message wrote on the back of it. Here was this airman, see, sitting on this bench with a broad. And the airmen's got his hands tucked down between his thighs, and the broad's making these eyes at him, and on the back I wrote a sort of love note . . ."

"What did you say?" asked Tiny.

"I don't remember after all this time. I just know I took a lot of trouble with it. I didn't write any old thing. I started off saying how I hoped she wouldn't think it a liberty, me writing to a lady like her from the shitty barracks I was in, only I thought shitty mightn't be the right word, so I crossed it out and wrote Prussian instead. I took trouble, see? I didn't just put down the first thing what come into my head."

"I hope she appreciated it," said Stege.

"You bet she did! Very puffed up she was—probably never been courted like that in her life before. Mind you, she was shy at first. I had to wait days before she'd agree to see me. Then she sent some kid round with a message and said I could go and call on her if I liked. She lived with her family, of course. An old house in the Bismarckstrasse it was. I knew I had to create a good impression, so I had a shave like, and smartened up the old uniform and had a bit of a wash down, and it was just as well I did, 'cause when I got there it was one of them posh places and it was the maid what opened the door to me. Very snooty she was too. Wanted to know if I'd got a card she could take in. 'I don't need no card,' I says to her. 'You ask anyone at Paderborn,' I says. 'I'm very well known round these parts.' So off she goes, walking like she's got a poker up her backside, and leaves me standing there in the hall. While she's gone I has a quick gander round to see what's what, and I take the opportunity to clean up my boots on a velvet cushion what they've got on the sofa. Velvet's one of the best things you can get for polishing boots on, and now I've got clean feet and all I'm beginning to feel like a proper gentleman."

"Just a minute," protested Tiny. "I thought you said you was in the hall?"

"That's right. That's where she left me."

"So how come you're using velvet cushions off the sofa to polish your feet on?"

"Because they've got this huge great sofa in the hall, that's why! Jesus, you can tell you ain't never been anywhere classy! I suppose you think the hall's a fucking little passage behind the front door, don't you? Well, it ain't, it's a great big space with furniture and pictures and all, just like a room. And where they sit and nosh is different from where they sit and yak. And where they sit and yak ain't downstairs, like you and me's used to, it's up on the first floor. And where . . ."

"And the head's got a mink cover on the frigging seat!" jeered Tiny. "Skip the boring details and just tell us the dirty bits. What happened next? She come down to this hall what's like a room and you pulled her onto this sofa with the velvet cushions and you got the meat in?"

"Pardon me," said Porta, "but I refuse to be rushed. Either you listen to the whole story and nothing but the story and get the artistic bits along with the physical ones, or I give up and you can start telling your own goddamn tales. Take it or leave it, but I got my pride same as what Schiller and all that had. You want to appreciate the juicy parts, you got to sit through the rest of it first. Like not having cake till you've had the bread and butter."

Tiny retired, grumbling, and telling us to give him a nudge when Porta got to the point where he screwed the girl. If ever he did. Steiner turned around with a blood-and-vomit-stained handkerchief and asked blearily, "What's going on?"

"Nothing!" Tiny sat up again, triumphantly. "That's just what I'm complaining of—*nothing's* going on. If that'd been me, now, I'd have raped her ten times before I'd even got as far as the house. And then I'd have had her on the sofa, and on the velvet cushions, and . . ."

"But what happened?" I said to Porta. "What happened in the end?"

Porta shrugged his shoulders sullenly. It was plain that Tiny had upset what he conceived to be his artistic soul and that now we should never hear the end of the tale.

"Tell her the bit about asking her father if you could marry her," urged the Old Man.

"Why?" said Porta. "It's not funny."

"That's a matter of opinion," said the Old Man, who had obviously heard the story many times before.

"Christ almighty!" said Porta angrily. "I only asked him if I could have her hand in marriage so's we could have it away together all nice and legal like! What's so funny about that, eh? I could've prodded her on a park bench, couldn't I? I could've slipped her a length any goddamn time I liked . . ."

"Pity you didn't," said Tiny sourly. "Might have had a tale worth telling then."

"I suppose," I said, "you never did marry her?"

Porta just gave me a contemptuous stare and turned away.

" 'Course he didn't!" said Tiny. "He never married her, he never fucked her, he never did one damn thing to her!"

At that moment the loudspeakers began crackling out an order for all chiefs of section in the Fifth Company to go to the armaments room for distribution of weapons. The Old Man knocked out his pipe and stood up.

"Time we were off," he said. "Who's going to carry Steiner?"

We moved to the door, all of us somewhat the worse for wear. Tiny was furious with Porta and Porta had reverted to being furious with everyone; Steiner had to be supported by Barcelona and the Legionnaire, and Heide appeared to be walking in his sleep. As we filed past the counter, Gerda's head suddenly sprang up from nowhere, her pale eyes contracted with hatred, her lips drawn back over her long teeth.

"I hope you all fry in hell!" she hissed.

It was the end of a good evening's drinking.

"Look, they can do what they bloody well like," declared the youth, vaingloriously certain of himself. "I don't give a damn for any of 'em! Far as I'm concerned, they can go and get screwed."

He was sitting on the draining board, his feet in the sink, eating pickled gherkins from a jar. As he spoke, his companions solemnly nodded their agreement and approval. The house was full of young people, boys and girls, all very vociferous and very sure of themselves; sure of their ability to stand out against authority and of their willingness to face death rather than fight for a cause they did not believe in. On the chairs and the tables, stretched out on the floor, squatting in corners, in the kitchen, the living room, the bedrooms and the bathroom, this band of young rebels shouted their agreement.

"It's not our war!" cried a disembodied voice from beneath a table. "We didn't start it, we don't want it, and we're not going to fight it!"

"People are dying every day, in their thousands, and the poor fools don't even know what they're dying for."

"They torture them at the Gestapo. People are scared to open their mouths and tell the truth any more," declared a young girl who was not quite as young as she looked and was doing her best to seduce a nervous youth who was still a virgin.

"Well, I'm not scared!" screamed a fragile-looking creature from his position on top of the unlit stove. "When my turn comes to be called up, I shall tell them exactly what I think of them!"

"Hear, hear," murmured his companions, while the nervous youth took off his spectacles and vigorously polished them, rather alarmed at his own daring at being in such company.

"What happens if the Gestapo comes?" queried some faint-heart sitting in the passage.

"Let them come!" A young boy seated on the kitchen table, who was in the habit of declaiming dramatic poetry, threw wide his arms and faced them challengingly. "Let them come! What do we care? The world is our oyster—and this land is our land, because we are the future! They can't force us to fight and destroy ourselves!"

One Sunday evening, five months later, their weekly meetings were brought to an end by the sudden arrival of three men. Three men in leather coats, wearing shoulder holsters.

They encountered a small core of stubborn resistance, but for the most part, the proud youth of Germany were swiftly dealt with.

The nervous youth, who greeted their appearance with shrill screams of hysteria, was silenced by one sharp slap across the face.

The young girl who was not as young as she seemed, and who never had succeeded in seducing him, managed to spit out a couple of obscenities before she was kicked in the stomach and pushed to one side.

The boy who had monopolized the sink was making love on the bathroom floor with his girl friend. They were separated by a few well-placed prods with the butt end of a pistol and sent downstairs to join the others.

The poet wet his pants with fright the very moment the intruders arrived. He offered no resistance of any kind.

In a long line, shuffling single file with their heads hanging, fifty-two boys and girls left the house and entered two green coaches that were waiting outside. The world was their oyster, but fear was an unknown quality and they were meeting it face to face for the first time.

For three days they were retained at Stadthausbrücke No. 8. Their treatment was not particularly harsh, but it was enough simply to be there; it was enough to learn the meaning of fear and to understand that courage had no place in their lives. Courage was for those with power.

After three days they were put into uniform and sent off for training. Several died during their preliminary courses of instruction; some through accidents, others because they chose to. And as for the rest, they battled on and tried to come to terms with their new situation and their new selves; tried to grow reconciled to the fact that when it came to the point, they were no different from all the other poor idiots whom they so heartily despised.

They didn't want to fight. It wasn't their war. They hadn't started it and they didn't believe in it. But they fought just the same.

IV

ON GUARD AT THE GESTAPO

We saw them coming up the steps, pushing an old woman between them. The two Unterscharführer, Schultz and Paulus. Kriminalrat Paul Bielert's most indefatigable headhunters.

We stood at the entrance to the building and watched them go in.

"I wonder what that poor old cow's supposed to have done?" muttered Porta.

I shrugged my shoulders and made no reply. What could I have said? How did I know what one miserable old woman, wearing a coat that stank of mothballs, might have done to offend the Gestapo? It was a perennial wonder to me how the average uninfluential citizen ever managed to avoid offending them.

As the old woman passed in front of us, she turned and smiled. She half opened her mouth, then Paulus gave her a shove forward and they passed through the doors. I wondered what she wanted to say to us, two strange soldiers standing in the rain with trickles of water dripping off our helmets and down the backs of our necks.

We turned and watched as they walked toward the elevators. The old woman could hardly keep up with the two men and their long-legged strides. Schultz gave her another push.

"Come on, granny. We haven't got all day. You're not the only one that's been invited to the party."

They pressed the button and stood waiting for the elevator to arrive. Paulus suddenly caught sight of Porta and me standing watching from the doorway and he waved an impatient hand.

"Get out of here! You're supposed to be on guard duty, and in any case this isn't a pantomime. Go on, piss off!"

"Watch it," growled Porta warningly. "You don't give orders to me, sweetheart!"

"That's what you think!" Paulus came striding toward us, his gray eyes two contracting pinpoints. "You seem to have forgotten that I'm an Unterscharführer . . ."

"Filthy shit, more like."

"You dare to talk to me like that?" demanded Paulus, almost as taken aback as I was myself.

"Why not?" said Porta with one of his evil grins. "You can't do nothing to me—not without I spill the beans about that raid you carried out at No. 7 Herbertstrasse. You haven't forgotten that already, have you? Because I can assure you that I haven't. In fact, I been thinking, Paulus— we got room for someone like you in our regiment. How'd you like to leave the SD and come and join us, eh? Guys have come to us for doing far less than what you've done."

The man's eyes widened, and then contracted again. "What do you know about Herbertstrasse?" he asked.

"I know you're a thief, for a start . . ."

Paulus drew himself up very stiff and raised a cold eyebrow. "Are you presuming to call an Unterscharführer of the SD a thief?"

"Right first time," said Porta cheerfully. "And I'll say it again if I feel like—whenever and wherever I feel like it. Why not? You got any objections?"

Paulus heard the elevator arriving. He pursed his lips to a thin line and strode away, not looking back in our direction. Porta watched him, a satisfied smirk on his lips. "That'll give him a few sleepless nights, the bastard!"

"Why?" I said. "What went on at Herbertstrasse?"

We turned back again, into the rain.

"To tell the truth," admitted Porta, "I don't really know, except it's where they picked up those two whores a few days ago. The ones that had been hiding a couple of deserters. Apparently they done a raid on the place, and whatever went on there it was enough to make old Paulus think twice, wasn't it? You see the way he changed color?"

"But surely to God you know more about it than that?"

Porta shrugged. "Only by hearsay. One of the whores that lives at No. 7—not the two they took away, another one. The place is lousy with 'em—well, she was telling me that Paulus and another jerk swiped the girls' ration cards and walked off with their savings. I wasn't sure it was true until just now."

"You mean, you tried it on without really knowing?" I said, aghast.

"Why not? Nothing venture, nothing win, as some other old geezer once said."

"And what now? You going to squeal on him?"

"Not before I've squeezed him dry," said Porta callously. "When he ain't no more use to me, I'll make damn sure he's sent off to Fuhlsbüttel—and on the day he finds himself landed in a disciplinary unit, I'm going to go out and paint the town the brightest bloody red you ever saw!"

"Always assuming you're still alive to do it," I grunted. "One of these days you're going to bite off just a bit more than you can chew. One of these days you're going to meet up with someone who turns around and tells you to go screw yourself."

"Balls!" said Porta. "You think I don't know what I'm doing? They're all the same, these types, right from Himmler on down. The minute you try a bit of the old blackmail on them, they all get the wind up and start shitting blue bricks —they've all got something to hide, see? All you got to do is find out what it is."

We stood in silence a few moments, contemplating the empty street. The rain blew into our faces and got into our eyes and down our necks.

"I wonder what that poor old girl had been up to," I said.

"I dunno. Opened her mouth too wide, I expect."

"Think they'll give her the full treatment?"

"Why not? Only reason they bring 'em in, to see how loud they can make 'em shout."

We tramped along by the side of the building, our heavy boots resounding on the pavements. The pale light of the streetlamps was reflected in our wet helmets and rifles.

"I could do with a glass of soda and slivovitz right now," said Porta longingly.

"Make it slivovitz and soda," I said, "and I'll join you—three-quarters slivovitz and the rest soda—and God in heaven!" I added irritably as I felt my shirt flapping damply against my back, "I'm sick to death of this pissing rain! I'm sick to death of the whole damn war, and everything to do with it! We're all sick to death of it! They're sick of it, we're sick of it, so why the hell don't we all call it quits and go home again?"

"Some hope," said Porta cynically. "It's only those what have to fight the fucking thing that are sick of it—and they're not the ones what can call it off. Them as starts it and them as finishes it aren't nothing to do with the likes of you and me. They don't give a shit what we feel about it, and they're not going to get sick of it all the time they're making all that money out of it, are they? They'll just go on until we're all dead and buried. Much they care! And them over there," pointed wildly in a direction that seemed to take in England and the rest of Europe, "they're just as bad as them over here. Revenge, that's all they want. Revenge and money, that's all any of 'em wants."

"It's like the Legionnaire said the other day," I agreed. "They call this World War II, but really it's just the same as World War I and every other war that's ever been fought. It's all one great big war that never ends. We think it ends and then another one starts up, but he's quite right, it's all the same one, just fought on different fronts at different times with different weapons . . ."

I remembered very clearly the Legionnaire saying that.

"It won't ever end," he said, "because *they* don't want it to. Why should they? As long as the war goes on, then capitalism can flourish. Stands to reason, doesn't it? So of course they're going to keep it alive. It might die down from time to time, but they'll damn well make sure the fire never goes out altogether. There'll always be someone there to fan the flames."

"That's treason!" shouted Heide. "I could denounce you for that! That's Communist talk!"

"Balls," said the Legionnaire distastefully. "Communist, capitalist, Nazi, I hate the whole damned lot of them. I'm just a soldier, doing what I'm told to do."

The Old Man looked at him a moment, then asked, "Do you enjoy being a soldier?"

"That's irrelevant," said the Legionnaire with a shrug. "It's just a job, same as any other job. No one ever bothered to ask me what I'd *enjoy* doing. I didn't have any choice in the matter."

"So that's why you do it?"

"Well, look at it this way." The Legionnaire leaned forward to face him closer. "Do *you* like being a soldier? Did *you* have any choice in the matter? Does anyone? Why do people go on paying their taxes? Or not driving without a license? Or paying for their food instead of stealing it? Because they *enjoy* doing these things? Or because they don't have any choice in the matter? Because they don't have any choice in the matter, that's why. It's either obey the law or go to the pokey. Or, as in my case originally, being a soldier or starving. Or as in our case now—your case and my case and Sven's and Porta's and Tiny's—being a soldier and doing what they say, or being stood against a wall and having our brains blown out." He sat back, shaking his head. "And if you call that any sort of choice, then I don't."

I sighed and watched the rain falling steadily off my helmet.

"Fucking guard duty," I said. "Seems like it goes on for weeks at a stretch."

"Let's pray for a pussy cat," said Porta. "A nice fat black pussy we can shoot at. Anything to relieve the monotony . . ."

We had retraced our steps and were back near the entrance to the building, with its crenellated wall, its loopholes and small turrets.

"Let's slip behind there and have a smoke," said Porta. "We can get out of the way of this god-awful rain then. No one won't come looking for us here."

We slipped behind the wall, settled ourselves in a dry spot and removed our helmets. There was only a quarter of an hour to go before Heide and Tiny would turn up to relieve us. Doubtless they would bring something strong and warming to drink with them.

"Who knows?" said Porta hopefully. "We stay here long enough, we might even give some poor jerk just the opportunity he's been waiting for to send the whole damn lot of 'em up in flames. In fact, anyone come up to me with a bomb in his hand and asked me to look the other way for a bit, I'd do it like a shot. He wouldn't even have to bribe me . . ."

"Talking of money," I said, squatting on my haunches, "what about those steel helmets the Legionnaire lifted from Supplies? What's happening to them?"

"They're with a Swedish janitor in the Bernhard Nachtstrasse at the moment. He says they're safe as houses, but they can't stay there forever. There's a locksmith in Thalstrasse who's willing to buy 'em, but he wants us to dump 'em all in a depot in Ernst Strasse—just opposite Altona Station. Problem is, getting 'em there. We can't use our own trucks, we'd never get away with it."

"How much is he willing to pay?" I asked. And then added, "As a matter of fact, I know where we can lay hands on a load of howitzer shells, but again it's a question of transport. We'd have to go early in the morning and we'd have to have an SS truck. Not only that, we'd need a special permit signed by the SS, or they wouldn't let us collect the stuff. They've been a bit jumpy ever since some geezer managed to walk off with a couple of engines that didn't belong to him—still, if we could get the necessary transport, it'd be worth a try. I was tipped off by a guy I know in the SS; he's got a chip as big as Mount Everest on his shoulder on account of he once tried to do a bunk and they caught up with him."

"This locksmith," said Porta. "He's giving us sixty-seven pfennig a kilo. We'd probably be able to screw him a bit more for the shells. Say sixty-nine—any rate, like you say, it's worth a try. Tiny could manage a nice new set of number plates, and if we took the big Krupp, we might get away with it. That's a twin brother to an SS truck, near as damn it."

"How about the permit?"

"Couldn't your pal in the SS wangle it for us?"

"Could be. How much do you think we'd have to pay him for it?"

"A kick in the ass," said Porta. "We've got a hold on him, don't forget. One squeak out of us and he's for the high jump."

"Yeah, but—" I broke off and closed a hand over Porta's wrist as I heard footsteps approaching. "Watch it! Someone's coming . . ."

We sat there a moment, our ears strained, and then Porta poked the muzzle of his rifle through the loophole. "If it's a Gestapo bastard, I shall shoot him," he decided. "Anyone says anything, we'll tell 'em we thought it was a saboteur. They're always going on about saboteurs."

"You crazy?" I said. "We'd never get away with it."

Porta suddenly lowered his rifle, obviously disappointed. "It's only Tiny and Heide."

We peered over the top and saw them slowly approaching.

They were talking earnestly and waving their arms about, and Tiny had a bottle clenched in one vast paw.

"Thank you, God, for the Emperor," breathed Porta. "And specially for his horse."

We heard Tiny's loud laugh, and then the lower tones of Heide, grumbling and cursing.

"He's a shit, he's a prick, and he's a bastard, and he's going to get what's coming to him. Great stupid queen—well, this time he's for it!" He paused, spat on the pavement and ground it in with the heel of his boot. "You wait till I get my hands on him. You just wait!"

"I don't like him, either," said Tiny.

"Biggest load of shit I've ever met in the whole of my life," said Heide vindictively.

Porta laughed and jabbed me in the ribs. "That'll be Feldwebel Brandt—wanna bet?"

"Like hell!" I said. "On a sure thing?"

"Well, it was time he was bumped off. Sounds like Julius might have something in mind."

"I'm game," I said. "I can't stand the bastard."

"Suppose I jump up and down on his belly till he farts his guts out," we heard Tiny suggest in his helpful way.

"Jesus Christ!" There was a fanatical glare in Heide's eyes. "Only to think of the swine makes me feel sick! I still don't know how it happened—" He stood still and held out his arms appealingly. "Tiny, just tell me—aren't I the cleanest, smartest, best-groomed soldier in the whole regiment? In the whole division? In the whole damned Army?"

Tiny looked at him and nodded vigorously. "Yeah. Yeah, I guess that's right."

"Of course it's right! Look at my chin strap—look at it, go on, look at it! I'll give you my next five years' pay if you can find even the slightest mark on it—well, you can't, I promise you that, so don't yank my goddamn head off!' Heide jerked himself away from Tiny, who had taken the offer literally and was peering closely at his chin strap, clutching it with one big paw. "You know what," continued Heide, "when I was going through training—and this is Gospel truth, so help me God—they used to end up looking at our asses if they couldn't find anything else to get us on. And you know what? My ass was the cleanest bloody arse in the whole company! And still is! You could look up my ass any day of the week, any minute of the day, and you'd find it as clean as a new pin. I swear to you," cried Heide, growing ever more excited, "that I wash the damn thing out three times a day!"

"I believe you!" shouted Tiny, becoming infected with some of Heide's own enthusiasm. "I believe you, you don't have to show me!"

"Look at my comb!" Heide pulled it out of his pocket and thrust it beneath Tiny's face. "Cleaner than the day I bought it! And just tell me, what's the first thing I do when we've had to dig ourselves in somewhere? What's the first thing I do?"

"You clean your fingernails," said Tiny positively. "I've seen you do it."

"Precisely. I clean my fingernails. And what do I do it with? I do it with a nail file—not with the point of my bayonet, like you and the others."

"That's right," nodded Tiny. "That is quite right."

"And what about this!" Almost beside himself, Heide dragged off his helmet and pointed to his head. "Not a hair out of place! All cut according to regulations—combed according to regulations—even the fleas march single file on the right! But Leopold Brandt, the Feldwebel of the devil, God rot his balls—Leopold Brandt has to haul me up on account of my part isn't dead straight! Me!" screeched Heide, turning purple. "Me of all people!"

"It's a diabolical liberty," said Tiny earnestly.

"It's more than that, it's a bloody outrage!"

"It is," agreed Tiny. "It's an outrage."

"The man's a nut!" cried Heide. "He even had me standing at one end of the courtyard while he climbed up onto the roof of Third Company HQ and looked at me through a goddamn range finder! Just so he could *prove* the bloody thing wasn't straight!"

"That's madness, that is," said Tiny.

They walked forward, caught sight of us and slipped behind the shelter of the wall to join us.

"What's all this?" demanded Porta. "You got it in for Brandt, have you?"

"I'll tell you something," confided Heide, "only keep it under your hats. If we can manage to get friend Leopold as marker on number three next time we have rifle practice with real ammunition—" He paused significantly, nodded and winked, "that'll be the end of that creep."

"How come?"

Tiny turned to whisper in Heide's ear. "Shall we tell 'em?"

"If they swear to keep their big mouths shut."

Porta and I instantly swore. Tiny took a jubilant swig of slivovitz from his bottle and handed it on to Porta.

"It was like this," he said. "It was me what thought of it in the first place, and it's me what's arranged it all—it come to me when I was out on the rifle range last week, this sudden idea about how we could polish the bastard off. It was just a question of having the opportunity." He took back the bottle and had another swig. "Well, I had the opportunity a couple of days ago. I was sent off with another guy to change the plate on number two. While we was doing it, he had to go off to the latrines to pee—seeing as how Hinka blows his stack if the place starts stinking of urine; he can't stand anyone pissing on the Third Reich. Anyway, while he was gone, I took the opportunity to take the plate off of number three and fix it on again a bit too low down, see?" He demonstrated, with one hand beneath his chin. "Result is, anyone stands on the butt and his head's unprotected and liable to get blown off—and nobody to say who's responsible for it."

"Very clever," I said, "but how can you guarantee that it's Leopold who's on number three at the right time?"

Tiny tapped his head with a finger. "I'm not as stupid as you may think, I got it all worked out. First, it's the Legionnaire what draws up the lists, so he can easy arrange for Leopold to be on number three. Second, we all know that Leopold likes showing off when he's out there. And third, we always finish up by firing with telescopic sight, and it's always at number three—right?"

"I guess so," I said. "But I still don't get it."

"Well now, someone—" and he looked meaningly at Heide and Porta, "someone has to go out and finish the job by fixing a few explosives in the loophole where Leopold's going to stick his ugly head—and then it won't be your fault if you fire a bit to one side, will it?"

"It's a cinch!" Heide rubbed his hands together. "Can't fail!"

"Only one thing," I said. "Suppose the Old Man finds out? There'll be hell to pay—you realize it's premeditated murder?"

"What, killing a shit like that?" Porta sounded genuinely surprised. "That's not murder, that's a service to your country!"

"Yeah? You just try telling that to the Old Man."

"Look," said Heide, coming over to me and holding up a clenched fist by way of warning, "you don't have to come in with us on this, nobody's forcing you, but one squawk and you've had it."

"I'm shedding no tears for Leopold," I told him, pushing his fist away. "I just don't fancy swinging for a bastard like that."

"Nobody ain't going to swing," said Porta. He took some dice from his pocket, crouched down, blew on them, rattled them in his hand and blew on them again. "A game, anyone?"

Tiny squatted down to join him. He looked on with interest as Porta repeated his performance with the dice.

"What's all the show for? Everyone knows they're loaded."

Porta looked up, indignant. "That's just where you're wrong. I wouldn't dream of using loaded dice with you. As a matter of fact, I've got two sets. This is the good one."

"Ha bloody ha," said Heide.

Slowly, Porta turned his head to look at him. Slowly he tossed the dice from hand to hand.

"That reminds me," he said, "you owe me two liters of slivovitz and twelve pipes of opium. Due yesterday. Should have kept your mouth shut, I might have forgotten about it—and from now on, the interest goes up to 80 percent. You know, Julius, you'll have to start taking a grip on yourself. Too many debts aren't good for a man." He pocketed his dice, stood up and took out a small black notebook. He smeared a tongue liberally over his finger and began leafing through the pages. "Let's have a look, see where we stand —here we are. Julius Marius Heide, Unteroffizier, 27th Regiment, 5th Company, Section Two, Group Three—that's what I've wrote down." He fixed Heide with a stern eye. "I suppose you won't deny that *is* you?"

"You know damn well it is!" snapped Heide. "Wise guy!"

Porta raised a warning eyebrow. He held the book nearer to his face and bid Tiny shine the beam of his torch over it.

"April 4—9 bottles of vodka. April 7—3 bottles of slivovitz. April 12—I've got that down as your birthday. That's hard, that is. You owe more from that day than any other—712 marks and 13 pfennigs, 21 bottles of slivovitz, 9 pipes of opium, Danish eau-de-vie, a half case of Dortmünder, free entry to the brothel for a month . . ."

Porta's voice droned on with the long list of Heide's debts.

"Then we come to the 20th—that's Adolf's birthday, that

is. Let's have a gander what you had on that day—should mean something pretty special to you, Julius." Porta gave him a knowing leer. "After all, you was a member of the Party, if I mistake not."

"Was," agreed Heide. "You know damn well I'm not any more."

"Only because they threw you out," said Porta brutally. "Couldn't stand the sight of you any more. Anyway, on Adolf's birthday you lost 3,412 Reichsmarks and 12 pfennigs. And you can add 80 percent onto the whole lot. The rate you're going, doesn't look like you'll ever be free of debt, does it?"

"Hey, I wish I could write!" exclaimed Tiny, suddenly snatching the notebook from Porta and wonderingly examining the entries. "I bet you if I could write I'd be a millionaire by now. Know what I'd do? I'd dope one of them rich types and pinch his checkbook! Then all you'd have to do is sign a few checks and grab the dough."

He beamed round at us with a grin of triumph. No one had the heart to disillusion him. Porta returned to his pursuit of Heide.

"Look here," he said amicably, "we've been buddies a long time, you and me. I don't like to feel you're worried about being in debt to me all the time—how about wiping it off?"

"You mean cancel it?" said Heide, unable to believe his luck.

"Something like that," agreed Porta with a sly grin.

Heide turned instantly to Tiny and me. "You heard him! You bear witness to that!"

"Take it easy," said Porta. "No need to get so excited. Wait till you've heard my conditions."

"What conditions?" asked Heide, at once suspicious, as well he might be.

"Well, to start with, I want those three bales of cloth you've got hidden away in Beanstick's room—and then I'll have the two barrels of Dutch herrings what you left with that dentist in Hein Hoyer Strasse."

Heide's amazement was almost pitiful. His mouth dropped open, his eyes widened, and he stammered as he spoke. "How the heck did you know about that?"

Porta's little pig's eyes sparkled maliciously. "I know a lot more than you think! I know everything there is to know

about you. I make it my business to know, when people owe
me as much as what you do."

"The—the carpets in Paulinen Platz?" asked Heide, too
shaken to be circumspect.

"Of course." Porta hesitated a moment, then made a quick
stab in the dark. "Give me the carpets as well and I'll over-
look the rest and we'll call it quits."

His stab in the dark hit its target; it was obvious from
Heide's reaction that there was, indeed, something in addition to the cloth, the herrings and the carpets.

"How do I know you won't try blackmailing me?"

"Give you my word." Porta raised his arm in a three-
fingered salute.

"Your word!" scoffed Heide. "I wouldn't trust you farther
than I could throw you. You can have the herrings and the
cloth and I'll go halves with the carpets."

"Who's calling the tune around here, me or you?" Porta
wanted to know. He jabbed a finger into his chest. "It's me
you owe the money to and it's me as says what I'll take for
it. I'll have all the carpets."

"That's a bit steep!" protested Heide. "Eight hundred
carpets! That's a hell of a lot more than I owe you . . ."

"Take it or leave it," said Porta. "But if you don't play ball
with me, I certainly don't play ball with you."

"You mean you'd squeal?" asked Heide indignantly.

"You bet—over and over, about everything I can bloody
well think of! I haven't forgotten what you did to that
peasant that time.* I've had it in for you ever since. I don't
forget that easy."

Heide shrugged his shoulders. "Oh well, if you're going to
keep raking up the past—but I'll tell you one thing. Both
the herrings and the carpets are hot as hell, so don't blame
me if you get picked up for them. Just remember that I
shan't know anything about them."

"Don't kid yourself," said Porta. "They nab me and I'll
make damn sure they nab you as well."

"Well now, you just listen to me," hissed Heide. "I could
break you right here and now if I wanted—you know why?
Because I happen to know a guy who works in one of the
SS depots. And I happen to know that they're after someone
who's got away with a hefty load of steel helmets—they've
already got a cell ready and waiting at Fuhlsbüttel."

---

*See *Panzers of Death.*

"So what?"

"So it's you that stole the damn things!" screamed Heide.

"For God's sake," I said nervously. "You'll bring half the frigging Gestapo down on us if you go on shouting like that."

Heide dropped his voice to a venomous whisper. "You go on pushing your great beak into my affairs and you'll find yourself breaking stones in some labor camp before you're very much older."

It was Tiny, with one of his totally irrelevant observations, who intervened and prevented probable bloodshed.

"The day we bump off Leopold," he remarked—quite suddenly, it seemed to the rest of us, though he had doubtless been turning it over in his mind for some while—"I'm going to have a binge of sausage and slivovitz." He licked his lips and rubbed a hand over his belly. "I'm going to have a real celebration, a real blowout."

"One thing," I said. "Leopold and his pals ought to be damn proud of us. They're always bawling at us about being hard as Krupp and his precious steel—well, pretty soon they're going to find out that we are. They've done a good job on us, I guess."

"Krupp and his steel!" scoffed Tiny. "Soft as butter, that stuff. You watch this!"

He sent his fist crashing into the concrete wall; his fist remained unbroken, but the wall shuddered violently and a small crack appeared in the center and branched out in two directions. We looked at it awed, impressed as always by Tiny's feats of strength. He was a giant compared to the rest of us, and on many occasions we had seen him split open a brick with his bare hands. He had once broken a cow's neck with one flat-handed blow across its throat. Porta was also able to split open a brick, but it always took him a couple of attempts. Steiner had once tried it and broken every bone in his hand. The rest of us were content to stand by and watch, and Tiny had latterly taken to practicing with an iron bar, contemptuously dismissing bricks as child's play.

We heard footsteps approaching, and we stood listening. They sounded like the measured steps of a soldier.

"Who is it?" whispered Porta. "Tiny, go and have a gander."

Noisily, Tiny emerged from our shelter. "Halt or I'll shoot!"

The footsteps stopped abruptly and we heard a well-known voice. "Stop horsing around, it's only me."

"Who's you?" demanded Tiny.

"For crying out loud!" said Barcelona. "If you can't recognize my voice after all these years, you need your ears tested!"

"Can't help that," said Tiny obstinately. "Got to have the password before I can let anyone through."

"Piss off!"

We heard Barcelona's footsteps start up again, then abruptly cease at a wild shout from Tiny. "Give me the password or I'll fire!"

"Look, you great big oaf, it's me, Barcelona! Put that rifle down and stop assing about!"

Heide crept up to Tiny and hissed urgently at him through the darkness, "What's got into you? Let him through before there's a nasty accident."

"I got to have the password," chanted Tiny. "I'm a good soldier, I am. I know what's expected of me, I can't just let any Tom, Dick or Harry walk past."

It seemed to be deadlock. Barcelona stood uncertainly a few yards off. I held my breath, wondering what new maggot had got into Tiny but aware from past experience that it was asking for trouble to cross him when he was in one of these moods.

"Oh, for Christ's sake!" snapped Barcelona, suddenly losing patience. He launched himself at Tiny, hurtled past him and fell headfirst into our midst.

Tiny lowered his rifle and came in after him. "That had him worried," he announced smugly. "Nearly shitting green he was."

Barcelona turned on him. "What d'you think you're playing at, you brainless ape? What the hell *is* the password, anyway?"

Tiny shrugged a shoulder. "How should I know? You're the Feldwebel round here, not me. If you don't know what it is, how can we be expected to?"

"Are you out of your tiny bird-brained mind?" asked Barcelona witheringly. He saw the bottle of slivovitz and held out a hand. "Let's have a swig—the Old Man sent me round to tell you that with any luck we'll be having a quiet time of it tonight. The Gestapo's busy having a witch-hunt through the ranks, and Bielert's putting his own men through the hoop, so they're not likely to have any time to spare for us."

"What's brought this on all of a sudden?" I asked. "What's the point of it?"

"It's the great periodic purge," explained Barcelona. "They do it now and again, just to keep 'em on their toes."

"What are they getting them for?"

"Anything and everything. Everything from first-degree murder to pinching a handful of office paper clips—thuggery, buggery, rape and incest—you name it, they've done it. Bielert's got half the bloody Gestapo lined up downstairs waiting to go into the cells. I tell you, if he carries on like this all night, he'll be the only one left there in the morning."

"And a good job too," I began, when Porta suddenly interrupted with a wild cry.

"Hang on! We ought to be able to cash in on this, if we volunteer to give 'im a hand . . ."

"Who?" said Tiny, looking startled. "Bielert?"

"Of course Bielert! Who else, for God's sake?"

"But what for?" babbled Tiny.

Barcelona gave a wolfish grin. *"Qui vivra, verra,"** he murmured.

Fifteen minutes later the guard was changed and we were free to return to the guardroom. Barcelona had already gone back with news of Porta's suggestion, the Old Man had already offered our services to a surprised Bielert, and the scene was already set. We swaggered in together, and Porta at once took command of the situation. "I'm the one who's going through their pockets."

"Fair enough." The Legionnaire nodded his approval. "You've certainly got a nose for the loot."

"Just watch your step," said the Old Man grimly. "What you're proposing comes under the heading of misappropriation of funds."

"Aw, stop whining!" said Porta with a contemptuous wave of the hand.

There was a knock at the guardroom door. The Old Man walked slowly over and a secretary pushed three SD men into the room.

"All candidates for the jug," he said abruptly. "Take good care of 'em." He tossed three yellow forms onto the Old Man's desk and left the room.

Barcelona opened the register and entered the details, the men's names and ranks and the crimes for which they had been arrested. In the top left-hand corner of the yellow forms it was explained that the prisoner would be referred to

*Who lives will see.

an SS tribunal within forty-eight hours, but that he was meanwhile being guarded by a disciplinary company. In other
words, us.

Porta had taken his stand in the middle of the room. He
leered a welcome at the three prisoners.

"Take a good look," he suggested with false bonhomie,
"and see what you think of me—we're going to be stuck in
each other's company for the next few hours, so we might
as well try to get on together. It's entirely up to you, of
course, whether we do or we don't. Speaking for myself, I'm
an easy enough guy to get along with. But I'm like a cat,
see? Rub me the wrong way and it does bad things to me.
My name's Joseph Porta of the 27th Regiment and I'm an
Obergefreiter, backbone of the German Army and don't you
forget it. All right, let's have those pockets emptied!"

Reluctantly the three men laid out their possessions on the
table. Unterscharführer Blank looked understandably anxious
as he produced five marijuana cigarettes. Porta picked them
up and sniffed at them.

"You ought to be ashamed of yourself," he said. "Carrying
this sort of trash around with you. You know bloody well
it's against regulations."

"One of the prisoners gave them to me," muttered Blank
in an attempt to make his crime less heinous.

"Sounds a good enough excuse." Porta shrugged. "A prisoner give 'em you, and now a prisoner's given 'em me." He
put them carefully into a pocket and turned his attention to
Scharführer Leutz. "How about you? You had any little
gifts given you, eh?" Without waiting for Leutz' reply, he
picked up five paper sachets and opened one of them. "This
gets worse and worse," he said in outraged piety. "We only
need the pipes and we'll have a real opium den down here,
won't we?" He glared at Leutz. "How could you bear to use
the filthy stuff? You, what's supposed to be one of the pro-
tectors of the Fatherland?"

Leutz lowered his gaze to the floor. I guessed he was
smarting at his own invidious position, being rebuked by this
fool of an Obergefreiter and unable to do a thing about it.
He looked up again, his expression defiant. He moved forward slightly and I saw his muscles flex, but at the same
moment he caught sight of Tiny and stopped short. Tiny
was idly toying with a spade; a big, sturdy spade with a
thick wooden handle reinforced with iron bands. Even as

Leutz watched, Tiny nonchalantly broke the spade in half and tossed the pieces away. He glanced across at Porta.

"I'm getting out of practice," he complained. "How about lending me one of that crew to have a go on?"

"Later," said Porta. "If they don't behave themselves." He put the opium away with the marijuana cigarettes and turned to examine a gold wristwatch, picking it up and listening approvingly to its tick. "Not bad," he said, absently pocketing it.

Leutz took a few deep breaths but said nothing. Porta cast an avaricious eye at Oberscharführer Krug and was at once attracted by the enticing sight of a gold ring on one finger. Two strands of gold were twisted around each other to represent snakes, and the heads were diamonds. Porta held out his hand.

"I'd better take that off of you or you won't get to sleep tonight worrying about it." Krug protested bitterly, and Porta snapped an impatient finger. "Keep your mouth shut when you're addressing an Obergefreiter," he said grandly. "And get a move on with that ring. I'd like to know who you stole it from in the first place."

Krug changed his tactics. He put his hands on his hips and swelled out his chest. The Old Man wrote studiously at his desk, never once taking his eyes off the register.

"Can you not see," roared Krug, "that I am Oberscharführer?"

"I'm not blind," said Porta arrogantly. "But so long as you're my prisoner, I don't care if you're a goddamn general, I'll treat you like the shit you are."

Krug grew mottled and crimson. "I shall make a report of this! I demand that you treat me with respect, according to the regulations."

"Respect!" jeered Porta. "You're not even fit to wipe my ass! And the sooner you realize that you're no longer in a very healthy position, the better for you." He held out his hand again. "I'll tell you who'd like that ring," he said to the rest of us. "Old Hot Pants down at the Hurricane. She's given me good service, that girl. It's only fair she gets a little something to remember me by. And if you're a good boy," he informed Krug, "I'll tell her it was a present you give me, and whenever we're having it away together, we'll spare a thought for you in the Dirlewanger Brigade."

I saw a nervous tic ripple down the side of Krug's forehead at mention of the Dirlewanger Brigade. It was supposed to be top secret, but we knew very well, and Krug and his companions knew very well, that it was an SS disciplinary brigade whose unique mission in life was to hunt down and to kill, by any means available, the partisans who swarmed in the thick forests around Minsk. The Brigade was led by SS Brigadenführer Dirlewanger. He had been handpicked for the position from his prison cell, where he had been serving a sentence for crimes of violence, and he had an almost psychopathic streak of sadism in him. In fact, on one occasion he had so overstepped the mark that even Himmler and Heydrich had called for him to be court-martialed and condemned to death. There was a long list of indictments against him, starting with the least brutal, the rape of several Polish prisoners, but the murderer was under the powerful protection of SS Obergruppenführer Berger who, after more than one hour's talking, was able to persuade Heydrich and Himmler that for the sake of the Fatherland and for the sake of survival it was necessary to tolerate Dirlewanger and his coarse methods of warfare. Heydrich, particularly, was impressed by his argument, since it coincided very largely with his own precept of opposing terror with worse terror and violence with worse violence.

Dirlewanger ultimately met the death he deserved, though unfortunately not until January 21, 1945. It was he himself who had originally introduced the barbaric torture of roasting men slowly over an open fire, and one day in Poland he found himself on the receiving end. A party of German soldiers discovered him hanging by his feet from a tree, his head, dangling a few inches above some smoldering ashes, done to a turn like a piece of roast pork. According to some Polish partisans, the operation had been carried out by eight of his own men, who had circled about him singing joyously as he suffered and died.

He had screamed for four and a half hours. Today, in the War Museum in Warsaw, there is a picture recalling the event, with Dirlewanger's hated face plainly discernible amid the leaping flames of the fire.

Krug glared up at Porta from beneath lowered brows. He had no illusions about his probable fate, he could guess only too well what was in store for him. He had seen a great many men, old comrades, some of them, sent off to the Dirlewanger Brigade, but it was a fact that he had never seen a single one of them come back again. Rumor had it that not only the men themselves vanished forever, but that all traces of their identity, their papers, their possessions, their very names in the records, were similarly expunged.

Krug had but one chance, and that a slender one, being totally dependent upon the whim of the governor of Torgau military prison—and that one-armed bastard, reflected Krug grimly, was known to have no love for the Gestapo. Only one thing for it, and that was to be on his best behavior as a prisoner and to take every possible opportunity to declare his own loathing of the SS. The governor was bound to have his spies everywhere, and sooner or later word would be sure to reach him about the prisoner Krug's behavior. Perhaps, with any luck, he would then be able to avoid the Dirlewanger Brigade . . .

"Well?" said Porta.

Krug shook his head free of forebodings and looked defiantly at Porta. With two swift, soft steps Tiny was at his side, standing mountainous and threatening by his elbow. In the circumstances, it doubtless seemed a trifle futile to continue his protests. Krug took off the ring and sullenly handed it over.

"That's better," said Tiny, giving him a shove through the door, out into the passage and toward the cells. "Let's go and lock you up for the night. You'll be nice and cozy here until your pals come to pick you up tomorrow morning."

"God help him," said Porta cheerfully. "Doesn't stand a chance, poor bastard. Good as dead already."

Tiny opened a door and they pushed Krug into the bare cell. Tiny stood swinging a bunch of keys, while Porta was lost in admiration of his ill-gotten ring.

"How's it feel," asked Tiny curiously, "to be a living corpse?"

Krug found himself starting to sweat. He mopped at his brow with a dirty handkerchief, in the corner of which could be seen a set of initials that certainly did not belong to him.

"P.L.," read out Porta slowly. He was referring to another set of initials—those engraved on the inside of the ring. "Who's P.L., Krug?"

A hectic rash of sweat broke out on Krug's forehead. "Paula Landau—she died at Neuengamme."

"And she gave you the ring for looking after her so nicely," suggested Porta with a sneer.

Krug waved the handkerchief helplessly to and fro, his entire face now drenched in a dew of perspiration. Paula Landau. The fear of discovery had been with him ever since he had taken the ring from the dead girl's finger—the almost dead girl's finger. It was not his fault that she had died; she had been more corpse than living human being from the very day they had brought her to Neuengamme. There was nothing Krug could have done to save her, and no one would have thanked him if he had. It was not death he had on his conscience, it was the ring. He had stolen that ring, and that in itself was considered an act of treachery punishable by death. Of course, if he hadn't purloined it, someone higher up in the hierarchy would certainly have done so, but it seemed unlikely that any tribunal would accept this as a valid argument in his defense.

Krug flashed a furtive glance at Porta, then swiftly bent and unscrewed the heel of his boot. With flushed face he stood up and thrust two fifty-dollar bills at his tormentors. "It's all I've got—you're welcome to it, it doesn't look as if I shall be needing it any more."

It was a tacit plea for the subject of Paula Landau to be dropped, and Porta accordingly dropped it; not from any motives of sympathy, but simply because it seemed that there was nothing of any particular advantage to himself to be gained from pursuing the matter.

"What they get you for, anyway?" asked Tiny. "Whatever it was, I hope you didn't admit to it?"

Silently Krug bowed his head.

Tiny looked at him incredulously. "Jesus!" he said. "They make 'em stupid in the Gestapo, don't they?"

Krug shrugged his shoulders. "There wasn't any point in denying it. They'd set a trap for me, they had all the evidence they needed. There was nothing I could have said."

"Always deny everything," chanted Tiny, as if reciting a lesson he had learned by heart. "So what they pinch you for then? Caught you snitching things, did they?"

"No. I was just trying a bit of—er—well—blackmail, I suppose. I guess I went too far. Overstepped the mark."

"There's always some silly twerp that has to get himself nabbed," said Tiny philosophically. "It's a question of knowing when to stop. Like me, for instance, if I could lay my hands on ten pipes of opium, I'd only take eight of 'em. Pays off in the long run."

"That's all very well," protested Krug feebly, "but as far as I'm concerned here and now, you've taken every damn thing you can lay hands on."

"Oh well, you're different," said Tiny comfortably. "Dead

men can't talk, see? And you're as good as dead, pal—I
know, because I've had a gander at your papers. I may not
be able to read, but I'm not color-blind, and I know as well
as the next man what a dirty great red mark means—it
means Dirlewanger, and Dirlewanger means death." He
leaned forward and spoke confidentially to Krug. "You ever
seen what happens to fellas when Uncle Joe's partisans get
hold of 'em?" Krug shook his head, mesmerized by horror,
and Tiny turned triumphantly to Porta. "Tell him—go on,
tell him what we seen! Tell him about that guy what had
been eaten alive by ants."

"That's nothing," said Porta scornfully. "They know all
about that trick in the Gestapo. But what about that one
where they string you up from a couple of trees and leave
the birds to peck your eyes out?" He turned to Krug and
addressed him conversationally. "You heard of that one,
have you? Tie you up by the legs, each leg to a different
tree, and just leave you there to rot . . ."

"Nasty," said Tiny. "Very nasty—I only remember one
person ever surviving. That was that broad, Natasha de
Mogilev. You remember her?"

"I remember the mess she was when they cut her down,"
said Porta. "They'd carved two bloody great swastikas into
the cheeks of her ass and strung her up stark naked and
the birds had had a go at her face."

"Mind you, she asked for it," said Tiny. "She was selling
information to our side and framing her own people right
and left."

"Threw herself under a train in the end," mused Porta.
"But what about that SS guy they done in? What was his
name? Ginge?"

"That's right! They stuck him on a pole and roasted him
like a pig!" cried Tiny enthusiastically.

"And he wasn't even in the Dirlewanger bunch. Just an
ordinary Waffen SS officer." Porta looked kindly over at Krug.
"You want a piece of advice?" he asked. Krug nodded, his
face pale and clammy. "First chance you get there, down
there at Fuhlsbüttel, climb into a noose and hang yourself—
it's no good hoping they'll let you off the hook, because you
don't stand a chance. And don't start imagining they'll send
you to an FGA.* The only SS men we ever get are the ones
what've done something pretty small, like swiping the office

---

*Feldgefangenabteilung (disciplinary camp).

blotting paper or pissing on the CO's potted plants, but you've really gone and shit your copybook, you have. Far better do away with yourself while you've still got the chance . . ."

Porta and Tiny left the room. The heavy door clanged shut behind them. Tiny's key grated in the lock and their footsteps crashed back along the corridor. Krug stood a moment where they had left him, then slowly collapsed to the ground and lay there, staring at the concrete in blank desperation. All his life he had been told he would come to a sticky end, and now it seemed as if he had. He felt that Porta's advice had probably been good, but he knew he could never follow it. Even now he could not quite bring himself to believe in his own misfortune. And yet, as he stared around the cell, the nightmare grew clearer, closer, more realistic. The room was bare and clinical and quite incredibly clean. There was an abundance of cold air, yet no bed, no blankets, no stool. And if this was the Army for you, how much worse would the Dirlewanger Brigade be!

Krug fell at last into a troubled half sleep, only to be woken every twenty minutes or so by someone tramping up the passage in heavy boots, or by the banging of cell doors. The cells were all full, and from the amount of activity throughout the night, it appeared that Bielert was continuing his frenzied purge through the ranks. Not that that was any comfort to Krug, shivering on the bare floor of his cheerless cell. He found the prospect of dying in the company of his former SD comrades scarcely any more inviting than the prospect of putting his head in a noose.

Back in the guardroom work had slackened off and Heide and Porta had settled down to a game of cards. Inevitably, the peace was soon shattered by loud oaths and venomous shouts of accusation and counteraccusation flung back and forth across the table. On this occasion, it seemed proven beyond any reasonable doubt that Porta was the culprit; he had been holding the ace of spades up his sleeve and had somewhat maladroitly introduced it into his hand at a point when the kitty had assumed worthwhile proportions.

Heide jammed his knife hard into the table, only centimeters away from Porta's arm. "You're cheating again!"

"So what?" said Porta brazenly. Cheating was, after all, an accepted hazard of cardplaying.

"You had the ace of spades!" screamed Heide. "I saw it!"

"Well, one of us has to have it," retorted Porta. "What makes you think you've got sole claim to it?"

Heide grew stiff and pale. While Porta unconcernedly laid out his hand for all to see the incriminating card, Heide pulled his knife out of the table and brought it crashing down within an inch of Porta's shoulder. Porta moved just in time. Quick as a flash, his hand shot out in a sharp chop across Heide's throat. Heide, too, just avoided the blow. When it came to a fight, they were well matched.

Porta snatched up a bottle, smashed it against the wall and hurled what was left of it into Heide's face. Heide saw it coming and had time to duck. He gave a shriek of triumphant laughter and rushed in again with his knife. I saw it poised to strike, and then there was a scream of pain as Porta jammed a knee hard into Heide's crotch. The knife clattered to the floor. Heide rocketed backward, propelled by Porta's hands closed tight around his throat. We watched with interest as Porta got Heide up against the wall and began bashing his head to and fro. Heide crumpled slowly to the ground and Porta followed him, plainly out for blood.

"That's enough!" The Old Man's voice cut sharply into the sudden silence. "Give it a rest, for God's sake!"

"I'd like to kick his ugly face in!" panted Porta.

We looked at Heide's face. Far from being ugly, it was, in fact, the only presentable, respectable, unmarked face among the lot of us. We could all, except Heide, boast more or less permanent disfigurements. Tiny had lost an ear, I had a broken nose, Barcelona a glass eye, the Legionnaire a puckered scar, and so on, but Heide's face was fresh and clean and carefully shaven, and I could suddenly understand how Porta felt about it, and why he had this urge to kick it in. Why, after all, should not Heide too have a few reminders of the war to carry him through the rest of his life?

"Kick him to death!" urged Tiny recklessly.

"Hold your mouth!" snapped the Old Man. "How many more times do I have to tell you that it's me that gives the orders around here?"

He took up his submachine gun and perched on the edge of the table with it, swinging a leg and watching us. We eyed him uncertainly. We felt pretty sure he would never use it, the Old Man just wasn't that type; nevertheless, whenever he was really serious, we always took good care to humor him.

Heide came slowly to his senses. He held his aching head in both hands and looked up at Porta with the light of hatred still in his eyes. "Cheater," he hissed between his nice white teeth. And then he spat out a mouthful of blood and gingerly felt his throat, which was bruised and purple with the marks of Porta's fingers still standing out clearly.

"Think yourself lucky you've still got a head on your shoulders," sneered Porta. "One of these days I'm really going to town on that lovely face of yours. When you've lost an ear and an eye and a mouthful of teeth, you won't have quite so high an opinion of yourself."

Heide slowly got to his feet, dragging himself up by the wall. "Just because you're as ugly as sin," he said haughtily, "it doesn't mean to say you have to be jealous of other people's good looks. You ought to try washing and shaving once in a while, it would do wonders for you."

He had a point there; he really did have a point. But before Porta could make one of his usual obscene rejoinders, we were interrupted by the arrival of two SD men and the old woman we had seen earlier on in the evening. She had aged by several years in the few intervening hours. From an upright and fairly well-preserved elderly lady, she had turned into a bent and wrinkled old crone, with black hollows beneath the eyes and a mouth wrinkled up like a prune. They stood her in a corner and handed over the usual sheaf of papers to the Old Man.

"For you. Just fill 'em in in the normal way."

"Hang on a minute, don't be in such a hurry." The Old Man looked at the prisoner, looked back at the papers and then up at the SD men. "You've come to the wrong place. We don't have any dealings with civilians. We belong to the Army, not the Gestapo."

One of the men bent down and spoke a few words into the Old Man's ear. The Old Man frowned, looked again at the prisoner. "I see. Well, in that case . . ."

"Please yourself, of course," the man shrugged a careless shoulder. "I just thought she'd be better off with you—not that I give a damn either way. It's all in a day's work as far as I'm concerned. Mind you," he passed a weary hand across his brow, as if he had the cares of the world upon his shoulders, "it's not an easy job. It takes it out of you more than you always care to admit. There are moments when I find myself wishing I could do something slightly less taxing, but . . ."

He shrugged again, eloquently. Porta at once hooted and Tiny let out a noisy fart.

"Bring on the violins!" jeered the Legionnaire. "Nobody obliged you to be a cop, did they? The Army's crying out for men, in case you're interested . . ."

"What, him?" said Porta. "Him in the Army? Don't make me laugh!"

Before the object of their scorn could retaliate, they were interrupted by an unexpected voice from a forgotten quarter.

"Children, children, don't fall out with each other! Harsh words can never be taken back and you'll only regret it later."

Startled, we turned to look at the old lady in her corner. She smiled at us gently, leniently.

"There is already so much unhappiness and discord in the world," she said in her tremulous, bleating voice. "I beg of you not to add to it. You're all good boys at heart, but war is a trying time and it plays upon the nerves and makes one behave as one would never dream of doing in times of peace." She paused, but we were far too flabbergasted to speak. "You must try to follow the example of your excellent chief," she told us. "Herr Bielert. Such a gentleman, and so very kind. He insisted on arranging for a car to take me home." She gave us a charming smile from her puckered old mouth. "He was so horrified when I suggested I might walk!"

Tiny opened his mouth to say something, but Barcelona gave him a hard kick in the leg and he closed it again.

The two SD men stood by the door looking foolish. One of them waved a hand at the sheaf of papers. "Now perhaps you can understand why we brought her to you."

"All right," said the Old Man curtly. "Leave her and get out of here."

The old woman politely shook hands with her two guards, as if she had been paying a social call.

"Thank you so much for looking after me. And remember, any time you happen to be near Friedrichsberg, drop in and see me. You know my address. I always have a supply of candy and illustrated magazines to offer my visitors. Young people always enjoy my magazines."

Muttering uncomfortably, they shuffled out. At the foot of the stairs one of them turned.

"Good-bye, Frau Dreyer."

He blushed scarlet as he said it. Frau Dreyer raised a gracious hand as the Legionnaire closed and locked the door behind them, putting a barrier between our two worlds; they were the Gestapo, we were the Army, and as far as we were concerned, that was the way it was going to stay.

The little old woman opened her handbag and pulled out a packet of candy which she handed around to us. We nodded our appreciation and helped ourselves avidly. Tiny, in fact, helped himself twice.

"Don't you worry," he told her. "You're with the Army now." He nodded and winked, and we looked at him apprehensively. You never knew, with Tiny, what he was liable to say next; he was not the ideal companion for a sensitive old lady. "We know how to deal with these bastards in the Gestapo," he continued boastfully. "Why, I remember once I . . ."

He broke off with a loud howl of pain as Barcelona gave him another kick.

"I don't think Frau Dreyer's really very interested in that sort of thing."

"What sort of thing? Why not?" demanded Tiny, instantly aggressive. "I was going to tell her about that time in Pinsk, when we helped those three whores get away from the Gestapo."

"Well, don't!" snapped Barcelona.

Frau Dreyer herself intervened.

"Let the poor boy speak. He's just a big overgrown child, I'm sure he couldn't harm a fly and I should like to hear his story."

Tiny looked at her with wide-open eyes. Porta sniggered.

"He's nothing but a great big liar. He tells lies like you and me eats or sleeps. He does it natural like. Can't help himself, if you know what I mean. Like for instance, say today was Monday the 19th, he'd tell you it was Tuesday the 20th. Not for any reason. Just out of habit. You can't ever take what he says to be true."

"He'd sell his soul for half a pfennig," added Steiner.

Tiny was about to protest in the way which came most naturally to him. He picked up a chair and prepared to bring it down on Porta's head, but the Legionnaire caught him by the arm and whispered a few words into his ear.

The Legionnaire could always work wonders with Tiny. He put the chair down and retired muttering to a corner.

The rest of us, smiling vaguely at the old woman, sat down to play craps. Frau Dreyer watched us a while, and then, to our intense relief, settled herself in a chair and went to sleep.

For half an hour she slept, and then Porta's loud braying laughter woke her up again. We tried not to notice, but her quavering voice soon floated across to us.

"If you don't mind," she said, "I think I should like to go home now. Do you suppose my car would be ready yet?"

Porta gave a wild yell of glee as he threw six aces.

"Herr Bielert did promise me a car, you know."

We gritted our teeth and did our best to close our ears. She was just a stupid old woman who had no idea what the hell was going on. Perhaps she was a congenital idiot, or perhaps she was in an advanced stage of senility. She certainly didn't seem to appreciate that she was now in the hands of one of the world's most pitiless judicial systems.

Heide scooped up the dice, shook them energetically, making as much noise as possible, and shot them elegantly across the table. Six aces. As Porta before him, he gave a loud whoop of joy. Then, in silence, he picked them up from the table and prepared for another go.

"Herr Feldwebel," went on the thin piping voice, which was beginning to grate on all our nerves, "would it be too much trouble to ask you to see if my car is ready? I really am becoming extremely sleepy sitting here. I should like very much to be taken home now."

Heide sent the dice flying over the table again. Another six aces. No one said a word. I could feel the tension mounting. Porta licked his lips, picked up the dice and looked at them suspiciously. Heide smiled.

"Sorry to disappoint you, but they're not loaded. What you have yet to learn is that it takes intelligence to play this game. An intelligence which some of us have and some of us haven't. And just to prove it, I'll throw you another six—double or quits."

"Don't be a fool," said Barcelona. "It won't turn up again."

"Want to bet?" Heide grinned, raked up the dice, raised his arms above his head like a prizefighter and gave the leather dicebox a good long shake before bringing it down onto the table. He left it there, his hand firmly holding it down for at least a minute, calmly taking time off to light a cigarette. It was one of Porta's, but Porta was staring so hard at the dicebox that he never even noticed.

"Oh dear, how my poor feet do ache!" sighed Frau Dreyer, a note of the dreaded self-pity creeping into her voice. "I put on my best shoes to come here, and they do pinch me so—and I've been here since early this evening, you know . . ."

Heide blew out a mouthful of smoke and drummed his fingers on top of the dicebox.

"Come on, come on," muttered Steiner. "Let's get going!"

"There's no real need for all this suspense," said Heide smoothly. "I can tell you what's under there without looking: six aces."

"Like hell!"

Heide smiled sweetly. "You don't believe me? Well now, I'll tell you what I'll do. We won't make it double or quits, we'll make it ten times or quits."

Porta began chewing frantically at a fingernail. He ran a hand through his red hair and screwed up his face in a frenzy of indecision.

"This is lunacy," declared the Legionnaire. "You can't possibly *know* that there are six aces under there . . ."

The voice droned on from its corner.

"It's two o'clock, Herr Feldwebel. There's another three hours to go before the trams start up again. What shall I do if the car doesn't come?"

Slowly Heide began tightening his grip on the leather dicebox. His voice had been quite steady, but I saw the sweat standing out along his hairline. We all leaned forward with him. Tiny had a cigarette hanging forgotten from his lips. Porta had chewed his finger almost to the bone. Any minute now we should know the truth.

"Are you so sure?" said the Old Man, not daring to take his eyes off the box to look at Heide. "Are you really so sure?"

"I'm sure," confirmed Heide, and a bead of sweat trickled down his top lip and splashed onto the table.

Someone's rifle clattered to the floor, but our concentration was intense and the noise scarcely penetrated the outer edges of consciousness.

"I can hear a car. I can distinctly hear a car. Perhaps it's come for me at last."

Frau Dreyer rose from the chair and began buttoning her threadbare coat.

Slowly, very slowly, Heide lifted the dicebox.

He had thrown six aces.

The tension broke abruptly. Tiny hurled his chair against the wall and pounded both fists on the table. Steiner shouted aloud. The rest of us leaned back and let out our breath in great sighs. Porta tore his fascinated gaze away from the dice and looked up almost pleadingly at Heide.

"How d'you do it, Julius? Tell us how you do it—six aces three times running! I've never seen that in my life before."

"Like I said, it takes intelligence." Heide wiped the back of his hand across his brow and resumed his usual air of arrogance. "If you count up what you owe me, I guess you'll find it wipes out my debts to you."

Porta frowned. "I'll play you one more throw."

The sweat at once broke out again on Heide's face. He stared into Porta's small and greedy eyes and was plainly tempted. But at last he stood up and threw back his chair. "Not interested. I've done it three times, that's quite enough. You do it too often, it gets boring."

"Balls!" said Porta. "You know damn well you couldn't do it again, not if you tried all night!"

Heide shrugged. He could afford to. He looked across at Frau Dreyer. "Why did the Gestapo come for you?" he asked coldly. Not that he really cared, but it was one way of silencing Porta.

"Oh dear, it was my neighbor," said Frau Dreyer in hushed tones. "She wrote them that I had insulted the Führer."

We turned around, our attention caught. Insulted the Führer! That could be interesting. Stege leaned toward me and whispered gravely, "The poor old girl could be shot for that."

We all looked at Frau Dreyer who had become, quite suddenly, an object of quite incredible wonderment. Not because she was liable to be condemned to death—God knows, we were well accustomed to that—but because she could sit there in all innocence and not realize the enormity of her crime and its probable consequence.

"How had you insulted the Führer?" said Heide.

Frau Dreyer touched delicately at her nostrils with a small handkerchief that smelled of lavender.

"Well, it wasn't anything really, you know. Or at least, only what everyone else has been saying. It was during that very bad air raid we had last year; you remember, they

bombed Landungsbrücke and the boarding school behind
Bismarck's statue. Frau Becker and I—Frau Becker, that's
my neighbor—we went along to have a look at the damage.
And it was then I made the remark which so upset poor
Herr Bielert, though really how was I to know, when everyone else had been saying it for days? 'It was better under
the dear Emperor,' I said. 'At least they didn't fly over in
their airplanes dropping bombs on us. And in any case,'"
she looked at us, sternly, "'a man like Adolf Hitler, what
does he know of running a country? I'm sure he tries his
best, but he was born in poverty and he knows nothing of
the ways of the world.'"

We stared at her in a shocked, incredulous silence. Barcelona swallowed once or twice before saying, "Did you—
did you repeat all that to Herr Bielert?"

"Of course," said Frau Dreyer with a proud lift of the
head. "He asked me my opinion, and I gave it. I am not
yet too senile to have an opinion, I should hope."

"No, but you—you shouldn't have—you really shouldn't
have—" Words failed Barcelona. He opened his eyes helplessly at the rest of us.

Porta hunched a careless shoulder. "Let's see what the
dice have to say about it—will she or won't she?" And he
ran a finger across his throat and winked at us ghoulishly.

We sat around the table and each one pressed his left
thumb against the edge. Heide shook the dice. "What'll it
be?"

"The little bird on the park railings," suggested Tiny.

"Okay."

"One," said Steiner.

"One to six," said Porta.

"One to six," we chanted in chorus.

The dice rolled across the table.

Eight soldiers playing at dice in the cellars of the Gestapo,
much as the Roman soldiers, in their time, had played at
the foot of a hill near Jerusalem.

"This is disgraceful," said the Old Man suddenly. "Pack
it up, for heaven's sake."

And he turned his chair around, facing Frau Dreyer, and
began speaking energetically about God knows what; anything to keep her attention away from the macabre game
that was in progress.

The dice lay on the table: four aces, two sixes . . .

"She's had it," muttered Barcelona. "The dice are always right."

"Everyone agreed, one to six?" asked Heide.

Porta nodded. "Six for life, one for death . . ."

We looked across at Frau Dreyer. She was earnestly telling the Old Man the history of her late husband.

"He was killed at Verdun," we heard her say. "He was in the 3rd Dragoons at Stental. It was nice at Stental, I liked it so much, we had such a good time there. My husband was in the Dragoons from 1908 until his death—he fell on December 23, 1917. He'd gone out to find a fir tree for Christmas and he was killed by a stray bullet on the way back. He was a good soldier and a very brave man. He was with Hauptmann Haupt and Oberleutnant Jenditsch when they took the fort of Douaumont . . ."

"Douaumont!" cried Tiny, his face wreathed in smiles. "I know all about Douaumont! The Prussians was only in there for about five minutes before the Frogs threw 'em out again, ass over tit to the other side of the Rhine—and you fuck off!" he added angrily in Heide's direction. "What are you trying to clobber me for? Keep your great big feet to yourself."

"Frau Dreyer's husband was killed at Verdun," Heide reminded him. "Couldn't you choose your words more carefully?"

"It's only the truth, what I'm saying." Tiny stuck out his lower lip mutinously. "You ask anyone if it ain't."

"He's right," said Porta. "The Frogs knocked 'em about so bad at Douaumont that the Crown Prince himself got one hell of a balling out from the old Emperor."

Barcelona frowned at him and turned back to Frau Dreyer. "What did Herr Bielert say to you, exactly?"

She sighed and frowned and dragged her eyes away from a photograph of Himmler, which seemed to mesmerize her. Across the foot of the photograph, printed in gold letters, the caption read:

HEINRICH HIMMLER Reichsführer of the SS
Chef der Polizei*
Minister des Inneren†

---

*Chief of Police.
†Minister of the Interior.

"Herr Bielert was so kind. He listened to all that I had to say, and I could tell it upset him, and I thought perhaps I'd been offensive in some way, but then he told me it was all over and done with and I wasn't to bother my head over it any more."

And she looked back up at Himmler and smiled at him.

"Did he tell you what was going to happen to you?" asked the Old Man. "Did he write down what you said about Herr Hitler?"

"Oh, yes, indeed, he was most punctilious. He dictated it all word for word to another gentleman who was sitting in the room with him. I'm afraid I became rather sleepy, I think I must have dozed off, but when I opened my eyes again, I found they'd written quite a book between them—and then Herr Bielert told me I was to go to Berlin."

"To see the Führer?"

"Oh, dear me, no! I'm sure he's far too busy to bother with people like me." She looked again at the photograph of Himmler, and her forehead puckered. "I can't quite remember—there were some initials, I know, but . . ."

"RSHA?" suggested Barcelona into the cold silence that had fallen on the room.

"Ah, yes! RSHA! That was it!" Frau Dreyer clapped her hands together and looked at Barcelona. "Do you know it, Herr Feldwebel?"

Barcelona looked around at the rest of us for help, but we turned away and left him to it.

"Yes, well—it's a—well, it's a—a big department in Berlin."

"What do they do there?"

"They—er—" Barcelona scratched a hand desperately through his hair. "Well, it's a sort of cross between a—a registry office and an employment bureau."

"I like it!" approved Porta boisterously. "I like it, I like it! But you left out the most interesting bit."

"What's that?" asked Frau Dreyer innocently.

"Well now, I'll tell you. The RS . . ."

"For God's sake!" said the Old Man. "Hold your tongue!"

"I wonder if they wish to offer me employment." Frau Dreyer sighed and kicked off one of her shoes. "I fear I'm rather useless. I suffer from my feet, you know—I should have gone to the chiropodist this afternoon, but of course I had to miss the appointment because of coming here to see Herr Bielert."

We nodded, solemn and awkward and wishing she could be spirited away, struck dead, turned to stone, anything to save us this embarrassment. She leaned back in her chair and began talking, rambling on in that way old people have, more to herself than us.

"I was out when they came for me. I'd gone to settle up with Herr Berg in the Gänsemarkt. Once a month I go. I was early, of course—I always am. I like to sit down in the station for a bit and watch the people go by. And then at this time of year they have such a splendid show of flowers to look at. I know Herr Gelbenschneid, the stationmaster. I know him very well. He has green fingers, his roses are some of the best I've ever seen. I wish I could grow them like that, but there you are, if you don't have the touch, there's nothing you can do about it."

She shook her head, resigned, and Tiny shook his with her in sympathy.

"Well, now, I knew as soon as I got to the top of my road that something had happened. I saw the car, you see. A big gray one, and I knew it belonged to the SS because I'd seen them before. At first I thought they'd come to see my neighbor. Frau Becker. She has a son in the SS. He's an Untersturmführer in the 'Reich' division. She's very proud of him, naturally. Before he was made an officer he was in another regiment—what was it? SS Westland, I think. My youngest son was in the SS, you know. I didn't want him to be, but he would have his own way. Attracted by the uniform, I shouldn't wonder. Young boys are so easily swayed by these things. Anyway, he's dead now. They sent me his Iron Cross. I remember he was very angry with me when I told him his father wouldn't have been at all pleased at him going into the SS. 'You ought to wait,' I said to him. 'Wait till you're called up, like your brothers.' Three brothers, he had. Two of them went into an infantry regiment, and the oldest went into the Pioneer Corps. He's dead now as well. The other two were reported missing. They might still be alive, I don't know, I try not to think about it too much. But the youngest boy, he was always one to have his own way. When I told him to wait for the call up and not go throwing his life away, 'Mother,' he said to me, 'Mother, I should by rights report you for spreading defeatist talk, but just for this once I'll pretend not to have heard you. Never again, mind you. Next time I shall report you whether you're my mother or not.' Oh dear, he was so angry with

me—didn't even want to kiss me good-bye when he went
—and now he's dead, like all the rest of them, and I've
nothing left save his Iron Cross. I keep it in the drawer
along with all their baby clothes. Their little vests and their
little knitted shoes . . ."

She suddenly looked across at us and smiled. Tiny smiled
back, in a rather sickly fashion, I thought.

"But anyway, you see, as I walked down the road I
realized that the car was parked outside my door, not Frau
Becker's, and I thought for a moment it was Paul come back
from the grave—Paul was my youngest son, of course, the
one I was telling you about. Well, the young man that got
out of the car, he looked just like him, I'm sure. Six feet
tall, wide shoulders, narrow hips, blond hair, blue eyes—he
was always the most handsome of the four—and this young
man was so like him it gave me quite a turn. And when he
spoke he was so gentle, so polite, so obviously well brought
up. He must have come from a good family, you know. The
only thing I didn't take to was the black leather he was
wearing. He seemed to be all black leather from head to
foot—so cold, I always feel, so very impersonal—but then,
perhaps it's a uniform."

Smiling now at Tiny, now at the photograph of Himmler,
she took us through the entire scene. I was able to picture it
so well: the blond young god from the SS, with his arrogant
blue eyes and his black leather boots, and the silly old
lady, faded and trusting and too busy comparing him with
dead baby Paul to notice the menace lurking behind his
facade of polished charm.

"Frau Dreyer?" he had politely inquired, as he stepped
out of the car.

And the old woman, all of a flutter, had presented herself
to him and held out her hand and had it crushed in a big
black gauntlet, and the young man had gone on to verify the
fact that she was indeed the Emilie Dreyer who lived at
Hindenburgstrasse No. 9. And all the time standing there
with suave smile on his face and a Walther 7.65 in his
pocket, and old Frau Dreyer never suspecting a thing. He
turned and opened the car door, to usher her into the back
seat. They wanted her at headquarters, there were matters that had to be talked about.

"Oh, I'm so sorry, but I can't possibly manage today! I
have an appointment with Dr. Jöhr, to have my feet seen to,
you know. I suffer very badly with my feet."

And the SS man had laughed aloud at that. A visit to the chiropodist! That was the poorest excuse he had ever heard.

Frau Dreyer never knew why he found her innocent statement of fact so amusing. She went on to explain, in case he might not have appreciated the seriousness of the problem, that Dr. Jöhr was a busy man with a large practice, and if you didn't cancel an appointment at least twenty-four hours in advance, you still had to pay for it.

The SS man laughed even louder. He at least had a good sense of humor.

"Don't you worry about your feet, old lady. We'll get in touch with Dr. Jöhr and see that he doesn't charge you."

"But you see," she said, "it might be weeks before I can make another appointment. He's such a very busy man . . ."

Losing patience with the daft old bag, the SS man had taken her by the shoulder and pushed her toward the car. As he did so, she had suddenly realized that his left arm was missing, and this had completely sidetracked her from the problem of her feet. Such a dreadful thing to have happened! Such a tragedy, such a disaster, such a . . .

"Do you mind if we don't discuss it?" he said curtly.

She showed him the SS ring that had belonged to Paul. She told him about Paul, about his Iron Cross and how he had died for his country, but the young man seemed curiously uninterested. He had bundled her into the back seat of the car and slammed the door on her, and they had driven off at full speed to the Gestapo. They went everywhere at full speed, those people.

The driver was a very different type from the other young man. A rough, tough, crude type of person. No manners, no breeding. He had a glass eye, which had been ill made and looked more like a blood alley than a glass eye. And his face was thick and coarse, and Frau Dreyer felt from the beginning that he was out of sympathy with her.

"Watch it, grandma!" were the first words he had addressed to her as she was hustled into the car; and then, turning to his companion, "I hope the old bag behaves herself in the back."

"You get on with the driving and leave everything else to me," was the young man's retort.

Frau Dreyer felt that the implied rebuke had been justified.

"It was not up to a man of that class to address me as grandmother," she told us. "And as for calling me a bag, I find that to be totally lacking in respect toward one's elders and betters."

"Yeah, I know what you mean," said Tiny. "But if I was you, I wouldn't get too hot under the collar about it. I mean, it's not like calling someone a . . ."

Just in time, Porta clapped a hand over his mouth. "In future," he begged him, "just confine your remarks to a simple yes or no and then we'll all rest a lot easier."

"Get out of it!" shouted Tiny, indignantly breaking free. "I'll say what I damn well like and it's no concern of yours. And I'm certainly not saying yes any more, I can tell you that for nothing. First time I ever said yes it got me two months in the poky. I swore blind after that I'd stick to no."

"So long as you do," said Porta. "That's all we ask." And he turned back to the bench on which he was stacking up one of his marked packs of cards. He always put them away very carefully in their original wrapping paper, sticking it down with an application and regard for detail that was totally missing from the more official tasks that were given him.

Barcelona and Heide were idly playing craps again. Frau Dreyer went on with her tale as if there had never been any interruption.

"I couldn't help feeling he was rather an unpleasant man altogether. He drove so fast, you know, really quite dangerous, and on several occasions I swear it was a miracle that people escaped. But he just laughed, as if it were a great joke. Then at Harversterhude they stopped to pick up a young girl. I don't know why they wanted her—they dropped her off at another building before we got here, I don't know exactly where—but I must say that even the young man who was so charming to me behaved in a *very* ungallant way toward her. Perhaps she may have done wrong, I wouldn't know, but I really cannot see that there was any need for them to hit her as they did. A gentleman should never hit a woman, never! And if he does, he only shows himself to be no gentleman, and so I said to the young man. Don't you agree with me, Herr Feldwebel?"

"I do indeed," said the Old Man gravely.

"I wouldn't have hit her," said Tiny. "What'd be the point of it? I can think of something I'd far rather do. What's the point of clobbering 'em if you can . . ."

This time, it was the Legionnaire who shut him up. Frau Dreyer blandly continued.

"When we arrived here," she explained to us, "they showed me into a sort of waiting room up on the third floor. There seemed to be a great many other people there who had come for interviews, and they left me in with them for some time. Not very polite, I thought. After all, I hadn't *asked* to see Herr Bielert, you know. It was he who had sent for me. So I do think they might have made a little more effort—however, I suppose they are busy men and there is a war on. I think an apology is all I would have asked. Well, even when they took me out of the waiting room I still didn't get to see Herr Bielert. Instead, they insisted on going through all my pockets and my handbag and taking away a great many letters of a personal nature. I know they were only doing their job, I know there is a war on and we all have to beware of foreign agents, but I still can't help feeling that they were overreaching themselves just a little—and I am still at a loss to know what right they have to read my letters. Anyway, when they had searched me they took me off to a second waiting room. I didn't like it in there at all. An old man with a gun sat on a chair and wouldn't let any of us speak. It was most boring, and not only that, I was hungry."

They had left her there for several hours, and then the blond one-armed Oberscharführer had collected her and taken her to a small room elsewhere in the building, where two men in civilian clothes had asked her if she had ever said the Führer was a fool.

"Well, of course," she told us, "I denied it at once. I said someone had been spreading horrid lies about me. And then they asked me if I wouldn't please try to help them, because you see it was their job to look into all this sort of thing and make sure no one had ever said anything bad about the Führer, and really in the end they were quite nice about it all and told me I should take my time and try to remember exactly what it was I'd said."

"Didn't you ever tell your neighbor, Frau Becker, that you thought the Führer had been foolish ever to start the war?" Bielert had asked her.

"Oh, yes," she said to him. "I did say that and I'd say it again. I think this war is a piece of sheer folly."

And then, to her bewilderment, they had all laughed heartily and the one man had written down her words on a sheet of paper.

"You see, Frau Dreyer, it's just as we said—you called
the Führer a fool."

She had been taken aback then; assured them that by
saying the war was a foolish action, she had not intended to
imply that the Führer was a fool. She wouldn't—hadn't—
couldn't . . .

"But surely," Bielert had insisted, "anyone who commits a
foolish action is a foolish person, and hence a fool."

She had to admit the logic of it.

"But, as I told him, I wasn't the only person who said such
things. Everyone was saying them. I was only repeating what
I'd heard."

Of course, Bielert had at once jumped in to ask who, and
where, and when.

"Well, there's Herr Gelbenschneid, the stationmaster, for
a start. I have frequently heard him say that this war is the
worst thing that's ever happened to Germany. And then
there's Frau Dietrich, the nurse at the chiropodist's. She
told me only the other day she wished the war had never
been started and the sooner we were defeated the better
as far as she was concerned. And then . . ."

In her ignorance, she had dictated a whole list of names
to Bielert's avid note-taking companion, who had promptly
passed them on to the Oberscharführer—presumably for
immediate action.

"And then," said Frau Dreyer wonderingly, "they wanted
to know if I'd ever been in a mental home."

"As a matter of interest," said Porta, turning around,
"have you?"

"Well, no, I haven't, and it seemed such an odd question
that I quite took fright and began to cry. To tell you the
truth," confessed Frau Dreyer confidentially, "I was scared
they were going to fine me. For saying things I shouldn't
have, you know—even though I didn't realize they were
wrong. I asked them if I mightn't apologize rather than pay
a fine, because all I have is my widow's pension, you see,
and I simply couldn't afford it. Well, they were really very
nice about it all. They said I shouldn't have to pay a fine,
so not to worry about it, and they would accept my apologies on behalf of the Führer. And then, I remember, they
grew very friendly and began asking me questions about my
boys. They were so interested in them, it quite took my
mind off everything else! And we talked of this and that,
and it turned out that Herr Bielert was a good friend of

Bent, who used to be my Kurt's closest companion in the old days. He became an SS Obersturmführer, and quite often he used to come round and visit when Kurt was on leave. Now, he was a brave boy, such a row of medals on his chest, and yet, you know, he didn't believe in the war, either. I remember once, it was just before Kurt's birthday, just before the battalion was sent to the front, I remember Bent telling me that the Führer was only a man, not a god, and that like all men he sometimes made mistakes. And as for Himmler—I can't tell you how angry he and Kurt became whenever one mentioned Himmler! You would have thought the poor man had done them some personal injury! Why, I remember . . ."

"Hang on a second," said the Old Man, frowning. "You didn't tell him all this, did you? You didn't tell Bielert?"

"Oh, yes," she said blithely. "They were so interested, you see, and Herr Bielert told me that Bent had always been an intelligent boy and that he was wasted at the front, so they were going to call him back to Hamburg and promote him. I wanted to write and let him know straightaway, but they said not to, because they wanted it to be a surprise for him."

"Of course," agreed the Old Man solemnly. "And what else did you talk about while you were there?"

"Well, now—" she gathered up the wrinkles in her forehead, trying to remember. "We spoke of my nephew Dietrich. He's a student of theology, you know. For some reason Herr Bielert seemed to think that he might have said bad things about the Führer. He asked me to tell them what Dietrich had said, and I told them I couldn't recall that he ever said anything. And then Herr Bielert grew quite angry and shouted at me; I couldn't understand what it was that I'd done to displease him, while the other man kept shaking his head at me and I grew so confused I really don't know what I should have done if Herr Bielert's telephone hadn't started to ring. And they all ran out with their revolvers and I was left alone for some while until another man came and took me away."

"Brought you down here?" asked the Legionnaire.

"Oh, no," she said. "They shut me up in a little room, and then they came for me again and took me back to see Herr Bielert. And that was when they wrote down everything I'd told them and I had to sign it for them." She smiled. "When I'd done that, they were pleased with me again. They gave me coffee and cake and told me I should be taken care of."

We looked at her silently. It was incredible that anyone could be so naive.

"I wonder if my car will be here soon?"

She addressed her appeal to the Old Man, who made vague noises of encouragement and looked across at the rest of us. We shuffled our feet and stared at the floor.

"One day when you can spare the time," said Frau Dreyer graciously, "you must drop around to visit me. Let me know beforehand and I'll see if I can't make one of my fruit cakes for you. All the boys like my fruit cake."

We mumbled our thanks and she smiled at us and nodded her head up and down on its frail neck, and then, to our unspeakable relief, her eyelids drooped and she drifted off into an exhausted sleep, snoring gently and rhythmically.

Porta had finished stacking his marked cards. He suggested a game and we agreed, provided that we played with Barcelona's pack.

Two hours later we were still playing, so engrossed in the game that we could hardly bear to leave the table long enough even to stagger across to the handbasin for a piss. Frau Dreyer slept on.

We were disturbed by an impatient rapping at the door. Barcelona went across to answer it and found himself confronted by two SD men carrying submachine guns.

"Heil Hitler!" they greeted him severely. "You got an Emilie Dreyer down here?"

At the sound of her name, the old lady woke up. She stumbled across the room, heavy with sleep.

"Is that my car?"

"That's it, lady. Your car. Get your things together and come with us. We're taking you to Fuhlsbüttel."

"Fuhlsbüttel?" She hesitated. "But I don't want to go to Fuhlsbüttel, I want to go home."

The SD man laughed. "Don't we all?"

"But Herr Bielert said . . ."

"Herr Bielert said he'd lay on a car for you, and he has. And we're all going off in it together for a nice little ride to Fuhlsbüttel. So be a good lady and hurry along, I don't want to have to get rough with someone old enough to be my grandmother."

For the first time, Frau Dreyer began dimly to perceive something of the truth. She turned, trembling, to the Old Man and held out her hands. "Herr Feldwebel . . ."

"God will protect you," said the Old Man, very low and almost as if he were ashamed of himself. "Go with them, Frau Dreyer. It's all you can do. All any of us can do."

"Yes, of course," she said doubtfully.

She stood a moment, helpless, her lined old face quivering. We handed her her handbag and her coat and silently she pattered after the SD men. One of her shoelaces was undone and both her thick wool stockings were crumpling around her ankles. The heavy door slammed behind her. We heard the other doors slamming as well, as the prisoners were taken from their cells. They were led into the courtyard, packed into the big green vans that would transport them to Fuhlsbüttel.

In one of them sat a little old lady who even now could not understand the crime she had committed.

In the guardroom no one spoke and we avoided looking at each other. We were ashamed of ourselves and of the uniforms we wore.

After a while, Tiny left the room. Still without a word. We returned halfheartedly to our cards, but before we could deal out another hand, Tiny was back again.

"Krug's dead in his cell!" he panted excitedly. "Hanged himself with his braces!"

The tension was now broken. We crowded out of the room and along the passage to witness the scene. Krug swung from the ceiling like a misshapen rag doll. His face was blue and bloated, and his protruding eyes stared at us glassily. His neck seemed quite incredibly long. Beneath him, on the floor, lay his kepi.

"Best thing he could have done, really," said Barcelona.

We looked up dispassionately at the swaying body.

"No need to feel sorry for that rat," declared Tiny.

I don't think any of us did. Not even Stege attempted to speak up in his defense.

"We'll have to put it in the report," said the Old Man. "There'll only be repercussions if we don't."

We trooped back up the passage to the guardroom. While the Old Man seated himself at his desk and took up a pen, the rest of us now quite happily returned to our interrupted game of cards.

"Pity he couldn't have had the decency to wait till he got to Fuhlsbüttel," said Porta, rapidly shuffling the pack while the rest of us watched him like hawks. "Still, some people just naturally have bad taste."

They were black marketeers, the pair of them. Born to get themselves constantly into trouble and always to get themselves out of it again, respecting each other's treachery and cunning even as they sought to outdo one another. They stole everything they could lay hands on, sold everything that came their way, from women to spent cartridges.

The SS driver weighed the cigarette in the palm of his hand a moment, regarding it thoughtfully. He then raised it to his nostrils and gave a suspicious sniff.

"I think you're a filthy liar," he declared at last. "Take it to pieces and let me see for myself."

"Do you doubt my word?" demanded Porta arrogantly. "If I tell you there's opium in each cigarette, then there is opium in each cigarette."

He spat contemptuously at the SS pennant flying from the big gray Mercedes. The driver at once returned the compliment by hawking in the direction of the monument set up in memory of those soldiers who had given their lives in World War I.

With this exchange of formalities completed, they returned to business.

"I've got a nice little haul of car tires," offered the SS man. "Just up your alley—only trouble is, they're a bit hot at the moment."

"You'll be a bit hot," said Porta, "if ever they lay their hands on you. Bet you a pound to a pinch of pig shit you'll end up with us one of these fine days!"

The SS man hunched an indifferent shoulder. "The chance you take," he said laconically. "If you're interested, I can let you have the address of a good strip show."

"I know plenty of strip shows."

"Not like this one. Not around here. Not with stark naked lovelies in it."

Porta licked his lips. A hot splash of color branded his cheekbones.

"Completely naked?"

"Near as maybe. Shoes, stockings, garter belts—just enough to titillate. Can't complain of that, can you?"

Porta scraped his throat a few times. "Can you hire 'em out for an evening, say?"

"Why not?"

They put their heads close together and began to discuss terms.

V

PORTA AND THE SS

One day, quite suddenly and with no warning, Lieutenant Ohlsen was arrested. He was accused of having associated with a group of officers who had come under suspicion, and of having himself uttered defamatory words against the Führer. We later discovered it was his wife who had denounced him.

They came for him one morning, two military police and a lieutenant, slinking silently into camp in a manner so furtive that they at once drew attention to themselves. Doubtless their aim was to pick him up with the minimum of fuss and smuggle him out before too many questions could be asked, but fortunately we had wind of their presence and were able to alert Colonel Hinka. Not that there was much anyone could do, but at least we could put up a good fight. Some officers we should gladly have seen arrested, but Lieutenant Ohlsen was not one of them. He had been two years with the company and had served with the Regiment since 1938, and we had no mind to stand by and watch as they marched him off.

On hearing the news, Colonel Hinka at once sent his adjutant to arrest the two MPs as they left company headquarters. The guards were alerted and all exits closed. No one was to leave the building.

The adjutant smiled suavely at the officer who was with the police. "Colonel Hinka would like to have a few words with you, Lieutenant. If you'd care to come with me, I'll take you to his office."

The lieutenant and the two policemen followed him, stubbornly dragging Ohlsen along with them. He was the prey they had been sent to fetch, and they had no intention of letting him go at this stage of the proceedings.

In Hinka's office the storm burst. Hinka, furious that any upstart cops should try arresting one of his officers without first asking his permission, swore that no one should leave the premises until the matter had been sorted out to his own satisfaction. He picked up the telephone and rang through to the Kommandantur in Hamburg. They swiftly denied all responsibility. He tried Hanover, with no success. He tried the Abwehr,* who wanted nothing to do with it. Finally, in desperation, he got through to the Army Personnel Bureau in Berlin and demanded to speak with General Rudolf Schmudt.

Needless to say, such an abnormal amount of activity on what should have been a morning like any other morning did not escape the ever watchful eyes of the Gestapo.

It was not long before a familiar gray Mercedes drew up with two SS Unterscharführer and a small dapper civilian, dressed all in black. The civilian looked at once both seedy and sinister. Like a bank clerk going off to his grandmother's funeral, with his shiny black homburg, his heavy black overcoat, his gloves, his scarf, his umbrella, and his cramped rounded shoulders and shuffling footsteps; like a weasel after a rabbit, with his small close-set eyes shifting furtively from side to side, bright as diamonds and as hard, missing nothing and ceaselessly on the alert.

Captain Brockmann could hardly believe his eyes when he passed this curiously clad creature creeping up the stairs. He stood a moment, staring after him, then hurried across to the sergeant in charge.

"Who the hell was that clown?"

"I dunno, sir. I asked him for his pass, but he just walked right on up the stairs like he never heard me. Like he was a ghost or something."

---

*Counterespionage.

"A ghost!" The captain gave a short bark of laughter. "An escaped lunatic, more like. No one who was even remotely normal could walk round in that ludicrous getup." He snatched the telephone from its hook and dialed a number. "Klaus, there's a guy dressed in black from head to foot wandering about the place as if he owns it. Have him picked up and brought straight to me under escort."

He laughed and rubbed his hands together as he replaced the receiver. Whoever this little black maniac was, they were going to have some fun with him. Captain Brockmann had something of a reputation in the regiment as a wit and a wag, though he occasionally went too far for everyone's liking. Only a month earlier he had succeeded in pushing Lieutenant Köhler to suicide. But nobody was likely to care what happened to this funereal nonentity creeping around the building with his rolled umbrella and his stooped shoulders.

Brockmann rang up one or two of his particular cronies among his fellow officers and invited them along to the party.

The intruder was stopped in the corridor by a Feldwebel and taken down to Brockmann's office. He went without a murmur, a twisted smile only on his lips and a gleam of anticipation in his diamond-bright eyes.

Brockmann was waiting for him, legs straddled, hands on hips, while his pals lolled about in easy chairs and smoked and prepared to watch the fun.

"Well?" bawled Brockmann, swaying forward slightly on the balls of his feet so that his boot leather creaked. "What the hell do you think you're doing, wandering about the barracks as if they're a public amusement park? Civilians aren't allowed on the premises without a special pass—and even if they've got a special pass, they're expected to show it to the sergeant on duty and not just stroll in without so much as a word." He swayed a bit more, until he was creaking all over like a sailboat at sea. "Are you deaf and dumb or something? Why didn't you reply when the sergeant asked to see your papers?"

The civilian stood with bowed head, looking down with interest at the floor. Brockmann took his riding crop from the desk and brought it lashing down against the side of a boot. He then held it behind his back, rocking back and forth on his heels and swishing the crop gently to and fro so that his spurs jingled. As he did so, he sucked industriously at a hollow tooth and rolled a comical eye at his fellow officers. They grinned encouragingly as they smoked their cigarettes.

"Do you realize I could have you locked up and left to rot—and no questions asked? An old black crow like you, you could be dangerous. For all I know, you've got your pockets stuffed full of time bombs—planning to blow up the whole barracks!"

The civilian looked up. He stared mildly into Brockmann's face, his expression faraway and calculating, as if this present moment were of no concern whatsoever and he was deliberating upon more important matters.

Brockmann jerked his riding crop at the big black umbrella. "Have you got a license for that thing?"

"Of course not, the man's a saboteur!" decreed Lieutenant Berni, stubbing out his cigarette and coming across to have a closer look. "Sticks out a mile. Traditional saboteur's outfit, that."

Everyone laughed. They began circling around the man, examing him from all angles, noting the greenish sheen of his homburg, the sunken neck and the rounded shoulders, the ridiculously long overcoat and the enormous gloves that hung puppet-like from the sleeves.

"Do him good to be in the Army," declared Lieutenant Reichelt. "See a bit of action, get some of that tension out of him."

Not that Reichelt had ever seen any action. Before the war he had been a wine and spirit merchant, and now he bought his safety with brandy and champagne. Reichelt was having a good war. He had built up a reputation as a ladies' man, and he never ran fewer than three mistresses at a time, discarding them all after a few weeks and finding himself three new delights.

"Brockmann, I think you ought to examine his papers," said Schmidt, who was the commissary general and whose war was going as smoothly as Reichelt's.

Instead of women, Schmidt had food. He lived for food. He not only ate it, he also stole it and sold it to a butcher in Lübeckerstrasse. The butcher in Lübeckerstrasse traded almost exclusively in food stolen from the barracks. Schmidt was not his only supplier.

"You'll probably find," added Schmidt, "that he's lied his way out of military service. He ought at least to be in the

Territorials. You'd like that," he told the impassive civilian. "Do you no end of good."

The man remained silent. Schmidt wrinkled his brow in perplexity.

"You don't think the guy's touched in the head, do you?"

There was a rap on the door, and before anyone could answer it, it opened and an SS Unterscharführer entered the room. He was big and brutish and well over six feet tall. On his sleeve were the letters SD; on his kepi, pushed carelessly to the back of his head, gleamed a silver death's head. He ignored Brockmann and walked straight up to the civilian. He saluted smartly.

"*Heil* Hitler, Standartenführer! We've just had a message from the RSHA over the car radio. Said to pass it on to you immediately, sir—No. 7 command has just completed operations successfully."

The Standartenführer nodded his head, as if well satisfied. His eyes glittered behind his spectacles.

"Very well, Müller. Tell them that I want the prisoners to be held in the strictest secrecy. No one is to interrogate them before I arrive. I'll be with you in a moment."

Müller saluted again and left the room. The civilian turned to the assembled officers. "I thank you, gentlemen, for the entertainment. It has been most enlightening. I have to be going now, but I feel sure we shall meet again. *Heil* Hitler!" He followed Müller from the room.

The officers looked at one another apprehensively, no longer so sure of their own omniscience.

"What the hell was all that about?" demanded Brockmann. He strode across to the door, opened it and shouted, "Sergeant!"

"Yes, sir?"

"Find out who that man was and let me have the answer within five minutes if you don't want to land in trouble."

"Yes, sir."

Brockmann came back into the room and laid down his riding crop with a hand that was not quite so assured as it had previously been.

Schmidt licked his lips. "Gestapo?" he suggested nervously.

From the silence, he knew that he was right. It had to be the Gestapo. Schmidt wiped a plump pink hand over his brow and felt a sudden constriction across the chest. There were some sausages and some cases of ham, Italian haricot beans and one or two other little bits and pieces that he had been hoarding up, ready for the butcher in Lübecker-strasse—and with the Gestapo on the premises, one never knew—one never felt quite safe . . .

Muttering his excuses beneath his breath, Schmidt left the room and hurried on trembling fat legs to his own department. Within a matter of moments the whole depot had been turned upside down, as Schmidt's staff dropped whatever they had been doing and rushed to carry out new orders. Twenty minutes later, two trucks left the barracks full to overflowing with ham and haricot beans. They were deposited in a safe place with Schmidt's opposite number in an artillery regiment, and the whole operation cost Schmidt several pounds in weight and nineteen cases of champagne. The nineteen cases of champagne canceled out all the profit he would make on the ham.

Not everyone in the barracks knew that the Gestapo had been there. And even among those who had heard rumors, not everyone flew into a panic. A certain Obergefreiter, supposed to be on guard duty at the time, was even chatting quite amiably with the driver of the Mercedes. They were discussing business together, and had been doing so ever since the Standartenführer had entered the building.

"Well, come on!" urged the SS driver. "Out with it! How much do you want for the——" He glanced around suspiciously and lowered his voice. "For them?" he substituted. On his right sleeve he wore a white armlet with the letters RSHA.

"They're worth quite a bit," said Porta. "How much are you prepared to offer, that's more to the point?"

The man hesitated. A crafty expression appeared in his eyes. "A thousand?" He plunged a hand deep into his pocket and came out with a bundle of notes. Porta laughed in his face.

"You lost your marbles?" he jeered. "What do you think this place is, a goddam charity home? A thousand! You must be joking!" He pushed back his helmet, settled his rifle more comfortably and pushed both hands into his pockets. "You know, nobody ain't forcing you to buy the goods," he said kindly. "I mean, you don't *have* to have them if you don't want 'em—I only offered 'em to you on account of I thought you might be smart enough to handle 'em. No good letting an amateur get his mitts on 'em, he wouldn't know how to get rid of 'em and like as not he'd land us all in trouble. But seeing as you're obviously a guy what knows his way around . . ."

"Look, I could get the damn things for free if I really wanted 'em that bad!" The driver turned and spat contemptuously on the memorial for the glorious dead of World War I.

"Is that so?" sneered Porta. "I wasn't born yesterday, it's no good thinking you can take me for a ride!"

And by way of retaliation he took a hand from his pocket, bent over the Mercedes and vigorously blew his nose on the SS flag which fluttered from the bonnet of the car.

The SS man pretended not to have seen. He simply turned and spat for the second time on the glorious dead of the 76th Infantry Regiment.

"Seems to me," he said, "seems to me you don't know who I am or who I work for." His chest swelled out as he spoke. His face glowed with simple pride. "That's my boss that's gone in there just now. Gone to speak to your CO, he has."

"So what?" said Porta coldly.

"So you'll change your tune a bit when I tell you who he is. I bet you'll be so scared you'll give me your precious cigarettes for free." The SS man smiled unpleasantly and held out his right arm, displaying the letters RSHA on his sleeve. "I can be bought—at a price," he admitted. "Say, twelve pipes of opium?"

"Bought?" Porta leaned forward and spat on the SS flag. "Why the hell should I want to buy a creep like you?"

"Silence, pal. You don't buy me, you buy my silence."

"That's a laugh!" Again Porta spat. The swastika pennant, flying so bravely a few moments ago, was beginning to sag under the weight of so much moisture. "You can keep your fucking silence! You think I care two hoots for a prick like you?"

The SS man's top lip curled in a self-satisfied sneer. He felt very sure of himself. He leaned out through the window of the Mercedes.

"You'd better care, that's all I can say—because if you don't watch you're step, you're liable to land yourself in real hot water. My chief is none other than Standartenführer Paul Bielert!"

A note of trimphant reverence entered his voice as he pronounced the name. His eyes blazed with the devout fervor of a missionary telling a bunch of habitual drunks about Jesus Christ.

Porta walked up very close to the car and spat yet again on the pennant. "I don't give a hoot in hell for Paul Bielert!" he declared. "Paul Bielert can go screw himself! Fuck Paul Bielert!"

The SS man narrowed his eyes and stared at Porta in stupefaction.

"You dare to say that about the Standartenführer?" He shook his head, bewildered. "You must be a raving nut—a certifiable lunatic—you can't go around saying fuck Paul Bielert and get away with it! Bielert's just about the biggest bastard in the whole of Germany! He'll have your guts for suspenders if he ever gets to hear of it." His voice took on a note of pious wonderment. "Even SS Heinrich shits blue bricks whenever he hears the name Bielert. Only one man I ever heard of what could stand out against him and that's Gruppenführer Heydrich—and we all know what *he's* like."

Porta leaned against the side of the car and looked down at the earnest driver. "How about you, then?" he said casually. "If he's as bad as you say, you must be pretty scared of him yourself."

"Everyone's scared," retorted the driver. "And so would you be, if you had any brains in your head. And just remember this, pal—it's all very fine and grand standing out here cursing and strutting, but you won't be so damn cocky when the time comes!"

"Time?" said Porta innocently. "What time?"

"The day of your reckoning, that's what time, pal—the day when you have to stand up and face the Standartenführer."

"What makes you think I ever will have to?"

"I don't think, I know—because I can go to the authorities any time I damn well feel like it and spill the beans about your drug trafficking. And when you're standing in front of Bielert, you'll wish you'd never tried to push your luck so hard. Only the other day he had nine men executed, just for the hell of it. When I say executed, I mean heads off, down on the old chopping block. Nine at a blow! Nine heads rolling about in the basket! I'm telling you—you get in his hands, you don't stand a chance. He doesn't have men butchered because they've committed crimes, he has 'em butchered because it amuses him!"

"Christ," said Porta scornfully, "that's nothing. I had a CO once, he was practically a homicidal maniac. Lindenau, his name was. Papa Lindenau we used to call him—as a mark of our affection you might say." Porta grinned, as if savoring some particularly delightful memory. "He was burned to a cinder at Kiev Pavlo. I watched it happen." He laughed uproariously for a few minutes, then looked down again at the SS man. "I tell you, Bielert's a babe in arms compared with Papa Lindenau."

"How do you know?" asked the man jealously. "You've never had anything to do with the Standartenführer."

"That's what you think. You'd be surprised the people I've had dealings with in my time—the people I happen to be on personal terms with."

"Personal terms?" The driver frowned. "What do you mean by that?"

"People in my position," said Porta with dignity, "have dealings with both them at the top and them at the bottom. And when we have dealings with people, we tend to get on personal terms with them—you have to, otherwise you couldn't have dealings, could you? I mean, you know too much about each other, see? Like if I offer you something and you buy it, you could say we was on personal terms with each other—if you get my meaning."

The driver remained silent a moment, reluctant to believe what Porta was saying yet not quite able to dismiss it outright. Porta closed one eye, took careful aim, and for perhaps the tenth time scored a bull's-eye. The driver leaned farther out of the window and stared accusingly at the bonnet of the car.

"You keep your bloody spit to yourself!" he screamed. "Look at my flag! It's ruined!"

"Yeah," Porta agreed with a slow smile. "Looks like it's been out in a rainstorm."

Red-faced, the driver stormed around to the front of the car and tried unsuccessfully to dry the pennant on his sleeve.

"You do that again," he told Porta, returning to the driving seat, "and you'll be asking for trouble."

"Think I care?" jeered Porta.

The SS man slammed the door shut and, putting his head out of the window, looked suspiciously up at Porta. "Have you really had dealings with the Standartenführer?"

"Wouldn't you like to know."

"Well, I'm asking you—have you?"

"You think I'd tell you? Why don't you try running to him like you said and telling your little tales? You'll soon see whether I've had dealings with him or not—but one word of warning," Porta bent down and put his face very close to that of the driver, "I don't advise you to try it unless you fancy a good long stay in Torgau."

"Who said anything about Torgau?" The driver withdrew his head and stared up at Porta in hurt innocence. "Who said anything about running to the Standartenführer?"

"You did. Just now. Remember?"

"Forget it." The driver hunched a shoulder. "One says these things—just a lot of bullshit really. Didn't mean a word of it." He attempted a laugh. "I thought you were going to tell me about your old CO? Papa Lindenau who got burned to death at Kiev Pavlo?"

"How about the cigarettes?"

"I'll take them, don't worry, I'll take them!" said the driver eagerly. "Just name your price—and I'll tell you what, I'll throw in the address of a place I know as well."

"What sort of place?"

"Very classy. Very superior establishment." The driver closed one eye. "Take it from me, it's a cut above the usual."

"Well—I'll consider it," said Porta graciously. "But no more talk of running off to Bielert, eh? Little men like you shouldn't really ought to meddle with this sort of thing. You don't know what you're getting yourself into. Now take me, for example—" He puffed out his chest. "You don't get into a disciplinary regiment for nothing, you know. You people in the SS, you have it too easy. Makes you soft. I'm not at all sure I'm doing the right thing, offering you this stuff. How do I know you're not going to ball it all up? And if you do, you mark my words, your pal Bielert ain't going to be very happy about it. He's a professional, I'll give him that. But you—" Porta pulled a face, "you're just an amateur. Like as not you'll lose your nerve at the last minute and we'll all be up the creek."

"I never have before!" protested the man indignantly.

"No, but this is pretty hot stuff. I've never sold you stuff like this before."

The driver licked his lips.

"Look, I'll make it three thousand instead of one—and I'll throw in a case of powdered milk as well. How about that?"

"Where's it come from, this powdered milk?"

"Denmark," said the man proudly. "Filched it from the Todt Organization over there."

"Is it safe?"

"As houses. And I'll let you have that address I promised you. Can't say fairer than that now, can I?"

Porta seemed to reflect a while. He scratched under one arm, pushed his helmet from the back of his head to the front. Thoughtfully he sucked at one of his few remaining teeth.

The SS man, now coveting the opium above anything else in the world, grew desperate. "Just remembered something else," he said. "I got a whole bundle of photos you can have, if you like."

"Photos?" said Porta disdainfully. "What would I want photos for?"

The driver gave a sly wink. "They're worth having. You take my word for it." He made a few vaguely obscene motions with his hands. "Not the usual sort of crap, believe me! Real arty sort of stuff. Everything you've ever dreamed of. All tastes catered for. Enough to make a castrated monkey take himself in hand."

"Don't know any castrated monkeys," objected Porta; but he nevertheless seemed drawn to the idea. "Where are these photos?"

"I got 'em on me." The driver grinned craftily. "Not the sort of stuff you can leave lying around just anywhere."

"Let's have a gander."

Porta held out a dirty hand, which the driver ignored with a scathing "Like hell! You think I was born yesterday?"

"Okay. You know what you can do with your stinking pictures!" Porta withdrew his hand, shouldered his rifle and prepared to leave.

The driver at once leaned out of the car and clutched at his arm. "Don't be in such a hurry—we can come to some arrangement."

They eyed each other warily.

"Let me see the pictures."

"I'll hold 'em up and let you take a look from a distance," the driver temporized.

"You know something?" said Porta contemptuously. "I could sell this stuff elsewhere for three times the price you're offering. I'm only letting you have first option because I got a kind of funny idea you're liable to become one of us pretty soon."

"One of you?" The driver shot him a quick look of alarm. "What d'you mean, one of you?"

"One of our outfit. Well, look at it this way—you've dabbled your dirty little hands in too many pies to get away with it forever. You just ain't smart enough. Sooner or later they're going to catch up with you, and the rate you're carrying on it's going to be sooner rather than later. And when that happens, bud, I guess we're going to have the pleasure of your company—marching along beside us, hiding in the trenches with us. And then you'll know you've really arrived. After a short spell in Torgau, of course."

"Yeah? You think so? Well, that's just where you're wrong, see? If the day ever comes when they chuck me out of the SS and into a disciplinary regiment, it won't be with your scrubby outfit, it'll be with the cavalry. They've got their own mob, and that's where I'll be heading."

"Ah, now you're talking about the 37th Uhlans," said Porta. "Only trouble is, you're all out of date. They don't exist no more. The 49th Kalmykrytter division made mincemeat out of 'em some time ago. Only about ten survived and they didn't bother to reform the regiment, so you're out of luck."

The driver stared at him, his eyes almost starting from his head.

"Is that the truth?"

"Would I tell a lie?"

There was a long silence. Porta stood by the side of the car, nonchalantly picking dirt from beneath his fingernails.

"If I—er—came to you then," said the driver at last, "how do you think I'd make out?"

Porta shrugged. "Hard to tell. Some last, some don't. Some go under, some come to the top."

"Do you have any buglers in your company?"

"Fancy being a bugler, do you?" Porta looked down at him and grinned. "That's a change of heart, ain't it? A minute ago you wouldn't even look at us. Not quite so cocky now, are we?"

"I never was cocky," protested the driver vehemently. "I wouldn't be such a fool. It never does to be too damn sure of yourself in this god awful world. Everyone knows you don't make old bones, being under the Standartenführer. I'd probably stand just as much chance with your crowd. Suppose they did send me to you—is there anything you could do to help me?"

"Help you?" said Porta, at once suspicious.

"To be a bugler. Hang on a minute, I'll show you." He plunged a hand into the glove compartment and emerged with a bugle, brash and shining, and bearing the gold ribbon of the cavalry.

"Look here." He pointed to four rosettes pasted to the instrument. "See these? I won them at competitions. I've played this bugle all over the place. I played it at one of Adolf's blowouts, when all the nobs came to nosh with him. I played it for old King Carol, I played it back in 1938 when Chamberlain came over and had his head talked off. There was even a picture of me in the English newspapers. They had my name and all. People paid more attention to me than what they did to Adolf and Chamberlain."

"Not surprising," said Porta dryly. "Who'd want to listen to them two clowns driveling?"

"Look, if you don't believe me . . ."

"I believe you, for God's sake!" Porta pushed the bugle angrily away as the man raised it to his lips. "Don't blow the damn thing, we'll have the whole fucking barracks running out to take a look."

"I just wanted you to know . . ."

"Then save it. Wait till it happens and I'll see what I can do."

"Will you have a word with your CO about it?"

"Look," said Porta, "you got the wrong idea, see? I don't have to have words with no CO. It's me what practically runs this company. I say you're going to be a bugler, then you're going to be a bugler and that's all there is to it."

The driver looked at him doubtfully, and Porta clapped a suddenly friendly arm about his shoulder. "Come down to Bernard the Boozer's some time and bring the blower with you. Show us what you can do."

"And what about the cigarettes?"

"Well, what about 'em? You want 'em or not?"

"I want them all right—it's just a question of the price. If only you'd take my photos, I swear you wouldn't regret it. I'll tell you this for nothing, you'll never find any as good as this little lot. They're worth twelve pipes of opium on their own. Look—just take a look."

He pulled a small folder from his pocket and selected a picture. Porta stared down at it coldly, apparently unmoved. Only the glittering of his small eyes betrayed his eagerness to lay hands on it, which did not pass unnoticed by its owner. Slyly he pushed back the photograph and drew out another, depicting a scene of such pornographic boldness that it took even Porta by surprise. Unable to contain himself any longer, he stretched out a hand for it. The SS man grinned and at once moved it out of reach.

"Not bad, eh? And that's one of the milder ones—you wait till you've seen some of the others!" He licked his lips and winked. "Give you wet dreams for a month on end!"

Porta groped for some of his lost dignity. He stepped back a pace and sniffed. "I can get plenty of the real thing," he said. "What do I want with pictures?"

"Wait till they send you back to the trenches. I bet it's not so easy there . . ."

"There are ways," said Porta darkly.

"Yeah? Well, if that's the way you feel—" The SS man flipped quickly through the photographs, dwelling here and there on one that especially took his fancy, titillating Porta still further with a coarse chuckle or a prim downturning of the lips. "Mind you, you're passing up a good investment. Should have thought you were smarter than that—after all, you get tired of looking at 'em, you can always trade 'em in for a new set or sell 'em off to someone else for a good price. Still, if they don't do nothing for you, that's all there is to it . . ."

"Wait a minute." Porta held out a hand. "Let me have a quick look, make sure they're all genuine and what you say they are. I been caught that way once already and it ain't going to happen again."

"How come?"

"Some prick sold me thirty-five photos. He showed me the first four and I was dope enough to take his word for the rest. When I got 'em back home I found I'd been done—the others was all pictures of lousy scenery and bits of building and suchlike. I spent eight days looking for that bastard. I'm still looking—I even promised Tiny a couple bottles of vodka if he could lay hands on him for me. And I'll catch up with him one day, that's for sure. I never forget a face. And when I lay my hands on him—" He bent down to the car window, and suddenly there was a knife in his hand; he ran it swiftly through the air, only centimeters away from the driver's throat. "He won't live to sell any more dirty photos, you can take my word for that."

"I do," said the driver, his top lip twitching. "There's no need to demonstrate."

"Just thought you'd like to know."

"You surely don't think I'd be fool enough to try the same trick? Not on a friend. Not on someone like you."

"Why not?" growled Porta. "I'd try it on you fast enough, if I thought I'd get away with it. I'd try it on with anyone what was fool enough to let me. And you and me, pal, we're blood brothers, we are. What I'd do, you'd do, and we both know it. So let's have a gander at those snapshots before we decide anything."

"Well, I dunno—" The driver scratched thoughtfully at the lobe of his ear with the ignition key. "I'll make a deal with you: I let you have a quick whip through the photos and you let me have a cigarette while you're doing it. Just to hold it—kinda security."

"Okay."

The exchange was effected. Porta could hardly get his hands on the photographs fast enough. The driver sat holding his opium cigarette, watching Porta's face change as his little elephant's eyes gobbled up one piece of pornography after another.

"Like 'em?" he asked casually.

Porta swallowed a few times, cleared his throat, made an attempt to speak in his normal register.

"Not bad," he allowed. "Some of 'em are quite horny. I suppose," he said grudgingly, "I could always let 'em out for hire when I've had an eyeful—Tiny's fool enough to promise me a year's pay just to have 'em in his hands for a while. Yeah, all right, it's a deal."

The remaining eleven cigarettes were handed over. Porta put the photographs in his pocket and the driver produced three bundles of bills, each with a band around it. Porta stood stolidly counting them.

The driver sat and sniffed his opium cigarettes. They were firm and well packed, the best he had seen in a long time. He wondered if it would be worth the trouble and expense to get Porta drunk one day and try to discover where he obtained his supply . . .

"Hang on," said Porta. "I'm a hundred marks short."

"You can't be. There's a thousand in each pack, I counted 'em myself."

"Count again, then."

He did so. Three times. One hundred marks short. He shook his head in bewilderment, but the call of the opium was strong and he had no mind to jeopardize his chances for the sake of a hundred marks. He handed over another bill.

"That's better." Porta slipped an elastic band around the

three bundles and buttoned them away in a pocket. "And don't forget that address you promised me."

"I'll give it you right away. It's near the Alster. A white house with a black roof, you can't miss it." He scribbled something on a sheet of paper and handed it over. "It's a strange-looking place, used to belong to some Chinks."

"Did they leave any of their broads behind? I could just fancy a nice little bit of Eastern Promise. They say," said Porta carelessly, "that they can do it standing on their heads with their feet in the air."

"I wouldn't know about that, but you'll get your money's worth all right. Just tell 'em you've come from Rudolf. Rudolf Kleber. They know me. They—" He broke off, suddenly stiffened. "Watch out, he's coming back!"

Instantly, Rudolf was transformed into the perfect chauffeur, sitting patient and upright behind the steering wheel, his opium cigarettes disappearing into a hidden pocket by some practiced sleight of hand.

Porta stepped back a pace or two and snapped into the regulation guard position. He looked as if he had stood without moving for a hundred years. Only his eyes swiveled around, watching as three men came out of the building. Paul Bielert, dressed in black from head to foot; the SD Unterscharführer, one hand on his holster; and Lieutenant Ohlsen walking between them. They stepped into the car and the long, low, gray Mercedes rolled majestically from the barracks.

Porta watched until it had disappeared. He wondered for a moment where they were taking the lieutenant and why, but he had more pressing matters on his mind and he soon deserted his post, left the barracks to look after themselves, and slipped away to the garages. There, crouched behind a pile of oil drums, he gloated over his spoils. He went through the photographs, studying each one in minute and luscious detail, until the excitement became unbearable and he had to put them away for a more auspicious moment. He took out his bundle of bills and counted them again. Then, from another pocket, he took out a single hundred-mark note. With a satisfied grin, he slipped it under the elastic band with the rest of the pile. That would teach that fool Kleber to keep his eyes open!

Eventually he deigned to return to his post, where he found Heide waiting for him. "Where the devil have you been?" he snapped. "Tiny's been along twice already and both times you weren't here!"

"Piss off," said Porta in his usual amiable fashion. "You give me a pain in the ass. I had more important things to do than hang around playing at toy soldiers."

"Cut it out!" Heide shouted. "You're supposed to be on guard and you'll bloody well *be* on guard! You take your orders from me, you don't make them up for yourself!"

"Who says?" jeered Porta.

"I do!" yelled Heide. He paused and took a deep breath. "Perhaps you didn't know it, but we've had the Gestapo here today. They've just run through the barracks like a dose of salts. Looking for you, I shouldn't wonder. I always said you'd end up with a rope around your neck."

"Not this time, chum. They've come and they've gone, and it wasn't me they was after."

"Well, anyway," said Heide sullenly, "I'm sick and tired of continually having to cover up for you. Next time it happens, you can bloody well take the consequences and go hang for all I care."

"Okay. Suits me. I can look after myself."

Nonchalantly Porta slipped a hand into his pocket and brought out the photographs. Nonchalantly he began to study them. He passed through them just fast enough to whet Heide's appetite; just slowly enough for him to get a glimpse. Heide momentarily forgot his grievance. He craned his neck over Porta's shoulder. "Where'd you get that lot from?"

"Easy, easy," said Porta, at once shuffling the pictures together and holding them out of sight. He laid a finger on the side of his misshapen nose. "None of your business."

Heide breathed avidly down his neck. "Let's have a look."

"With pleasure. You can have them for an hour if you like."

Heide at once stretched out a hand, two patches of color burning his cheekbones. Porta flipped casually through the photographs once again.

"Smashing, ain't they? Take a look at those tits . . ."

"Well, come on, let's have 'em then!"

"Mind you," said Porta judiciously, "it'll be a waste unless you got the time to enjoy 'em properly. If I were you, I'd take 'em down to the shithouse and shut yourself up for an hour or two. Like that, you'll be well away . . ."

Heide was beginning to sweat. "How much do you want for them?"

"Nothing. They ain't for sale. Only just got 'em, didn't I?"

"Well, then, what—what do you—" Heide's mouth was twitching so much he could hardly speak.

"You can hire 'em, if you want. Hundred marks an hour for the whole lot, five marks for singles."

"You crazy?" Heide's speech abruptly returned to him. "Hundred marks an hour to look at a bunch of scrubby old whores? You must be joking!"

Porta hunched a shoulder and put the photographs away inside his empty gas mask case. "Take it or leave it, nobody's forcing you."

He strolled away again, leaving Heide in an indecisive sweat of desire and indignation. It was not long before Heide caught up with him and was muttering hotly into his ear.

"Give them to me. Here's your hundred marks. I suppose you know it's daylight robbery?"

"Well," Porta looked around at him, "if you're so over-sexed you can't stop yourself looking at dirty pictures, it's hardly any fault of mine, is it?"

His face livid with lust and burning with shame, Heide snatched at the pictures, thrust them deep into a pocket and walked off without a word. At the end of his guard duty he disappeared into the latrines and was seen no more for a full hour.

"They've taken Lieutenant Ohlsen off with them," announced Barcelona, as Porta returned to the guardroom.

"Yeah? So what?" said Porta. "He can take care of himself. What they nab him for, anyway?"

"Nobody knows, but I can tell you one thing—all the top brass is up in arms about it."

"Fat lot of good that'll do."

"Old Hinka's foaming at the mouth, and the adjutant's flat out on the carpet. According to Feldwebel Grün, we shan't be seeing Ohlsen back here again. Looks like we'll have a new CO pretty soon."

"It's obviously something serious," said the Legionnaire, who had just come in and had caught the tail end of our remarks. "I saw them as they drove off. An SS Mercedes with Auntie Bielert in the back of it. And you know what that means—Section IV/2A. They're only concerned with the big stuff there."

"What can he have done?" I wondered.

"Trouble with stupid officers," Porta lifted an indifferent shoulder, "they never know when to stop talking—yak yak yak, here, there and everywhere, anyone could be listening to 'em. But they're so much in love with the sound of their own voices, they don't care if people do eavesdrop. They *like* 'em to eavesdrop—hell, they sometimes talk so loud you can't *help* but eavesdrop. And then they sit back on their great fat asses with their chests covered in bits of tin and think they're safe and that nobody can't touch 'em, just because they're fucking officers; don't seem to realize that when it comes to dealing with people like Bielert, you might just as well be a private as a lieutenant for all the good it'll do you."

"I bet you a pound to a pinch of pigshit," said Steiner, "we won't never see Ohlsen again."

"That's for sure," agreed the Legionnaire.

Tiny suddenly clattered into the room, making more noise than usual and plainly spoiling for a fight. He tossed his rifle into a corner, bounced his helmet onto Barcelona's feet and spat, in passing, into someone's cup.

"What's eating you?" grumbled Barcelona, kicking the helmet to the far side of the room.

"I'll tell you what's eating me!" Tiny roared, like a bull in its death agony. "I've only spent the whole of my guard duty sweetening up some broad along by the electric fencing . . ."

"What were you doing along by the electric fencing?" demanded the Old Man suspiciously.

"Sweetening up this broad, like I said. I . . ."

"You had no right to be there," objected the Old Man.

"Well, I was, so balls to that!" retorted Tiny.

"And what happened?" I asked. "Wouldn't she play?"

"Oh, she'd play, all right," said Tiny bitterly. "Only trouble was, just before I got started, I had this crazy urge to pee . . ."

"So?"

"So I peed—" He turned and held out his hands appealingly. "You ever peed on an electric fence?"

A great roar of laughter went up. Tiny scowled.

"You think that's funny! I damn nearly got myself burned to a cinder—and her just standing there sniggering, with her pants in her hand, laughing fit to bust, and me trying to stop pissing and not being able to—Jesus Christ almighty!"

He smote a fist heavily onto the table, furious at the injustice of it all. "A dame all ready and waiting to be screwed, and me just standing there pissing my guts out!"

"Very frustrating," said Porta. "Accept my commiserations. I know what it's like, I've had it happen to me. Not because of an electric fence, of course, we're not all that stupid, but the same sort of situation . . ."

"And now I feel as randy as a goat!" bellowed Tiny.

"I've got the very thing you need to help you," Porta told him with a wink. "A set of photographs—all genuine, all unique—better than the best you ever saw. I'll let you have 'em for an hour for a hundred marks. Just as soon as Heide's finished pawing over 'em. What d'you say?"

Tiny promptly forgot his grievance about the electric fence. "Can I have 'em on credit?"

"On credit?" Porta stared at him. "On credit?" he repeated, his voice rising by half a horrified octave. "What d'you think I'm running, a goddamn charity or something?"

"All right, all right," said Tiny hastily. "No need to get hopped up. Hundred marks, you say?"

"A hundred marks," confirmed Porta.

"I'll get it!" Tiny made for the door. "I'll get it, I tell you! Just don't let 'em out to anyone else before I get back!"

"I wonder if I could get some copies made?" mused Porta, returning to his chair. "That way, I could lend 'em around the whole barracks . . ."

"Let me see," said the Legionnaire, "I was nineteen when I saw my first execution. It was at Casablanca, I remember. Some idiot who'd been twelve years in the Army and suddenly gone berserk. Taken it into his head to go galloping off God knows where—thought he could get away with desertion, poor fool. Of course, I've seen hundreds of others since then, but somehow you never manage to forget the first one."

"I was only eighteen," said Barcelona. "It was in Madrid, when I was with the Thälmann Battalion.* We had to shoot a kid of about my own age behind the abattoirs. He hadn't done anything, poor jerk. He just had a rich father, that was all. So we shot him—and Christ, what a hash we made of

---

*German battalion of Communist volunteers.

it! No training, no experience—we blew half his head away!"

"Personally, I never trouble my head over executions." Heide shrugged a contemptuous shoulder. "Can't see the difference between shooting a man who's standing up against a brick wall and shooting a man who's hiding in the trenches. It all comes to the same thing. It's all war."

"You remember that time we had to shoot that telephonist jane?" demanded Tiny, with his usual eagerness for the gruesome. "That was a real farce, that was! It was Sven's fault. Him and Stege. Wanted to act the gentleman and save her unnecessary suffering—and while they was stalling, she just took to her heels."

"I remember!" Porta gave a loud crack of laughter. "We had to chase her back into the building and all up and down the goddamn corridors . . ."

"And old Gustav bleating along behind us telling us not to shoot or we'd fuck up his books . . ."

"That's right, she had to be done away with proper, according to regulations, else her papers wouldn't be in order."

"We had to carry her out screaming in the end . . ."

"She was a murderer," said Heide coldly. "I saw her file in Hauptfeldwebel Dorn's office. She killed her best friend."

"Yeah, but only because her best friend happened to have pinched her fiancé," I objected.

"Fiancé, my ass! She just slept around with him and took what she could off him—he was a rich bloke, remember?"

"Next week we're on duty at Fuhlsbüttel," said Steiner suddenly. "I've arranged to go sick that week. I've already seen the Feldwebel down at the infirmary. It's costing me two cartons of cigarettes, but I guess it's worth it; I know for a fact they've got at least five executions laid on for that week."

"Don't worry me none," declared Tiny. "So long as they give us a bit of extra cash for being there, I don't care how many executions they got going. Way I see it is, if we didn't do it, there'd be a hundred others who would."

"Precisely," said Heide. "And in any case, we're supposed to be soldiers. We just do what we're told to do."

VI

PREVENTIVE DETENTION

In the offices of the Gestapo, Stadthausbrücke No. 8, Lieutenant Ohlsen sat facing Paul Bielert across a wide desk.

Lieutenant Ohlsen was holding a document in his hand. Bielert was thoughtfully smoking a big cigar. With a smile on his lips, and his eyes narrowed, he watched the smoke as it twisted and curled on its way to the ceiling. Ohlsen was his 123rd arrest that week. Gruppenführer Müller in Berlin could hardly do otherwise than express his satisfaction with Bielert's industry. Though, mind you, Müller was a fool and a swine. Not a patch on Obergruppenführer Heydrich.

Bielert shifted his position slightly and thought about Heydrich. They had assassinated him, the fools. And yet he was one of the best men they had had. A man Bielert had not objected to working for. Intelligent, self-assured and unscrupulous. A very angel of the devil. Even SS Heinrich had thought twice before crossing swords with him. And who knew, wondered Bielert, as he had often wondered before, who knew if Himmler and the Führer himself had not had a hand in his murder? Scared that the man was growing too powerful, and hence dangerous. Certainly the whole affair had been handled in a highly unsatisfactory manner. There were still far too many unanswered questions for Bielert's liking.

Why, for instance, had none of Heydrich's assassins been allowed to survive to tell their tale? The order of SD Gruppenführer Nebe, who was in charge of the mopping-up operation, had made it very clear that death and not capture was what was required: "Take no prisoners. They must all be killed, by whatever means available—even if it means violating the sanctity of a church, should they attempt to take refuge in one. Burn the church if necessary, but let none escape."

The last of the assassins had been run to earth in Prague. He had given himself up without a struggle, and instead of shooting him on the spot, they had taken him back with them. He seemed perfectly willing to talk, but he had never been given the chance; he had been shot in Nebe's office. According to the official report in the papers, it had been suicide, and most people had readily believed it. Even the British had swallowed the story and had put it out on the BBC.

Bielert slid open a drawer in his desk and looked down at the pistol he kept in it. It was the pistol he had used to shoot the last of the assassins, there in Nebe's office. He had been glad enough to do so at the time, thinking only of revenge, but now he sometimes found himself wondering what the man might have said, had he been given the opportunity to talk.

Shortly after the inquest, Nebe had been removed from office. He had become increasingly cocksure and overzealous since Heydrich's death and was evidently considered an embarrassment. At first Bielert had been puzzled, but his cunning brain had soon put two and two together and he had begun to wonder if he might not be the next on the list. He had instantly put in for a transfer and been sent to Hamburg.

By way of a so-called reprisal for the murder of Heydrich, they had burned down the entire village where it had happened, just outside Prague. It was the military police who performed the operation. A rumor was spread about that the SS had been responsible for it, but in fact there were no more than five SS men in the whole commando unit. The liquidation had been entirely the work of MPs from Dresden and Leipzig.

Bielert laughed softly to himself. It had originally been

proposed that the Waffen SS should perform the task, but SS Obergruppenführer Berger had strongly opposed the idea on the grounds that it would be harmful to the current recruiting campaign for volunteers from Bohemia and Slovakia. He had probably been right, in theory. In practice, as it turned out, the recruiting campaign was in any case dealt a blow from which it never recovered.

The idea of burning the village had come from Himmler himself, and it seemed an excellent one. An act so terrible, on such a scale, would set the whole world by the ears. It would be understood at once that it was a reprisal; an act of revenge against the Czechoslovak resistance movement, which had supposedly assassinated Heydrich. And in the face of such an orgy of slaughter, of burnings and shootings and hangings, all for the death of one man, the people would surely turn and curse the resistance movement for bringing such misery upon them.

The only trouble was that the British almost immediately became suspicious. They lost no time in broadcasting their views on the affair, with the result that many hundreds of volunteers from Bohemia and Slovakia at once deserted and joined the resistance movement instead, while the recruiting offices fell suddenly silent and empty. Heydrich had been exterminated, certainly, but the rest of the plan had gone sadly astray. One might even say, thought Bielert, closing the drawer again, that it had backfired. And served them right, too.

He turned his attention to Lieutenant Ohlsen, who was frowning as he read through the warrant for his arrest. Bielert leaned back in his chair and smiled contentedly through a cloud of cigar smoke. It was a good idea—and his own—to give these intellectual types the chance of acquainting themselves with a few of the facts before the interview began. It unsettled them, made them less sure of their ground and more disposed to open their mouths and try to talk their way out of trouble. And in Bielert's experience, the more a man talked, the more trouble he made for himself.

He waited patiently. Ohlsen was now reading through the warrant for the third time, going through it with desperate care, to make sure he had missed none of it. They always did that. The first time they skipped through it and only half understood it; the second time they slowed down sufficiently to grasp a few of the essentials, although even then

their minds still refused to accept the hard fact of their
arrest; but the third time, their nerve began to go and they
began to be far more malleable. So Bielert sat back and
bided his time, looked at his well-kept fingernails and savored
the aroma of his excellent cigar.

Lieutenant Ohlsen appeared to be no exception to the
general rule. He was reading the document with painful
slowness, still tending toward incredulity and yet with a
growing horror of awareness which spread from the deepest
pit of his bowels and steadily up through his body, making
his palms sweat and the hair follicles prick at the back of his
neck.

To the President of the People's Tribunal,
People's Tribunal, 7.J.636/43 (52/43—693)

> Hamburg, April 3, 1943
> Stadthausbrücke 8
> Hamburg 2.

WARRANT OF ARREST

Lieutenant Bernt Viktor Ohlsen, born April 4, 1917, at Berlin-
Dahlem, currently serving with the 27th Armored Regiment,
is required to be interned by the State Secret Police. The 27th
Armored Regiment is at present stationed at Hamburg, at the
Altona Barracks.

An official inquiry is to be held into the conduct of the said
Bernt Viktor Ohlsen. He is accused of seeking to disrupt public order by spreading alarm and despondency and by gen-
erally encouraging acts of sabotage and insurrection. The facts
are as follows:

1) On January 22, 1943, while the Regiment was at the
   Eastern Front, the Accused made the following declaration
   to a fellow officer:
   "If you ask me, the Third Reich won't even see its
   centenary, let alone the millennium—everyone knows
   the war's as good as lost. It's not going to be long before the English and the Americans come up through
   the Balkans and Italy and invade Germany herself—
   and then Adolf and his pals can go jump in their
   ovens and burn themselves to cinders, and the sooner
   the better as far as I'm concerned."

2) On or about the same date, the Accused showed to a
   junior officer some Russian propaganda inciting German
   soldiers to desert.

The offenses committed are in violation of Paras 5 and 91,
Article I of the Penal Code. The arrest and preliminary

investigation of the Accused shall be carried out by the
State Police, Stadthausbrücke 8, Hamburg 2. The arrest
and detention of the Accused are subject to appeal before
the President of the People's Tribunal.

                              (Sgd) Dr. Mickert
                              President of the Court of Appeal.

Lieutenant Ohlsen came to the end of the document for
the third time. He laid it on the desk and looked across
at Paul Bielert with a gesture of resignation.

"What am I supposed to say?"

Bielert blew out an unhurried cloud of smoke.

"That, of course, is entirely up to you," he said smoothly.
"I am only the person in charge of the preliminary investigation. It is not up to me to tell you what you should say.
However, there is one word of advice I can give you."
He leaned forward across the desk, gesticulating toward Ohlsen with his cigar. "Remember always that we at the Gestapo are not fools. We know what we're about. We never
arrest anyone without very good reasons—and we never
make mistakes. We check the facts most carefully before
we even go to the lengths of bringing in a suspect for
questioning. In a case such as yours, therefore, you will only
make it worse for yourself if you attempt to deny any of the
charges—particularly since, in the final analysis, you will
end up by saying just whatever we wish you to say."

He smiled, and leaned back again. His eyes glittered with
malevolent enjoyment behind his thick-lensed spectacles.

"If I were you, I shouldn't worry too much about the
details. When it comes to it, it resolves itself quite simply
into a question of choosing whether you walk out of this
room on your own two feet or whether you're dragged out
like a sack of potatoes—it is entirely up to you. But whatever
you decide, it makes no difference to me. Either way, you
don't leave until you've made a full and satisfactory
confession."

He held his cigar under his nose a moment, delicately
twitching his nostrils at the aroma. He looked across at
Ohlsen and smiled amiably.

"Of course, you can make things far easier for yourself
if you do decide to be sensible. If you're willing to make
a confession straightaway, it saves both your time and ours.
We don't have the bother of going through all this rubbish,"
he disdainfully tapped a finger on a pile of papers that lay
before him on the desk, "and you will probably be detained

in Torgau no longer than two to three weeks, which I think you will agree is quite reasonable. After Torgau, of course, you'll either be sent to a disciplinary regiment as a private, or possibly put in an FGA for a few months."

Lieutenant Ohlsen ran a hand through his hair, until it stood on end like a brush. But meeting the glittering gray eyes of Bielert, he refused to flinch.

"Everything you say sounds perfectly straightforward," he allowed. "Even, in the circumstances, quite tempting; I suppose most of the poor fools you have sitting in this chair would be gullible enough to believe you. The only thing is, I've already served three years in a disciplinary regiment and I'm perfectly well aware of the fact that no one—I repeat, no one—has ever survived more than two months in an FGA."

"You're exaggerating, of course," Bielert said equably. "I have personally known several people who have been through the ordeal and are still very much alive today— naturally, they are the ones who have been sensible and cooperative, I will grant you that. But anyone who is willing to be reasonable is always given a fair deal. And frankly, Lieutenant, I don't see that you have any real choice in the matter. Owing entirely to your own lack of discretion, you have succeeded in landing yourself in your present position, so why not confess to your crimes and have done with it? I have, I can assure you, sufficient evidence against you to have you executed if you don't choose to cooperate with us." He picked up his pen and pointed it at the Lieutenant. "When I say executed, I mean—executed. Decapitated. Have you ever seen anyone decapitated, Lieutenant? It's not a wholesome experience, even for the audience. Anyway, that is the position in which you find yourself and it's up to you what you decide. But whatever you do, don't underestimate the Gestapo. I don't exaggerate when I tell you that our information services are so efficient that we even know what people say in their sleep—my men are all over the place. And I make no bones about it, some of them are pretty unscrupulous. I don't care who they are or where they've come from, whether they're generals or whether they're prostitutes, whether I've met them at dinner parties or in the urinal of some stinking bistro—so long as they can do the job, that's all I ask. If I felt so inclined, Lieutenant, it would take me no longer than a couple of weeks to have the whole of your life history from the moment you were

born, even down to the minutest details that you yourself
have probably never known—I daresay I could find out the
color of the very first pacifier you ever sucked."

Lieutenant Ohlsen made as if to interrupt, but Bielert
held up a restraining hand.

"One moment before you have your say. You shall be
given all the time in the world very shortly. Let me first tell
you some of the more salient facts as I have them. We
know, to begin with, that you have frequently spoken to
your men of treason and of sabotage and of desertion. You've
treated the Führer's name with disrespect and you've read
and discussed prohibited literature—in particular, *All Quiet
on the Western Front,* from which you've often quoted long
passages. All this is in direct violation of Paragraph 91. In
addition, your wife is ready to make depositions as to other
treasonable acts of yours—we have far too much against
you, Lieutenant, there's no point in trying to fight us. Why
not take up your pen and make a full confession, and we
can be done with the whole unfortunate business within
the hour. You can cool off in the cells for a week or two,
and then I imagine your sentence will be six to eight weeks
in Torgau. After that, as I said, a disciplinary regiment.
Stripped of your rank, of course, but at least a very much
wiser man." He smiled. "You'll know better than to open
your mouth too wide in the future."

"It all sounds eminently reasonable," murmured Ohlsen.
"Only one thing worries me: what guarantee do I have that
everything will take place just as you've promised? I have
heard of people being shot for lesser crimes than I'm supposed to have committed."

"One hears so many tales," said Bielert carelessly. "Just
as one should guard against talking too much, so perhaps
one should guard against listening too much. As for a
guarantee—of course, I'm afraid that's not possible; as you
will appreciate, I am not the person who will ultimately sit
in judgment on you. However, you can rest assured that I
have had a great deal of experience in cases such as yours,
and I do know what I'm talking about. Whatever sentence
is passed has to come through to me for confirmation, and
I am able to modify it as I see fit. If I find a judge has been
too lenient, it is in my power to have both him and the
accused sent to a security camp. Equally, I can, if I wish,
tear up an order for execution and have the prisoner released
immediately. It all comes back to this question of willingness

to cooperate. We are constantly on the lookout for new talent, and to this end we are always interested in those who wish to cooperate with us. You, for instance, could do both of us a good turn if you chose to come and work for me. I should be particularly interested to learn certain details about your commanding officer, Colonel Hinka. Also, you have a cavalry captain by the name of Brockmann in your regiment. I have a very special interest in Captain Brockmann. I will be honest with you, Lieutenant; it would give me positive pleasure to see Captain Brockmann's head severed from his shoulders. Still," he sat up very straight and squared his narrow shoulders, "let us get your affairs in order to begin with. Make your confession, serve your time in Torgau, and I can promise you that within three weeks I shall send an order for your immediate reinstatement in your company, with your present rank of lieutenant. It will all be made to appear perfectly normal to your colleagues, and once back, you can quickly prove to me that you have regretted any past errors. Not, of course, that we ever force men to collaborate with us against their will. It is your own decision entirely."

Lieutenant Ohlsen gave a cynical smile. "All this is very well," he said, "but there's one flaw in it—in the first place, you see, I categorically deny all the charges made against me."

Bielert sighed.

"Ah, Lieutenant, I thought you had more intelligence than to start running your head against brick walls! Whether you deny the charges or admit them is totally irrelevant. You yourself are irrelevant, if it comes to that. I have nothing against you in particular—it was more chance than anything which made me pick on you. It could have been any member of your family. I could, if I'd wished, have arrested the whole lot of them while I was about it, but I don't require the whole lot of them, I require only one—one member of each family in Germany. That's what I must have."

Lieutenant Ohlsen stiffened.

"I'm afraid I don't follow you. What does my alleged behavior have to do with my family?"

Bielert tossed the butt of his cigar negligently through the open window and shuffled a few papers on his desk.

"Nothing," he said. "Nothing at all. The point I am trying to make is that it might just as well have been your father or your sister or your brother as you—it was mere chance that you happened to be the one who was chosen." He looked across at Ohlsen with a cordial smile. "We could just as well have arrested your father."

"On what grounds?" demanded Ohlsen coldly.

Bielert glanced down at the papers before him.

"April 26, 1941," he read out crisply. "At a few minutes past eleven he was discussing politics with two friends. During the course of the conversation he made the following statements: One, that he no longer believed in the possibility of a Nazi victory, and two, that he considered the State to be an idol with feet of clay. That may not seem to you a very grave crime, Lieutenant, but you would perhaps be surprised what we can do with it if we choose! And then, of course," he pulled out another sheet of paper, "there's your brother Hugo. He's serving at present with the 31st Armored Regiment at Bamberg. We have information on him as well, you see—he has been known on several occasions to make some very curious remarks on the men who run the Third Reich. We could certainly issue him with an invitation to come along here for a chat. And then again, there is your sister." He selected a third sheet of paper and ran a finger down it. "Here we are—a nurse in an Air Force hospital in Italy. In September, 1941, she was on a hospital ship in Naples. On the 14th of that month she was heard to remark that she held Herr Hitler directly responsible for— let me see—'for all this shameful and senseless slaughter . . .'"

Bielert collected his papers together and looked across at the lieutenant. "And there you have it," he said simply. "We possess similar information on virtually every citizen who has a tongue to speak with. I have here," he indicated a wire tray containing a bulky file, "a case against a top official at the Ministry of Propaganda. A man in his position, and he knows no better than to pour out his heart to his mistress! However, he was sensible enough to make a full confession and offer his services the moment I taxed him with it. He could well be very useful to me. I've long had my eye on Dr. Goebbels and his wastepaper ministry! You see, Lieutenant, I believe in aiming high . . ."

He laughed, brushed a few ashes off the lapel of his jacket and tightened the knot in his tie.

"You have an odd sense of humor," remarked Lieutenant Ohlsen dryly.

Bielert abruptly pulled down the corners of his thin mouth. The gray eyes narrowed to slits.

"I am not interested in having a sense of humor, Lieutenant. My work is far too serious for such frivolities. I do what has to be done and it takes up twenty-four hours of every day. The security of the entire country rests on my shoulders. Mine and my colleagues'. We have a duty to perform. Anyone who is unable to fit into our society must be exterminated for the good of that society. I think you will agree it is no laughing matter."

"Not when put like that," murmured Ohlsen.

"Hm." Bielert cracked each of his knuckles in quick succession, then tapped a hand impatiently on the table. "Well, I can't afford to waste any more time talking to you, Lieutenant. Sign the declaration and I shan't bother with the rest of your impertinent family. They deserve to be locked up, but as I said, I can't deal with the whole lot of them. One from each family, that's all I require. It was Reinhard Heydrich's idea, and like most of his ideas it's fundamentally sound. Just wait until the war is over, Lieutenant. You'll see the day when the entire population of Europe raise their hands in salute whenever an SS officer goes by. As they do in Japan, you know. I was in Japan for several months, it was a most enlightening experience. Dutch and English officers prostrating themselves before their Japanese masters—" He leaned back luxuriously in his leather chair, his small, neat hands resting lightly on the arms.

Lieutenant Ohlsen tried to suppress a shiver, and failed. It needed only a pair of glittering black crows to transform the chair into a devil's throne, and Bielert into a creature dragged from the depths of Grimm's fairy tales.

He turned and looked out of the window. A steamer hooted mournfully on the Elbe. Two pigeons puffed and strutted on the ledge. From the flagpole hung the red flag with its swastika, limp in the still air. A flight of seagulls soared and swooped, squalling in a fretful heap over a crust of bread. Lieutenant Ohlsen turned his eyes away. He had never been able to bear the sight of seagulls since the day in the Mediterranean when he had been aboard a boat that was torpedoed. Himself lying wounded and unable to help, he had watched in horror as a pack of ravenous birds had alighted on the dying ship's captain and torn out his eyes. He had loathed seagulls ever since. At least the birds of prey, the crows and the vultures, even rats and hyenas, had the decency to wait until their victims were dead before tearing them to pieces. But not seagulls. Seagulls tore the eyes out of their living prey. They seemed to him to be the Gestapo of the bird kingdom.

He looked back at Bielert, a little gray man hunched in his armchair, indescribably evil, with a power that was terrifying, and he suddenly saw Bielert as a seagull; crouching over a warm body, sucking out its eyes and cramming them into his mouth . . .

Ohlsen stretched out a hand for the pen. He signed the declaration without even looking at it. He no longer cared. And besides, it was true. He had said far harsher things about the Führer than Bielert had accused him of. Perhaps, after all, he would be dying for a good cause. But he wished he knew who it was that had denounced him. He wished there were some way of getting word to Porta and the Legionnaire. They would take his revenge for him, no matter who it was, and revenge would be sweet even by proxy.

Paul Bielert leaned forward with a slight grunt and took the declaration. He looked at the signature and nodded, then offered the box of big cigars to Ohlsen.

"There! It's done—and it wasn't really so difficult, was it?"

Ohlsen said nothing. There was really nothing to be said. He knew he could have prolonged the matter, denied all the charges, refused to sign, but he knew also that it would have been futile. The Gestapo had all the power and there was nothing the individual could do.

Ten minutes later, two SD Unterscharführer entered the room. One of them laid a heavy hand on Ohlsen's shoulder.

"We're just going for a spin, Lieutenant. We've come to take you with us. You'll enjoy the outing."

They laughed uproariously. Unterscharführer Bock was reputed to be something of a joker.

Lieutenant Ohlsen left the room in silence, continued in silence through the building and out to the car. Unterscharführer Bock sat in front, next to the driver, and kept up a running commentary as they drove through the city. Down Mönckebergstrasse, across Adolf Hitler Platz; a detour because of the bomb damage, along the Alster, past the hotel Vier Jahreszeiten, across the Gänsemarkt; down the Zeughausalle and into the Reeperbahn. The Reeperbahn was crowded. It seemed to be full of people who had nothing better to do than drift from one bar to another, growing progressively and squalidly drunk as they did so.

"Pity we're in such a hurry," said Bock. "We could have stopped for a beer."

A long line of people stretched the full length of Kleine Maria Strasse.

"They're waiting to try out the new whores," explained Bock, hanging over the back of the seat and addressing Lieutenant Ohlsen, who made no attempt to show any interest. "We've just installed another twenty of 'em. There's service for you! Don't never let me hear anyone say the Third Reich isn't well organized. Tell me, Lieutenant, have you ever stopped to think exactly what National Socialism really is?" Ohlsen kept his head turned away, staring bleakly through the window. "Well, I'll tell you," said Bock. "It's the one and only workable form of Communism."

Ohlsen turned slowly to look at the man. "How do you make that out?" he asked wearily.

Bock laughed, flattered that he should at last have gained Ohlsen's attention.

"Well, now, the way I see it, over here we're what I call *national* Communists. We want to make Germans out of the whole world. Anyone got the wrong shape nose, the wrong type of hair, the wrong color skin, he's out. And that's as it should be, because they're not Germanic—right? Now the Russians, they're not nearly so choosy. They don't care what you look like, it's enough for them just to tap you on the shoulder and say from now on you're a Bolshevik and you've got to think like a Bolshevik. And that's all they care. No feeling of nationality at all. Mind you, I've got to admit it, in some respects the Russians know what they're doing a damn sight better than we do. Take priests, for example. Over here, we let 'em walk about quite freely, don't even make 'em wear a swastika. Over there, they hang the bastards. Hang 'em and be done with it. And I say that's the way we should treat 'em. Because otherwise we're just storing up a pack of trouble for ourselves, you mark my words. A pack of trouble—it doesn't pay to be too soft, and they're stronger than what you probably think they are. People are suckers for that sort of thing, all the mumbo jumbo and the bowing and the scraping and the going to confession and all the rest of it. For myself, I wouldn't have nothing to do with any of it. Catch me going anywhere near a goddamn priest!"

He laughed, and the driver laughed with him.

"Why is that?" asked Ohlsen mildly. "Do you have so much on your conscience?"

Bock looked out at the Königin Allee, with its church lying in ruins.

"I've not got nothing on my conscience, no sir. All I've ever done is carry out orders. Done what I been told to do. It's no concern of mine what the orders are, nor who gives 'em, so don't you try blaming me for anything."

The car drew up outside headquarters and a sentry bent down and spoke to the driver.

"Where from and where to?"

"Gestapo IV/2A, Stadthausbrücke 8. We're going to the garrison prison."

"Let's see your pass."

The sentry glanced for a moment at Lieutenant Ohlsen with a look that said quite clearly, Last time he'll ride in the back seat of a car, poor devil—probably the last time he'll ride anywhere at all.

He walked around to the front of the car to check the number plate. Resolutely, he saluted Ohlsen.

The big Mercedes drove on into the barracks. Lieutenant Ohlsen caught sight of a group of officers in white jackets walking up the broad steps to the casino. He himself had been to that casino, in earlier, happier days which now seemed a lifetime ago.

They drove on across the square and pulled up outside the prison. Bock laughed.

"Here we are, Lieutenant! A five-star hotel, all for your delight—private bathroom and a soft bed, what more could a man ask? Don't be alarmed that the doors are locked and barred. That's not to keep people from getting out, it's to keep 'em from getting in . . ."

He pressed a button at the side of the door, and far away in the depths of the prison could be heard the faint ringing of a bell. Soon there were heavy footsteps and the sound of keys turning in a lock. The door was swung slowly open by an Obergefreiter. Bock announced the arrival of Lieutenant Ohlsen as if he were the Queen of Sheba in person, and the Obergefreiter accepted delivery in phlegmatic silence as if he were taking receipt of a crate of vegetables.

"Is he one for the knife?" he asked laconically as he handed back the official forms, duly signed.

"Who knows?" laughed Bock.

He saluted and turned away, leaving Ohlsen standing helpless on the wrong side of the stout iron doors. He was marched along to a reception office, where an artillery Stabsfeldwebel lorded it behind a large empty desk. He was short and squat, with a bald head and an enormous chest, an overhanging forehead and small round eyes like boot buttons. He took his time reading through Lieutenant Ohlsen's papers, either because he had difficulty in reading or because he enjoyed wallowing in a sense of self-importance before a disgraced officer.

"Crimes against the state," he said, slowly running a square-tipped finger along the line of print. "Crimes against the state—" He looked contemptuously across at Ohlsen. "I don't like people that commit crimes against the state. I'd rather have your real honest crook than scum like you. You can trust the green uniforms, but you can't never trust the red. I'd even rather have a yellow than a red. They might drive you nuts reading the blessed Bible all day long, but at least they don't give no trouble. You people, though—you're just a bunch of idiots that won't never learn. Tilt at windmills," he said scornfully. "That's what you do. Tilt at windmills. Now, you listen to me," he abruptly changed his tone to one of official barking. "Empty your pockets and lay everything out on the table. And when I say everything, I mean everything—and that includes all the little goodies you've tried stuffing up your asshole. You can just spit 'em all out again. I wasn't born yesterday, you know; I've seen it all before—" He leered. "That's right, put 'em on the table. Work from left to right and make sure you keep 'em in a straight line. Use the edge of the table as a guide—space 'em out proper, two fingers between each item—lighter and matches over on the right, money down at the end on the left—and get a move on, can't you, we haven't got all day, there is a war on, you know!"

Lieutenant Ohlsen stood back and looked at his personal belongings spread out in a straight line along the edge of the table: lighter, pen, watch, pipe, notebook, and all the other oddments that a man normally keeps in his pockets. At the far end, on the left, were thirty-two marks and sixty-seven pfennigs.

Stabsfeldwebel Stahlschmidt noted every article, in detail, on a sheet of paper, and then attached a label to each one. On Lieutenant Ohlsen's notebook there was a red star—the cockade of a Russian commissar, a souvenir of Kharkov. Stahlschmidt tore it off with an oath, hurled it to the floor and trampled it vigorously underfoot.

"We don't keep that sort of trash here. I should have thought that was a crime against the state in itself, carrying about rubbish that belongs to the enemies of Germany."

He looked across at Lieutenant Ohlsen, his eyes gleaming with malicious anticipation; they had now arrived at the point where the lieutenant must be stripped of his medals and his uniform and be subjected to a search. Stahlschmidt always enjoyed that more than anything.

He licked his fleshy lips and rubbed his sweating palms down the side of his legs, casing Ohlsen through half-closed eyes. This one, he estimated, was not likely to give him any trouble, although prisoners in the past had been known to produce the most unlikely reactions, and it never did to take too much for granted. The essential, as far as the Stabsfeldwebel was concerned, was to push the prisoner over the borderline, where rage or panic or general desperation would prompt him to lash out against his tormentor. Then, and only then, could the Stabsfeldwebel really begin to savor the joys of his position; then, and only then, could he pass to the counteroffensive. With Obergefreiter Stever standing foursquare and solid like a human Mount Everest at the door, blocking any possible escape route and complacently witnessing the fact that his superior was acting purely in self-defense, Stahlschmidt could work out all his problems, all his neuroses, on the hapless prisoners.

Still watching Ohlsen, he picked up a long, slender riding switch and began tapping it pensively against his calf. He was remembering the scene that had been played out only a few days earlier with a fool of a colonel from the 123rd Infantry Regiment, who had been accused of sabotage. The man had borne all manner of insults and rough treatment with soldierly dignity until the moment he was ordered to remove his clothes, at which he had stalled and, indeed, lost his head and become completely hysterical. That had been an unexpected bonus!

Stahlschmidt's thick wet tongue flicked out again and moistened his lips as he remembered the apoplectic colonel.

"You may be an officer and the commander of a regiment," Stahlschmidt had sneered, secure in the safety of his own position; "you may be covered in bits of tin and honor and glory and all the rest of it, and you may come from a fancy blue-blooded family, but by Christ, as far as I'm concerned, you're nothing but a lousy stinking bastard that's broken the law and that's here to be punished! And if you live long enough, you'll be taken out and shot, and nobody's going to give a damn if your blood's as blue as the stinking Med . . ."

At this, the Colonel had exploded. Obergefreiter Stever, watching from the door, had leaned forward and pushed him neatly in the small of the back, so that he lost his balance and cannoned into the waiting Stahlschmidt. For a few moments they had tossed him back and forth between them, punching him in the stomach, jabbing him with the butt of a rifle, until the colonel, seizing his chance, had shot through the door and gone galloping up the passage with his shirttail flapping against his stringy old thighs. They had chased after him, up and down the corridors, and finally cornered him with the aid of Greinert, otherwise known as the Vulture. While Greinert and Stever had held him between them, Stahlschmidt had pulled out his pistol and forced him to take it in his right hand, pressing it against his temple.

The colonel had died badly. He had begged and pleaded and babbled hysterically, with tears down his cheeks, of the favors he could arrange for them if only they would spare his life. His last despairing words had been to offer them free use of his wife and daughters. Stahlschmidt had laughed as he forced the colonel to press the trigger and blow his brains out.

Naturally, one could not expect all prisoners to put on such a good show, nor to commit suicide, but looking at Lieutenant Ohlsen, Stahlschmidt found himself hopeful that this young man might also prove an entertaining proposition. He scraped his throat and swallowed hard in anticipation.

"Will the prisoner now please remove his garments and lay them out on the two chairs provided. Undergarments on the left, all the rest on the right. Boots to be placed halfway between the two."

He scraped his throat again, waited a second, then looked up to see how the lieutenant was taking it. To his acute disappointment, the lieutenant was taking it quite indifferently. His face was unchanged. The lines around the mouth had perhaps hardened, the expression in the eyes perhaps grown a little bleaker, but it was evident that he was not going to crack easily. The Stabsfeldwebel had seen the signs before; the signs of a man who could no longer find the energy to fight or to set himself up against the system. And they were the most tedious of all prisoners. They would do whatever they were told, accept all manner of insults and injuries without so much as raising an eyebrow; just sit quietly in their cells and wait to be interrogated, wait to be tried, wait to be found guilty and shot. All this without a flicker of emotion to indicate that they cared. And perhaps they didn't care, and it was this which so irked the Stabsfeldwebel. Because a man who didn't care was a man who was invulnerable, and a man who was invulnerable was a man without interest. You could jeer at him, taunt him, humiliate him all you liked, and it was only a waste of time and a source of frustration, for you might just as well pour a flood of scorn upon a brick wall and expect it to fall to pieces as expect a man who no longer cared to show any stimulating reactions.

Lieutenant Ohlsen slowly and impassively undid his jacket and hung it over the back of the chair.

"Don't take all day about it!" snapped Stahlschmidt. "You're not getting changed for a fancy dress ball!"

The lieutenant obediently pulled off his shirt and pants and flung them after the jacket. His expression was still blank. He showed no signs of shame, or anger, or humiliation. Stahlschmidt chewed at his meaty underlip with a set of yellowing teeth. Wait till the bastard was up before the governor! That would shake him out of his lethargy. That would teach him to sing a different tune. That would . . .

Lieutenant Ohlsen stepped out of his boots and stood naked between the two chairs. Stahlschmidt turned to look at him. His top lip curled into a hoop of derision.

"What a loathsome sight! Eh, Stever? What a horrible, loathsome sight—there's something very disgusting about naked bodies. You didn't look so bad with your uniform and all your lovely medals, but believe me, if you could see yourself now, you'd want to crawl into a hole and die. Look at you! Look at those great bony knees! Look at those horrible hairy legs! Look at those huge horny toenails! Jesus Christ, what a specimen, eh?"

He winked at Stever and began pacing around the lieutenant, casting derisory glances at him, every now and again poking or prodding him. The lieutenant bore it all with an air of weary patience, as if the Stabsfeldwebel were a child to be humored and tolerated.

"All right!" roared Stahlschmidt, coming to a halt. "Let's have you down on your hands and knees—down on the floor, down you go! Ten push-ups, and no cheating—Stever, come over here and take a quick dekko up his backside, make sure he's not got nothing hidden there . . ."

Obergefreiter Stever willingly left his post at the door and walked to the far side of the lieutenant. As he reached the last of his prescribed number of push-ups, Stever suddenly placed one heavy booted foot on his rump and gave him a shove that sent him flying. Stahlschmidt did his best to get in the way—even the lightest touch by the prisoner and he could claim to have been attacked by him—but, annoyingly, the lieutenant managed to control his fall. He crashed into the door, but he avoided the Stabsfeldwebel.

He staggered to his feet and stood patiently by the side of one of the chairs, awaiting the next absurd order. His eyes were blank, staring not so much at the Stabsfeldwebel as straight through and past him, and by his very indifference he remained aloof and impregnable.

Stahlschmidt breathed deeply. If this insolent lieutenant persisted in his present course of action, his stay in prison was likely to prove very uncomfortable indeed. It was Stahl-schmidt who for all practical purposes ran the prison. The governor came round occasionally on a tour of inspection, but it was Stahlschmidt who made all the decisions and organized the general treatment of the prisoners. Whatever he chose to do, Major Rotenhausen would close his eyes to it. Too close an inquiry into their affairs would have pleased neither man, and so long as Stahlschmidt remained reasonably circumspect, the governor was content to leave matters in his hands.

"Right!" Stahlschmidt stepped forward to the two chairs. "Belt and suspenders are left down here. We don't want you taking them off to the cells with you and getting ideas into your head." He leered into the lieutenant's face. "We don't have suicides in this establishment—not unless I personally arrange for them. Just remember that. I daresay there's nothing you'd like better than to put an end to your miserable existence before you have to face the tribunal and take the just punishment what's coming to you—I daresay you'd like to deprive society of the pleasure of having its revenge, wouldn't you? I know; I've met your type before.

Think you can get away with things without paying for them. Well, you can't and I'm here to see to it that you don't."

He rubbed his large misshapen hands together and took a turn about the room.

"It'll either be Torgau or Glatz. One of the two. That's where you'll end up—I hope it's Glatz, eh, Stever? You've got Colonel Remlinger at Glatz. He knows how to deal with people like you. He knows how to break you, he knows how to make you grovel—he runs that place with a discipline that would have made even old Fritz* turn pale. I've seen your death-or-glory boys fresh from the trenches and covered from head to foot in scars and medals, I've seen 'em walk in there proud as peacocks one day and sniveling like kids the next. They make you go up and down the stairs, four flights of 'em, on your hands and knees, you know that? They treat you like you deserve to be treated, lower than beasts of the field . . ."

As the lieutenant remained in his impassive trance, Stahl-schmidt took a pace backward and tried a new tack.

"Still, maybe I'm wrong at that. Maybe it won't be Glatz and it won't be Torgau. Who knows, eh? It might be the old chopping block—I seen 'em do that to a guy. Just once, I seen 'em do it and I couldn't bear to watch no more—bloodthirsty, it was. Very. They don't always come off clean at the neck with the first blow . . ."

A slight, involuntary ghost of a smile flickered across Ohlsen's lips. It seemed to Stahlschmidt as if he were laughing at him; laughing kindly and trying not to show it, as at a child's naive exaggeration.

Stahlschmidt stiffened.

"All right, that's enough of the talking! Get your clothes back on, and on the double before I lose patience! I'm a busy man, I've got things to do. It's all right for you, you're a nothing, you're a nobody, you got no responsibilities, but I got a position to keep up, I can't hang around all day telling fairy stories to the likes of you."

Lieutenant Ohlsen quickly dressed himself again. He was obliged to keep one hand on his pants, now that his suspenders had been confiscated. He was about to put his tie around his neck, when Stahlschmidt suddenly yanked it violently away from him.

"No ties allowed! What do you think this is, a fashion

---

*Frederick the Great.

house? And do your jacket up properly, I won't have slip-shod ways in my prison!"

The lieutenant silently folded the wide lapels of his jacket across his chest and buttoned them down. Stahlschmidt nodded approvingly.

"Good. That's better. I can see you're quick to pick up new ideas—we'll make a man out of you yet. You'd be surprised the number of officers who've come in here like you and been sent out again as real soldiers. Right! A little gentle exercise before you go to the cells. Arms above your head, jumping on the spot—starting now!"

The lieutenant put his arms above his head and began jumping on the spot. As he did so, his pants fell about his ankles and threatened to trip him up.

Stahlschmidt and Stever threw back their heads and roared with coarse laughter. Lieutenant Ohlsen went on jumping. He seemed almost unaware, and certainly uncaring, that his pants were around his ankles and that he looked ridiculous.

Stahlschmidt stopped laughing, dug Stever in the ribs and glared at him. Stever also stopped laughing. Lieutenant Ohlsen had ruined the joke; it simply wasn't funny any more.

Together they stood watching him, bewilderment and rage writ large on Stahlschmidt's face. He found himself wondering whether in fact the prisoner's mind had given way completely. Certainly there had been others whose spirit had broken and who no longer cared what became of them, but this idiot lieutenant was holding out far longer than most. It was conceivable that a man could be left unmoved by thoughts of his ultimate fate, the chance of imprisonment or execution, but sooner or later Stahlschmidt had never failed to produce a spark of reaction by subjecting them to the smaller humiliations of life—the handing over of their possessions, the stripping, the searching, the jumping on the spot. Was this stubborn fool of a prisoner completely insensitive? Had he no proper pride or sense of shame?

Stahlschmidt moved on to his next charade.

"Right! Down on the ground, flat on your stomach! Five turns to the right, five turns to the left, and don't take that belly off the floor or there'll be trouble!"

Lieutenant Ohlsen obediently fell flat on his stomach. Obediently he began pulling himself around in a circle.

Stahlschmidt moved over to him and deliberately stood on his fingers. Lieutenant Ohlsen winced. He bit his lips until they bled. Stahlschmidt renewed his efforts, walking back and forth over the prisoner's hands. Ohlsen saw a red mist of pain before his eyes, but no more than a low groan of protest was wrung from him.

After that, they gave him a rifle, a heavy Belgian rifle of antiquated design, and led him out in the corridor, where they called up Greinert the Vulture and had him assist them in putting the lieutenant through his paces.

"Rifle drill!" bawled Stever. "Down on your knees, prepare to fire!"

Greinert walked around with a critical eye, ready to jump on the smallest of faults, but he lacked the imagination to invent any, and unfortunately for him Lieutenant Ohlsen appeared not to have any faults. He knew what he was doing when it came to handling rifles.

"On your feet, ready to fire!" yelled Stever.

Lieutenant Ohlsen was on his feet in an instant, the rifle in regulation position. Stever at once began shouting out a new string of orders.

"Down on your stomach! On your knees! On your feet! Present arms! Stand at ease! Fix bayonet! Down on the ground! Stand to attention! Stand at ease! Ready to fire! Half-turn to the right! Face front! Running on the spot, start now!"

Lieutenant Ohlsen took it all in grim silence. They kept him at it until he was almost, but not quite, at dropping point.

"Stand to attention!" roared Stever, whose voice was growing hoarse.

The lieutenant stopped running on the spot. He pulled himself upright and stood stiffly to attention. For a second the building swayed before his eyes and he thought he was going to pitch forward, but the sensation passed and he retained his stance. Not, however, before the lynx eyes of Greinert had noted the slight movement. He stepped forward in a lather of excitement.

"He moved! He's supposed to be standing to attention, and he moved!"

Stever and Stahlschmidt, who had not noticed anything, handed over the field of battle to Greinert.

"Look at him!" screamed Greinert. "Shaking all over like a wet dog! And him an officer! Supposed to train new recruits, and doesn't even know how to stand to attention! Doesn't even know how to obey an order!" He moved closer to the lieutenant. "I said stand to attention, not dance an Irish jig! When I say stand to attention, you stand to attention. That means you freeze to the spot, you grow like a statue, wild horses couldn't drag you away and earthquakes couldn't shake you . . ."

Lieutenant Ohlsen spoiled this fine burst of poetry by involuntarily swaying forward again. The Vulture stepped back a pace, pulled down his jacket, pushed back his helmet. His breath came snorting indignantly down his nostrils.

"Things have come to a pretty pass," he said bitterly, "when a simple sergeant has to take an officer in hand and start training him in basic discipline."

Suddenly, and with no warning, his right fist shot out and crashed into the lieutenant's face. Ohlsen staggered backward, knocked off balance by the blow. He took a few uncertain steps, then regained his equilibrium and came once more to attention, standing stiff and straight and staring ahead, despite the blood that was pouring from his nose and dripping onto his tunic.

The Vulture at once launched into a fine display of histrionics. He raved and he roared, he mocked, he jeered and he intimidated, and he accompanied the whole tirade with a nonstop string of vitriolic obscenities. He raced off into a positive frenzy of fresh instructions, spitting them out one after another until the lieutenant was several moves behind him and would have had no hope of keeping up even under the best of conditions.

When Ohlsen was finally standing to attention once again, his face streaked with blood, his nose swollen, his chest heaving and his ears ringing, Greinert embarked upon a new set of tactics. He began by standing a few paces away and studying the lieutenant intently from head to foot, now and again giving a small, scornful laugh. When he had finished with this amusement, he walked closer and stared direct into his face, trying to make him lower his gaze or blink. When Lieutenant Ohlsen did neither, Greinert set off on a circular tour, walking very silently around and around and around, in never-ending circles . . .

It was a well-known trick. Most people broke after the first five minutes. Some, the toughest and most experienced, held out for ten. Very rarely did a man last a quarter of an hour.

Lieutenant Ohlsen survived for thirteen minutes. His head

was beginning to swim and his arms to grow lead weights. His knees were trembling and he had cramp in his fingers. Greinert had been watching and waiting for this moment. He took up his position behind the lieutenant and waited a while longer; and then, very gently, he stretched out a hand and gave a sharp push at Ohlsen's rifle. The rifle slipped from his numbed fingers and fell to the floor with a crash that rang startling loud in the silence.

"So now we come to it!" screamed Greinert. "An officer who can't even hold onto his rifle! Drops it to the ground like a toy he's got tired of!" He walked around to face the lieutenant. "Get down on your stomach and grovel!"

Ohlsen fell thankfully to the ground. Greinert gave him a kick.

"Pick that rifle up and crawl forward! On the double, we don't want to be here all day! And lick the rifle while you're doing it—I said lick it, damn you, lick it! Crawl and lick, crawl and lick, one-two, one-two—keep it up, no flagging, I didn't tell you to stop!"

And so the lieutenant crawled up and down the passage, licking his rifle till his tongue was sore. Each time he passed in front of Stahlschmidt and Stever, they trod on his fingers and abused him. Each time he passed in front of Greinert, he received a kick in the face, in the head, in the groin. He was bleeding from both nose and mouth. His hands were almost raw. His eyes were clouding over.

Someone dragged him to his feet and began using him as a punchball. They pushed him to and fro between them, battering him until he fell limply from one to another and finally slid unconscious to the floor. Greinert aimed one last vicious kick into his crotch, but fortunately the lieutenant was no longer capable of feeling pain. He lay on his back with his head to one side, a thin trickle of blood coming from his mouth and dripping to the floor.

"Hm." Stahlschmidt grunted and stood looking down at the inert form. He had been unable to break the man's mind, but at least he had had the satisfaction of breaking his body. "All right," he said, turning back down the corridor. "Throw him into No. 9 and forget about him."

Happily he returned to his office. It had, on the whole, been a good day. This stubborn fool of a lieutenant was the fourth prisoner he had passed through the initiation ceremony. Stahlschmidt rubbed his hands together and trod with jaunty step to the window. If only, one day, a certain

Lieutenant Hans Graf von Breckendorf could be passed through the initiation ceremony! If he could only have von Breckendorf crawling naked and shivering before him, jumping with his pants around his ankles, lying in a heap with blood trickling from his mouth—his joy would be complete.

Stahlschmidt swallowed and forced himself to sit down, before the excitement of the prospect should overcome him. He prayed nightly to a god he didn't believe in for von Breckendorf to be delivered to him. He hated von Breckendorf with a hatred that could only partially be appeased by the constant humiliation and brutality that he practiced on all the other officers who came his way. Never, as long as he lived, would he forget the way that he had been made to suffer at von Breckendorf's hands.

It was a Saturday afternoon, a hot, bright day in the middle of July. The Stabsfeldwebel had just come off duty and had gone straight to the canteen for a beer. He had undone his collar and pushed his cap to the back of his head, and he remembered even now the anticipatory saliva suddenly flooding his mouth as he walked toward the steps.

At the foot of the steps, barring his entrance to the canteen, was Lieutenant Graf von Breckendorf. He had been made a lieutenant on the eve of his nineteenth birthday, and he was arrogant and insufferable on account of it. He was sitting astride a magnificent dapple horse when Stahlschmidt came up, and as Stahlschmidt drew near, he extended a languorous arm and poked the tip of his riding crop into his throat.

"What's the meaning of that, Stabsfeldwebel? Do your collar up immediately, I will not tolerate men wandering about half undressed." And as Stahlschmidt did up his top button, von Breckendorf's eyes had narrowed and he had lowered the crop and pushed Stahlschmidt in the abdomen with it. "How disgustingly fat you're becoming! Locked away in that prison of yours, it's not good for you, I don't believe you have nearly enough exercise. It's not healthy for a man to sit hunched over a desk all day. Come along with me and I'll put you through your paces."

Stahlschmidt had had no alternative but to obey. The horse set off at a trot, and he had to run along behind to keep up, breathing in the sweet, suffocating smell of hot horse and saddle leather and human sweat.

Von Breckendorf had sent him through every obstacle on the obstacle course. Stahlschmidt had emerged from the barbed wire with his uniform in shreds and his face torn to ribbons, but von Breckendorf had appeared not to notice. He had immediately dragged him off to the stables, sent him into the ring and made him run around it several times while he rode behind him cracking his whip and saying "Hup!" each time they came to a jump. Even then von Breckendorf had not wearied of the entertainment. He had given Stahlschmidt ten minutes to go away and change and to come back dressed in full combat uniform, including his gas mask, and he had then run him around the ring thirty-six times, von Breckendorf on horseback, Stahlschmidt on a leading rein. Anytime Stahlschmidt staggered, he felt the cut of the riding crop across his shoulders. He had been on the point of passing out when finally von Breckendorf had let him go.

"I think you'll find that's got some of the loose flab off you," he had said, smiling benignly. "Good day, Stabsfeldwebel. I feel sure we shall meet again sometime."

Stahlschmidt hoped so. With all his heart he hoped so. Each morning he woke to a new day full of new expectations. Each morning he hurried to his office and ran a febrile eye through the sheaf of papers that had been left on his desk. One day, please God, he would see the name of Hans Graf von Breckendorf among them . . .

Nobody had ever seen fit to tell Stahlschmidt that Lieutenant Graf von Breckendorf had been killed over a year earlier at Sebastopol. Had he ever found out, it would almost certainly have broken his heart.

During the next few days, the prison staff was kept more busy than usual, and several happy inmates were locked away in their cells without first having to undergo the initiation rites. A large-scale offensive had been launched against those officers who entered into overfriendly relations with the people of occupied countries, and as a result, the number of arrests was increasing daily by leaps and bounds. Anyone who was even heard to say a good word for an enemy nation came under the gravest suspicion, and one indiscreet infantry officer at Oldenbourg, chancing to remark that he found Winston Churchill a great deal more inspiring than certain other people, found himself under arrest almost before he had finished speaking.

A cavalry officer who chose to salute with two fingers raised in the V for Victory sign was rushed straightaway to see Herr Bielert: infringement of the famous paragraph 91. The cavalry officer was never seen again.

The vast majority of those accused not only made full confessions within the hour, they also volunteered the names of friends and relatives, whether they were guilty or not. Paul Bielert was having a most gratifying war.

As for Lieutenant Ohlsen, in cell No. 9, he found himself a regular visitor to Bielert's sparsely furnished office, with its inevitable vase of pinks from which Bielert helped himself to a buttonhole every day. He soon grew so accustomed to these visits that they ceased even to be a diversion.

For the rest of the time he lay huddled in his cell, pressing his aching head against the stone wall in an attempt to find some relief from the pain. He thought back to the trenches, which now seemed a model of comfort compared with his bleak prison cell. He wondered often why no one from the company had come to see him. Possibly they thought he was already dead. It would be quite typical of the Gestapo if they had announced his execution days or even weeks before it took place.

He was strictly guarded, and isolated from the other prisoners save during the exercise period, but even then it was impossible to exchange more than the odd snatched word here and there. Both Stahlschmidt and Greinert were ceaselessly on the watch, prowling to and fro, and Stever and some of the other guards were in the habit of sitting on the wall to watch the fun. The exercise period, far from being a relief from the cramped monotony of the cells, was in fact a nightmare. The prisoners were obliged to run in circles for a full half hour, with their hands clasped behind their necks and their legs held stiff. It was most amusing to watch, most exhausting to perform. It jarred the entire body and cramped the muscles of the leg. But it was Stahlschmidt's very own personal invention and he was naturally proud of it.

When the SD had come the first time to collect Lieutenant Ohlsen for interrogation by Bielert, they had taken one look at his battered face and swollen nose and laughed until they almost cried.

"What's happened to you, then? Fell down the stairs, did you?"

Stahlschmidt had earnestly explained that the Lieutenant was subject to bad dreams and had thrown himself out of

bed in a fit one night, which only increased the general
hilarity.

"It's an odd thing," remarked one of the Unterscharführer,
wiping his eyes, "how many of your prisoners manage to
fall out of bed—I wonder you don't start tying them in at
night. For their own protection, of course . . ."

On the wall of Ohlsen's cell, a father had scratched a few
pathetic lines to his son, bidding him farewell and com-
mending him to the care of the world. Erich Bernert, Colonel,
4.15.40. Lieutenant Ohlsen wondered what had happened
to Erich Bernert, Colonel, and whether his son was old
enough to be told about him. And then he fell to thinking
about his own son, Gerd, whose mother and her family
had placed him in a National Socialist Education Camp near
Oranienburg. Lieutenant Ohlsen was very well aware that
once he was dead, the leaders of the Hitler Youth would
lose no time in taking Gerd to one side and poisoning his
mind against him. Probably they had already begun on the
task. Your father was a traitor, your father was an enemy of
the people, your father betrayed his country. And then
there were his in-laws, the proud-faced stiff-necked Länder,
who never had approved of him. He could hear Frau Länder's voice, ringing out rejoicing, as she heard the news of
his death. A traitor to his country, he had spoken out against
the Führer, and in her mind he would be no better than a
sexual pervert or a murderer. She would tell her stylish
friends all about him, in hushed tones, over the afternoon
teacups. She would revile him for having brought such shame
upon the family, and yet at the same time she would dine
out on the story for weeks to come.

Lieutenant Ohlsen began to feel that he was already dead
and forgotten. He no longer cared what became of him,
he was not scared of death, he almost welcomed the idea as
a release from pain; and yet it was hard to sit alone in his
cell and think of the world outside, laughing and crying,
fighting and playing, totally unaware of his existence. How
easy it was to cease to be! How swiftly people forgot,
how little they cared . . .

And then, one day, he had some visitors. The Old Man
and the Legionnaire came to see him, and at once the
curtain lifted and he was no longer a ghost, he was part of
the world again. He might not be able to walk out and join
them, but at least they had remembered him. And although,
obviously, neither the Old Man nor the Legionnaire could

set him free or change his ultimate fate, he knew now that his treatment would not go unrevenged. And that made it easier. There was a certain satisfaction in knowing that those who had sneered at you, humiliated you, beaten you half to death, were themselves under sentence of revenge and never knew it.

The little Legionnaire had taken note of all three of them, Stahlschmidt, Stever and Greinert, and the Legionnaire would remember. The Legionnaire always remembered.

Stever was present throughout the visit, and found himself strangely troubled by the sight of the Legionnaire. He had tried, at first, to join in the conversation, but the Legionnaire had coldly rebuffed him. Swallowing this treatment, Stever had then handed around his cigarettes, even though smoking was strictly forbidden. They had all looked the other way without even saying thank you.

At the end of the visit, the Legionnaire had looked up at Stever with narrowed, calculating eyes.

"You're Stever—that right? And the big fellow in the office, the one with three stars on his shoulder, that's Stahlschmidt? And your pal I saw you with before we came in— the one with the crooked nose—he's called Greinert?"

"Yes," said Stever, wondering why it mattered.

Good." The Legionnaire nodded his head and gave a most unpleasant smile. "Good. I shall remember that. I never forget a name—or a face. Good day."

And he had strolled away down the passage singing a song under his breath. Just loud enough for Stever to catch the words: "Come, come, come, oh Death . . ."

Stever returned slowly to Lieutenant Ohlsen's cell. The Legionnaire had upset him. There was something unnerving about the man. Stever sat down on the edge of the bunk and looked across at Ohlsen.

"That little fellow," he said warily. "That little fellow with the scars all over his face—he a friend of yours?"

Lieutenant Ohlsen silently inclined his head. Stever picked nervously at an earlobe.

"Nasty piece of work," he observed. "Looks like he'd knife his grandmother in the back for half a cigarette. Gave me the cold shudders, he did. Wouldn't surprise me if he was some kind of a nut. Probably certifiable. I don't know how an officer like you can bear to have him around you."

Lieutenant Ohlsen shrugged his shoulders. "I don't 'have him around me.' No one 'has the Legionnaire around him.'

He's what you call a loner—he's only got one real friend, and that's death."

"What do you mean, death?" Stever shivered. "I don't know what you mean. Is he a murderer or something?"

"On occasion. If he feels like it. He has been known to kill those who offend against his own personal code of morals. It's a bit different from yours or mine, you see. Not nearly so elastic, for a start. The Legionnaire won't accept any excuses. He sets himself up as his own judge and his own executioner. That's part of his moral code: a man shouldn't sit in judgment unless he's prepared to carry out himself the punishment that he decrees—and the Legionnaire is always prepared."

Stever wiped a hand across his brow. "People like him shouldn't be let loose. He's enough to give you the willies. I've met some beauts in the RSHA before now, but that pal of yours has 'em all beat. Makes your flesh creep just to look at him."

"He's not pretty, I'll grant you that," Ohlsen smiled. "But I think he has a certain sort of charm, don't you find?"

"Charm be damned!" said Stever. And then, suddenly fearful, "Here, you don't think he's got anything against me, do you?"

"Why ask me?" said Lieutenant Ohlsen. "He doesn't let me into his secrets. No one ever knows, with the Legionnaire, until it's too late. You may have remarked something else about him, Stever; he walks like a cat. No sound at all. He wears rubber boots, of course, but it's more than that. It's a skill he's acquired over the years. He could walk up behind you on a gravel path covered in twigs and bits of broken glass and you'd never hear him coming—until it was too late."

"Well, anyway," said Stever, rallying a little, "I don't see that I've done anything to upset him. I've never seen him in my life before, and I've no wish ever to see him again." He took off his helmet, wiped his head, put the helmet back on. "I'm only an Obergefreiter," he said fretfully. "It's not up to me to give the orders around here. I'm just the poor cunt that has to carry them out."

"Of course," agreed Lieutenant Ohlsen with a comforting smile. "You don't have to explain. You don't enjoy kicking people in the gut, but you have to do it nonetheless . . ."

"Exactly," said Stever. He leaned forward. "I'll tell you something, Lieutenant. It's Stahlschmidt, he's the dangerous one around this place. He's the Stabsfeldwebel, he's the big wheel. So if the little guy with the scars feels like carving anyone up, do me a favor and tell him to go for Stahlschmidt, will you? Marius Alois Joseph Stahlschmidt, that's his name, and he's a bastard. You're quite right, Lieutenant; I can't stand to see men beaten up and smashed to pulp. Specially not officers. But what can I do? I'm only an Obergefreiter. As a matter of fact, I'm thinking of putting in for a transfer. I tell you, I can't take this place much longer. Not only that, but it's asking for trouble, ain't it? I mean, some of the guys that come here are let out again. Not very often, but it does happen. And what about the ones that are sent off to disciplinary regiments? Stands to reason *some* of 'em are going to survive, doesn't it? And one day they're going to come back here, I bet, looking for Stahlschmidt. And when that happens, I'd rather be somewhere else, thank you very much. I mean, they might not know that I'm just doing my job and carrying out my orders, right? I mean, you didn't until I told you, did you?"

Lieutenant Ohlsen gravely shook his head. Stever suddenly stood up.

"Look, I'll show you. I was transferred here from a cavalry regiment in Paris." He pulled out his military notebook and thrust it at the lieutenant. "See that? The 12th Cavalry, I was. And then the lousy bastards sent me to this shithole— I didn't want to come, make no mistake about that. Only thing was, I didn't have no say in the matter, did I? I've often asked for a transfer, believe you me, but what can I do, Stahlschmidt doesn't want me to go, he's got used to me and he needs me—like when he goes too far and clobbers people too hard and they die on him, he's got to have me to give him an alibi. Be a witness like. Explain how it was only in self-defense and all that crap."

"I see." Lieutenant Ohlsen handed back the notebook. "Tell me, Stever, don't you believe in a God?"

Stever looked alarmed, as if he suspected some kind of trick, some kind of double meaning.

"No, not really. Can't say I do."

"Have you ever tried saying your prayers?"

"Well—" He shuffled his feet uncomfortably, "once or twice I did, yeah. When I was in shit up to my neck and couldn't see no way out—but I can't say it does much good, myself." Stever buttoned his pocket and turned with sudden enthusiasm to Ohlsen. "Now, you listen here, Lieutenant. I'm going to take good care of you from now on. Now we've had this talk and we understand each other. You want something to read, maybe? Most officers seem to get a kick out of reading. Well, I'll nick a few books from somewhere and let you have 'em. Only take care Stahlschmidt don't see 'em, for God's sake. As for Greinert, you don't need to worry about him—he's got his own cells to look after. This lot down here, they belong to me. And just before I go, Lieutenant, I got a little present for you; brought it specially for you, I did. I've had one or two, but these'll last you a few hours." He slipped a pack of cigarettes under the mattress on the bunk and winked conspiratorially. "You and me can be pals, eh? Only smoke 'em near the air vent, so's the smell don't hang around."

He moved toward the door, and then turned.

"We get our chocolate ration this evening. You like chocolate, Lieutenant? I'll bring you my ration. I'll put it behind the water tank in the can, then next time you go for a piss you can pick it up, okay? And you will speak to your pal about me, won't you? Tell him what I said about Stahlschmidt being the guy he really wants. I don't need to tell you, Lieutenant, I'm risking my neck for you, what with the smokes and the chocolate and the books and all. Even talking to you like this, I could be nabbed for it—but somehow I liked the look of you right from the first moment I saw you. Don't you remember I winked at you behind Stahlschmidt's back? Don't you remember that?"

"I can't say I do," admitted Ohlsen.

"Well, I did," said Stever. "And another thing—don't you worry about me getting the jitters, or nothing like that. I'm not scared of nothing and no one. Anyone knows me'll tell you that. I got my two Iron Crosses in Poland, and it was tough out there. Real tough. Talk about the Russian front, that's got nothing on Poland. I was the only man in all the company that got the Iron Cross—you tell your friend that. And tell him I haven't always been stuck in this dump. I been at the front as well. At Westa Plata, for instance. I wiped out a whole section single-handed. That's as true as I stand here, so help me. I got the EKII* for that. And in Warsaw I destroyed four air raid shelters full of partisans. I destroyed four air raid shelters single-handed with a flamethrower. Not a single one got out alive. That's when they

---

*Iron Cross 2nd Class.

give me the EKI. So you see, I know what's what, and I can't be accused of not doing my bit. I was mad to get to Stalingrad, only the bastards wouldn't let me."

He opened the door, went out, but turned and put his head back in again. "Tell me," he said. "This friend of yours with the ugly mug—he the sort that would use a knife?"

"That's right," Ohlsen nodded. "He's pretty slick with a knife, the Legionnaire . . ."

Stever slammed the door and tottered on weak legs down the passage to the toilet. He ran the cold water faucet over his head for a few minutes, feeling suddenly sick and faint.

Lieutenant Ohlsen, alone in his cell, contemptuously brushed the blanket where Stever had been sitting, then stretched out full length on the bed, his hands behind his head, staring up at the ceiling with a smile on his lips. The revenge had already begun and he himself was able to take a hand in it.

Stever left the toilet with his hair dripping water and hurried back along the passage to Stahlschmidt's office. He burst in without troubling to knock at the door.

"Did you see No. 9's visitors, Stabsfeldwebel? Did you see that little guy with the scars? Did you see the look in his eyes? Did you . . ."

"Pipe down, Stever, pipe down." Stahlschmidt gazed across at his subordinate through eyes that had narrowed to two calculating slits. "I saw them, so what? They're of total unimportance. And as for the one with the scars, in my opinion he was quite obviously drunk. Stark raving drunk. I watched him going down the passage. He was singing some sentimental rubbish about death."

"Death?" whispered Stever.

"Well, either he was drunk," said Stahlschmidt, "or else he's suffering from shell shock. I shouldn't wonder if that was it. He was practically bent double under all the medals he was wearing. These frontline heroes are usually a pretty unstable lot."

Stever wiped his sleeve across his forehad and sank into a chair.

"I don't know about unstable—right off his nut, if you ask me—and dangerous with it! That man is dangerous, you mark my word! Christ almighty, with a face like that, he ought to be locked up! Did you see that scar he had? Running right down his face? It kept changing color, I swear it did! And his hands, I've never seen anything like 'em!"

"You have a very vivid imagination, Stever. They just looked like hands to me."

"Hands that were made for strangling," said Stever hoarsely.

Stahlschmidt made an impatient noise somewhere down the back of his throat and picked up the visitors' permit that was lying on his desk. "Willie Beier and Alfred Kalb," he murmured.

"That's it!" cried Stever. "Alfred Kalb! That's him, I recognize the name!"

"All right, there's no need to shout." Stahlschmidt was examining the permit through his magnifying glass. His face suddenly twitched. "Take a look at that signature," he said.

"What's the matter with it?" asked Stever, squinting slightly.

Stahlschmidt looked up in annoyance. "Obergefreiter Stever, I have always regarded you as a reasonably intelligent person. Not brilliant, but not a complete moron. You do have a certain semblance of brain. If you hadn't, I'd have had you sent packing to a disciplinary company long ago. However, that's beside the point. The point is, I don't like working with fools. They dull the intellect and slow the reactions. And if you're going to start fumbling and muttering and scratching your ass every time I put a simple question to you, then you might just as well get out of here right now before I throw you out."

"Let me have another look." Stever begged nervously. "I'm—I'm not quite myself today." He snatched up the paper and examined it under the glass. He turned it this way and that, he took it to the window, he closed each eye in turn, he almost stood on his head, but still he could see nothing very remarkable about the signature.

"Well?" said Stahlschmidt.

"Yes!" Stever laid down the paper and the magnifying glass and stepped back a pace. "Yes, now you come to mention it, there is something rather odd about it. I'm afraid my eyes aren't quite as quick as yours. I'd never have noticed it if you hadn't pointed it out to me."

"Hm! It's taken you long enough to get there. Either you need glasses or your brain's starting to go soft—you'll have to get to bed earlier at night. Have a good eight hours' sleep and don't drink so much. Make sure your bowels are in good working order."

Stahlschmidt opened the bottom drawer of his desk, took out a bottle of whisky and filled two glasses.

"Still, I'm glad you tumbled to it in the end. The signature has almost certainly been forged. It's a good thing you spotted it."

Stever's eyes widened. His hand, which had automatically reached out for the whisky, wavered a moment, then changed direction and picked up the permit once more. For the life of him he could still see nothing wrong with the signature.

"Of all the permits we've had in this office," Stahlschmidt was saying, "have you ever seen one that's been signed by Standartenführer Paul Bielert in person? Not printed or rubber-stamped, but actually signed by him in pen and ink?" He shook his head. "Of course you haven't! The Standartenführer wouldn't so degrade himself as to sign his name in person to every fucking little bit of paper that came his way. Even I don't, so I'm quite sure he wouldn't—even I use a rubber stamp." Stahlschmidt looked up at Stever and his lips twisted in what might have been a smile. "And so do you on occasion, don't you, Stever? A rubber stamp with my signature on it . . ."

"Me?" gasped Stever, in tones of outrage. "I've never done that in my life!"

"No?" Stahlschmidt raised a derisive eyebrow. "Well, perhaps you've not been aware of it at the time—perhaps you suffer from amnesia? Sudden blackouts? Dizzy spells? I give you the benefit of the doubt, you see, because it's obviously a very serious offense to use another man's signature without his knowledge and authorization."

"Of course it is!" exclaimed Stever self-righteously. "That is why I would never, never—" He broke off. "I mean, why on earth should I?" he demanded.

"Oh, my dear Stever, I can think of a dozen reasons." Stahlschmidt sprawled back in his chair with his legs spread out under his desk, enjoying the sensation of having Stever at his mercy. "Perhaps you had some gambling debts? Perhaps you wanted to requisition some article that you could sell on the black market? I'm sure you don't need me to tell you all the things a rubber stamp can be used for! As I already said, you're a person of fair intelligence, and people of intelligence are the biggest scoundrels on earth."

"But Stabsfeldwebel, you're a person of great intelligence yourself!" burst out Stever triumphantly.

This time, Stahlschmidt raised both eyebrows simultaneously, as high as they would go.

"Watch what you're saying, Stever. Just remember your position. You're only an Obergefreiter, don't go putting on airs." He reached out for the permit again. "Let's have another look at his forged signature. With a bit of luck, Willie Beier and Alfred Kalb will soon be joining their friend the lieutenant in our cells."

Stever rubbed his hands together and snatched eagerly at his glass of whisky.

"God, if that happened, I swear I'd mend my ways! I would, really! I'd feel that Him up There was kind of saying, Well, I do exist, this is proof of it—know what I mean? And I'd go to mass at least once a—once a month. Yes, I would. Once a month I'd go. To *early* mass," said Stever impressively.

"You don't think that's rather excessive?" murmured Stahlschmidt.

"I'd do more than that, I'd go down on my knees and pray!" shouted Stever. "God, if I had that scarred little bastard in here, I'd—I'd put his eyes out for him!"

"You mean like Greinert did to that major he took such a dislike to?"

"Exactly! I'd do it with my thumbs, just like he did— stuff a bit of rag into his mouth so's nobody would hear, and dig both his eyes out."

"Sounds delightful," murmured Stahlschmidt. "But I wonder, would you really have the guts to do it, when it came to the point?"

"With that rat, yes!" Stever tossed off his whisky and set the glass back on the table with a jaunty flourish. "I feel more like myself again now—I can already see those two being marched through the doors under escort . . ."

Stahlschmidt nodded and smiled. He looked again at the forged signature and felt very sure of himself. And even if he were proved wrong, he could always blame Stever. He picked up the telephone and dialed a number.

"I want the Commissariat. Feldwebel Rinken. This is Stahlschmidt here, Stabsfeldwebel Stahlschmidt of the garrison prison . . . Oh, it's you, is it, Rinken? Why don't you announce yourself, for God's sake? I could be talking to anybody, couldn't I? Listen, I've got a job for you, I want you to . . . What? What's that you say?" He remained silent a moment, then exploded down the receiver. "You'll bloody

well do what I tell you and no questions asked! I don't
doubt you're busy, and so are we, working our balls off
doing all the stuff you should have done and haven't, so
don't try that one! In any case, it's perfectly simple and
straightforward, a piece of piss—I just want you to arrange
for two men to be picked up and brought over here as soon
as possible. Got a pencil? Good. Make a note of their names
—Willie Beier and Alfred Kalb—all right? You got that?
Good. They came to visit one of the prisoners here and I
don't like the look of them. Particularly the Kalb man.
He's either suffering from shell shock or else he was as
pissed as a newt. Anyway, the point is, they got in here on
a forged pass, so I want them brought in for questioning
as soon as possible, and—" He broke off, suddenly suspicious. "What are you laughing at?"

"You!" Rinken's loud guffaws could be heard at the far
side of the room, and Stever looked up inquiringly. "Really,
Stahlschmidt, have you lost your grip or something? What
the hell have these two lunatics got to do with me? They're
your pigeon and you're welcome—under Heeresarmeevor-
schrift* No. 979, April 26, 1940, para. 12, clause 8, it's
exclusively your concern if something like that occurs in
your territory, and you're obliged to make a report on it.
And until we've got your report, our hands are tied. All I
can say is, I hope for your own sake you've made a mistake.
It's not going to sound too good, is it? A couple of men
allowed to walk into your jail as bold as brass with forged
papers that no one checks? Visiting a prisoner under your
very nose when they had no right to be there—" He
clucked disapprovingly. "I shouldn't care to be in your
shoes right now, and that's a fact! You ought to have nabbed
'em before they left."

Stever, who had crept up to the desk and had been
listening, sprang away at these words and stood, white and
trembling, by the door, as if prepared for instant flight.

Stahlschmidt drummed his fingers on the desk and
screwed his neck a few inches out of his collar.

"Look here, Rinken, don't be a fool! There's no need to
get all het up! Strictly off the record, I only called you
because I'm not altogether *sure* that the pass was forged. I
think it is, but I want to check, and I want you . . ."

"Like hell! A second ago you were telling me to have

---

*Army Bulletin.

them picked up because they'd quite definitely got in on a forged pass . . ."

"No, no, I said I *thought* they had . . ."

"Thought, my ass!" said Rinken crudely. "No use trying to wriggle out of it, Stahlschmidt, I've got a witness who'll testify if necessary. He's listening in on the extension."

"Screw the witness!" roared Stahlschmidt. "You don't think I give a damn about any lousy witness, do you?"

"Whether you do or don't," said Rinken darkly, "I've already explained that the affair is nothing to do with us. You'll have to put in an official report. Time and again you've told us that what goes on in your jail is your business and no one else's. If you'd had any sense at all, you'd already have this couple under lock and key. But since you haven't, and since the matter has now been brought to my notice, I suppose I shall have to get in touch with Lieutenant Colonel Segen and tell him about it. We'll have the two men brought in for questioning and we'll soon get to the bottom of the story—but I still want a written report."

Stahlschmidt kicked savagely at his wastepaper basket and forced himself to speak calmly. Perhaps he had been a trifle precipitous. The affair was not progressing as he had anticipated.

"Look, thinking it over, Rinken, you're quite right. It's my affair and I shouldn't have bothered you with it. I'm sorry, I wasn't thinking, I . . ."

"That's quite all right." Rinken's voice purred down the receiver, full of cream and honey and general complacency. "We all make mistakes. I don't mind having a word with Segen about it. Just let me have your written report, that's all I ask."

"But look, it's really not worth your while . . ."

"One thing I should be interested to know," interrupted Rinken. "Whose signature had they forged?"

"Bielert's."

"Bielert's? I see. In that case, the matter really is serious. I'll take it up without delay, written report or not."

"But look here . . ."

"Incidentally, Stahlschmidt, did you know they're forming a new disciplinary infantry regiment? I hear they're crying out for experienced NCOs. Why don't you put your name forward?"

"Rinken, please!" Stahlschmidt sounded almost humble. With a great effort of will, he forced a note of supplication into his voice. "Don't go bothering Colonel Segen about it. Let the matter drop. To be perfectly honest, I don't really have any idea whether the damned pass is forged, it was just an idea that occurred to me. But in any case, the two men are no longer in the area, they . . ."

"No longer in the area?" repeated Rinken joyously. "Really, Stahlschmidt, don't you have any method of controlling people's exits and entrances? It sounds to me as if the public at large can wander in and out as if you're running an art gallery rather than a jail. Who let these men in, in the first place? Who let them out again? Who checked their credentials?"

"I did," said Stahlschmidt irritably. "You know I did. You know it's me that sees to all that sort of thing. God knows, there's no one else I can rely on."

Rinken laughed sardonically.

"Speaking of relying on people, I've been relying on you, Stahlschmidt, to pay me back that hundred marks you owe me. You hadn't forgotten it, I hope? One hundred marks, plus twenty-four percent interest."

"I hadn't forgotten it. I never forget my debts, especially to friends. But the thing is, Rinken, I'm not too flush at the moment. I've—I've had a lot of extra expenses. A couple of new uniforms and a pair of new boots. You know how it is —you can't go around in rags. Not when you're a Stabs-feldwebel. And then the prices they charge these days! I had to pay four times more for those boots than I should have done. And in any case, you know, you lent me that money as a friend. Without interest. You never said anything at the time about twenty-four percent."

"Really, you astound me," said Rinken coldly. "First of all you ring me up with wild tales of forged passes and two raving criminals running in and out of your prison with no one even asking their names, and then you start babbling about new uniforms and expensive boots and expecting me to pay for them, and finally you try to deny ever borrowing any money from me!"

"No, no, only the interest!" protested Stahlschmidt.

"You owe me a hundred marks plus twenty-four percent interest," said Rinken stubbornly. "You deny the interest and you refuse to pay me back the hundred marks. That's more than enough for me. I shall speak to Colonel Segen about you. You can't expect to do that sort of thing and get away with it, you know."

There was a click and the line went dead. Rinken had hung up. Stahlschmidt sat a moment, staring aghast at the telephone, wondering how it was that the affair had back-fired so disastrously.

"What did he say?" asked Stever, taking a few hesistant steps away from the door and back into the room.

"None of your fucking business!" snarled Stahlschmidt.

He paced furiously up and down a few times, kicking any object that was unfortunate enough to lie in his path, smashing his fist into the filing cabinet, spitting on the photograph of Himmler. And then he suddenly lunged back to his desk and clawed up the telephone again.

"Paul? Is that you, Paul? It's Alois here." His voice flowed gently, sweetly, coaxingly down the line. "Listen, I'm sorry about that money I owe you. You're quite right about the twenty-four percent, of course you are, but you know how it is—one protests as a matter of principle! We all do it, don't we, Paul? It's just habit, it doesn't mean anything, it doesn't mean I'm trying to wriggle out of it . . ."

"That's as may be," said Rinken coldly. "All I'm interested in right now is getting my money back. I'll give you until midday tomorrow and not a moment longer. One hundred marks plus the interest."

"Look, I swear to you," said Stahlschmidt, "I swear to you, Paul, you'll have it all back. I'll put it in a plain envelope and send Stever round with it."

From the far corner of the room, Stever shook his head violently. Stahlschmidt ignored him.

"All I ask, Paul, is that for the sake of our friendship you tell me how the hell I'm to get out of this fix! It's all been a ghastly mistake, but there must be some way out."

"As far as I can see, there are only two things you can do," said Rinken, still very cold and curt. "You can either go to your CO and make a clean breast of it, and hope he's fool enough to swallow it—which he probably won't be, and then he'll start poking around and asking questions and you'll be worse in the shit than ever. Or else, of course, you can take the bull by the horns and ring straight through to the Gestapo. Only thing is, you'll need to be very careful what you say to them. Have a rehearsal first, I should, if I were you. And even then, of course, you'll have had it if the pass turns out to be genuine. Bielert will come down on you like a ton of bricks. And then again, on the other hand, if it *is* a forgery, you'll be in even worse trouble, because then they'll want to have a word with the two guys you let in, and you can imagine how pleased they'll be when they discovered you've let 'em go . . ."

There was a moment's silence. Stahlschmidt sat chewing a pencil, holding it between his back teeth and gnawing at it.

"Paul," he said at last. "Are you there, Paul? I just had a new idea. Mightn't it be simpler if you just forgot I ever called you in the first place? Come round tonight for dinner. I'll invite one or two of our pals. Feldwebel Gehl might be able to dig up some girls from somewhere. Come around *about* eight and we'll . . ."

"Hang on," said Rinken suspiciously. "Did you say *forget* it? A man in my position?"

"Well, you could," urged Stahlschmidt. "Couldn't you?"

"I don't know," said Rinken slowly. "I do have myself to think of. I have no desire to be sent off to a disciplinary company at this stage of my career."

"But nobody would know," whispered Stahlschmidt.

"Well—well, no, perhaps you're right. Except that I still want an official report, mind. About that dinner invitation— eight o'clock you said?"

"Eight o'clock," confirmed Stahlschmidt. "I'll take care of the drinks, food, the entertainment. You're a good guy, Paul, I've always said so. I think I'll just tear up this damn pass and forget it ever happened."

"I shouldn't do that," said Rinken. "I don't think that would be at all wise. If it is official, there'll be copies galore all over the place. And if it isn't—well, quite honestly, I think you should do a bit of discreet checking. Otherwise there'll be hell to pay if ever the story comes out."

"You're right," said Stahlschmidt, sweating heavily around his collar. "You're quite right. I'll telephone my CO. He's as thick as pigshit, he won't ask any questions."

"I think you ought to get it cleared up once and for all," said Rinken. "I'll keep quiet at this end until I hear from you."

"That's good of you," murmured Stahlschmidt, hating Rinken more by the minute.

"Mind you," said Rinken jocularly, "I wouldn't relish being in your shoes right now. It wouldn't surprise me if tonight's blowout ended up as a farewell party—you might even end up in one of your own cells!"

"My God," said Stahlschmidt, "if that's your idea of a joke,

I don't think much of your sense of humor. With friends like you about, I don't need enemies."

Rinken's only answer was a cheerful guffaw.

"And anyway," said Stahlschmidt irritably, "they'd never do a thing like that."

"Why not?" asked Rinken. "It's always nice to be among old friends—you could talk about the good old days when you were in charge of the prison and they were as the dust beneath your chariot wheels . . ."

Chuckling to himself, Rinken put down the receiver. Stahlschmidt sat staring at the telephone, wondering for a moment if he was sickening for some disease. The room was spinning about his ears, he felt sick and giddy and a cold perspiration had broken out all over his body. You never could tell nowadays—so many odd diseases seemed to be going around. He groped for his pulse and turned to Stever.

"I think I'd better go and see the MO. I feel really quite ill. You can take over for a few hours. Or a few days, it might be, if they keep me in bed."

Stever began to tremble.

"I don't think that's a very good idea, Herr Stabsfeld-webel. Surely Greinert is more qualified than me? He's been here longer than I have."

"Greinert's a fool."

They sat staring at each other a while, then quite suddenly Stahlschmidt picked up the telephone and asked to speak to Major von Rotenhausen, the prison governor.

"Sir? Major Rotenhausen, sir? It's Stabsfeldwebel Stahlschmidt here, sir."

"Yes, Stahlschmidt? What is it?"

"I have to report, sir, that two men of the 27th Armored Regiment—a Willie Beier and an Alfred Kalb—visited one of the prisoners today on a pass that I now think might be a forgery."

There was a long silence while Rotenhausen tried to take in what had been said to him and tried to think of a pertinent question to ask. At last he found one. "Whom did they visit?"

"Lieutenant Bernt Ohlsen."

"Who's he? Whose prisoner is he?"

Stahlschmidt closed his eyes. He sank in upon himself, huddling up in his chair. "The Gestapo—IV/2A—" His voice was the barest whisper.

"And who signed the pass?"

"Standartenführer Paul Bielert," said Stahlschmidt, and almost fell off his chair.

Rotenhausen hung up. He gave no indication of what he intended to do, or if, indeed, he intended to do anything at all. Once again Stahlschmidt was left with a silent telephone receiver in his hand. He replaced it helplessly in its cradle.

"Well," he said to Stever with a bracing joviality, "we're in the shit and no mistake—what the devil do we do now?" Stever looked at him, a hump of immovable misery. "That son of a bitch Rinken!" railed Stahlschmidt. "Who does he think he is, jumped-up bag of skin and bones! Just because he helps his frigging CO put on his overcoat every day—" Stahlschmidt turned and spat vehemently in the direction of the overturned wastepaper basket. "You know what he used to do before the war, don't you? He was a milkman, that's what he was! And you can bet your sweet life that's what he'll be again as soon as the war's over. Well, come on, Stever, get your brain to work, man! Don't stand there like a solidified turd, start thinking!"

Stever elaborately cleared his throat, then "Herr Stabsfeldwebel," he said, "I'm quite sure you'll be able to find a way out." And he looked Stahlschmidt straight in the eye, very firmly tossing the ball right back at him. Stever intended to make it quite clear that he had had nothing to do with the affair.

Stahlschmidt outstared him. He waited until Stever dropped his gaze, then smiled grimly.

"If I go under, you go with me," he murmured, too soft for Stever to hear. "Make no mistake about that—I don't drown alone!"

For ten minutes more he paced about the room, watched furtively by Stever, who had no desire to stay but was too scared to go.

The monotony was broken by the sudden screaming wail of the sirens. The two men looked at one another.

"Here they come again," said Stever.

"That'll be the Canadians," said Stahlschmidt.

They stood listening a moment, then Stahlschmidt jerked his head toward the door and picked up the whisky bottle.

"Come on. Down in the cellars and pray like hell that they drop a bomb on the Gestapo."

"And Major Rotenhausen?" suggested Stever.

"And Major Rotenhausen," Stahlschmidt nodded emphatically. "And Rinken as well, the prick! I would send a personal note of thanks to the head of the Canadian Air Force."

They hurried down to the cellars, stayed there for the duration of the air raid, approximately twenty minutes, and finished off the bottle of whisky between them. When they emerged, it was only to discover that the attack had concentrated on the southern area of the port and had been nowhere near the Gestapo. Or Major Rotenhausen, or Rinken.

"Not even an indirect hit," mourned Stahlschmidt, as they returned to his office.

He looked at Stever and Stever looked back at him. There was no hope in that direction. Stever was not a man to come up with bright ideas.

"Well, there's only one thing for it—I'll have to take a chance and call the bastards, see if I can't explain it to them. It'll be worse in the long run if they find out for themselves."

The trembling of his hand as he dialed the dreaded number of the Gestapo—10 001—belied the bravado of his voice.

"State Secret Police. Stadthausbrücke Section."

Stahlschmidt swallowed a mouthful of saliva. Stumbling over his words, stammering, stuttering, gasping for air, he managed to stagger through his report.

"Just one moment, Stabsfeldwebel. I'll have you transferred."

Stahlschmidt moaned gently and ran a finger around the inside of his collar. A new voice came on the telephone; crisp and sharp and authoritative.

"Hallo, yes, can I help you? This is the Executive Service, IV/2A."

Once again Stahlschmidt tripped and stumbled through his story. Even to his prejudiced ears it no longer seemed to have any ring of truth or probability.

"And who signed this pass?" the voice demanded.

"Herr Standartenführer Paul Bielert," croaked Stahlschmidt, and he humbly inclined his head to the telephone.

"You can drop the 'Herr'!" snapped the voice. "We gave up that plutocratic fawning a long time ago."

Stahlschmidt at once let loose a flowing string of apologies and excuses, almost prostrating himself across the desk as he did so.

"If you've quite finished?" said the voice. "I'll hand you over to the Standartenführer himself."

Stahlschmidt gave a terrified yelp. The telephone went dead. He looked at the hated instrument and knew a moment of intense desire. If he could only wrench it away from the wall and hurl it into the courtyard, might not all his troubles be ended? Or perhaps if he were to be taken suddenly ill—he felt ill. He felt very ill . . .

"Hallo?"

Stahlschmidt clutched in terror at his throat.

"H—hal—hallo?"

"This is Paul Bielert speaking. What can I do for you?"

The voice was low and agreeable; kind and soft and somehow inviting. For one rash, insane moment Stahlschmidt was almost tempted to make a full confession of his folly, to grovel and to sob and to go down on his knees. Instead, he opened his mouth and began jabbering the utmost futilities into the telephone. The story fell out pell-mell, disjointed, incoherent. At one moment he was declaring on oath he had known straightaway that the signature had been forged; the next moment he was flatly contradicting himself by saying that even now he was unsure and wanted only to check. He denounced Rinken, he denounced Rotenhausen, he denounced the entire prison staff. They were all lazy, useless, deceitful bastards without a brain between them. He, Alois Stahlschmidt, was left to carry the load for everyone. He was left to . . .

"One moment, Stabsfeldwebel." The voice broke in, persuasive and almost apologetic. "I don't like to interrupt you in full flow, but has anyone ever told you that you are not, perhaps, as bright as might be desirable?" Stahlschmidt gulped noisily into the telephone and his neck grew slowly scarlet. "If this pass really were a forgery," continued Bielert, still in his soft, persuasive voice, "does it not occur to you that the names of the visitors might also have been assumed for the occasion? Have you already checked on this? Have you checked on their company? Have you searched the prisoner since the two men left him? Have you searched his cell?"

"Oh, yes! That was Obergefreiter Stever's job, Standartenführer."

"And has Obergefreiter Stever done it?"

"Oh, yes! Yes, yes, yes indeed! I saw to it myself!"

"And what did he find?"

"Ah—well—nothing, sir." And Stahlschmidt turned to look accusingly at Stever, who was staring with bulging eyes, sheeplike and incredulous.

"In that case, it must surely have been a very superficial search?"

"The trouble is, sir, you see, as I was explaining, it's quite impossible to trust anyone in this place to do a job properly. I find myself quite unable to delegate. Unless I set to and . . ."

The voice again broke in on the frenzied explanations. It was no longer quite so gentle as it had been.

"Now you listen to me, Stabsfeldwebel! I hold you and you alone to be responsible for the whole of this miserable affair, and if the prisoner is found dead in his cell because of it, you may rest assured that I shall personally arrange for your execution."

Under the desk, Stahlschmidt's kneecaps began to bounce and his legs to knock together. For the first time in his life, he wished he were out fighting at the front.

"As for the pass," continued Bielert, "you can bring it round to my office yourself. I suppose by this time you'll have managed to alert half Germany?"

Slowly and brokenly Stahlschmidt recited the list of people who knew of the incident.

"One can only be thankful," said Bielert sarcastically, "that you haven't yet written to the newspapers about it. Or perhaps you were on the point of doing so when you decided to telephone me and ask my permission?"

An odd sound, a strangulated yelp of panic, forced its way out of Stahlschmidt's mouth. Stever looked at him in awe. He had never seen his chief in such a pitiable state. Thank God he himself was only a miserable Obergefreiter!

Stahlschmidt slowly let fall the receiver and stared around the room with red-rimmed eyes. Who knew but that that fool of a prisoner might not even now be in the act of swallowing poison smuggled into his cell? He turned wildly to Stever.

"Obergefreiter! What are you standing there for? Get a move on, for God's sake! I want the prisoner's cell searched from top to bottom. I want the *prisoner* searched from top to bottom. Jump to it, man, don't just gawk!"

Stever made a sudden dive for the door. He shot through it and sprinted up the passage, crashing headlong into

Greinert, who was coming in the opposite direction at a more leisurely pace.

"What the hell are you up to?" he wanted to know. "What's all the mad rush all of a sudden?"

"You'll know soon enough!" panted Stever. "Get a couple of men and bring them along to No. 9. We've got to search the bastard inside and out."

Greinert shrugged his shoulders and sauntered off. A few moments later he was back with two more men and together all four of them began the search. They tore off Lieutenant Ohlsen's clothes, they ripped up the mattress on his bunk, they heaved at the iron bars on the window, they broke everything that was breakable, including the chamber pot. They tapped the walls, the floor and the ceiling, while the lieutenant sat naked on the bunk, watching them with an amused smile.

Stever did a disappearing act with the pack of cigarettes he had pressed on the prisoner earlier in the day. Greinert ran howling and shouting up and down the cell. The other two men took hold of the lieutenant and searched him thoroughly, peering in his mouth and down his ears, forcing his legs apart, examining his body in minute and unscrupulous detail. Lieutenant Ohlsen bore it all with weary patience. He opened and shut his mouth a dozen times for them, but they failed to discover his false tooth where the little yellow phial was secreted. There was enough poison in that phial to kill ten people. The Legionnaire had brought it back with him from Indochina.

All the time the search was going on, Stahlschmidt was pacing back and forth across his carpet, and had soon blazed a perceptible trail from the door to the windows, from the windows to the bookshelves, from the bookshelves back to the door.

The bookshelves were full of fat legal volumes, most of which Stahlschmidt had "borrowed" from libraries or smuggled out of shops and other people's offices. He fancied himself as something of a lawyer. He always told his mistresses that he was a prison inspector, and in his local bistro, Le Chiffon Rouge, he was known as Herr Inspektor. He had learned a number of legal paragraphs by heart and he was accustomed to quote them parrot-fashion whenever the occasion arose. He had quite a following in the Chiffon Rouge and his advice was frequently sought on legal matters—though rarely by the same people twice. Too many had

been disappointed in the past to go back for a second helping. The fact was that Stahlschmidt could never bear to
confess ignorance on any subject; whenever he found himself at a loss, he simply quoted an imaginary precedent, in-
vented on the spur of the moment, and went on from there.

As Stahlschmidt paced past the windows for the sixth
time, the telephone rang. He stopped in his tracks, staring
distrustfully at the instrument, root of all his sudden mis-
fortunes. Slowly he walked across to the desk; warily he
picked up the receiver. He spoke in a voice that was low
and reluctant.

"Garrison prison . . ."

As a rule, he would snatch up the receiver and scream,
"Stabsfeldwebel Stahlschmidt speaking! What do you want?"
But not any more. Never again. That wretched pass had
ruined all that for him.

"You sound a bit down," said Rinken's voice, maddeningly
full of cheer. "What's up? Spoken to the Stapo, have you?
Any luck?"

"Cut it out!" snarled Stahlschmidt. "I'm sick to death of
this place! I've a good mind to put in for a transfer. You
work hard, you do your best, you're a damn sight more con-
scientious than anyone else, *including* your commanding officer—and what happens? I ask you, what happens? You get
kicked in the teeth for your pains, that's what happens!"

"Ah, well, we live and we learn," said Rinken in an annoyingly smug voice. "But don't give up hope. If you really
want a transfer, I'm sure I can arrange it; that disciplinary
company I was telling you about still wants NCOs. They'd
welcome you with open arms—shall I give 'em a ring?"

"Fuck that, I'd sooner you gave me some good advice for
a change! I've had Bielert himself on the phone. He wants
me to take the pass round to him personally."

"So? You're not scared of Bielert, are you? There's no
need to be, unless you've got something on your conscience . . ."

"Don't play the innocent with me, Rinken! You know
damn well there's no one in the whole of Germany with a
completely clear conscience. Even the SD guards at Fuhlsbüttel and Neuengamme shit blue bricks when they have to
go anywhere near Stadthausbrücke."

"Best put your brown pants on!" joked Rinken.

Stahlschmidt swore violently and slammed down the receiver.

Of course, what he could not possibly realize was that there was far more to the affair of Lieutenant Ohlsen's visitors than met the eye. To begin with, he did not know that a few days ago the Legionnaire, the little Legionnaire with his scarred face and his hard eyes and his supple hands with their long fingers, had paid a visit to Aunt Dora at the Ouragan. (That was the very day before Aunt Dora had disappeared. Officially it was understood that she had gone to Westphalia to visit a sick friend, the widow of a Gauleiter. Unofficially—well, unofficially, one wondered . . .)

However, the Legionnaire had visited her at her establishment and they had sat down at a table in the corner and pulled the thick curtains together until they were in a private alcove of their own. Before them, on the table, were two glasses, a bottle of Pernod and a bowl of roast chestnuts. They gnawed the chestnuts open with their teeth and carelessly spat the skin out on the floor. Aunt Dora bent her head to her glass and sucked up a mouthful of Pernod.

"So Paul's nabbed your little lieutenant, has he? For opening his big trap too wide. Well, all I can say is, he must be a bit soft in the head, going around shooting his mouth off like that. I mean, it's asking for trouble, isn't it? Might just as well climb upon the roof and shout it through a megaphone."

"You've got a point there, granted." The Legionnaire squinted at the glass in his hand. "Some people just aren't fit to survive. Now you and me, we know how to look after ourselves, but Ohlsen—" He shook his head. "A babe in arms! Gestapo could run rings around him. Still, I've known the fool for a long time, I can't just leave him there to rot. I've got to do something about him."

"If you say so." Aunt Dora spat out a mouthful of chestnut and looked at it in disgust. It was brown and bitter. "Damn the woman! Can't even roast a chestnut! You'd never believe the trouble I had getting a cook. And now I've got one, I'd just as soon do without for all the use she is to me!" She tossed off the remains of her Pernod and poured herself another. "It's the same with all the staff these days. Even the girls aren't what they used to be. Just lower-class whores, most of 'em. Straight off the street, no style at all, can't even rely on them. Take that slut Lisa—the one that's supposed to be at the check desk—she's been off sick four times already this month. Sick, my fanny!" Dora picked out another chestnut and crammed it into her mouth. "I know what she's up to, she can't fool me! There aren't no flies on old Dora!"

"I'm quite sure there aren't," agreed the Legionnaire. "But why on earth don't you get foreign girls? I thought they were a dime a dozen these days."

"They are, but I wouldn't let them anywhere near the place," said Dora bitterly. "Half of them are Gestapo spies. You think I want foreign trash breathing down my neck, reporting my every move? I'd be whisked off to Stadthaus-brücke in no time!"

The Legionnaire smiled. "Come, now, Dora, I'm sure you don't have anything on your conscience!"

Dora cackled and punched him amiably in the chest.

"This lieutenant of yours, though." She poured out some more Pernod. "What have they got him for? One of their famous paragraphs?"

"Ninety-one B," said the Legionnaire, taking a chestnut and grimly surveying it. He sank his teeth into it and ripped off the outer shell. The long scar which ran down the length of his face looked red and painful. "I'm afraid he's for the high jump," he said briefly.

"Just for shooting his mouth off?"

"'Just,' Dora?" said the Legionnaire. "You know as well as I that that's fast becoming the number one crime of the century. In any case, they wanted someone to hold up as an example of what happens to people who talk too much. They've got it all planned out, I had a look at his papers— Porta introduced me to a seedy character who works in the commissariat; goes under the title of 'Doctor,' but almost certainly isn't. Anyway, I managed to find his weak spot—" The Legionnaire gave Dora a wink and a charming grin, "and he let me see the papers. Easy when you know how. Some people will do anything to get what they want."

"And what do they plan to do to your lieutenant?"

The Legionnaire frowned.

"Execute him. Read out the list of his crimes in front of the execution squad—they figure that way they'll break even the toughest of 'em. It's no fun, seeing a man executed. It's not a question of shooting, it's a question of—" He chopped a hand into the back of his neck. "Takes a lot of courage to go away after that and commit any crimes of your own."

"Courage!" said Dora scornfully. "Everyone talks about courage! What's courage supposed to be? Something you've got when your head's safe on your shoulders and your belly's full and you've got a glass in your hand! Don't talk to me about courage! You try being in the hands of those bastards for more than ten minutes and see how far courage gets you! There's only one way to deal with the Gestapo, and that's to know something about them that they don't want anyone else to know. You've got a hold over them, you're all right. Without one, you're done for."

"I couldn't agree with you more." The Legionnaire leaned across the table and spoke confidentially. "How about Bielert, Dora? You know things about Bielert, don't you? Enough to help Ohlsen keep his neck on his shoulders?"

Dora shook his head.

"I doubt that, sweetie. I might be able to manage a pass for you so's you could go and see him, but anything else and I'd be risking my own neck. I know a thing or two about Paul all right, but even a lapdog'll bite if you kick it hard enough. And you know Paul—he's unreliable. Like a wild beast. So long as you've got the upper hand he'll behave himself and do what you want. But you try pushing him too far and he just loses control of everything. Goes mad and hits out in all directions. Besides, I can't help feeling this lieutenant of yours has gone and stuck his neck out. It's asking for trouble, carrying on like he did, shooting his face off to every Tom, Dick and Harry. And someone I don't know from Adam. If it were someone like you, I might consider taking the risk, but not for some unknown jackass that can't keep his mouth shut. It's playing with fire, interfering with Paul's prisoners."

"Yes, I know." The Legionnaire pursed his lips and looked down into his glass. "That man collects prisoners like other people collect butterflies."

"He's a dangerous bastard, that one." Dora picked out another chestnut and thoughtfully dipped it into the melted butter at the bottom of the dish. "I've half a mind to lie low for a bit myself, as a matter of fact. Just sort of disappear. Give the keys to Britta and go into retirement until the Tommies arrive."

The Legionnaire laughed. "Don't tell me they're on to you, Dora? Not you, of all people!"

"I don't know." Dora scratched at her tangled hair with a dirty fork. "But there's a voice at the back of my head keeps saying, 'Pull your pants up, Dora, and scram.' I've noticed, just recently, we've had rather too many visits from a certain type of person—know the ones I mean?"

"I believe I do," murmured the Legionnaire. "The sort of guy who comes in for a Pernod and nearly chokes to death over it?"

"Exactly," said Dora. "Beer types. Spot them a mile off. Hats pulled down over their eyes like something out of a cheap spy movie."

"Pernod has its uses." The Legionnaire picked up his glass and smiled. "It sorts out the wheat from the chaff—the man in the street from the man in the Gestapo. Hey, Dora, remember that one whose throat we cut?"

Dora shuddered and began scratching compulsively between her pendulum breasts.

"For God's sake don't remind me of it! It brings me out in gooseflesh even now—I still remember the mess my garage was in. Blood all over the floor . . ."

At that moment the ghostly wail of the air raid sirens started up.

"Shit!" said Aunt Dora. "That means the cellars."

"With a couple of bottles?" suggested the Legionnaire. "You never know how long we're going to be there . . ."

A table was pushed back and a trapdoor opened. Clients and staff arrived on the double, jostling each other down the narrow steps into the cellar. A supply of bottles was passed down from hand to hand, the trap closed, and the assembled company stretched themselves out and prepared to enjoy the enforced intimacy. Only Gilbert, the porter, remained upstairs. It was necessary to have someone on guard to watch out for looters.

The raid lasted an hour. Dora staggered up the steps and tottered back to her table in the corner. Her glass of Pernod was still where she had left it. She picked it up and stared at it with slightly glazed eyes.

"Tell you what," she said as the Legionnaire rejoined her. "I'll give Paul a ring and see what I can do for you. Come round here tomorrow morning, if you're able to get out of barracks. About eleven o'clock. If I can dig a pass out of the old bastard, then I will. If not—" She shrugged. "If not, it means I'm losing my grip and I'll probably be joining your lieutenant on the scaffold."

The Legionnaire laughed. "That'll be the day, Dora! I'll be round at eleven, and you'll have the pass, want to bet?"

He went out into the street and was immediately approached by a girl on the lookout for trade.

"Got a cigarette, lover-boy?"

The Legionnaire brushed her out of his way and walked on. She hurried after him, panting endearments down his neck. The Legionnaire suddenly stopped. He swung around on her, his face contorted and his eyes blazing.

"Piss off out of it and leave me alone! I'm not interested!"

He took one step toward her, but that was enough; the girl fled, and for the next two days scarcely dared set foot outside the front door.

A couple of hours later, Dora kept an appointment with Standartenführer Bielert on the corner of the Neuer Pferdemarkt and Neuerkamp Feldstrasse, alongside the abattoirs. Bielert enjoyed the abattoirs. He often passed an afternoon there, watching the slaughter.

He and Dora walked together across the Pferdemarkt and entered the restaurant of the Hotel Jöhnke, taking their places at a table set somewhat apart from the rest. Dora went straight to the point.

"I had to see you, Paul. I need a pass, a visiting pass or whatever you call them, and I need it in a hurry." She ran her fingers through her hair and looked at him distractedly. "I'm always in a hurry these days, it's dreadful. Honestly, you've no idea the trouble I'm having with staff. Rush here, rush there, do this, do that—you can't get them for love or money, I'm having to do half the cooking and housework myself now."

"That's nonsense, Dora." Bielert smiled. "I've told you often enough, I can supply as many people as you need."

"Foreigners!" scoffed Dora. "Thank you, no. I'd rather go down on my knees and scrub my own floors than have Gestapo agents running loose about the place. But I must have my visiting pass!"

"Whom do you want to visit? And where?"

"Someone in prison. A lieutenant."

"I see." Bielert pulled out his cigarette case and thoughtfully inserted a cigarette into his long silver holder. "You know, my dear, you're really becoming very demanding lately. A pass is a valuable commodity these days. Greatly in demand."

"Don't come that crap with me!" said Dora scornfully. "You can get me a pass just by snapping your fingers, if you feel like it."

"In that case," he murmured, "I suppose it all depends on whether or not I do feel like it."

"You'd better," said Dora. "And buy me a rum, will you? A nice hot one."

They sat in silence until the drinks arrived. Bielert looked consideringly at Dora.

"Suppose you begin by telling me who it is that really wants this pass? And just who it is they want to visit?"

"Here you are. It's all written down there."

She handed him a piece of paper. Bielert studied it a moment and raised one almost nonexistent eyebrow. "Lieutenant Bernt Ohlsen," he said slowly. "Imprisoned for crimes against the state—and you want me to allow him to receive visitors?"

"Why not?" Dora shrugged.

"Why not? Why not, you say? I'll tell you why not!" Bielert screwed the paper into a ball and threw it angrily to the floor. "Because the man is a criminal and a traitor and a danger to his country! I have nothing but scorn and hatred for men of his type! If I had my way, they'd be exterminated wholesale. Them and their families. Their wives and their children and their mothers and their fathers! All of them!"

His face had twisted itself into a sudden mask of white, trembling hatred. Dora watched him dispassionately. She had heard it all before. At the far end of the room, several people quietly stood up, called for their checks and disappeared. Bielert ranted on regardless.

"I have a list of names so long," he boasted, "that even Gruppenführer Müller was taken by surprise. It's not only that we're at war. It's more than that. We're living through a revolution, and I count myself as one of its chief engineers. I have a loathsome job, I know. A filthy, degrading job. But a very necessary job and one that I believe in. The end will justify the means, and without men such as myself to carry the thing through to its conclusion, the revolution would suffocate on its own vomit tomorrow."

"Yes—of course—you're so right," murmured Dora vaguely; and then her eyes lighting up: "Talking of Müller, I saw him only the other day! He came into my place, quite unexpectedly, out of the blue, just like that! We got as pissed as newts together, I can tell you—it was quite a reunion after all these years!"

"Müller?" said Bielert, his nose twitching anxiously as he stared at Dora. "Which Müller are you referring to?"

"Why, Gruppenführer Müller, of course—the one you've just been telling me about. My God, I hadn't seen him since the day he got his promotion to Untersturmführer! We had such a laugh together!"

"I wasn't aware that you knew Heinrich Müller," said Bielert, frowning at her. "How did you meet him? You've never been to Berlin in your life, that I know for a fact."

Dora looked at him and laughed. "Oh, Paul, don't tell me you even keep a tail on *me*? On your old friend Dora?"

"Who said anything about a tail?" demanded Bielert irritably. "I just have your safety in mind, that's all. One never knows what unlikely turn events may take these days."

"You're so sweet to me!" Dora smiled and raised her glass to him. "But surely you mean *your* safety, rather than mine? After all, if anything should ever happen to me—if events ever *should* take an unlikely turn—it would rather put you on the spot as well, wouldn't it?"

"We live in troubled times," replied Bielert. He took a small sip of brandy and knocked some ash off his cigarette. "Tell me, Dora, what did you and Müller talk about?"

"Oh, this and that, and old times," she said airily. "And strangely enough, at one point, people who had committed crimes against the state—like this Lieutenant Ohlsen, only far worse. Müller was asking me about some Communists I used to know once. He was specially interested in any that had left the Party and gone into the Gestapo."

Bielert's eyelids flickered very slightly.

"I see. And were you able to help him?"

"Well, I was and I wasn't," said Dora frankly. "I gave him one or two little tidbits to be going on with, but it wasn't till after he'd left that I remembered this."

"What is 'this'?" asked Bielert, a shade too smoothly.

Dora pulled up her dress, plunged a hand up the leg of her thick woolen pants and brought out a letter.

"Here you are," she said. "Funny thing, I was turning out my closets a while back and I came across a whole heap of old junk. And in the junk I found this letter. All about some cell or other—" She unfolded the letter and read it, frowning. "Cell 31—a Communist cell, you know the sort of thing. It talks about a Paul Bielert, who was head of this cell. It's quite a coincidence, isn't it? Someone having your name, I mean."

"Quite," said Bielert. He took the letter from her and glanced through it. "Very interesting. Do you mind if I hang onto it?"

Dora smiled at him. "Do what you like with it. Matter of fact, I've got one or two others that might interest you—all on the same subject, of course."

Bielert colored slightly.

"How is it you've managed to lay hands on correspondence that dates from 1933 and earlier? Who did you get it from?"

Dora looked down into her glass and shrugged a shoulder.

"You've still got a lot to learn, haven't you, Paul? You've still got a good way to go before you catch up with me. You've done well for yourself, but you always were inclined to be backward." She put out a hand and patted his arm consolingly. "Poor old Paul! When you were learning how to milk cows in the reform school, with all the old monks doddering about and driving you crazy and you just muttering under your breath about revenge, I was already taking steps to make sure of my future. I picked up everything I could lay hands on and stored it away for a rainy day. By the time you started playing little kids' games with your pals in cell 31, I'd already acquired the magpie habit. It was a piece of cake, getting hold of your letters. Of course, I didn't know then if they'd ever be any use, but I thought I might as well keep them. Just in case—" She squeezed his arm a moment, then sat back in her chair. "Why do we have to rake all this up? I don't want to get you into trouble. All I want is one simple little pass with your signature on it."

"Come round to the office tomorrow. I'll have it ready for you."

Dora laughed. "You must be joking! Me set foot in your office? I'd never be allowed out again! No, thank you, I'd rather you sent one of your men round to my place with it."

Bielert stared at her coldly. His fist clenched and unclenched on the table and his eyes narrowed, but his voice remained soft and low.

"You know, Dora, I'm beginning to wonder if it might not be a good idea for me to send several men round to your place—they could bring you back with them in the car and you could pay us a little visit. I'm sure it would be quite enlightening for both of us."

"I'm sure it would," said Dora, matching his tone. "And I'm quite sure it's not the first time the idea has occurred to you."

"Well, no, but now and again it does come to me more forcibly than usual."

"The only trouble is, Paul, that you couldn't possibly have me shut away in a cell without having yourself shut away in another one only a few hours later. There's so much I could tell . . ."

They smiled at each other in mutual hatred and understanding.

"Well, well," said Bielert, carefully extracting his cigarette butt from the holder. "You shall have your pass. I'll send Grei round with it at three o'clock."

"That suits me fine. Grei and I get on with each other very well. Did you ever know him before the war, I wonder? I can still remember the time when he used to sing nothing but the *Internationale*. Of course, he's changed it to the Horst Wessel now, but who can blame him? Only a fool tries to swim against the tide."

Bielert stood up.

"One word of warning, Dora: watch your step. You have many enemies."

"You too, Paul. I hope you follow your own good advice."

Stever had been in the Army for five years, and he was a good soldier. Stahlschmidt, on the other hand, had been in the Army almost thirty years, and he was a very bad soldier. And as for Rotenhausen, who was an officer and the governor of the prison, it was arguable whether he could be called a soldier at all. It was not, in any case, thought Stever, the length of service that counted so much as whether a person had the aptitude.

"And I have the aptitude," said Stever aloud to himself.

He looked at his reflection in the mirror and smiled and saluted. He enjoyed being a soldier. Both Stahlschmidt and Rotenhausen were too busy lusting after power. Neither of them realized that they were but tools in the hands of the Nazis.

I realize it, thought Stever, prancing and posturing before the long mirror. That's why I shall survive.

Stever had no particular desire for power. Power brought not only increased prestige but increased personal risk, and Stever could do without that. He was happy with his present position and his present way of life. He was paid regularly, was nowhere near the front line, and had a regular supply of women and clothes.

The clothes were supplied free by a tailor who lived in the Grosser Burstah and whose son had once been a prisoner in one of Stever's cells. All Stever's suits and uniforms were handmade and the envy of his comrades.

As for his women, he chose them carefully and had a semipermanent entourage. In Stever's mind, human beings fell into four categories: men who were soldiers and men who were civilians; women who were married and women who were single. Stever despised civilians and found single women more trouble than they were worth. He always went for the married ones. At the age of fifteen he had made the discovery that most married women were sexually undernourished, and he had taken upon himself the task of easing their lot.

There was something very satisfying about married women. In the first place, they never wanted to become emotionally involved, they never made any demands other than the purely physical, and this suited Stever down to the ground; he found it impossible to imagine existing for anyone but himself and for anything but his own gratification. The idea of being expected to consider another person's wishes was terrifying and alien to his nature.

Secondly, he found that married women were always very anxious to be pleased. In nearly all the marriages he had encountered, the batteries had seemed to run dry after two or three years, and then Don Juans such as Stever were able to step into the breach and make good the deficiencies.

He found young girls too much of a responsibility, too much of a trial, while virgins were a positive menace.

"Shove a hand up their cunt before they're ready for it and they'll scream the place down and have you arrested," he gravely explained to Obergefreiter Braun, who found it difficult to get women, though he was far better-looking than Stever. "Have to spend hours touching 'em up and whispering at 'em and telling 'em how lovely it's going to be and how much you want 'em, and all that balls—and half the time," he added, "you're in such a hell of a state when they finally drop their pants that you screw the whole thing up anyway. And half the time they don't like it and keep complaining you're taking advantage of 'em and go on moaning all the time you're on the job—game's not worth the fucking candle," he said in disgust. "Stick to the married ones, bud. They know the score and there's no damn rigmarole to be gone through before they let you have it."

"I see," said Obergefreiter Braun, puckering up his fore-head. "I'll try one of them next time."

"That's the idea," said Stever, cramming his cap on his head and stepping smartly out of the barracks.

No one seeing Stever outside the prison, with a pleasant smile on his lips and a helping hand for little old ladies who couldn't cross the road, would ever have taken him for the same man who casually battered prisoners half to death before throwing them into their cells to rot. And if anyone had asked Stever himself about it, he would have been quite puzzled.

"I'm only an Obergefreiter," he would have said. "I'm only carrying out orders."

And besides, he had never actually killed a man. He prided himself on that. He had been through the entire war without firing a shot at anyone. And that was a record to boast of. Stever had no man's blood on *his* conscience.

VII

PRISON DISCIPLINE

Major Rotenhausen turned up once every month to introduce himself to the latest batch of prisoners and to take his leave of those who were leaving. He never said farewell to those who had been condemned to death, since as far as he was concerned, they no longer existed; only to those who were leaving to serve their sentences in one of the military prisons, Torgau or Glatz or Germersheim.

His favorite visiting hour was eleven o'clock at night, when all the prisoners had settled down and were alseep. He enjoyed the inevitable panic and confusion as guards raced around the cells shaking unwilling men into wakefulness in order that they might be presented to the prison governor. It gave him a pleasurable sense of his own position and importance.

He made one of his surprise visits four days after the affair of the forged pass. It was a few minutes before midnight and he went to the prison straight from an evening's play at the casino. He was in a particularly good humor. He had dined well, he had drunk a little too much and he had passed an entertaining evening. He was the picture of sartorial elegance, and he knew it. His gray cape, lined with white silk, billowed gently in the breeze. His leather boots creaked energetically as he walked across the courtyard. His long legs looked superb in their sleek gray pants, and his epaulettes gleamed golden in the darkness. Major Rotenhausen was one of the garrison's best-dressed men; three years earlier he had made a rich marriage, and he was now president of the casino. Men looked at him and envied him, and Rotenhausen held his head high and felt himself to be the pride of the German Army.

Most people who came to the garrison accepted Rotenhausen at his own value, assuming automatically that he was a man of influence and a power to be reckoned with. There had been only one occasion, as far as the garrison could recall, when some stranger, some upstart officer from God knows where, had walked into the place and upset all the accepted rules of etiquette, had ignored Rotenhausen and set all the other officers by the heels.

He was a young colonel, no more than thirty at the most. He had lost an arm at Minsk and was stationed temporarily in Hamburg, a halfway halt between the hospital and a return to the front line. He had received virtually every available decoration, and his chest was a blaze of medals. His uniform itself caused several disdainfully raised eyebrows. Apart from the tunic, which was custom-made, the rest had all very obviously come right off the rack. Men looked at his boots, his pants, his kepi, even his leather belt and holster, and silently sneered. His pistol was a P.38. All the other officers carried the Walther, a neat little job which they felt to be more fitting to their status, but the unknown colonel was apparently indifferent to such niceties.

He belonged to an Alpine Regiment, the edelweis flash stood out boldly on his left sleeve, and although at first the garrison had no idea who he was or why he was there, this fact in itself was enough to put them on their guard.

Within half an hour of his arrival, the colonel called a meeting and informed the startled company that he had provisionally taken over the command of the garrison.

"I am Colonel Greif of the 9th Alpine Regiment," he announced into the horrified silence. "I am here for a temporary period."

He shook hands with no one; merely fixed them all with his bright unblinking gaze and continued with his introductory lecture.

"I've always got on well with the men under my com-

mand, and I expect to do the same with you. Just pull your
weight as I pull mine and we shall all do fine together. Only
one thing I cannot stand and will not tolerate, and that's a
shirker." The steady brown eyes flickered back and forth
across the ranks of the assembled officers. "I suppose you are
aware, gentlemen, that the units at the front are crying out
for replacements. I'm sure you don't need me to tell you, but
if for some reason you haven't been out there for a while,
you might not quite realize how desperate the situation has
become; there are men in my regiment, for instance, who
have had no leave for the last three years."

He asked every officer present how long he had been in
the garrison, his eyebrows rising ever higher and his lips
turning down at the corners at the replies. The number who
had ever been anywhere near the front was but a minute
percentage of the total.

"I can see, gentlemen," said Greif, "that things are going
to have to change around here."

And change they did; and abruptly. Within three days
of the colonel's arrival, all the fantasy uniforms, the capes
and the cloaks and the stylish kepis, the highly polished
boots and the neat little pistols, had been reluctantly packed
away and exchanged for more regulation attire. The garrison became a place of hard work, filled with sweating,
hurrying men and drab uniforms, instead of presenting its
more usual aspect of a fancy dress ball in full swing.

"We're at war, for God's sake!" was Greif's constant cry.
"This is a military establishment, not a toy soldiers' fort!"

Even the officer commanding the 76th Infantry Regiment,
old Colonel Brandt, had to bend before the storm and
abandon his lorgnette.

"If your sight is defective, then go and get yourself some
spectacles," said Grief curtly. "But don't ever let me see any
more of this affectation."

And Brandt had to stand there and take it. Had to stand
to attention and suffer insults from this strip of piss, this one-
armed, ribbon-bedecked, jumped-up colonel from nowhere
who was young enough to be his son!

The garrison suffered not in silence but in a continuous
state of low dissatisfied muttering. Men gathered together
in small secretive groups and spoke in veiled tones of various
accidents that might possibly befall the colonel. One lieutenant even had the brillant idea of denouncing him—
annonymously, of course—to the Gestapo. While they were

still trying to work out what to denounce him for, the garrison as a whole received a shock from which it never quite recovered: Colonel Greif had a social call from no less a person than Heydrich.

Heydrich of all people! The devil's adjutant! The idea of denouncing Greif to the Gestapo was tacitly abandoned and men began to grow suddenly restless and seek after change. Requests for transfer began to pour in. No man in his right senses would wish to stay on in Hamburg under someone who was a friend of Heydrich. Even the front line was preferable to the Gestapo.

Rotenhausen was not among those who joined in the first mad scramble to get out. He stayed his hand a while—not because of any low cunning but simply because his reactions were slow. And God protected him, thus confirming his own exalted view of himself. Only a few days after Heydrich's visit to the colonel, Greif was advised by telegram of a new posting. He packed his bags and set off within hours for the Russian front. He was never to see Germany again. He died in a snowdrift just outside Stalingrad, and when the Russians discovered him, on February 3, 1943, he was stiff and cold and had been dead for some time.

The garrison celebrated his departure for four days and nights nonstop. The champagne flowed and the old carnival uniforms were pulled out of their hiding places. Men strutted and peacocked to their hearts' content and Colonel Brandt bought himself a new lorgnette.

Greif's replacement was a brigadier general of doubtful intelligence and possibly suffering from a premature onset of senility. The garrison were charmed by him. A most delightful old fool, even if he would insist on slobbering over their wives' hands and whinnying like a horse whenever he presented himself to them.

"General van der Oost, madame—of the infantry, of course!" And then he would straighten himself up, creaking and grunting, tug at his jacket, heave at his collar, clear his throat and trot out one of his standard jokes. "I'll venture to guess you don't know why I'm in the infantry, eh?"

Obviously no one ever did, and no one ever cared, but the answer came just the same.

"Well, I'll tell you—I'm in the infantry for the simple reason that I'm not in the artillery, d'you see; never could stand the artillery, matter of fact—dreadful business, all that noise all the time, gives me a shocking bad head."

One day he staggered into the casino and stopped the whole proceedings with a great roar of delighted laughter.

"Gentlemen, I'm happy tonight! Do you know why I'm happy?"

By this time his officers had grown accustomed to his simple turn of wit. They did know why, but he was a brigadier general and he suited them very well, so they shook their heads and humored him.

"I'll tell you why!" The general held out his arms, delighted. "I'm happy because I'm not sad!"

Even when they had all guffawed deferentially, van der Oost was not satisfied. Beaming, he advanced on them and cracked another witticism. "Yesterday I was damnably sad—simply because I wasn't happy, d'you see."

Better an old fool like van der Oost than an objectionable young hothead like Greif. The garrison and their new commander were on excellent terms. Van der Oost asked no more than that he be allowed to keep them in a state of constant amusement. Men quickly found that if they laughed at his jokes, he would blindly sign any piece of paper that was set before him, whether an illegal requisition for a crate of margarine or an execution order. There was even a rumor in the garrison that the brigadier general was unable to read.

"Well, well," he always remarked after scrawling his signature across a document. "Well, well, well, there you are, d'you see. Always up to date, eh?" And he would lean back in his chair and wave a hand at his empty trays. "In-tray, out-tray, pending—nothing in any of 'em, d'you see. That's the way to do it, gentlemen. Keep up with the work and it never gets on top of you."

"They executed three infantry soldiers at Fuhlsbüttel yesterday," said his adjutant one morning, by way of making conversation.

"Ah, yes," said van der Oost. "They have to, don't you see—each war demands its sacrifices. Without sacrifices there wouldn't be any war, you know. Wouldn't be any war."

He always slept during the Kriegspiel.* He would drop off at the beginning and wake up halfway through with loud cries of encouragement and advice.

"The foreign armored divisions must be destroyed, gentlemen! Must be destroyed before they manage to reach

---

*War game.

Germany and cause a congestion. The essential in a battle of this kind, d'you see, is to make sure the enemy run out of munitions. What's a tank without shells, eh? Like a railway without a train."

And the officers would nod their agreement and conscientiously begin moving the pieces as he directed. But somehow, no matter how hard they tried, they never were able to devise a scheme for cutting the enemy's supply line. In the end they hit on a solution, and at the start of each game would solemnly announce to the general that the enemy lacked munitions, whereupon, quite contented, he would rub his hands together and beam his approval.

"Well done, gentlemen. That means we have won. All we need do now is bomb the enemy's factories and then we shall have them at our mercy."

And off he would fall to sleep, convinced of his own brilliance as a military strategist.

One day the garrison cat upset the whole field of battle by depositing a litter of kittens in the middle of Hill 25. All the little tanks, all the little field guns and all the little armored cars were scattered pell-mell about the table, some upside down, some on their side, some even on the floor. It looked as if a miniature bomb had scored a direct hit. And it had to happen—as is the way with cats and their choice of inapposite moments for giving birth—just on a day that the garrison had invited their neighbors over to take part in a game.

Van der Oost lost his temper for the first time since he had been there. He demanded that the cat be hauled up before a court-martial. There was nothing for it but to humor him and join in the farce. Two Feldwebels cornered the cat and held her throughout the trial. It was the nearest they had come to danger in their entire military careers. The cat was sentenced to death on the grounds of having sabotaged the officers' instruction course in the art of warfare. However, the next day found the general in a better temper. He reprieved her on condition that his batman attach her collar to a leash and take charge of her. Some time later the cat disappeared; the batman had sold her to a butcher and the general fretted his heart out until another cat was found to take her place.

Two years had passed swiftly and pleasantly since the terrible advent of Colonel Greif and his brief reign of terror. The garrison was a happy and hedonistic place, and Major Rotenhausen increased his sphere of influence from day to day. He had discovered that the brigadier general had a passion for brandy, and he had also discovered where he could lay hands on a continual supply of it. Major Rotenhausen and General van der Oost understood each other very well.

Humming briskly to himself, Rotenhausen marched across the dark courtyard to the prison—to his prison, the prison he commanded. He smiled and flicked his riding crop against the side of his leg. He never went riding—he was terrified of horses—but the crop looked good and was useful for bringing recalcitrant prisoners to heel.

Stabsfeldwebel Stahlschmidt had been warned by telephone of the visit, and he came to meet him. Rotenhausen rather distantly returned his salute. Stever was also there. They had had to search half the town for him and had eventually run him to earth in a private club, where he had been watching an obscene film in which naked people of various shapes and sexes committed atrocities on one another. Stever had still not completely returned to the mundane world of the prison.

"Very well, Stabsfeldwebel. I suggest we get down to business straightaway," said Rotenhausen, vigorously switching at himself with his crop. "I'm a busy man, as you know, so let's waste no time."

Stahlschmidt led the way to his office. It was not only clean, it was not only tidy, it was impeccable in every detail; every single object in it was placed according to the rule book. Rotenhausen walked around it a few times, peering into hidden corners for patches of dust, examining the wire baskets for papers that had no right to be there, taking out a metal rule and measuring the distance between the edge of the desk and the edge of the in-tray, the edge of the desk and the inkwell, the inkwell and the out-tray, the out-tray and the blotting pad. Stever stood stolidly at the door watching him. Stahlschmidt walked about behind him and every now and again closed an eye in Stever's direction. What fools these officers were! He knew that Rotenhausen had long cherished a desire to fault him on some small point of order. Had he himself been an officer, thought Stahlschmidt, he would not have taken so long about it. But then, he was smarter than Rotenhausen and that was why Rotenhausen would never catch him out.

Having measured everything on the desk that was even remotely measurable, Rotenhausen sighed with weary boredom and demanded to see the list of the prisoners. Smiling, Stahlschmidt handed it over to him. He read it through with the aid of a monocle, which he had great difficulty in keeping in his eye.

"Stabsfeldwebel, this list is deficient. I see no mention of the number of new prisoners—I see no figure for the number of men who are to be transferred . . ."

"Here we are, sir, down here." Stahlschmidt jabbed a fat red finger at the foot of the page. "Seven new prisoners, sir. One lieutenant colonel, one cavalry captain, two lieutenants, one Feldwebel, two privates. Fourteen to be transferred, sir. All of them to Torgau. There's one brigadier general, one colonel, two majors, one captain, one Hauptmann, two lieutenants, one Feldwebel, three corporals, one marine, one private. There are also four men condemned to death. Their appeals have been rejected and all necessary arrangements have been made for their execution."

"Well done, Stabsfeldwebel." With a twist of the lips, Rotenhausen dropped his monocle and laid the paper on the desk. "It gives me great pleasure to find everything so well organized. You obviously know your work and take care over it. You're a man in whom one can have all confidence. Hm." He beat himself hard with his riding crop. "No slovenly ways here like there are at Lübeck, eh? Everything goes like clockwork with you, doesn't it, Stabsfeldwebel?"

"I do my best, sir."

"Let me just give you one word of warning, however: watch out for accidents—you know the sort of thing I mean? If a prisoner happens to break an arm or a leg, that's perfectly all right with me, but do try to avoid breaking their necks!"

"Me, sir?" Stahlschmidt frowned. "Me break their necks, sir?"

"You know what I mean!" said Rotenhausen irritably. "Just take great care, that's all I'm asking—if not, we shall both find ourselves in trouble. There's a man called Bielert at Stadthausbrücke. You may have heard of him. A most disagreeable type. He's started taking rather too much interest in our affairs these past few weeks. Nosing about the garrison, asking questions about the prison, the way it's run, how many people in it, you know the sort of thing. He even had the infernal nerve to come bursting into the casino at two A.M. the other day. Such behavior would never have been tolerated in the days of the Emperor—a man like that would have been thrown out on his ear. A lieutenant who didn't know him took him at first for a priest. I ask you! Strange type of priest! He was one of Heydrich's disciples, you know. Not a man we should be wise to cross, Stabsfeldwebel. We know better than that, don't we?"

"Well, if I'm to understand you correctly, sir . . ."

"If you are to understand me correctly, Stabsfeldwebel, just remember this: that unless you want to end up in the forests of Minsk fighting partisans, you will behave with circumspection and do nothing that might bring this man Bielert down on our heads. If you want to hit the prisoners around a bit, I've already said that's all right with me; God knows they deserve it, and in any case I should be the last person to interfere with a man's pleasures. But use a bit of discretion, that's all I ask. There are plenty of parts of the human body you can bash to your heart's content and nobody any the wiser. Remind me to show you when we start on the interviews."

In the corridor, the guards had lined up all those who were to have the honor of being presented. First of all, the newcomers. And to start with, a forty-eight-year-old lieutenant who had been sent there on a charge of refusing to obey orders. His introduction to Rotenhausen took exactly three minutes and four seconds, and he was then carried away almost senseless by two Gefreiters. There was hardly a mark on his body.

"Well, you didn't last long, did you?" sneered Stever, jabbing the groaning man in the belly. "Three minutes! Hardly a record, is it? We had a Feldwebel here once, he held out for two hours. Still on his feet at the end of it. Rotenhausen had to give up and take a rest in the end, before he could get strength enough to finish him off."

Lieutenant Ohlsen was in the corridor with all the other guests. They were standing in a line with their faces to the wall, their hands clasped behind their necks.

Two heavily armed guards marched up and down, ready to fire on the least provocation. It had occasionally been known for a prisoner driven to desperation or blind rage to leap at the major and attempt to throttle him. No one, of course, had ever survived such a foolhardy attack. They always ended up as lifeless bodies in one of the discipline cells down in the cellars, trussed like chickens with a label tied around one ankle.

Stever yelled out Lieutenant Ohlsen's name. Ohlsen

jumped round, marched into the office where Rotenhausen
conducted his interviews and sprang smartly to attention.

The major was enthroned behind the desk. Before him
lay his riding crop. Stahlschmidt stood at his elbow. He was
holding a rubber truncheon, coated with the crusted and
coagulated blood of ages past. Stever stood inside the door,
just behind the prisoner.

"*Heil* Hitler!" barked Rotenhausen.

"*Heil* Hitler," responded Ohlsen tonelessly.

The major smiled. He leaned forward and picked up a
sheaf of papers.

"I've been reading through your file," he told Ohlsen. "To
me, your case doesn't look too good. In fact, in the light of
my past experience I can confidently predict that you will
be sentenced to death. Probably decapitated—unless you're
lucky, which I doubt. If you are lucky, of course, you'll be
shot, but I shouldn't hold out too much hope if I were you.
I have a feeling for these things." He looked across at
Ohlsen. "Death by decapitation is both dishonorable and
unaesthetic. There's too much blood, and a headless body
is not a pleasant sight—absurd and revolting at one and the
same time. Do you have any comments you wish to make?
Do you want to ask me for anything? Do you wish to lodge
any complaints?"

"No thank you, sir."

"I see." Rotenhausen leaned back in his chair and
squinted at Ohlsen. "The prisoner is not holding his head
straight," he observed.

Stahlschmidt at once stepped forward with his right arm
raised and his fist clenched. Stever moved in to help with
the butt of his submachine gun.

"Better," said Rotenhausen appraisingly. "But still not
quite right."

A pain ripped its way through Lieutenant Ohlsen's body.
It came so suddenly and was so intense that he felt it must
surely be tearing his inside to pieces. He staggered and
swayed and only just managed to remain on his feet.

Rotenhausen turned to Stahlschmidt. "He moved!" he
said. "Don't they teach people how to stand to attention
these days?"

Stahlschmidt bunched his fist again. Stever moved in with
two ramrod blows from the butt of his submachine gun hard
into the kidneys.

Ohlsen fell forward onto his knees. Tears sprang from

his eyes and he felt as if red-hot pokers were being rammed up the muscles of his back.

Rotenhausen shook his head. "This is too bad," he remarked, gently reproving. "Does the prisoner now refuse even to stand up? Must he grovel on the floor in that obscene fashion?"

He nodded at Stahlschmidt. Lieutenant Ohlsen lay on the floor, screaming. Stever was hitting out with the frenzy of a maniac. Stahlschmidt concentrated on kicking. After a few moments a thin trickle of blood oozed from the prisoner's mouth. Rotenhausen at once banged on the table with his crop.

"Obergefreiter, get that man on his feet!"

Stever dragged him up. Ohlsen groaned and then shouted as new pains tortured his broken body. Thoughts of his son suddenly flitted through the dark mists of his mind and he muttered to himself.

"Is the prisoner daring to complain?" asked Rotenhausen, outraged.

They didn't know what he was doing, but they beat him up a bit more, just to teach him a lesson. They then disposed of him, throwing him back senseless into his cell.

From the new prisoners they passed to the old; to those who were to be transferred to Torgau. Each man had to sign a declaration to the effect that he had been well treated and had no complaints to make.

One brigadier general refused to sign.

"I suggest, for a change, that you listen to my point of view," he said, very cold and calm and reasonable. "I'm being sent off to Torgau for a maximum period of two years. It might very well be less, and it certainly won't be more. If I choose to tell the authorities of the things I've seen in this prison—two cold-blooded murders, just for a start—you'd be sent down for about twenty-five years. Now just reflect a moment what that means. It means, first, that after I've served my sentence I shall be transferred to a disciplinary regiment. I shall almost certainly be given back my old rank of brigadier general and end up in command—they're short of experienced officers, so they've really no alternative. And once I'm back in a position of authority, I can promise you I shall move heaven and earth to have you people sent to my division."

His words fell into a shocked silence. Stever looked hopefully for guidance at Stahlschmidt, but Stahlschmidt made no move. It was plain from his expression that for once he was nonplussed. He had met stubborn prisoners, foolhardy prisoners, prisoners who tried insulting him or even attempted physical violence; but never in all his career had he encountered one who dared to threaten. Prisoners were not in a position to threaten, and he wished Major Rotenhausen would explain as much to the brigadier general.

Rotenhausen lolled nonchalantly in his armchair. He took his time lighting a cigar, then picked up his riding crop and flexed it gently across his knee. He looked up thoughtfully at the brigadier general.

"Do you really suppose," he drawled, "that a man of your age would last six weeks in a disciplinary regiment? I guarantee that after you'd been there three days you'd be looking back on your spell with us as one of the cushiest times of your life."

He smiled. The brigadier general met his eyes and Rotenhausen looked away. "I'll make you an offer," he said. He took his pistol from its holster, leaned across and laid it on the desk, within the general's reach. "There you are. It's all yours. Take it and use it."

There was a long silence. The general made no movement. Rotenhausen suddenly rose from his armchair, walked round the desk and cracked his whip only inches away from the general's face. Stahlschmidt caught his breath. If the idiot went berserk and the general arrived at Torgau with purple bruises all over his face and half the bones in his body broken, there would be hell to pay. Let Rotenhausen talk his way out of that one, if he could. At least Stahlschmidt would have had no part in it.

"You'd like it, wouldn't you, if I were to beat you black and blue?" Rotenhausen threw back his head and laughed. "Just suit you fine, wouldn't it? Then you really could go bleating to Colonel Vogel at Torgau about the nasty way we've treated you here. Well, I'm sorry to disappoint you, but we're not such fools as all that. In fact, we're not fools at all, as you'll very soon discover. We go strictly according to the rule book here. There are other ways of breaking a prisoner's resistance besides using violence." He turned to Stever. "Obergefreiter, in ten minutes' time I want the prisoner standing ready in the courtyard in full combat dress. Fifty kilos of damp sand in his rucksack, and try to find a couple of nice sharp stones to slip in his boots. And while you're about it, make sure they're old boots—old and stiff and preferably half a size too small. All right?" He smiled, and Stever nodded enthusiastically. "We'll start him off with a couple of hours' gentle exercise. See how he gets on."

"Yes, sir!"

Stever's round, amiable face split wide open with a grin of anticipation. Stahlschmidt laughed aloud, appreciative of the joke. Not quite such an idiot after all, old Rotenhausen!

Only the brigadier general remained impassive, giving no hint as to his thoughts. He was not a young man and it seemed unlikely he would survive two hours of Rotenhausen's "gentle" exercise, with or without boots that crippled him and a rucksack full of sand on his back. Even if, by some miracle of willpower, his heart held firm, Rotenhausen would almost certainly invent some new diversion to finish him off. And the general knew that under Prussian military law Rotenhausen was well within his rights. There was no rule against killing a man by such treatment.

"Prisoner—about—turn!" Stever held the door open and jerked his head at the general. "Forward—march! On the double! One-two, one-two . . ."

As the unfortunate general disappeared down the corridor at a fast trot, Major Rotenhausen picked up his cape and swung it carelessly over his shoulders, put his pistol back in its holster, settled his kepi on his head, tilting it saucily over one eye. He had studied the effect in the glass and he knew that it made him look dashing and fearless.

"Come with me, Stabsfeldwebel. I'll teach you the best way to deal with a recalcitrant prisoner without incurring any awkward complications or giving rise to too many questions. It's all a matter of technique."

Stahlschmidt snatched up his own cape and followed the major from the room. He automatically set his kepi on his head at the same rakish angle as Rotenhausen. He always wore it like that and it was more than possible that Rotenhausen had copied him. It occurred to Stahlschmidt in the nick of time, however, that the major might just think it was the other way round, and silently cursing, he readjusted it, so that it sat at the regulation angle low on his forehead. He knew that he looked the complete idiot, like an ape done up in its Sunday best, but better that than incur a jealous scene.

Rotenhausen strode in front of him. He had thrown his cape over his shoulders and had drawn on a pair of gauntlets. The gold braid of his epaulettes gleamed in the darkness of the prison. Stahlschmidt followed him with contempt.

Bloody Prince Charming poncing off to a masked ball, he thought scornfully, and he began to imitate Rotenhausen's walk, tossing his own cape over his shoulders and gesticulating right and left to an imaginary crowd.

They went out into the covered courtyard. Stever had performed a quick-change act on the general, and they were already standing there waiting.

"Just looking for a couple of suitable stones, sir," panted Stever, who had obviously thrown himself heart and soul into the job and was more exhausted than the prisoner.

He turned to face into the courtyard, standing legs apart and hands on hips, and began barking out the first of a long string of orders. "Right turn—stand to attention—left turn—running on the spot—forward at a run—faster, faster, faster! Knees up, up I said! No flagging, keep it up—halt! Down on your stomach—forward crawl—twenty times round the courtyard . . ."

The brigadier general was sweating under his heavy load. His eyes beneath his helmet were bulging from their sockets as he gasped for breath and fought to carry out each fresh order as it came. He knew only too well that the least hesitation, the least sign of weakness, would give Rotenhausen the opportunity to pounce. He would doubtless be shot for refusing to obey orders. The brigadier general had served forty-three years in the Prussian Army. At the age of fifteen he had entered the military academy at Gross Lichterfelde. He had worked his way up, he knew all the tricks in the book, he knew his own rights and he knew those of others. And at the moment, Major Rotenhausen was within his rights.

"Prisoner—halt!"

The general staggered thankfully and incredulously to a stop. But there was to be no respite. Down in a squatting position he went, and around the courtyard he began painfully to hop like an arthritic frog. His body cried out in protest but his brain refused to listen to its urgent appeals. He went on hopping, and the stones in his boots cut his feet and the unyielding leather, a size too small, stubbed his toes and rubbed blisters on his heels.

Stahlschmidt was openly laughing at the sight. Stever shouted words of encouragement each time the general passed him at the end of the courtyard.

The hopping came to an end and the jumping began. Long jumping, high jumping, jumping on the spot; jumping feet apart, jumping feet together; jump up, fall to the ground, crawl forward; jump up, fall to the ground, crawl forward; jump up, fall to the . . .

After twenty minutes of this treatment, the general quite suddenly fainted. It was against the rules to shoot an unconscious man for refusing to obey orders, but it took Stever barely two minutes to revive the prisoner.

The exercise continued as if the interruption had never been. Rotenhausen finished his first cigar and lit another; he finished the second cigar and lit a third; and then the brigadier general began to break. At first they noticed only a low moaning as he toiled around the courtyard. It seemed that he was moaning in spite of himself, without even realizing it. Later, the moaning raised its pitch and grew in intensity. Later still it became a wail, which rose and fell and died away and came again and again with ever increasing urgency. And then the wail became a shriek of protest, a shout of agony, a long inhuman scream of a man tortured beyond the limits of his endurance and reason.

All over the prison men woke up and heard this mindless call of despair and ran with dread to the windows of their cells. Only a few, those who had been inmates for a long time, remained in their bunks and resisted the temptation to respond to the summons of the tortured man. They knew what was happening out there. They had seen it before. Special training, they called it . . .

The cry was broken now at intervals. And at each interval there came a long, shuddering breath and a rolling rattle in the throat. Stever was in the center of the courtyard, his submachine gun pressed hard against the general's abdomen, just above the navel and just below the dome of the diaphragm. Stever knew what he was doing. You left no traces that way. You might rupture the stomach perhaps, but who was to say that that might not have occurred spontaneously during the normal course of a rigorous exercise? And since when had rigorous exercise been frowned upon in the Army?

Rotenhausen was no longer smiling. He was enjoying himself too much and concentrating too hard to smile. His mouth was drawn back over his teeth in a thin and twisted line. His eyes shone with the gleam of the fanatic.

"Prisoner! On your feet!"

With Stever assisting with his submachine gun, the general staggered upright. He swayed forward as if he were drunk. Stever ran alongside him around the courtyard, jabbing him gently with the butt of the gun.

"Halt! Five minutes' rest! The prisoner can sit down. Have you anything you wish to say?"

The general, an old man now, with palsied limbs and shrunken cheeks, stared unseeingly ahead out of eyes that were covered by a milky film. He had the air of a corpse enclosed in a diseased but still living body. Slowly he shook his head. His lips silently framed one word: no. He had nothing he wished to say.

Stever stared down at the general in contemptuous amazement. Was the man a complete fool? What was the point of setting himself up in opposition to authority? What could he possibly hope to gain by it? Another half hour of suffering and he would be dead—and all for nothing, as far as Stever could see.

The five minutes came to an end. The prisoner was hauled to his feet. He made another two laps of the circuit and then pitched forward, headfirst, and lay still. Stever was on him in an instant, beating him wantonly about the head and shoulders, kicking at his feeble old legs, reviling him for being a fool.

Again the general staggered to his feet. Stever looked at him with hatred. Why couldn't the old dolt give up and die? Any more of this and there would be no sleep for any of them tonight. As it was, there were only three hours to go before reveille. He promised himself that the next time the general faltered, he would give him such a blow as would finish him off once and for all.

The prisoner stood upright—or as upright as he could. His shoulders drooped, and the straps of the rucksack cut deep into them. He was trembling from head to foot. His helmet was askew, his white hairs were plastered in wisps over his forehead, and tears were streaming from his half-closed eyes. Painfully, he ran a swollen tongue around his lips, which were torn and bleeding. In a voice that was no more than a feeble croak, he gave Rotenhausen best; he had no complaints to make of his treatment and he wished to sign a declaration to that effect.

"I assumed you would, sooner or later," said Rotenhausen simply. "Everyone else does, so why not you?" He took out another cigar and paused to light it. "I trust, by the way, that you are not sufficiently small-minded to regard this period of exercise as being in any way connected with your previous refusal to sign the declaration. That of course would be quite contrary to all my principles. The fact is, we do occasionally select a prisoner at random and put him through the hoop, so to speak—purely for his own good. It gives him a taste of what to expect in a disciplinary camp, and therefore a far better chance of ultimate survival. Why do you keep gasping like that? Are you thirsty?"

The general nodded.

"Well, now you know the sort of thing you're likely to have to put up with, don't you? I hear that in Russia the men are expected to march for half a day or more without a drink."

There was still a further twenty minutes to go before the stipulated two hours were up, and even though the general had capitulated, Rotenhausen saw no reason to cut short the exercise period.

The old fellow set off yet again around the courtyard, with the faithful Stever plodding and prodding at his side. He weathered another ten minutes, and then, quite suddenly, he stopped and heaved and vomited blood. Stever butted him violently with his gun.

"Get on, damn you! Get on!"

The final minutes of the drama were played out in slow motion, with the general dragging himself around the ring at the pace of a tortoise and Stever walking with him and meditating on the possibilities of a sly blow that would put an end to all their miseries, allow the general to die in peace and himself to get some sleep.

Back inside the prison, the general collapsed. This time it took Stever almost five minutes to revive him. Rotenhausen ordered that he should have his clothes removed and be taken for a shower, so Stahlschmidt and Stever led him away between them, stripped him naked and held him beneath the cold water for ten minutes. They then put his clothes back on him, dripping wet, and marched him off to the office to sign his declaration. They had to hold the paper for him, and support his arm and hold the pen in his hand before he could do so. Rotenhausen watched in some amusement.

"Why couldn't you have signed it right at the beginning?"

The general seemed not to hear the question. He stared blankly ahead, and the light of life in his eyes was barely flickering.

"I'm speaking to the prisoner!" snapped Rotenhausen. "I expect an answer!"

The answer came, but it was both unexpected and involuntary; the general quite suddenly began to relieve himself, there in Stahlschmidt's impeccable office, standing there unconscious with the urine running down his leg and onto the carpet.

Rotenhausen gave a shout of indignation and jumped back. Stahlschmidt was almost beside himself. He forgot the presence of the major and knew only that some filthy swine of a prisoner was daring to spoil his carpet. He ran at the general, shaking him back and forth screaming abuse. Stever stepped in with the truncheon and began methodically, and with a certain lack of enthusiasm, to beat the prisoner in the stomach and the back and across the shoulders. He was sick of the old man's pointless resistance, he wanted him to die, quickly and quietly, and let them all get to bed. But still he made sure that he hit him only where no telltale marks would be left. He finally pushed the prisoner to the floor, bent him forward and rubbed his nose in the mess.

Major Rotenhausen shook his head.

"This is a most disgraceful happening. To think that an officer could behave in such a fashion! You have my full permission to do what you like with him from now on, Stabsfeldwebel. I have totally lost interest. He is evidently not a gentleman. Only remember what I told you earlier: no traces. That is all I ask."

Stahlschmidt clicked his heels together. "I'll see to it, sir!"

Rotenhausen picked up the inspection register, wrote a few words in a large, plain hand and signed it with a flowing signature:

Inspection of garrison prison carried out. All in order. Prisoners due for transfer called for final interview: no complaints made.

P. ROTENHAUSEN
Prison Governor.

He raised two laconic fingers to the rim of his kepi and left the office, well content with his night's work. He went straight round to see his mistress, the wife of a lieutenant, who lived at Blankenese. While he was there, enjoying the delights of the house, Brigadier General von Peter quietly died.

Obergefreiter Stever launched a few languid kicks at the inert body, but it no longer moved. Stahlschmidt bent over it.

"Thank Christ for that! Now perhaps we shall have a bit of peace."

"I thought he'd never go," grumbled Stever.

"Pissing on my carpet! To think they make officers of pigs like that—the very idea!" Stahlschmidt turned to Stever. "There's no need to go spreading the story around the prison, by the way."

Stever smothered a yawn. "I shouldn't dream of it, Stabsfeldwebel."

"You'd better not." Stahlschmidt waved a hand at the old gray body lying limp on the floor. "Get rid of that rubbish, I don't want stinking corpses cluttering the place up. And tell that lieutenant in No. 9 to come and scrub my carpet. Just the sort of work for an officer."

"What do we put in the report?" asked Stever, carelessly picking up the brigadier general by one of his legs.

"I don't know—" Stahlschmidt scratched at his chest a moment. "Has he got any marks on him?"

Stever let the leg drop and closely examined the body. "A few bruises, that's all—they could have come from anything."

"Good. I'm glad to see you know your job. What would you say to taking over from me when I leave?"

Stever goggled at him. "Are you leaving, Stabsfeldwebel?"

"Not just yet awhile, but I shall be." Stahlschmidt flexed his arms and did a casual knee bend. His long leather boots creaked impressively. "I aim to move on to Potsdam. To the garrison prison at Potsdam. And then, my dear Stever, you'll be able to have this lovely office all to yourself as your very own. How would that suit you?"

"Sounds fine to me," said Stever. "Would that mean promotion?"

Stahlschmidt tapped the KVI* on his chest.

"You too could wear one of these—you don't have to go and beard the Russians in their den to get a medal."

---

*Kriegsverdienstkreuz 1 Klasse (Military Merit Medal, 1st Class).

"But how could I—I mean, how would it—well, frankly, I don't care too much for the idea of going off to a training school for two years just to learn how to be an NCO."

"Who said anything about going off to a training school? You don't think I bothered with all that crap? Use your head a bit and it's not necessary."

"But how do you get around it?"

"Impress people. Make your mark. Pressure them. Learn a couple of bits of rubbish by Goethe or Schiller or some other old goat. Trot 'em out whenever there's an opportunity. Con people. Play it right and you can get wherever you want. Like I'm going to get to Potsdam." Stahlschmidt laughed happily and flexed the muscles of his arms.

Stever looked doubtful. "Easier said than done," he muttered.

"Some of us can, some of us can't," Stahlschmidt said complacently. "Come on, let's get that filthy corpse out of here. Go and find Gefreiter Hölzer, ask him to give you a hand. Arrange a suicide in the prisoner's cell—you know the sort of thing, you've done it before."

"Stool by the window?" said Stever.

"That'll do. And twist the old fool's sheet around his neck and tie a knot—at the back of the neck, mind you. Not at the front. I knew a stupid bastard at Innsbruck made that mistake. Deserved a rope round his own neck, if you ask me. While you're doing that, I'll give the MO a ring and tell him what's happened. This time of night, he'll sign a death certificate without even looking at the corpse."

They had a quick glass of brandy from Stahlschmidt's secret cabinet and then each went about his work. Stever and Hölzer carried the corpse out of the office and back to its cell, where they arranged a squalid and effective suicide.

At the door of the cell they paused and looked back at the hanging body.

"Let's wait outside," suggested Hölzer.

Stever laughed. "You know, it slays me—it really slays me when christers start sounding off about heaven and God the Father and the angels and all that balls. Look at him hanging there! Can you imagine a sight like that ever flying around heaven with a bare ass and a couple of wings and a halo and all?"

"Don't tempt providence." Hölzer shivered slightly. "Just lately, I get cold fingers all up my spine every time I see a

damn priest in the street. I have to cross over the other side
of the road, you know that?"

"Superstitious claptrap," said Stever.

"No, it's not. It's more than that. I'm not superstitious and
I'm not religious, but I sometimes get the feeling that one of
these days it's going to be our number what turns up."

"So? We all got to die, haven't we?"

"Yeah, but not like that." Hölzer looked at the general's
limp body and looked away again. "That's what I'm scared
of. And we've had so many of 'em pass through here, I can't
help feeling it's going to be like—well, like a kinda retribu-
tion, see?"

"Aw, piss off!" said Stever, closing the cell door.

"I mean it," insisted Hölzer. "You know what, I was in a
club downtown the other day and I met these three guys
from a disciplinary regiment what's in Hamburg—tank corps
or something. Real tough lot. Slit your throat as soon as look
at you—and they very near did. Pissed to the eyeballs, of
course. So just to amuse themselves, pass the time away,
you might say, they tie a bit of rope around my neck and
shove a pistol in my belly. Know what they said? They
said, this is just a dress rehearsal. Next time it'll be the real
thing. And God help me, I believed them! I still do, come
to that. And so would you if you'd been there."

Stever's air of patronizing superiority had faded slightly
at the mention of a disciplinary regiment. His hand went up
and plucked nervously at his throat.

"What were they like, these three? One of 'em wasn't
a little guy with a dirty great scar down his face, was he?
Smoked cigarettes all the time?"

"That's right," said Hölzer, astonished. "You know him?"

"Yeah, he visited one of the prisoners just the other day.
Nasty bit of goods."

"You're not kidding," agreed Hölzer earnestly. "He put
the shits up me, I don't mind telling you. In fact, the whole
place is beginning to put the shits up me. This prison, this
town, everything. There's a club where I go—Aunt Dora's
place. You ever been there? Just lately it's been swarming
with Bielert's men. Like flies around a heap of turds. Dora
don't care, they can't touch her, she's well in with Bielert,
but what about the rest of us?" He moved close to Stever.
"Last night I opened my mouth a bit too big—said something stupid to her—I was plastered, didn't know what I
was about—and before I knew whether I was on my ass or

my elbow, I was being flung out the door by a couple of Gestapo bullies."

Stever forced a laugh. "Why? What'd you do to annoy the old cow? Not fucking enough?"

"Come off it!" protested Hölzer indignantly. "I'm there every night of the week when I'm not on duty. I take on the lot of 'em—regulars and casuals. She gets her money out of me, I'm not fussy so long as it's the right sex. The end of last week, I tell you, I was so fucked out I couldn't hardly move."

"So what'd she bawl you out for? What's your trouble? What's all the bellyaching?"

"I dunno," Hölzer shrugged. "I guess I just feel the writing's on the wall. Everywhere I go I keep seeing these guys from the 27th—they've got it in for me, I can feel it in my bones. To tell you the honest truth, I don't think I can take much more of it. I'd sooner be at the front than here."

"You gone off your rocker?" Stever inquired mildly. "If you think these bastards from the 27th are like wild animals here in Hamburg, just try imagining how they'd be at the front!"

"They wouldn't be at the front," muttered Hölzer.

"Well, perhaps not that particular bunch," agreed Stever. "But others just like 'em—or worse. And that's the sort you get out there, you mark my words. They're bad enough when they're back here in civilization, but stuck out there in the trenches with 'em, you'd be a goner and no mistake. They're psychopaths, the lot of 'em! Damn psychopaths running about with their pockets stuffed full of hand grenades and God knows what all else—blow you up as soon as look at you—knife you in the back on the slightest provocation—" He shuddered. "No, thank you! I'd rather spend the rest of the goddamn war in this shithole than get tangled up with a bunch of homicidal nuts! The thing is, not to let it get you down. Don't take it to heart so much. I mean, the prisoners and all that—whatever they get, they've asked for it. In any case, it's none of your business. You just do what you're told and don't worry about the rest."

"Yeah." Hölzer heaved an almost rib-breaking sigh. "Yeah, I guess you're right—but I'm damned if I know what to do about it. You ever walked around day after day feeling kinda—well—kinda sick with fear?"

"What d'you mean, sick with fear? What kind of fear?"

"I dunno," Hölzer sighed again. "Fear of what's going to

happen next—it just gets worse and worse. Every day there's some new horror I can't seem to cope with. Like tomorrow, for instance."

Stever wrinkled his forehead. "What's happening tomorrow?"

"That guy in No. 20's for the ax. He's quite a decent sort of guy, really. His family came to say good-bye to him the other day. I had to stand and listen to 'em all weeping and wailing over him—fit to make your stomach curdle. And then asking me afterward if there's nothing I can't do for him, nothing I can't do to save him. Why pick on me? What can I do? Or say?"

"Nothing," Stever told him firmly. "Not your job, is it? They want anything like that, they got to go direct to Adolf or Heinrich."

"That's what I told 'em. But even if they did it, what good would it do? No damn good at all, and they know it and I know it. And night after night," said Hölzer bitterly, "I drink myself stupid trying to forget it all. I screw some tart until we're both fucked out, then I booze until I'm paralytic, and then for a couple of hours I'm dead to the world and it's like being in paradise, you're unconscious, you don't know nothing, you don't have to watch guys die or listen to kids screaming—and then it's morning again and you're back where you started, only worse—because it gets worse all the time . . ."

"See here, you got to watch it," said Stever seriously. "You're in a bad way, you are. You got to try to be logical about these things. There's a war on—right? Whether you like it or not, you didn't start it, so it's no good you worrying about it. Second, how many prisoners do we kill off a week? Half a dozen? Maybe less, maybe a bit more. And some weeks we don't have any executions at all—right? Now, out at the front they're killing off whole battalions in the space of an hour—all day and every day—and you think anyone's losing any sleep over it? Not on your life! And just remember this: most of them poor dopes out in the trenches are there because they plain can't help it, because the bastards up at the top have sent 'em out there, but the scum we got locked up in these cells are here because they damn well *deserve* to be here. They done something, they got to pay for it. So there ain't no call for you to go weeping no crocodile tears over them."

"Yeah, but the thing is," confessed Hölzer nervously, "I

can't stand the sight of that ax coming down. It's bad enough being in a firing squad, but just having to stand and watch while some fellow's head's hacked off his shoulders—" He shivered. "And it's not even as if most of the guys here have done anything really wrong."

"That's not for you to say," said Stever severely. "If you've broken the law you've broken the law and you got to pay for it, and that's all there is to it, and in this country there's a law that says thinking's not allowed. It's as simple as that, and no one but a fool would ever let on he'd got anything but sawdust inside his head—am I right?"

"I guess so."

"So there you are. You and me are good citizens. We know the law and we keep it. We watch which way the flag's flying, and we fly with it until it starts to change—and as far as I'm concerned, I don't give a hoot whether I'm saying *Heil* Hitler or Long Live the Party, it's all one to me."

Hölzer shook his head. "It's no good, Stever. I still want to get out of this place. I figure it's not going to be so long before the flag does start to change. And when it does, Stahlschmidt's going to be one of the first to go to the wall—and I don't want to be in here with him. I want to get out while there's still time."

"Don't be a fool, Hölzer. There are easier ways. Nothing simpler than to pick one or two of the right sort of prisoner, help half a dozen or so make a getaway—some of 'em are bound to survive and there's your guarantee for life! But as for going off to the front to be a hero, that's just fucking stupid. Go down to the barracks where the 76th are stationed. Go down there some time tomorrow. They're sending off a company to the front. Take a good long look at them as they set out, and I promise you a bottle of booze for every smiling face you see." Stever spat contemptuously. "You won't see one! They'll all look as miserable as sin, like they're marching off to be buried, because they all know it's as good as a death sentence. You stay here, on the other hand, and you got a fighting chance. Just say yes whenever it's demanded of you, crawl up Stahlschmidt's ass, lick the major's boots, and there you are, safe as houses! And when the final showdown comes, you've only got to remember one thing: you carry out orders, you don't give 'em. You didn't make the laws, you didn't ask to work here, you had no choice in the matter."

"Goddamn right I didn't," said Hölzer. His eyes suddenly gleamed. "If I had my way, I'd be in the Navy," he confessed. "The Army's not up my alley, never was. But the Navy, now—and that gear they wear—" He rubbed his hands together. "All the broads go for it, you noticed that?"

"Yeah." Stever turned back to the cell and opened the door. "Let's see how our pal's getting on."

The brigadier general's corpse swung sadly in slow circles, back and forth, round and round, on the end of its rope of knotted sheet.

"Changing color already," observed Stever. "Well, if we're to believe what they tell us in church, he'll be up there perched on a cloud and playing his harp by now. No rules and regulations, not a care in the world." He looked across at the body and grinned. "He wasn't such a bad old bastard at that. Old enough to be my granddad and he sure took a beating. I thought he'd never go." He closed the cell door again and they took up their position outside, awaiting the arrival of the doctor. "I did a good job on that one," remarked Stever with a self-satisfied nod. "Not a mark on his body, even Stahlschmidt agreed I knew what I was doing."

"Yeah."

They stood in silence a few moments.

"I am, of course, a specialist in my own field," said Stever.

"Yeah."

"The number of people that have passed through my hands since I been here—the number of people I've given the treatment to—know what I mean?"

"I know what you mean."

"You get a sort of feel for it—a sort of knack. You know what you can do and what you can't do. Some people never learn, they just get into a frenzy and beat a guy to pulp. Now to my way of thinking, that's butchery pure and simple. No skill in it, see? No art. Anyone can do it. But . . ."

Stever's monologue was interrupted by the arrival of the doctor. He swept like a whirlwind into the cell, took one cursory glance at the body, shrugged his shoulders and signed a death certificate with no more ado.

"Here you are." He thrust the paper at Stever and headed again for the door. "If only these wretched people would contain themselves in patience until the morning," he said irritably. "What do a few hours more or less matter to them, after all? Dragged out of my bed at all times of the day and night—" He turned and waved a hand toward the body. "Get that thing cut down and dispose of it."

He disappeared along the passage and Stever closed the door behind him. He looked at Hölzer with a grin. "See what I mean? What a grand job I did on the old dolt?"

They set the stool upright and Hölzer clambered onto it to untie the deceased brigadier general.

"It's all so crazy," he complained. "One minute we're stringing the poor bastard up and the next minute we're taking him down again. Up and down, up and down, like a goddamn seesaw."

"There's worse things than seesaws," observed Stever sagely. "I'd sooner go up and down on a seesaw than in and out of the stinking trenches."

They cut the body down and dragged it the length of the corridor, then down the stairs to the cellar. As they opened the door, they both let go of their charge at the same moment and it slid from top to bottom of the stone steps. With joint recriminations they clattered after it, caught it up again by the legs and heaved it behind them. There was a sharp crack as the head ran into something.

"Son of a bitch!" screamed Hölzer, exasperated. "What they want is undertakers, not fucking soldiers! This is it! I tell you, this is it! I'm going. I'm putting in for a transfer first thing tomorrow. I'm . . ."

"For Christ's sake," snapped Stever, "will you shut up moaning? On and on until you're driving me nuts!"

"This time I mean it," said Hölzer. "I've had a bellyful." He let fall his leg of the body. "Carting corpses around, scooping up heads after an execution, next thing they'll have us wiping their asses, that'll be the next thing!"

"All right, then!" Stever threw down the second leg and turned angrily to face Hölzer. "Go and get yourself transferred if that's what you want. But don't come whining to me when you're lying headfirst in mud at the bottom of some stinking trench with your balls blown off!"

"Don't you worry," said Hölzer between his teeth. "Your number'll be up long before then, you see if it isn't!"

Obergefreiter Stever planted his elbows on the bar of the Matou and settled down to be argumentative. He pointed a finger at Emil, the owner of the bistro.

"Just shows how little *you* know about it," he declared witheringly. "As a matter of fact, most of 'em go like lambs to the slaughter—you don't even have to show 'em the way; they get down on their knees and they put their heads on the block just like they was saying their prayers. It's quite a lovely little sight. No screaming, no shouting, no . . ."

"Do you mind?" said Emil coldly. "I have no desire to hear the details of how you murder people. I run a bistro, not a slaughterhouse."

Stever picked up his glass. "We've got a tank lieutenant with us at the moment," he went on, not at all discouraged. Quite a decent guy, as officers go. Takes whatever's coming to him and never a murmur. He's for the high jump pretty soon and I'll bet you a pound to a pinch of the proverbial that we don't hear a squeak out of him."

"That's as maybe. I still don't wish to hear about it." Emil wiped a damp rag angrily across the counter. "You're a sadistic swine, Stever."

"Who, me?" Stever finished his drink and pushed his glass across for a refill. "What makes you say that?"

He sounded quite hurt. Emil poured out his drink and banged the glass back at him.

"Because it's true, that's what makes me say it! Because you so obviously love your work—you stink of war and death and torture and you wallow in it like a pig in shit. You're not a man any more, you're a degradation!"

"Look here," said Stever earnestly, "you've got it all wrong! I know the job I'm doing might seem disagreeable to some people . . ."

Emil cut him short with a derisive cackle of laughter. "That's the understatement of the year! Listen to me, you rat—" He leaned across the counter and spat the words into Stever's chubby pink face. "One of these days you're going to find yourself swinging from the wrong end of a rope, and when that day comes, I shall be the first to open the champagne!"

Stever frowned. He withdrew slightly and called across to a girl sitting alone in the corner. She was waiting for customers, but it was too early in the evening; few people ever came to the Matou before ten o'clock.

"Hey, Erika!" Stever snapped his fingers at her and she slowly looked up. "Did you hear what he said? You don't think I'm a—a sadistic swine and a rat, do you?" His tone was appealing. He seemed genuinely in search of information.

Erika raised an eyebrow and looked at him with bitter distaste. "You're a swine, all right," she said. "Dunno about a rat—a sewer rat perhaps."

"But why?" Stever held out a hand in bewilderment. "What have I ever done to you?"

"What wouldn't you do," said Emil, "if we ever ended up in one of your cells?"

"No, no, no!" Stever shook his head. "It's not what I'd do, it's what I'd be made to do. You've got me all wrong. I feel sorry for the fellows we got in there. But what can I do for 'em? I haven't got no authority, no more than you have."

"You don't have to work there!" hissed Erika from her corner.

"What would you have me do instead? Put in for a transfer and run the risk of getting my head blown off? Would that suit you better? Look," said Stever, growing desperate, "I didn't ask for this job, it was all decided over my head by some pen-pushing oaf sitting on his fat behind in an office: Obergefreiter Stever's got to be a jailer. It could have been different. It could have been the Russian front. But it wasn't, it was Hamburg. Fate, that's what I call it, and I don't believe in fighting against fate. And as for what goes on—well, I ask you, is it my fault? Do I make the laws? Do I decide who's going to live and who's going to die? Do I, hell! Some fat slob passes the order down the line and I'm just the poor cunt that has to carry it out."

"My heart bleeds for you," said Emil.

"I'll tell you what," said Stever, turning back to him. "You got to bend with the storm in this life. When the war comes to an end and the wheel turns full circle—which it will, make no mistake—I'll still be sitting pretty with a stack of prisoners to look after. Only thing is, they'll be a different lot of prisoners. The old bunch'll be let out, and the new bunch'll be brought in. And people like you," he jabbed a finger into Emil's chest, "people who haven't been forced to carry out orders like I've been, people who've made a profit selling drinks to the chicken lovers*—they're going to find themselves laughing on the other side of their faces. And

---

*Chicken—a term of derision for the Nazi eagle.

that, my friend, is what those as are intellectual call nemesis."

Stever scornfully tossed two marks onto the counter and walked out of the bar.

VIII

EXECUTION

The following day, Lieutenant Ohlsen was called to Stahlschmidt's office and there presented with his Bill of Indictment, which he was required to sign in three places. He
was graciously permitted to take the document back with
him to his cell and was given an hour in which to read it
through and note its contents.

Left alone, Lieutenant Ohlsen solemnly unfolded the
paper and began to study it:

State Secret Police
Hamburg Division
Stadthausbrücke 8

BILL OF INDICTMENT

Wehrmacht Kommandantur, Hamburg
Altona Division

To: General van der Oost, Garrison Commander
76th Infantry Regiment, Altona

Council of War 391/X AK against Lieutenant Bernt Viktor
Ohlsen of the 27th Tank Regiment.

On December 19, 1940, Lieutenant Ohlsen was sentenced to five years' detention for failing in his duty as an officer when serving with the 13th Tank Regiment. After eight weeks in the prison at Glatz he was transferred to a disciplinary armored regiment. He is at present being held in preventive detention at the Altona Garrison on the order of the Gestapo, Section IV/2A, Hamburg. He has no counsel.

I accuse Bernt Ohlsen of planning to commit high treason, as follows:

1. On several occasions and using veiled words he has attempted to incite men to the murder of the Führer Adolf Hitler.

2. On several occasions he has made remarks injurious to the good name and reputation of various of the officials of the Third Reich, including the Führer Adolf Hitler. (Details of the above-mentioned remarks are attached to this Bill and marked Exhibit "L.")

3. In spreading gossip and false rumors the accused has aided and abetted the enemies of the Third Reich and acted in such a manner as to undermine the morale of the German people.

I ask that the accused be condemned to death in accordance with Article 5 of the Law for the Protection of the People and of the State dated February 28, 1933; and in accordance with Article 80, para. 2; Article 83, paras. 2 and 3; and Article 91B, 73 Stbg.

Incitement to murder of the Führer carries the penalty of death by decapitation under Article 5 of the Law of July 28, 1933.

The following documents are enclosed:

1. Confession of the accused

2. Voluntary statements by three witnesses:
   a) A garrison cleaner, Frau K.;
   b) Lieutenant P. of the Military Political Department;
   c) Gefreiter H. of the Political Service of Military Security.

The above-named witnesses will not be called to give evidence at the trial. Their statements shall be destroyed as soon as judgment has been passed, in accordance with Article 14 of the State Security Bill.

The entire matter is classified GEKADOS (Secret) and all documents pertaining to it shall be finally lodged with the RSHA, Prinz Albrecht Strasse 8, Berlin.

The preliminary investigation has been carried out by SD-Standartenführer Kriminalrat Paul Bielert.

(Sgd) F. WEYERSBERG
Prosecutor General

Lieutenant Ohlsen walked across to the window. He stared through the bars, through the gray, unwashed panes of glass, through to the unimaginable freedom that lay beyond. Seeing it in print for the first time, that monstrous request that he should be beheaded, he found himself suddenly unable to face the reality. It must surely be a hideous joke, one of the Gestapo's sick attempts at humor. At Torgau, he knew, it was frequently their pleasure to arrange for ten executions to be staged and only eight to be carried out. They worked on the not unreasonable assumption that by the time the last two men on the list had witnessed their companions' heads rolling into the basket, they would be willing to go to any lengths of collaboration to avoid the same fate for themselves. It was small comfort, but all he could think of.

That same day a letter from the Wehrmacht Kommandantur in Hamburg was sent to the Kommandantur at Altona:

Wehrmachtkommandantur, Hamburg

TOP SECRET

This correspondence must be read by two officers and then destroyed. Receipt must be confirmed by telephone.

Subject: Executions following Sentence of Death

It is anticipated that sentence of death will tomorrow be passed on the following four soldiers:

a) Infantry Oberleutnant Karl Heinz Berger of the 12th Grenadiers
b) Lieutenant Bernt Viktor Ohlsen of the 27th Tank Regiment
c) Oberfeldwebel Franz Gernerstadt of the 19th Artillery Regiment
d) Gefreiter Paul Baum of the 3rd Alpine Regiment.

Two of the above-mentioned will suffer death by shooting, the 76th Infantry Regiment to provide two firing squads, which shall comprise two Feldwebels and twelve men. A medical officer shall be present at the executions.

The two other accused shall suffer death by decapitation, and the 76th Infantry Regiment is instructed to call the executioner Röttger from Berlin to carry out the sentence, which shall take place in closed courtyard B of the garrison prison.

A minister of religion shall be present at the request of the accused.

It is the responsibility of the 76th Infantry Regiment to
provide the necessary four coffins.

The bodies shall be buried in the special cemetery, Dept.
12/31.

(Sgd) A. ZIMMERMANN
Oberstleutnant

Lieutenant Ohlsen was not to know it, but arrangements
for his execution had therefore been made well in advance,
even before the trial had started, even before the court had
passed sentence.

Humanitarianism was a quality unknown and unacknowl-
edged in the Third Reich, whose code of behavior was
based firmly upon a multitude of paragraphs and subpara-
graphs, and upon nothing so flimsy as humanity. The least
infringement of any one of these myriad paragraphs carried
a rigid penalty, taking no account either of the situation or
of the individual. The term "extenuating circumstances" was
altogether too vague for even a sub-subparagraph and was
therefore not recognized.

The room where the trials took place was as usual filled
from floor to ceiling. All the public benches were occupied
by soldiers, who came not for a vicarious thrill, nor through a
wish to learn, nor out of academic interest, but purely and
simply because they were ordered to be there. The witnessing of military trials was held by those in authority to
have a beneficial effect on servicemen.

Gefreiter Paul Baum of the 3rd Alpine Regiment, white
and terrified, was waiting to hear his fate. The court had
retired to deliberate.

The prosecutor rearranged his papers, preparing for the
next case. He had already lost interest in the trembling
Gefreiter.

Counsel for the defense sat playing with his gold pencil.
With his elbows on the table, he was twisting the lead up
and down, his thoughts far from the courtroom. He was
thinking of his mistress; or not so much of his mistress as of
the meal she had promised him that night; a meal of beef
and sauerkraut. Mistresses were a dime a dozen these days,
but meals of beef and sauerkraut were something of a
luxury.

A stenographer sucked the end of her pen and thoughtfully regarded the ashen Gefreiter—a sad, squat, peasant
type, with thick features and great red hands. She could

never sleep with a man like that. Not if all the rest were killed, she couldn't. She would sooner retain her virginity.

The peasant Gefreiter sat staring at the floor. He began to count the boards with his feet: condemned to death, not condemned; condemned to death, not condemned— He finished up with an unfavorable verdict and for a moment grew stiff with terror. Just in time, he remembered that there were more floorboards beneath the bench. He felt cautiously with his feet. Three of them—that made it "not condemned." Feeling slightly happier, he raised his head and looked across to the white-painted door in the corner of the court. Through that door would come the three judges when they had decided on his fate. He sat with his eyes screwed tightly shut, willing them to listen to the verdict of the floorboards.

The whole of the proceedings against this boy of eighteen had taken no longer than ten minutes. The president of the court had asked a few laconic questions. The prosecutor had spoken a great deal and counsel for the defense had contributed one speech of a few seconds' duration:

"Law and order must, of course, be maintained at whatever cost, without regard for human emotions or human frailty. Nevertheless, I would ask the court to show indulgence and understanding toward my client in this difficult situation in which he finds himself."

From the point of view of military ruling, the case against the Gefreiter was cut-and-dried. There were no loopholes, no grounds for argument, and counsel for the defense made his brief speech and sat down again to dream of his beef and sauerkraut.

The Gefreiter was growing too nervous to sit still. He shifted up and down the bench, clattering his feet, tearing at his fingernails, clearing his throat. Why didn't they come? Why didn't the white door open? How much longer would they keep him in suspense?

And then it occurred to him—if they were taking so long to decide, it could surely mean but one thing? They were unable to agree on his case. And where there was disagreement, there was hope. That was why there were three judges, to make sure that the decision did not rest solely upon the whims and fancies of one man. Each prisoner must be given a fair chance.

In their antechamber, the three judges sat back in their easy chairs drinking kirsch. Kriegsgerichtsrat Burgholz was

coming to the end of a very funny story. They had been
exchanging stories ever since they had retired to discuss the
case. But the case was hardly worth discussing and none of
them had even bothered to listen to the evidence. Their
verdict had been decided for them in advance.

After half a dozen glasses of kirsch, they reluctantly decided to return to the courtroom.

The white door opened.

The Gefreiter began shaking violently. The crowded
ranks of soldiers craned their heads for a better view.

The president and his two fellow judges, smelling strongly
of kirsch, seated themselves with due majesty behind
their horseshoe table. The president delivered their verdict: found guilty of desertion and sentenced to death by
shooting.

The Gefreiter swayed forward in a faint and was jerked
upright by the rough grip of a court Feldwebel.

The president calmly continued his speech, rejecting in
advance any appeal that might be made against either the
verdict or the sentence. He then patted his brow with a
perfumed handkerchief, threw a quick glance of indifference
at the condemned man and turned to the next case: Number
19 661/M.43H, the State versus Lieutenant Bernt Ohlsen.

The Gefreiter was led away and Lieutenant Ohlsen was
sent for. The stage management was good and the show was
being run with a precision to be proud of.

Obergefreiter Stever threw open the door of Ohlsen's cell
and called him out. "You're wanted!"

"Why? Is it time?" Lieutenant Ohlsen walked slowly to
the door, feeling as if his stomach had suddenly collapsed.

"That's it," said Stever cheerfully. "You're on next. Room
7, under Oberkriegsgerichtsrat Jeckstadt. He's a fat stinking
pig, if ever there was one," he added by way of a snippet
of interesting information. "He'll be one of the first to go
when the wheel's turned full circle."

Stever pushed Ohlsen along the corridor and down the
stairs, where he was taken in charge by two military
policemen outside the entrance to the courtroom. Stever
walked away, humming. Lieutenant Ohlsen was hand-
cuffed and marched off through the long tunnel that led
to room number 7. On their way they encountered the
Gefreiter, making the return journey. He was screaming
and struggling, and it required three men to hold him in
check.

"Will you pipe down and stop bawling?" shouted one of his guards irascibly. He fetched him a cuff on the ear. "Who the devil d'you think you're impressing, anyway? Certainly not me, I've seen far too much of it already. What the hell, you'll probably be far better off where you're going than stuck here with the rest of us!"

"Just think," put in another of them, twisting the Gefreiter's arm behind his back, "little Lord Jesus is probably all ready and waiting for you. Probably got a party going in your honor. What's he going to think when you turn up in this state? Bloody ungrateful if you ask me!"

The boy suddenly caught sight of Lieutenant Ohlsen, and guards notwithstanding, he fell to his knees and called out to him.

"Lieutenant! Help me! They want me to die, they're going to shoot me, I was only gone two days, I swear it was a mistake! It was a mistake, I didn't mean it, oh God, I didn't mean it, I didn't mean it! I'll do anything they want me to, I'll go to the Russian front, I'll learn how to fly a Stuka, I'll go down in a U-boat, I'll do anything, I swear I will! Oh, Mother of God," he babbled, tears making rivers down his cheeks, "Mother of God, help me, I don't want to die! *Heil* Hitler, *Heil* Hitler, *Heil* Hitler, I'll do anything they want me to, but let me live, please let me live!"

He lashed out with arms and legs and succeeded in throwing one of his guards to the floor. The other two closed in on him and he screamed penetratingly as he struggled.

"I'm a good National Socialist! I was in the Hitler Youth! *Heil* Hitler, *Heil* Hitler, oh, God, help me!"

He disappeared beneath three heavy bodies. There was the unpleasant sound of a head being thumped against the stone floor, and when the guards picked themselves up and continued on their way through the tunnel, they were dragging an unconscious Gefreiter behind them.

Lieutenant Ohlsen hesitated a moment and turned to watch.

"What's the matter with you?" One of his own guards jabbed him in the back, pushing him forward. "The court's not going to wait all day, you know."

Ohlsen shrugged his shoulders.

"Getting squeamish?" jeered the guard.

"Call it that if you like—but that was a child they were dragging along by his hair just now."

"So what? He was old enough to know what he was doing, wasn't he? They let one off, they got to let them all off, and before you knew it, the whole goddamn Army'd be up and away."

"I suppose so." Ohlsen turned to look gravely at one of the men. "Do you have any children of your own, Oberfeldwebel?"

"Sure I got children of my own. I got four of 'em. Three's in the Hitler Youth and one's at the front. SS regiment—Das Reich."

"I wonder how you'd feel if one day he was dragged out to be shot?"

The guard laughed. "A likely thing! He's an SS Untersturmführer. Safe as houses."

"Even houses fall down in wartime."

The man frowned. "What d'you mean by that remark?"

"Whatever you like."

"And suppose I don't like?"

"Please yourself." Ohlsen shook his head wearily. "All I know is, I can't stand to see them drag kids like that away to the slaughterhouse."

"Well, if I was you, pal, I'd save all your pity for yourself, because the way things are going, you're likely to need it." He nodded significantly and tapped the holster of his pistol. "And no talking once we get in there, see?"

Lieutenant Ohlsen took his place in the courtroom with an air of apparent indifference, and his trial began. Dr. Beckmann, the prosecutor, turned to him to ask whether or not he intended to plead guilty to the charges brought against him.

Lieutenant Ohlsen stared down at the floor. It was polished to a high gloss and he experimentally slid a foot across it to test whether it was slippery.

Slowly he raised his head and looked across at the three judges behind their horseshoe table. Two of them seemed to be asleep. The president, enthroned on his big red chair, was lost in contemplation of a fly buzzing around the lamp. Admittedly it was no ordinary, common or garden housefly. It was a cleg, or gadfly. A bloodsucking fly. Not very pretty to look at, but doubtless very interesting from an entomologist's point of view.

Lieutenant Ohlsen drew his gaze away from the gadfly and turned slowly toward the prosecutor.

"Herr Oberkriegsgerichtsrat," he began respectfully, "since

I've already signed a full confession for the secret police, your question is surely superfluous?"

Dr. Beckmann pinched his thin lips together in a sarcastic smile. He stroked a blue-veined hand caressingly over his pile of documents.

"Perhaps the prisoner will be so kind as to leave it to the court to decide whether or not a question is superfluous?"

"Oh, by all means," agreed Ohlsen, with a slight lift of the shoulders.

"Very well, then. Let us leave aside for the moment the crimes of which you are accused in the indictment." The little doctor turned and addressed the judges in a loud, high-pitched voice. "In the name of the Führer and of the German people, I beg leave to add to the list of crimes of which the prisoner is accused, those of desertion and cowardice in the face of the enemy!"

The two sleeping judges opened their eyes and looked around guiltily, dimly aware that they had missed something. The president gave up his contemplation of the gadfly.

Lieutenant Ohlsen sprang forward. "That's a lie! I've never been guilty of either!"

Dr. Beckmann picked up a sheet of paper and smiled slyly into it, sucking in his cheeks and making them more hollow than ever. This was the type of combat in which he excelled: a quick barb, a surprise attack, a well-placed arrow.

"I've never in my life even thought about desertion!" shouted Ohlsen.

Dr. Beckmann inclined his head. "Let us study the matter together. That is, after all, what we are here for, is it not? We are here to prove either your innocence or your guilt. If, of course, you are able to prove the accusation to be false, then you will be allowed to walk out of here a free man."

"Free?" murmured Ohlsen, raising a cynical eyebrow.

What was a free man? Had there ever been such a person, in his lifetime, in Germany? Certainly there was none now, in the Third Reich. From newborn babes to old men on their deathbeds, Germany was a nation of prisoners.

"Naturally," went on Dr. Beckmann, leaning menacingly across his table, "if you are proven guilty, your fate will be very different."

"Naturally," said Ohlsen.

The president nodded his head in approval.

Dr. Beckmann turned back to the judges. "With the court's permission, we will disregard the accusations contained in the original indictment in order to concentrate on the fresh charges that I have brought. These charges were made possible only this morning, when I received certain documents," he held up a bulky bundle, "from the Secret Police Special Service. The facts contained therein are quite clear, and if I may be allowed to question the prisoner for a few moments, I believe I shall be able to convince the court that there is no necessity for a preliminary investigation."

The president nodded again. "Very well. The court gives its permission. We shall disregard the charges in the indictment and you may proceed to question the prisoner."

Dr. Beckmann made a servile inclination and swung around to Lieutenant Ohlsen.

"On February 2, 1942, you were the officer commanding the 5th Company, 27th Tank Regiment? Is that correct?"

"Yes."

"Will you please tell the court where you were then fighting?"

"I will if I can remember." Ohlsen stared ahead, frowning, at the enormous photograph of Hitler behind the president's chair. Not a very inspiring sight. "It was probably somewhere near the Dnieper," he said at last. "But I couldn't swear to it. I've fought in so many places."

Dr. Beckmann tapped a thin finger on the table. "Somewhere near the Dnieper. That in fact is correct. Your division had been sent to the Vyazma-Rzhev area. You had received orders to take up a position with your company near Olenin, to the west of Rzhev. Are you able to remember?"

"Yes. The division was on the point of being surrounded. The 19th and 20th Russian Cavalry Divisions had outflanked us on the south, and more of them were coming up on the north."

"Thank you, thank you, thank you!" said Dr. Beckmann crisply. "The court is not in the least interested in hearing of the activities of the Russians. And as for your division being surrounded—" He looked up at the gallery, full of high-ranking and powerful officers, "since the division is still in existence, this seems to me a highly unlikely story."

A loud murmur was borne down from the gallery. It was,

of course, accepted teaching that no German armored division could ever be surrounded by the troops of an inferior nation such as the Russians. Doubt was therefore at once cast upon the veracity of Lieutenant Ohlsen's version of the facts. Dr. Beckmann smiled upward at his audience.

"Tell me, Lieutenant, are you able to recall that period of the war with any clarity?"

"Yes, certainly."

"Good. Let us see if we agree with each other. You had received an order, verbally, from your commanding officer Colonel von Lindenau, to occupy a position near Olenin because the enemy had at one point broken through and there was now a gap in the defenses. That gap, to be precise, was along the railway line two kilometers to the east of Olenin . . ."

"Which railway line?" asked one of the judges.

It was not of the least importance and he had no interest whatsoever in the answer, but it created a favorable impression if one asked a question every now and again.

"Which railway line?" repeated Dr. Beckmann, for once at a loss.

He tore furiously through his papers, muttering, "*Which* railway line?" to himself in tones of disgust and impatience.

Lieutenant Ohlsen watched him for a while. "Actually, it was the Rzhev-Nelidovo line," he then said helpfully.

Dr. Beckmann turned to him with an irritable gesture. "The prisoner will speak only when he is spoken to!" he snapped. He looked toward the judges and bowed. "It was the Rzhev-Nelidovo line," he told them, and shrugged his shoulders. "A branch line merely."

"Excuse me," said Lieutenant Ohlsen, "but in point of fact, it was the main line from Moscow to Riga."

A suspicion of color entered the doctor's pale pinched cheeks. "I have already explained to the prisoner," he said, "that he may speak only when spoken to."

"Just as you wish, but I thought we should have the facts right."

"We do have the facts right! The line in question may have seemed of great importance to you, but in our eyes it is totally insignificant."

"Nevertheless," persisted Ohlsen, "it's a pretty outstanding branch line that has two tracks and runs for about a thousand kilometers."

"We are not interested in how far it runs nor in how many

tracks it has," replied the doctor, tapping his documents. "If I say it is a branch line, then rest assured that that is what it is. You're in Germany now, you know; not in some Soviet bog. And here in Germany we have very different standards from those obtaining in Russia. But let us pass over this wretchedly unimportant railway line and return to the facts! You received an order from your commanding officer to take up your position to the east of Olenin, and you were told that nothing—I repeat *nothing*, neither God nor the devil nor the entire Red Army—was to shift you from that point. You were to dig yourselves in there and make sure of your position both in front and on both flanks. Is that correct?"

Ohlsen hunched his shoulders and muttered some words too low to be heard.

"Yes or no!" cried Dr. Beckmann. "Will the prisoner please answer!"

"Yes," said Ohlsen.

Dr. Beckmann smiled triumphantly.

"Very well. So having established agreement on the orders you received, we may now go on with the tale in order to give the court an example of your extraordinary cowardice and failure to do your duty. Your company was fighting as infantry, but it was by no means an ordinary company that you commanded. It was a company which had been very much reinforced—you may correct me if I am wrong. Obeying written instructions, a section of tanks fitted with antitank guns had been sent to you, and also a section of sappers armed with both light and heavy flamethrowers. Perhaps you would care to tell the court in your own words what the exact strength of your company was at that time?"

"Certainly," said Ohlsen. "We had two hundred and fifty men in addition to the reinforcements you just mentioned. Say three hundred men in all."

"And I think no one would call that a small company," murmured Dr. Beckmann. "On the contrary, rather on the strong side, would you not say?"

"I wouldn't argue with you," agreed Ohlsen.

"Suppose you tell us something of the armaments you had?"

Lieutenant Ohlsen sighed. He vaguely began to see now where the prosecutor's questions were leading him. He looked across at the judges. One had his eyes closed again, and the president was drawing ranks of dinosaurs on his blotting pad.

"We had two antitank guns, 7.5 cm., two mortars of 8 cm., and three of 5 cm.—they were Russian, by the way. Then we had two heavy machine guns, four heavy flamethrowers, four light flamethrowers. All section leaders also had submachine guns. Some men had rifles. And the sappers, of course, had mines and grenades and that sort of thing."

Dr. Beckmann listened to this recital with his head on one side.

"I congratulate you. You have a very remarkable memory. That is exactly how your company was armed. I have only one comment to make, and that is that your allocation of submachine guns was very much higher than average. You had over one hundred, in fact, and yet despite this you behaved in a manner which can only be described as gross cowardice."

"That is not true," muttered Ohlsen.

"Oh?" Dr. Beckmann raised an eyebrow. "I beg to differ, Lieutenant. Who was it who gave the order for the company to retreat? Was it one of your men? A noncommissioned officer? Or was it you yourself, the head of the company?"

"It was I who gave the order," admitted Ohlsen, "but only because by that time the company had been wiped out."

"Wiped out?" repeated Dr. Beckmann. "You have a very bizarre notion of the meaning of that expression, Lieutenant! In my book, it is used to signify annihilation—total destruction. And yet your presence here today proves beyond any possible shadow of doubt that the company most certainly was *not* annihilated! And your orders, Lieutenant—if I may recapitulate a moment—your orders were quite definite, were they not? Neither God nor the devil nor the entire Red Army . . ."

Lieutenant Ohlsen looked without much hope toward the judges. "Do I have the permission of the court to relate the events that took place on February 2, 1942?"

The sleeping judge woke up and looked about him in alarm; things were happening again and he was not aware of them. The president finished off the last of his dinosaurs and glanced at his watch. He was hungry and bored. He had sat through too many of these trials, they were trivial and irrelevant and a total waste of his judicial intelligence. It was high time such matters were dealt with

backstage, by the office staff, without going through all
this absurd rigmarole in court. And as for Beckmann—he
glared at him over the horseshoe table. What did the fool
think he was playing at, dragging the case on into his lunch
hour in this tedious fashion? All this nonsense about cowardice in the face of the enemy. Nobody wanted high
drama when the outcome of the trial had been settled beforehand.

"You have the court's permission," he grudgingly allowed.
"But kindly be brief."

"Thank you. I'll make it as short as possible." Ohlsen
looked back again at Beckmann. "After four days and nights
of continuous fighting, my company of three hundred men
had been reduced to nineteen. All our heavy guns had
been destroyed. We had run out of ammunition. Only two
light machine guns were still in working order. It would
have been suicide to hang on with nineteen men and no
weapons. We were fighting at odds of five hundred to one.
Both before and behind us were the Russians, and we
were under constant attack. To have stayed on when there
wasn't a hope in hell would have been an act of lunacy
and an act of sabotage—throwing away nineteen lives to no
purpose at all, when they could still be of value to Germany."

"An interesting hypothesis," admitted Dr. Beckmann. "But
may I interrupt you one moment, Lieutenant. The order of
the day from the Führer himself for all troops in the
Vyazma area was to fight until the last man and the last
bullet, in order to stop the advance of the Soviets. And
you—you, a mere lieutenant—you dare to call that an act
of lunacy and sabotage? You dare to insinuate that our
Führer, who is under the direct protection of God, is a
lunatic? You dare to sit in judgment upon him? You, who
are so insignificant that your life could be extinguished this
very moment and no one in Germany would even notice, you
dare to set yourself up against the Führer and countermand
his orders?"

Lieutenant Ohlsen watched with a mild and detached
curiosity as this self-contained and precise little lawyer
worked himself into a rage of fanatical self-righteousness on
the Führer's behalf.

"Herr Oberkriegsgerichtsrat," he at last calmly inter-
polated, "I can assure you that I had no intention of implying
that the Führer was a lunatic, nor of countermanding his

orders, which I imagined were to be taken as a form of encouragement to the troops rather than to be followed literally down to the last man and the last bullet. When I said an act of lunacy, I was referring to myself. I was taught that an officer should use his own initiative where the situation calls for it, and in my opinion it called for it then. You have to remember, if you will, that our position had altered radically since Colonel von Lindenau first told me to hold the . . ."

"We are not interested in what your position had or had not done!" cried Beckmann. "We are interested only in the fact that you were specifically ordered to fight to the last man and yet you pulled out with nineteen! Why did you not get in touch with your regiment?"

"Because the whole combat area was in such a shambles that we weren't able to contact the regiment again until four days later."

"Thank you." The weary voice of the president droned into the court. "I think we have heard enough. The accused has admitted giving the order to retreat from his position near Olenin and the branch railway. The charge of cowardice and desertion is quite clear." He looked directly at Ohlsen and tapped on the table with his pencil. "Do you have anything else you wish to say?"

"Yes, I do!" rejoined Ohlsen heatedly. "If you will take the trouble to look in my papers, you will see that I have received a number of decorations in recognition of deeds requiring courage over and above the call of duty. I submit that this is proof in itself that I am not guilty of cowardice. On the occasion we were talking of, I was not concerned with my own safety but with that of my few remaining men. Nineteen of us—and 270 of our comrades lying dead in the snow all round us. Many of those 270 had shot themselves rather than fall into the hands of the Russians. Of the nineteen that were left, every single one was wounded— some badly. We had run out of ammunition, we'd run out of food. We were eating handfuls of snow because there was nothing else to slake our thirst. Several of the men were suffering hideously from frostbite. I was wounded in three different places myself, and yet I was one of the more fortunate ones. Some of the others couldn't even walk without being supported. And because I valued their lives, I gave the order to retreat. We destroyed everything of value before we left. Nothing fell into the hands of the Russians.

We blew up the railway line in several places—and I repeat, it was not a branch line but the main line from Moscow to Riga. We also planted mines before we pulled out."

Dr. Beckmann laughed sardonically. "A likely story! But whether it's true or not, the fact remains: you disobeyed an order to stay at your post and you are therefore guilty of cowardice and of desertion."

Lieutenant Ohlsen bit his lip and remained silent, realizing the futility of further protestation. His eyes flickered briefly over the crowded courtroom, but he felt it to be hostile toward him, and he knew—as he had known from the beginning—that the verdict had been delivered long before the case had even come to trial. In the back row of spectators he saw a thin sliver of a man, dressed all in black with a red carnation in his buttonhole: Kriminalrat Paul Bielert, come to witness his final downfall.

The president had also caught sight of Bielert. The flint eyes behind the spectacles flickered and danced, sweeping the court like twin radar beams. The man was openly smoking a cigarette, despite all the notices forbidding this. The president leaned forward to tap on the horseshoe table and have him arrested, but just in time one of his fellow judges sent him a warning look and whispered a name in his ear. The president frowned and sat back again, breathing heavily and indignantly and not daring to lift a finger.

Dr. Beckmann had also remarked the arrival of Bielert. He developed a sudden series of nervous twitches, awkwardly shuffling his feet and dropping his papers to the floor. It always bode ill when the chief of IV/2A appeared on the scene. The man was dangerous and you never knew where or when he was likely to strike next. And was there anyone who could stand up and say, in all confidence, "I have nothing to fear"? Dr. Beckmann certainly could not.

There was an affair he had been mixed up in four years ago—but surely no one could now unearth the details of it? He had been uncertain at the time as to the wisdom of it—but Bielert would hardly go digging that far back? And besides, they were all dead except him. All those who had been in it with him—even Frau Rosen had been hanged in the end. There was no one save himself who could know anything of it. Only you never could tell with Paul Bielert. Four years ago he had been a mere Kriminalsekretär of no importance whatsoever. Who could have prophesied that he would rise to such heights in so short a time? Of course, the man had had the good sense to be a friend of Heydrich's. It had been a shock, discovering that.

Dr. Beckmann pulled out his handkerchief and with trembling hand mopped at his brow. On its way back to a pocket his hand paused involuntarily to clutch at his throat. Dr. Beckmann stared in rabbitlike fascination across the court and into Bielert's eyes. A cold seizure took hold of his spine. What was the man doing here? Why had he come? They were trying no one of importance, every case was straightforward and routine. So why was he here? In whom was he interested?

Dr. Beckmann shook himself out of his petrified stupor, put his handkerchief away and attempted to square his hunched shoulders. Who was the rude uneducated little man, after all? No one. Simply a no one. A rat that had crawled out of a sewer and still had the odor of putrefaction clinging to him. This was a court of Prussian law and he, Dr. Beckmann, was an attorney. And a former university lecturer. A respectable citizen, ranking far above Bielert in the social and intellectual hierarchy.

He decided on an impulse to take the bull by the horns. Forcing his lips into what seemed to him a smile, though anyone else might well have taken it for an arrogant leer, he nodded at Bielert across the courtroom. Bielert stared back coldly at him, eyes glittering, narrow lips compressed, cigarette smoke curling from his nostrils. Dr. Beckmann slowly froze. With the arrogant leer still painted meaninglessly on his lips, he turned back to the judges' table. He could feel the hard eyes boring into his neck.

He realized suddenly that the court was waiting for him to speak. He sprang forward and shouted defiantly, determined to demonstrate his patriotism beyond any possible shadow of doubt.

"I ask the court that the accused be sentenced to death by decapitation under Article 197B and Article 91B of the Military Penal Code!"

Dr. Beckmann sat down and began to search industriously through his papers. Heaven knew what he was searching for—composure perhaps. He wished only to impress Bielert with his devotion to duty.

The president rose and walked with his fellow judges out of the court and back to the antechamber. They seated themselves comfortably around the table, where a thoughtful minion had left a carafe of red wine. The president pushed it to one side and called for beer. Someone else wanted sausages, and sausages were accordingly grilled and delivered on a tray with cutlery, plates and mustard.

"Well—" The president stuffed his mouth with hot sausage and swilled it around with beer. "In my opinion we should grant the request of the prosecutor and have done with it."

"I couldn't agree more," said Kriegsgerichtsrat Burgholz, mopping beer off his chin.

There was a moment's comparative silence while they all concentrated on their sausages. The youngest of the three judges, Kriegsgerichtsrat Ring, made a halfhearted attempt to speak up on behalf of Lieutenant Ohlsen.

"I confess I have my doubts about the decapitation," he murmured. "It seems unnecessarily harsh, and it's hardly an aesthetic way to kill a man. Besides, we should surely take into account the fact that the prisoner has never previously shown any inclination toward cowardice. In view of his decorations and so forth, could we not perhaps show a certain amount of clemency and change the sentence to death by shooting?"

The president narrowed his eyes as he held up his beer mug and stared into its depths. "I think not," he said. "You must remember it's not only cowardice the man's guilty of. He has also plotted against the Führer and made dubious jokes about him. If we allowed that sort of thing to go unpunished, I shudder to think what the outcome would be."

Burgholz cleared his throat and affected an air of indifference. "What—ah—what were these dubious jokes, anyway?" he asked. He picked up his fork and drew furrows through a pool of mustard. "They can't have been so very bad, surely?"

"That is a matter of opinion," said the president gravely. He looked over his shoulder toward the door, opened his file of papers, selected a sheet and pushed it secretively across the table to his colleagues.

Ring was the first to laugh. He smiled, and then he sniggered, and finally he threw back his head and bellowed. Burgholz at first attempted a more suitable reaction, drawing his brows together and pulling down the corners of his mouth, but Ring bent forward and pointed out one particular gem and Burgholz was soon laughing so much his belly bumped against the edge of the table. Even the president gave a sly smile behind his hand. Ring beat in a frenzy on his thighs. Burgholz overturned a full mug of beer. The tears rolled down their cheeks.

"Upsetting your beer is surely not as amusing as all that, gentlemen?" With reproof in his voice, the president stretched across and took back the offending sheet of paper. The other two rearranged their faces into lines more becoming a judge.

"Of course not, of course not," murmured Burgholz, blowing his nose.

"This document," continued the president, "is an outrage of obscenity and propaganda at its most dangerous and vile. In my opinion it is our bounden duty to accept the prosecutor's plea for death by decapitation. An example must be made of this man. We must act according to the best interests of the state, and not according to the emotional dictates of the heart."

And picking up his pen, he wrote the word "Decapitation" at the foot of a document and signed his name with legal flourish. He pushed pen and document across the table to his colleagues. Burgholz signed at once, without even pause for thought. Ring hesitated, drummed his fingers on the table, frowned and sighed and finally with great reluctance wrote his name. Each letter seemed wrung from him by force. The president watched him with growing dislike. This man Ring was coming daily to be a bigger thorn in his flesh. He would have to see what he could do about having him transferred to a more dangerous theater of war. The Eastern front perhaps.

The document signed, they relaxed in their chairs and drank a few more beers, ate a few more sausages. Burgholz opened his mouth and gave a gentle, rolling belch. He looked up in mild surprise as he did so, staring wonderingly at his two colleagues as if trying to decide which of them was the culprit.

The president called in the clerk of the court and dictated the verdict and sentence with all the solemnity the occasion demanded. The three judges then picked themselves up and proudly goosestepped through the door and back to the court, followed by the clerk at a respectful distance. The press-ganged audience at once shot to its feet. Only Paul Bielert remained seated, leaning against the wall and smoking.

The president looked across at him and scowled. The

insolence of the man was beyond all credibility. But the
Gestapo were full of their own importance these days. It
was their hour of glory and they were making the most of
it in a power-crazed frenzy of terrorism. Their hour would
soon pass, reflected the president as he seated himself. The
Russians and the Americans were stronger than anyone
had ever suspected, and the time was not far distant when
the Gestapo would find their power evaporated and themselves in the position of their present victims. One day,
thought the president, rolling a hand back and forth across
the table as if he were kneading a breadcrumb, one day he
would have the pleasure of condemning Paul Bielert to a
death by decapitation. It never crossed his mind that he
himself might by that time be removed from the bench.
Who, after all, could attach any blame to a judge? A judge
did not make the laws, he only carried them out.

He looked again at Bielert; this time there was a thin,
sarcastic smile on the man's lips. With an uneasy frown, the
president turned away. He began speaking very quickly, in
a flurry of words.

"In the name of the Führer Adolf Hitler and of the
German people, I hereby pronounce the verdict of the
court in the case of the accused, Lieutenant Bernt Viktor
Ohlsen of the 27th Tank Regiment." He paused a moment
and took a deep gulp of air. Bielert's glassy eyes were still
on him, and for a moment the president had a queasy
sensation at the pit of his stomach, as if—absurd idea!—
it was his own sentence he was pronouncing. "After considering the matter, the court considers that the prisoner is
guilty on all counts in the original indictment and is in
addition guilty on the extra charges of cowardice and desertion. He is therefore dishonored and shall be sentenced
to death by decapitation. All his worldly goods shall be
seized by the state, and the expenses of the trial shall be at
the prisoner's own charge. His name shall henceforth be
expunged from the registers. The body shall be buried in
an unnamed grave. *Heil* Hitler!"

The president turned gravely to the condemned man,
standing stiffly to attention before him.

"Does the prisoner wish to say anything?" He repeated
the question three times, with no response from Lieutenant
Ohlsen, whereupon he shrugged his shoulders and gabbled
out the statutory advance rejection of any appeal that might

be contemplated. "All right." He nodded to the Feldwebel standing at Ohlsen's side. "Take the prisoner away."

As Lieutenant Ohlsen was being marched back through the tunnel, they met the next prisoner coming down. Twenty-three minutes later the president pronounced his fourth sentence of death that day and left the courtroom. He exchanged his judicial robes for his pearl-gray uniform and made his way home to a dinner of tomato soup and boiled cod. Four death sentences. It was raining outside, a persistent drizzle, and he had passed four death sentences and was going home to eat tomato soup and boiled cod. A typical day in court. Four death sentences. A persistent drizzle. Tomato soup and cod. The president buttoned his coat and walked briskly toward the waiting car.

Oberfeldwebel Stever was waiting for Lieutenant Ohlsen down in the cell block. The heavy door clanged shut behind them. Stever groaned as he pushed back the bolts.

"Well, so what's it to be?" he asked as he straightened up and they began walking along the corridor. "Another case for the butcher? That makes the third today, and the one that's just gone down there, I guess he'll be the fourth. Not that that's anything to get excited about. A month ago we had sixteen in one day—" He looked at Ohlsen and grinned. "Don't take it to heart, Lieutenant. It's happened to better men than you—and we all have to come to it sooner or later, one way or another. And you won't be the first or the last to go like that. And if the padre's to be believed, it's a better world you're going to and Jesus will be there to meet you."

"Well?" Ohlsen turned to look at him. "Is the padre to be believed or isn't he?"

"You know more about that than I do," Stever hunched his shoulders uncomfortably. I haven't really thought about it too much. I suppose when the time comes I'll have to. But as for all this stuff about Jesus and suchlike—well, yeah, I suppose it's always possible." He scratched his head and frowned. "You can't say you don't believe in it, see, just in case it does turn out to be true. But the old padre, he believes in it all right." Stever paused to assume a suitable expression and a priestlike voice. " 'M'm—pray and the Lord will hear you,' he says. 'M'm—the Lord will receive you—' he always says 'm'm' before everything. They call him M'm-Müller in the prison. A filthy old shit, mind you—always blowing his nose in his cassock—but I suppose he knows what he's doing."

"I hope so," said Lieutenant Ohlsen quietly, "because I intend to say my prayers with him."

"Jeez!" Stever cocked an eyebrow. "Not that I blame you. I mean, no sense taking chances, right?"

"It's not a question of taking chances." Ohlsen shook his head and smiled. "I happen to believe in it."

"Jeez!" said Stever again. "What are you, if you don't mind my asking? RC?"

"I'm a Protestant."

"Well—" They reached the door of Ohlsen's cell and Stever flung it open, "it's all one to me, come to that. The minute I set foot in a church I get the feeling they're all just a bunch of great babbling idiots. Don't do nothing for me—know what I mean? Still, that's not to say that when my turn comes I won't feel a bit different.'

"Very likely," agreed Ohlsen with a faint smile.

He walked across to the window and looked out between the bars at the falling gray drizzle.

"Look here," said Stever consolingly, "you're okay for the rest of today. They won't have set it up yet. They have to get the old so-and-so down from Berlin and I don't think he's even arrived. In any case, he has to have a gander at you first—work out how he's going to—" Stever trailed into silence and demonstrated with an imaginary ax above his head. "Know what I mean? It's a skilled job, after all. Not something anybody can do. Not if they want a good clean cut, that is. And there's the padre'll have to come and see you as well. It won't be old Müller, though, he's the RC. It'll be the other one. Dunno his name, but he'll be along all right, that's for sure. Then there's the nosh. They'll give you a good nosh, give you a good send-off—" He winked. "Don't want to meet St. Peter with a rumbling belly, do you?" He raised his hand in a farewell gesture and closed the door behind him.

Lieutenant Ohlsen began a distracted pacing of the cell. Five steps one way, five steps another. He tried walking the diagonals. He tried walking around the perimeter. He walked in squares, he walked in circles, he traced geometrical patterns all over the place.

The hours slowly passed. It was still raining when he heard the garrison clock strike six. He braced himself for a visit from the executioner any moment.

All night he listened to the striking of the garrison clock. The hour, the quarter hour, the half hour, the three quarters; the hour, the quarter hour, the half hour, the three quarters; the hour, the . . .

Despairingly he began thumping his head against the wall. No use listening to clocks, no use thinking, no use anything any more. His life was over. Let them come and take him when they liked, and the sooner the better. He felt that spiritually he had died on earth already.

Morning came and prison life pursued its normal course. A company of young recruits swung past his cell, singing at the tops of their voices, and Lieutenant Ohlsen watched them go by and tried to remember if he himself had ever been young. He knew he must have been, everyone was young once, and yet he couldn't remember it. Before the war it must have been. He tried to work it out in his head. He was born in 1917, and now it was 1943. He was twenty-six. Twenty-six didn't sound very old when he said it aloud, but it certainly felt very old.

They fetched him from his cell for the exercise period. He was treated differently now. He wore the red badge of a condemned man on his breast and he took his exercise with the other condemned men, fourteen of them, marching endlessly in circles. They all had red badges, but some had a green stripe across them, which meant they were to be hanged, and others had a white stripe, which meant they were to be shot. Some had a black spot in the middle. The black spots were due for decapitation.

While the condemned men were marching in circles, Stever was standing at the door of the prison, whistling. It was a faint approximation of a dance tune he had heard at the Zillertal. With one finger he beat out the measure on the butt of his rifle. *"Du hast Glück bei den Frauen, bel ami . . ."* ("You're lucky with women, my friend . . .")

After a while, even Stever realized that the tune he was whistling had parted company with the tune he had heard at the Zillertal. He looked at the exercise party and his whistling abruptly changed course. *"Liebe Kameraden, heute sind wir rot, morgen sind wir tot."* ("Dear friends, today we're fine, tomorrow we die.")

The prisoners broke into a trot. Single file around the courtyard, three paces between each man. Hands clasped behind the neck. Let them have no chance of communication before they died.

Stever suddenly took an interest in the proceedings. He slammed his PM firmly against his shoulder and bawled at the top of his voice, "Get a move on, you lazy bastards! Pick your feet up, put some vim into it!"

He encouraged the men passing by at that particular moment with sharp jabs in the ribs from his PM. The prisoners picked their feet up and began running. Some of them inadvertently shortened the gap between them and the man in front.

"Keep your distance!" screamed Stever, flourishing his PM above his head. "What do you think this is, a reunion party?"

The PM came crashing down on the nearest head. The condemned men quickened their pace and kept their distance. Stever began beating the rhythm with his foot.

"Out of step! Out of step!" he shrieked. "Watch the beat, damn you! No use running hell for leather like a pack of mad dogs, you'll never make it back—and who knows? Some of you might be reprieved at the last minute and then you'll need to be in shape if you're to survive in a disciplinary company—work you like hell there! One two three, one two three, one two three—keep it up there! No flagging!"

Several of the prisoners had turned their heads to look at him, the last despairing gleam of hope flickering even now in their eyes. Was Stever tantalizing them or could he have heard something? There was such a shortage of manpower, it could be that the country was no longer able to afford executions. Two or three divisions could already have been formed from the number of men that had been killed for crimes against the state . . .

"Eyes front, don't kid yourselves!" bawled Stever. "Germany can manage without . . ."

He broke off in some confusion as Stahlschmidt appeared and took up a position by his side.

"What are you shouting about? Are you chatting with the prisoners? Are any of these men talking?" He turned to watch them running past, and suddenly shot out an arm and pointed at one of them. "That man there! He was speaking! I saw his lips move! Bring him to me, Sergeant!"

Obergefreiter Braun, standing guard with his rifle, waded into the circle of running men and collared an Oberstleutnant who had the white mark of the firing squad on his chest. Stahlschmidt gave him a few sharp cuts across the back of the neck with his riding crop and pushed him back again.

"Swine!" yelled Stever. "Get a move on, keep your legs up, keep your distance! What do you think this is—musical chairs?"

"Obergefreiter," Stahlschmidt shook his head, "you have simply no idea. Just watch me, and perhaps you'll learn something." He swaggered into the middle of the ring, cracked his riding whip and opened and closed his mouth a few times, as if testing the mechanism. At length a fierce, strangulated shout filled the air. "Prisoneeeers! Haaaalt! Form twos!"

The prisoners fell over themselves in their eagerness to obey the order. Stahlschmidt flexed his knees a few times. It was good to be a Stabsfeldwebel. He wouldn't be anything else, not even if they offered him the rank of general. He had had every grade of prisoner pass through his hands save a Stabsfeldwebel. It seemed to him, therefore, by a logical process of deduction, that Stabsfeldwebels were in some way exempt from the punishments meted out to more ordinary mortals. Even if that matter of the two visitors on the forged pass was ever brought back into the light of day—but no, that was not possible. Bielert surely had more important matters to occupy his mind.

Stahlschmidt opened his mouth and shouted again. The prisoners began to march forward in a rigid double line, their heads turned to the left. They marched like this for nearly ten minutes, until one of their number fainted. They then went on marching for another five minutes on exactly the same course, back and forth over the limp body.

"Obergefreiter," said Stahlschmidt casually before he left, "if that man hasn't recovered by the time the exercise period's finished, I shall expect you to do something about it."

"Yes, sir."

Stahlschmidt walked away, leaving his subordinate with an unconscious prisoner on his hands. The man in fact came to his senses a few minutes later and stood leaning against the wall vomiting blood. Stever looked at him angrily. Why couldn't he take his punishment like everyone else? Why did he have to crack up at the last minute? It seemed likely that for once Stahlschmidt had gone too far. The man was a Gestapo prisoner, and the Gestapo were sensitive over their prisoners. They didn't object to anyone having a bit of fun, but there would be hell to pay if one of their men died before he could be executed. Herr Bielert was most punctilious over such matters. Stever had heard it said that he had once arrested the entire staff of Lübeck Garrison prison for a similar mishap. And Stahlschmidt had already shit his copy book once over the business of the forged pass.

Stever watched the prisoner vomiting for the fourth or fifth time and wondered if it might not be a good idea to pay a visit to Herr Bielert. Tell him a few of the facts about Stahlschmidt. After all, none of it was Stever's fault and it would be grossly unfair if any of the blame should fall on his shoulders. He, after all, was nothing but an Obergefreiter, and Obergefreiters only carried out orders.

The following Sunday, Lieutenant Ohlsen heard the sounds of hammering in the courtyard, and two or three hours later Stever paid him a visit. He went straight to the window and began conscientiously to test each bar. He winked at Ohlsen. "Just checking," he said. "Just in case you're thinking of sawing your way through them."

"With what?" asked Ohlsen.

"Who knows?" said Stever darkly. "Prisoners get up to some very odd tricks."

"Has anyone ever actually succeeded in cutting his way out?"

"Not yet, but there's always got to be a first one, hasn't there? And I don't want that first one to be in *my* block. They can do what they damn well like in anyone else's, but not in mine. Here—" He pulled out two cigarettes, lit them both and handed one to Ohlsen. "Hold it down low, so no nosey parker looking through the door can see it. I don't mind risking my life for any poor bastard that's going to make the long journey, but I don't see any point in asking for trouble—get me? And there would be, if they caught you at it. Not supposed to fraternize with the prisoners, that's orders."

Lieutenant Ohlsen lay down on his bed and smoked his contraband cigarette. Stever looked out of the window into the courtyard.

"Hear that racket going on out there? You know what they're doing? Had a look, have you? You can't see much from here, of course, but I daresay you can make a pretty good guess."

"Mm-hm." Ohlsen shook his head, wearily.

Stever grinned. He made a quick, decisive chopping gesture across the back of his neck.

"They're getting it ready. Party of sappers out there putting it up—not just in your honor, of course. There's ten of 'em due for it altogether. All going off on the same day. They usually do it like that. Wait until there's a whole bunch, it saves money. They have to get the executioner down from Berlin, see. Him and his team. They figure it ain't worth bringing 'em down more than once a month." Stever turned back to the window. "They brought the coffins today as well; nothing fancy, but not bad. Not at all bad. Nothing to worry about on *that* score. And the baskets. They brought them too."

"Baskets?" queried Ohlsen.

"Yeah—for the heads."

There was a moment's silence, and then the lieutenant gave a rather ghastly smile. His face was white and his lips seemed almost purple. "So they're putting it up, are they? They're putting it up at last."

"Yeah, but that doesn't necessarily mean it'll be today they'll call for you," said Stever in rallying tones. "I remember one time, they put the thing up and it stayed up for two months without nothing happening. That was on account of the SD not agreeing with what they said at the trial. Judges wanted to let the guy off and the SD was out for blood. They got him in the end, of course. They always do. It was a colonel, I remember. Peppery old. He was in this same cell as you've got—No. 9. We always keep this one for people like you."

"Like me?"

"Well—you know." Stever smiled apologetically. "The ones that have had it in advance, see?"

"You mean you already know what the verdict's going to be when a prisoner first comes here? Even before he's had his trial?"

Stever glanced around the cell, looked over his shoulder, peered out of the window again and moved confidentially close to Ohlsen. "I oughtn't to tell you, it's something I'm not officially supposed to know myself. But I don't imagine you'll be with us very much longer, so—" He winked. "Just keep it under your hat. When a prisoner's delivered to us from the Gestapo, we get his papers as well. And down at the bottom, on the left-hand side, there's a little mark. The judge has a duplicate set with the same little mark on it.

And all the little marks mean something special, see? In your case, the little mark meant—" Again he went through his execution mime. "The Gestapo had already decided what they wanted, so we knew what was going to happen to you before ever you went for trial."

"And suppose the court had decided differently?"

Stever shook his head. "They hardly ever do. Not worth their while. Wouldn't get them anywhere."

"No, I suppose it wouldn't," agreed Ohlsen bitterly.

"Mind you," said Stever, "we don't leave none of these papers lying around. Anything secret, it goes up in smoke the minute it's finished with. Even carbon paper. Even typewriter ribbons. They're all destroyed. And as far as I'm concerned, I don't know anything anyway. I tell you," he nodded his head sagely, "if ever the time comes when this place falls into enemy hands—and I guess it will, sooner or later—I got it all worked out what I'm going to say. Me and the Vulture, we been over it together several times—I'm only an Obergefreiter, I don't know nothing, I just did what I was told to do. Which, of course, is true," said Stever virtuously. "And I defy anyone to say it isn't . . ."

He sat down on the bed beside the lieutenant and jabbed him in the ribs.

"What's it matter which side you're on? So long as they pay you good and you don't have to work too hard. I got a real cushy job here, and I bet the enemy'll be glad to keep me on when they take over—I mean, they won't have enough of their own men to keep the place going, they'll need people like me, stands to reason. And so long as they pay me, what do I care? So long as they pay me enough to have a screw whenever I feel like it—" He nodded and winked again. "You should see the babe I got at the moment! She not only knows a thing or two, she's got real hot pants into the bargain—go on all night if you let her. And do it just about any way you fancy—sit on you, give you a blow, you name it, she'll do it. Talk about the Kama Sutra, it's got nothing on her!"

He licked his lips and glanced sideways to see if he was whetting the prisoner's appetite, but Lieutenant Ohlsen appeared not even to be listening. Stever stood up, scowling. He objected to wasting his efforts.

"All right," he said, "if you don't appreciate my conversation, I'll take it elsewhere and leave you to talk to yourself." He walked to the door, adding, "You'll soon get pissed off with your own company."

There was still no response. Stever left the cell as noisily as he could, slamming the door behind him and rattling his keys. He peered in through the spyhole, but Lieutenant Ohlsen was sitting in the same position as before. He seemed not even to have noticed Stever's exit.

On the following Monday morning, Major von Rotenhausen paid an official visit to read out their sentences to the various condemned men. He trembled nervously throughout, twisting one foot around the other and pinching his thighs together as if he needed desperately to relieve himself. At his elbows stood Stever and Greinert, PMs at the ready. Major von Rotenhausen had a deep-seated dread of violent outbursts from the prisoners, and he was not a man who believed in putting on a brave front at the possible expense of his own safety.

Shortly before midday, a large, fishy eye appeared at the spyhole of cell No. 9 and stared long and calculatingly at the occupant. It remained there for almost ten minutes, and then silently removed itself.

An hour later Stever came on his rounds and stopped for a chat.

"The executioner's here," he cheerfully informed Ohlsen. "He's already had a look at you. Do you want to see his axes? He's brought three of 'em with him, they're in one of the cells up the corridor. Great big sharp things, make a cutthroat razor look like a kid's toy. He keeps them in special leather scabbards. The Vulture's already had them out and played with them. He's got a thing about knives and axes. Anything that cuts. He's dying to have a go at someone's neck."

"The padre hasn't been round yet," said Ohlsen. "They can't do anything until he's been."

"Don't worry, he'll be here. Not even the Prussians are that bad. They wouldn't send a man off without letting him say his prayers first."

"But when do you think he'll come?" insisted Ohlsen.

"Soon. He always rings up first to check if he's needed, and then he arrives about two hours afterward. I don't know whether he's called yet or not. Probably not. I think he's out blessing some troops that are going off to the front. Something like that." Stever laughed reflectively. "Funny, isn't it?

Priests and chiropodists, they got more work than they can
cope with just now. Before the war, nobody wanted to
know. Now it seems people can't live without 'em."

"Or die without them," murmured Ohlsen.

That evening, the long, wailing cry of a human soul in
torment echoed around the building. The prisoners woke up
shuddering in their cells. The guards either cursed or
crossed themselves, according to their temperament and be-
liefs. The cry rose and fell, dropped to a moan, then
gathered force again and became a slow shriek of mental
agony. Seconds later, Stahlschmidt appeared on the scene.
There was the sound of blows. The wailing ceased and an
uneasy calm descended on the prison.

The priest arrived next morning at half-past ten. He was
a small, bent man, with a receding chin and a mouth like a
goat, mild blue eyes that swam in pools of excess liquid, and
a nose that had a constant trembling pearl at the end of it.
He had forgotten his Bible and had to use the one that belonged to the cell. But he brought some artificial flowers
wrapped in pretty paper and a small figure of Jesus wearing
a somewhat crumpled crown of thorns.

Outside the cell stood Stahlschmidt and Stever. Stahlschmidt had his eye glued to the spyhole and was
ghoulishly noting every detail of the scene. He kept up a low
running commentary to Stever, ceded his position for a few
jealous seconds, then brutally elbowed his subordinate out
of the way and resumed his gloating watch.

"It's nearly over now—they're sitting on the bed, side by
side, holding hands. Very touching. Very nice. Now the old
goat's starting to cry—there he goes! Pissing his eyeballs
out . . ."

"What for?" said Stever in surprise. "It's not him they're
chopping up."

Stahlschmidt shrugged his shoulders, not sure of the answer.

"I guess it's because he's a priest," he said at length. "Man
of God, see? He probably feels it's part of his duty to show
a bit of emotion when he's preparing someone for the other
life."

Stever tipped up his helmet and scratched his head.
"Yeah—yeah, I guess you're right."

They moved away from the cell. Stahlschmidt jerked a
thumb back toward it.

"One thing's for sure," he said. "You and I won't ever be

in that position. We're not going to have any bum priest mumbling and farting over us and telling us stories about God and the angels. We know how to keep our mouths shut and our heads on our shoulders." He looked at Stever. "Don't we?" he said meaningly.

Stever gave a faint, imbecilic grin. The idea was still with him to get in touch with the Gestapo and safeguard his own position. He glanced involuntarily toward Stahlschmidt's thick red neck, and he wondered if even one of the razor-sharp axes from Berlin could cut through it at one blow.

"What are you staring at?" asked Stahlschmidt suspiciously.

"Nothing," babbled Stever. "I was just—just looking at your—your neck."

"My neck?" Instinctively Stahlschmidt raised a hand to his throat. "What about my neck?"

"It's very strong," muttered Stever.

"Damn right it is! It's the neck of a Stabsfeldwebel. And the necks of Stabsfeldwebels, my dear Stever, do not easily part company from their bodies. Unlike the necks of other people, such as lieutenants and captains and Obergefreiters."

Stever shuffled his feet on the stone floor. "The axes they use are very sharp," he muttered.

"So what?" asked Stahlschmidt coldly. "What's the matter with you today? Are you losing your nerve? Do you want me to send you to a headshrinker? Or are you drunk? Is that it?" He peered closely at Stever, who took a step backward. "Surely you've learned by now that Stabsfeldwebels are never among those executed? Have you ever seen one here, in this prison? Of course you haven't! We're the backbone of society, that's what we are, and they wouldn't dare lift a finger against us. Have you ever thought how it would be if we were to go on strike? Chaos! Complete chaos! Adolf, Hermann, Heinrich, they'd all collapse like a pack of cards!"

"I suppose you're right," said Stever, reflecting that if he went to the Gestapo, Stahlschmidt, in his own prison, might be the first Stabsfeldwebel ever to face the firing squad.

"Bloody right I'm right!" roared Stahlschmidt. "And you just remember that in future!"

During the afternoon exercise period, Stever and Braun searched the cells of the condemned men, Stever taking one side of the corridor and Braun the other. They made one or two interesting discoveries.

In cell 21, Braun unearthed a slice of hard black bread hidden inside the mattress. In cell 34, Stever found two centimeters of cigarette butt pushed down a crack in the floor. In the cell next door was a pencil stub. And in cell No. 9 was the most interesting find of all.

They collected all the treasures and tied them in a blue towel, taking them along to Stahlschmidt's office for his inspection. These few pathetic scraps of personal belongings were objects of intense emotional value to the condemned men, and he enjoyed gloating over them.

Lieutenant Ohlsen returned from the tortures of the exercise period and stopped in dismay on the threshold of his cell. Bare though the room was, Stever had succeeded in turning it upside down, and it was immediately obvious to its occupant that the place had been searched. Ohlsen flung himself at the bed and felt frenziedly under the mattress; nothing was there. He fell sobbing to the floor as the door opened and Stever crept silently in. He was holding a small yellow capsule between finger and thumb.

"Is this what you're after, by any chance?" He stood, jeering, inside the door. Ohlsen scrambled to his feet and made a despairing lunge at the capsule, but Stever's truncheon crashed mercilessly down on his head and shoulders, beating him halfway across the cell and cornering him by the window.

"Stand to attention when there's an Obergefreiter present! You ought to know the rules by now!"

Lieutenant Ohlsen shakily pulled himself upright, wiping the back of his hand across his nose.

Stever looked down at the capsule and shook his head. "You're a deep one and no mistake. Where'd you get it from? How long have you had it? You can't have had it long or I'd have known about it." He held it tantalizingly just out of reach. "Going to swallow it just before they led you out to the scaffold, were you? All the trouble they take to get up a nice funeral for you, all the money they spend on you, and this is the way you try to repay them! Ought to be ashamed of yourself! Mind you," he said sagely, "I can't say I'm all that surprised. I kinda guessed you were up to something. You were taking it all too calm. You got to remember I've had a lot of experience in these matters—I seen more men die than you've had hot dinners. Some people," said Stever, "think I'm slow. And that's where they make their mistake, because I know everything what goes on in this prison, and I've even got eyes in the back of my ass. That way, I save myself a pack of trouble. I know all the rules by heart, and I stick to 'em. Anyone tells me to do something that sounds a bit off, and I get 'em to put it down in writing. That way, see, they can't never get me for anything. Someone comes up and says, 'Stever, you've committed a murder, you've done something wrong,' I just show 'em the order, written down in black and white. And I'm only an Obergefreiter, I only do what I'm told."

He held the capsule in the palm of his hand and looked at it curiously. "How do these things work? Kill you straight out, do they?" He laughed. "I think I'll give it to Stahlschmidt's cat. It tried to scratch me the other day and I told it at the time I was going to wring its neck as soon as I got the chance. This'll do just as well!"

Lieutenant Ohlsen stood at attention. His lower lip was trembling and his vision was blurred by the tears that coursed down his cheeks and splashed to the floor. That capsule had been the ace up his sleeve, his precious trump card, his one salvation. The knowledge that he had it in his power to decide when and where he should die, by his own hand and no one else's, had sustained him during the long weeks of imprisonment. And now he cursed himself bitterly for a fool not to have taken it the minute the trial was over. Who but a pathological optimist would have hung on so long, despairing and yet hoping for a last-minute reprieve that would never come?

He looked across at Stever and held out an appealing hand. "Give it to me, Stever. For God's sake, give it to me!"

"I'm sorry," said Stever. "I just can't do it. Against the rules, see? Besides, the Gestapo's out for blood and if they don't get yours, the chances are they'll want mine instead." He shook his head. "You wouldn't ask that of me, would you?" he said reasonably. "We're both bound by the same laws, you know. But look here, I've got something else might interest you. I couldn't give it you before, Stahlschmidt never lets condemned men have letters in case the ink's poisoned. It did happen once—not here, in Munich. Quite a song and dance there was, and now Stahlschmidt always holds onto any letters that come. But I managed to smuggle this one out for you. Against the rules, of course. I was taking a big risk. You ought to be very grateful. I thought it might be from that little guy with the scar. The one that came to see you that time."

Lieutenant Ohlsen wiped his eyes on his sleeve and list-lessly took the letter. Stever watched him with narrowed eyes. "Just read it," he said. "Don't try eating it."

The lieutenant ran his eyes quickly over the few lines of writing. They were from the Old Man, but nothing could interest him, nothing could comfort him, now that his capsule was gone.

Stever held out an impatient hand, snatched the letter back and began to read it himself.

"Who's this Alfred he's on about? It's that character with the scar, ain't it?" He looked across at Ohlsen, who nodded. "I don't know what it is," said Stever, "but I still got the feeling he holds a sort of grudge against me. I don't see why he should. After all, I'm only an Obergefreiter, it's not my fault if people got to die."

He brooded uncomfortably a few moments, then his face slowly cleared. "I tell you what. You could do me a good turn, if you felt like it. After all, I done you one bringing you this letter. All you got to do is write a few words about me on the back of it. Obergefreiter Stever is a good soldier what always carries out his orders—he has treated me well —something like that. How about it, eh? With a PS saying about how I'm a friend to all the prisoners. And then put your name and rank and the date and all, that'll make it official, see?"

Stever pulled out a pencil and offered it to the lieuten-ant. Ohlsen raised an eyebrow. "Prove it," he said. "Prove you are a friend to a prisoner and I'll do it for you."

"Prove it?" Stever laughed. "You've got a nerve!"

"You don't think you've got an even bigger one?" mildly suggested Ohlsen.

Stever bit his lip. He looked down at the letter and read again the dreaded name of the type with the scar. "What do you want?" he asked sullenly.

"Give me back the capsule. That's all I ask."

"You must be raving! I'd be for the high jump myself if they found you'd gone and killed yourself before they could get their hands on you."

Ohlsen shrugged. He was suddenly past caring. "It's up to you," he said. "I've got to die anyway, so I'm not that interested. I thought I was, but I'm not. Now that it's actually come to the point, I'm not. But if I were you, Stever, if you value your life at all, I should think very seriously about getting a steel corset made for yourself. You can't escape from the Legionnaire, you know. He always catches up with people sooner or later."

Stever gnawed anxiously at his bottom lip. "I'd like to help you, I really would. I'd do anything to get you out of this fix—only I can't give you the capsule, it's more than my life's worth . . ."

"Please yourself," said Ohlsen, turning away and not bothering to stand at attention. "I couldn't give a damn either way."

They came for him just after the evening meal. They took him out to the courtyard through an underground passage. The priest led the way, intoning a mournful prayer. The executions were to take place in a small, enclosed courtyard that was safe from the prying eyes of unauthorized persons. The scaffold was set up, and on the platform were the executioner and his two assistants, dressed in frock coats, top hats and white gloves.

The condemned men were to be executed in pairs, and Lieutenant Ohlsen's partner in death was already waiting. When they were both present, the prison governor checked their identities and the first assistant stepped forward and cut off their epaulettes, depriving them of their rank and finally dishonoring them.

Lieutenant Ohlsen stood watching as his partner slowly climbed the ladder. The priest began to pray for the salvation of his soul. The two assistants helped the man to position himself and tied him down. The executioner raised his ax. The crescent-shaped blade flashed bright in the sinking rays of the sun. The executioner opened his mouth and shouted out his justification of the deed he was about to perform.

"For the Führer, the Reich and the German people!"

The ax fell. It met the resistant flesh with a faint thump and sliced straight through it. It was a clean blow. Strong and well placed by a man who was an expert. The head rolled neatly into the waiting basket and two jets of blood spurted from the surprised neck. The body twitched and contorted. With quick, deft movements the assistants tipped it off the platform and into the waiting coffin. The head was snatched up and set between the legs of the corpse.

The audience relaxed. Oberkriegsgerichtsrat Dr. Jeckstadt, president of the court which had passed sentence, slowly lit a cigarette and turned to Dr. Beckmann. "Say what you like about execution," he remarked, "but you can't deny that it's quick, efficient and simple."

"When it goes according to plan," muttered a Rittmeister, who was standing behind Jeckstadt and had overheard him.

"I must confess," said Dr. Beckmann, "that I find it an unpleasant spectacle. I never seem able to stop myself wondering how it must feel to be up there, waiting for the ax to fall—a curious sensation . . ."

"My dear fellow," said Jeckstadt comfortably, "why torture yourself with fruitless speculation? These people have betrayed their country and they deserve their just punishment. But you and I," he smiled, as at an absurd idea, "you and I are never likely to find ourselves in such a situation! One thing is quite certain, my dear Doctor—if it weren't for us legal fellows, the country would soon be in chaos. We are, if I may make so bold, virtually indispensable."

"Of course, you're quite right," agreed Beckmann, turning back to watch the second show of the evening. "No country can survive without its legal system."

Lieutenant Ohlsen climbed slowly and steadily up the ladder. The assistants positioned him. His mind was a blank. Almost a blank. He remembered that in the seconds before dying a man's whole life is supposed to pass before his eyes, and he wondered almost fretfully why his own life was not even now unfolding before him, spreading out its memories for his last-minute contemplation.

He began consciously to force his mind back into the past, back into his own precious private memories, his own personal history, but before any very vivid pictures could come to him, the ax crashed down and his life was over.

Down in the depths of Porta's stomach, fourteen pints of beer, nine vodkas and seven absinthes were fighting for possession, while Porta himself staggered across the room toward the piano. He walked bowlegged because he was too drunk to control his muscles. He rolled from side to side, belching and clutching at tables and chairs to support himself. Now and again, during his passage across the room, he swept bottles and glasses to the floor. Three times he himself fell to the floor and had to be picked up again.

At last he reached his goal, but the effort had proved too much for the disputatious contents of his stomach. Sprawling

across the piano, Porta opened his mouth and let everything
pour out.

The pianist fell backward off his stool. "Filthy shit!" he
cried. "Look what you've done to my fucking piano!"

By way of reply, Porta merely shot out an involuntary
hand and swept a full glass of beer over the keyboard. He
rolled around to the front of the piano and collapsed heavily
onto the stool. With a frown of concentration on his face and
his fingers large as pork sausages, heavy as lead weights, uncertain of their direction as straws in a gale, he began
drunkenly to play the semblance of a well-known tune.

Bernard the Boozer jumped up on a table and thumped
at the ceiling with two bottles of champagne. The room
rang with the sound of drunken voices in something roughly
approaching unison:

> *Vor der Kaserne, vor dem grossen Tor,*
> *stand eine Laterne und steht sie noch davor*
> *so woll'n wir uns da wiedersehn*
> *bei der Laterne woll'n wir stehn*
> *wie einst, Lili Marlene.*

> (Close to the barracks, beside its massive gate,
> there stood a streetlamp which still stands as before.
> Under that streetlamp we'll meet and stand again,
> as once, Lili Marlene.)

Only Tiny did not join in. He had a girl on his knee and
was systematically undressing her, with the same careless
determination with which one might pluck a chicken. The
girl was alternately kicking and screaming, not sure whether
to enjoy herself or be outraged.

The pianist, unable any longer to stand the sight of his
piano covered in beer and vomit, made a determined effort
to oust Porta from the stool. Porta stopped playing, wound
his arms lovingly about the man's neck and hung on. Seconds
later the unfortunate pianist found himself flying headfirst
across the room in the direction of the kitchen. He fetched
up against the wall, at the feet of Heide and an almost
comatose Barcelona.

At the same time as these festivities were going on, a procession of people trod solemnly along a passage in the prison
of Fuhlsbüttel. There were six SD soldiers, a priest, a
doctor, several court officials and an old lady. They walked
haltingly, almost reluctantly, toward a green baize door at

the end of the passage. It seemed that they were anxious to postpone the moment when they would have to turn the handle and enter. But the moment inevitably came, and the procession moved slowly through the door and into the room beyond.

A quarter of an hour later the door reopened and the procession reappeared. They were walking faster now. Six SD soldiers, the priest, the doctor and the several court officials. Only the old lady was no longer with them.

IX

A BIRTHDAY PARTY

The noise that poured out from the Three Hares on the Davidsstrasse could be heard in hideous clarity several streets away, even as far as the infirmary on Bernhard Nocht Strasse, where envious patients tossed and turned and cursed. It was the noise of sheer, exhilarating, incapable drunkenness and it bellied forth into the night in a continuous crescendo of sound.

The owner of the Three Hares, popularly known as Bernard the Boozer, was celebrating his birthday in a private room at the back of the bistro. Only the most favored of the establishment's regulars had been allowed in.

Tiny was one of the first to arrive, early in the afternoon. He had found the Boozer enthroned on a small stepladder, directing the operations for the evening's entertainment. Paper garlands and Chinese lanterns were being strung across the room, crates of beer and champagne stacked in the corners.

"Someone told me it was your birthday," began Tiny.

Bernard nodded. "Someone was right."

"Okay," said Tiny. "In that case, I'd like to wish you happy birthday. Just wanted to get my facts right first."

"Yeah?" Bernard looked at him and smiled knowingly, then swung around on his ladder and shouted at a youth who was staggering beneath a crate of beer. "Not out there, you fool! Over there in the corner!"

Tiny's eyes hungrily followed the crate on its journey across the room, then switched back casually to the Boozer. "You—er—having a bit of a blowout?"

"That's it." Bernard blew his nose between his fingers, directly over a large pan of meat. He looked down at it indifferently. "It's all right, it's only a stew, it can do with a bit more seasoning. Anyway, everything tastes pretty much the same once it gets into that mess. One of the girls emptied the coffee grounds into it last week—nobody said a thing. All mixes in together, you can't taste the difference."

"No," said Tiny. "I guess not." He gazed in wonderment at the rows of bottles ranged behind the bar. "Who's going to get through all that lot?"

Bernard looked at him a moment, then turned and spat through the open window. "My pals," he said simply.

Tiny grunted, not sure whether to lay immediate and automatic claim to being among the Boozer's most intimate circle of acquaintances or whether to pursue some other tactic.

"We're going away again soon," he ventured, wiping the back of his hand across his panting mouth.

"Yeah. That's the way it goes." The Boozer nodded his head without sympathy.

"We're being sent back to the front," Tiny persevered. "The battalion's almost up to full strength again. We've got a whole lot of new tanks and stuff—only keep that under your hat, it's supposed to be top secret. I can trust a pal like you to keep his trap shut, but don't go spreading it around."

"Shouldn't dream of it," said Bernard. "Don't know anyone who's interested." He pulled himself upright, stepped onto the top rung of the ladder and casually attached a paper chain to the portion of the ceiling immediately above his head. The ladder remained firm, but the Boozer wobbled perilously. He had been drinking beer since long before breakfast.

"Watch it," said Tiny, stretching out an enormous callused hand. "Don't want to go breaking your neck on your birthday." He settled Bernard back on his perch and gave him an ingratiating smile. "How many years does this make it?"

"Forty-two—and you can get a couple of bottles of beer over here and drink my health if you like."

Tiny's arm instantly stretched out to the nearest row of bottles and his vast hand closed over two of them. He passed one over to the Boozer and raised the other to his mouth, closing his teeth over the cap and starting to prize it off.

"Hang on a minute," said Bernard. He held out a hand and looked Tiny squarely in the eye. "Where's my present? You can't come here drinking my booze and saying happy birthday without bringing me a present."

"That's right," Tiny agreed cordially, lowering the bottle. "Got it right here with me. Good thing you mentioned it, I got a memory like a sieve." He sank a hand into the depths of a pants pocket and emerged with a minute packet done up in crude pink paper.

Bernard examined it with interest. "What is it?"

"You'll never guess," said Tiny, wrenching open his bottle. "Not in a million years. It's just what you've always wanted."

Bernard tore open the paper to disclose a cheap bottle opener. He hurled it across the room with an oath. "That's the tenth goddamn bottle opener I've received today! Don't you imbeciles have any imagination?"

"It's the thought that counts," said Tiny. He tipped back his head and poured half the bottle of beer straight down his throat. "Didn't no one ever tell you that?"

"Fuck the thought!" growled Bernard. "Who wants five hundred lousy bottle openers?"

"Oh, well," said Tiny wisely. "That's birthdays for you— never get what you really want."

Tiny stayed on after drinking Bernard's health. He stayed on to help with the stage managing and to drink his host's health a few more times in an indiscriminate variety of beer and liquor. And when the first of the guests began to arrive, he stayed to look after them and make them welcome. And then the guests drank Bernard's health, and Tiny joined in, and then more people came and more toasts were drunk, and even before the celebration had officially begun, Tiny had his head out of the window and his fingers down his throat, making way for the next round of drinks.

Porta arrived midway through the evenng. It was evident that he had stopped somewhere en route. He forged through the crowd and hit Bernard lustily on the back "Happy birthday! Happy birthday! Happy—did you get my present, by the way?"

"What present would that be?" Bernard looked at him suspiciously.

"Well, it was a bottle opener in the shape of a woman— Tiny was going to bring it."

"Yeah, I got it," said Bernard contemptuously.

"That's okay, then. It was from Tiny and me both. Joint present. We chose it together. Just what old Bernie the Boozer could do with, we said. Save his teeth. Save his false teeth. We thought you'd go for that. We thought you'd . . ."

"Aw, shove it!" snarled his host, pushing him to one side.

At some stage in the evening, before we became paralytic, we sat down to dinner. There was much pushing and jostling and general vituperation, one or two fights broke out and one or two chairs were broken, but finally everyone was seated more or less to his satisfaction. Bernard called on the two serving girls, who were dressed—overdressed, according to some people present—in black briefs and tiny aprons the size of postage stamps.

"Hey, Helga!" Porta called out to one of them as she came toward him with a plate. "Tiny tells me you've gone and shaved yourself like a French tart! That right? Can I have a feel?"

Helga slammed a plate of cabbage in front of him and stalked away without a word, her buttocks moving haughtily from side to side in their tight black pants. Porta whinnied like a horse and slapped a fist straight into his dish of cabbage.

At the end of the meal we feted Bernard with a birthday drinking song. It had nothing whatever to do with birthdays, being almost exclusively devoted to sex in its bawdiest manifestation, but Bernard accepted it as a fitting tribute to a man celebrating his forty-second year on earth.

We had drunk so much that there was not one among us who had not yet thrown up. With an inebriated sense of our own powers, we snatched up our host, tossed him into the air and caught him as he came down. The third time we all collapsed heavily to the floor, with Bernard buried beneath us. Porta staggered onto the table and stamped for silence. Heide supported him by banging two bottles together. The bottles promptly broke and a shower of glass rained down on the group on the floor.

"Shut your goddamn traps!" shouted Heide. "Joseph Porta wants to speak!"

At last we sorted ourselves out again and a sort of silence fell on the room, broken only by belches and the breaking of wind, by the sound of a man retching or the pouring of beer.

"Bernard the Boozer," began Porta sternly, "Bernie the Boozer, our old pal Bernie, you're forty-two today and we all know you're the biggest shit that ever walked, but we love you for it all the same!" Porta threw out his arms in an expansive gesture and almost fell off the table. "We're all shits together!" he cried in tones of ringing exultation. "That's why we're here tonight, drinking the health of the biggest shit of the lot! And now we'll have another song —one, two, three!"

He beat time with his feet on the table. One foot he raised too high and brought down too hard. It missed the table altogether and crashed down into Heide's lap. They disappeared together in a cursing tangle over the side.

At the far end of the table, Tiny had taken possession of Helga and was tugging maniacally at her black pants. Helga was kicking and biting for all she was worth. One or two people were placing bets on the probable winner.

Heide stayed under the table, leaning drunkenly against someone's legs and talking to himself. He talked about war and being a soldier. It was all very tedious and it was not surprising that he soon fell into a stupor.

Barcelona, finding himself next to Bernard the Boozer, began telling him compulsively about Spain. Barcelona always told anyone who would listen, or at least keep a decent silence, about his experiences in Spain. Somehow his demonstration of bullfighting and a battle with tanks somewhere near Alicante became inextricably merged until Barcelona was charging up and down the room with his head lowered in imitation of a bull, and of an imaginary submachine gun firing straight into the floor.

"What the hell's that meant to be?" demanded Porta, crawling out from under the table and blinking as Barcelona flashed past.

Barcelona screeched to a halt, regarded Porta with drunken dignity and sat down. "It was at Alicante I scored one of my greatest military successes," he said very coldly.

He picked up a spare glass of beer and poured it down his chest, then wiped his mouth with an air of apparent satisfaction.

"The hell with your successes," said Porta. "What about that Spanish whore you screwed? Tell us about her."

Barcelona hiccuped so violently in remembrance that had the Old Man not kept a firm grip on his collar, he would have fallen to the floor.

"Stewed to the eyeballs," said Porta in disgust.

Barcelona leaned toward him, with the Old Man still hanging onto the back of his neck. "Obergefreiter Joseph Porta," he said, slurring everything into a single word of elephantine proportions, "for the one hundred and twentieth time I'm warning you: address me correctly when you speak to me. I am a Feldwebel, the backbone of the German Army."

"Backbone, my ass!" said Porta scornfully. "An old soak like you?" He rolled across to the bar, collapsed against it, clawed up the nearest bottle and wrenched off the top. It went off like a gun—it was champagne—and half the guests instantly dived beneath the table. Porta raised the bottle to his lips and drank in great gulps.

"I am a lover of the arts!" screamed Barcelona into the hubbub.

Porta turned back to look at him. "Well, fuck you!" he said. "Feldwebel, sir," he added sarcastically.

"Not only me," continued Barcelona, "but my very dear friend Bernard as well. He also is a lover of the arts." And he leaned across and planted a heavy wet kiss on the Boozer's forehead as a mark of their great friendship. The Boozer smiled foolishly. As he swayed back to his original position, Barcelona crashed into the Old Man and they seesawed perilously for a while on the edge of the bench. "Who," shouted Barcelona, recovering his balance, "who in this drunken band of cretins and sex maniacs has ever been into a museum and tasted the beauties of art? Who," he went on, growing a bit muddled, "has ever drunk at the tree of knowledge? Which of you lousy philistines has ever heard of Thorvaldsen? Eh? Which of you has ever heard of him? You probably think he's a pimp on the Reeperbahn—well, he isn't."

Barcelona wagged a finger in the air and paused to look at it. That pause was the start of his undoing. It seemed to him that in some miraculous way he was wagging a dozen fingers simultaneously. Which was remarkable, when he was ready to swear that he had only five on either hand. And two hands made ten, and that was including thumbs. He watched for a while in fascination. He began speaking hypnotically of artists and heroes, passed on to a roof-raising speech about liberty, shouted angrily at us that we were all brothers and that he loved us, and ended up in the inevitable impasse of general obscenity and abuse, without ever realizing how he had arrived there.

He broke off in the midst of a string of curses and stared in amazement as the world rose up before his eyes and began slowly to close in upon him. He blinked and shook his head, and the world receded.

Barcelona was moved to thump vigorously on his chest, indicating his row of multicolored ribbons and decorations and declaring in passionate tones that none of them meant a damn thing to him and that he would be only too glad to be rid of them. He offered them all around as free gifts, attempted to claw them off his tunic and scatter them among us, but the effort was too much. He fell forward, headfirst onto the table, and lay with his head in a pool of beer singing a somewhat curious song about bird droppings.

After a while, someone sitting opposite, taking a sudden dislike either to the singer or the song, reached across and pushed him backward onto the floor. Barcelona's last words before he gave way to temporary oblivion were a fanatical *"Viva España!"*

For a moment, Bernard the Boozer sat contemplating the inert figure of his art-loving friend. The sight seemed to move him very deeply. With the aid of Porta and the Legionnaire, he crawled walruslike onto the table and prepared to make a speech, and there he stood, swaying in pendulum fashion from side to side, with the Legionnaire hanging onto both ankles and Porta waiting to catch him should he fall.

"My friends!" He held out both arms to embrace us. The electric light bulb went crashing to the floor. A paper chain came adrift and festooned itself around Bernard's neck. "My friends, I trust you've all got enough to drink and there's nobody going thirsty. Because I can tell you, here and now, that there's enough liquor in my cellar——" At this point he swayed backward, into the waiting arms of Porta, and there was a pause while he was set back on an even keel. "There's enough booze in my cellar to keep the whole German Navy afloat—and you're welcome to it! You're my friends and you're welcome to it! Drink it all! Drink it until it's coming out of your eyes and your ears and your ass-holes. My friends—" This time he swayed forward, and the Legionnaire held onto his ankles while Porta ran around to the front and caught him before he reached the table. He tilted him back again, toward the Legionnaire. "My friends, I hope you think of this little place of mine as being a home from home—a real home from home, where you can piss and shit and fornicate just like you would by your own fire-side. Being a publican is not just a job, it's a vocation—you know that? 'S a real vocation. Where do you fellas go when you're pissed off and want cheering up? Back to barracks? Back to the wife and kids? Like hell!" With a joyous ges-ture, Bernard swooped around in an arc that brought him dangerously close to scraping his nose on the table. By some miracle, the force of his momentum was strong enough to carry him onward, until he had again reached the per-pendicular and the Legionnaire was able to reach up a hand and prevent his going off on another turn. "Like hell!" roared Bernard undaunted. "You don't go anywhere near 'em—this is where you come! Round to good old Bernie's place! Round to the boozer! Bernie the Boozer, that's what you call me—and not for nothing, my friends! I'm not called that for nothing! I been in the business a good long time and I know what it's all about, and when you guys come here in search of a bit of comfort, I make damn sure you get it! Not one of my boys ever goes away from here without a gutful!"

"That's right," affirmed some wag from the far end of the table. "A full gut and an empty pocket!"

Bernard smiled benevolently, not catching the implica-tions of this remark.

"In my establishment," he declared, "the common soldier is king. Privates, corporals, sergeants—they're all welcome! There's only one class I won't abide, and that's officers. Officers, my friends, are the most antisocial, ass-licking, yellow-bellied . . ."

The rest of his feelings on officers were lost in a general storm of cheers and catcalls. Bernard raised both arms above his head, clenching his fists and prancing about the table like a triumphant boxer. The Legionnaire and Porta hovered anxiously at his side.

"Gentlemen!" roared Bernard, his voice rising above the

swelling hubbub, "we belong to Hamburg! Hamburg is our city! Hamburg is the last bastion of Europe!"

The cheers rang out again from all and sundry. Most of us had no affection whatsoever for Hamburg, but that did nothing to dampen our enthusiasm. We yelled and stamped and threw our arms around one another in a fervor of love and loyalty. Much encouraged, Bernard stamped energetically on someone's fingers and tramped down to the far end of the table, treading in plates and overturning glasses as he did so.

"Sylvia!" He lurched sideways, extended a hand and grabbed one of the passing serving girls. "Where are you going, wench? What d'you think you're doing? You're on duty as long as the liquor lasts. Bring on some more beer and keep the party going!"

Loud whistles filled the air. Feet stamped, hands clapped. Men opened their mouths and shouted wordlessly, for the pure delight of making a noise. Some of those who had temporarily withdrawn from the scene recovered their senses, threw up and returned to the fray. Bernard stumbled back down the table, waving his hands frantically toward the piano. "Let's have a song! Ready for the song of Hamburg, fellas! All together, now . . ."

The choir of voices filled the room. Harsh, unmelodious, out of time, out of tune, we bawled together Bernard's song of Hamburg:

> *Das Herz von Sankt Pauli*
> *das ist meine Heimat,*
> *in Hamburg, da bin ich zu Haus.*
>
> (The heart of St. Paul,
> that is my home,
> in Hamburg, there I'm at home.)

The song was brought to a halt by Steiner, who staggered back from the washroom to announce that the first dead-drunk, out-like-a-light of the evening, was to be found on the floor. A roof-raising cheer went up and the entire party at once crushed its way into the washroom to inspect the victim. It was a Feldwebel. He was out cold and no amount of rough handling would bring him back again. With wild cries of jubilation, the six fittest men transported him outside and flung him into the gutter. Porta laughed so long and so loud that he dislocated his jaw, but Tiny soon put it back in place for him with a well-timed upper cut.

During the next hour, another seven of the guests ended up in the gutter. Bernard the Boozer's birthday party died slowly out in a stale sea of overturned beer and a hovering pall of smoke. The floor was covered in debris and drunken bodies. The Boozer himself lay upended in a packing case.

The eight of us from the 27th, strung out arm in arm across the width of the pavement and halfway across the road, supported each other through the night on our way back to barracks.

"I'm thirsty!" howled Porta; and the narrow, crowded buildings of the Herbertstrasse flung the words back at him, echoing and reechoing.

As we swayed past an underground station, we saw an old man fighting with a brush and a bucket of glue to stick up a notice, and we naturally stopped to help him. For some reason he took fright and went hobbling off into the dim dawn light, leaving us to cope rather ineptly with the poster.

"Whozzitsay?" demanded Porta.

Steiner held it up and managed to read out the first word—NOTICE—before Barcelona pulled it away from him and dunked it in the glue.

"Who the hell—" Porta lost his balance, fell to the ground and foolishly attempted to pull himself up by my ankles. We collapsed together. "Who the hell sticks these damn things up at this time of night?"

It took us the best part of fifteen minutes to get that poster posted. We overturned the glue, we lost the brush, we tore the thing in half, we stuck it over ourselves and each other, and we finally got it back to front onto the wall and wondered why we couldn't read it. It wasn't until the Leigonnaire, leaning against the rest of us for support, solemnly peeled the thing off and turned it around that the mystery was solved.

"Whozzitsay?" Porta fretfully demanded for the second time; he was on the ground again and couldn't see.

Steiner and Barcelona stood with their heads together, taking each other's weight and attempting to bring the lettering into focus. The poster was upside down now. It looked like Russian to me. Steiner muttered the words aloud, and Barcelona politely corrected him as he stumbled over the more difficult syllables. Steiner kept saying "Thank you" and "Sorry," and Barcelona kept on saying, "Don't mind if I put you right, do you?" and it was altogether quite a charming scene except that the rest of us found it almost impossible to stand still and wait, one or other of us constantly falling down and having to be picked up again.

"Friends!" shouted Barcelona at last. He turned to us with a finger on his lips and his eyes open wide. "Don't panic! Keep calm! It's a message from the Gestapo!"

Steiner, left suddenly without support, pitched forward toward the poster, bumped into the wall and sank slowly down it on his way to the ground. "I'm so thirsty," he moaned.

"Whozzit*say*?" demanded Porta querulously for the third time.

Barcelona put out a hand to steady himself. "It's someone who's to be hanged." He brought the words out with difficulty. His eyes were round and owlish. His mouth was slack.

Porta, apparently satisfied, turned and vomited down the steps of the subway.

The Old Man sat down with his back against a street lamp. He made an attempt to speak, waited a moment, then tried again. The words came out one by one in a slow-motion blur. "Who—is—to be—hanged?"

Barcelona put his head right up against the poster. "Traitor to the Führer—to the German people—and to her country—will be executed today at 1715 hours—Emilie Dreyer . . ."

We picked up Steiner and Porta and continued in our way, arm in arm on a zigzag course toward the Palace of Justice. Barcelona and the Legionnaire were roaring and hiccuping:

> *Dragoner sind halb Mensch, halb Vieh.*
> *Auf Pferd gesetzte Infanterie.*
>
> (Dragoons are half man, half beast,
> Horseback-mounted infantry.)

"That woman—that woman they're going to hang—" I looked around for help in finishing the sentence, but no one was in a fit enough state. "That woman," I said again. "Did we—have we—was she the one we . . ."

There was a silence.

"Could be," said the Legionnaire.

"So many people die," said the Old Man wisely. "They
go to war. They die. You can't remember them all."

"We're going to war soon," said Heide. "The battalion's
been alerted."

"Cheers!" cried Tiny. "I'm a hero!"

We turned into the barracks. Porta suddenly sank down
on all fours, onto the beautiful velvet lawn outside staff
headquarters. With some difficulty he pulled himself up
into a sitting position. The rest of us stood swaying in a row
above him.

"Let's sing a song for all them lazy sleeping shits," he
proposed. "Let's have a little singsong—Colonel Hinka's got
a whore in his bed." He attempted a sly wink, but one eye
refused to close without the other. "I know his whore, she's
a filthy clap-ridden slut that won't even give the time of day
to an Obergefreiter. Let's give 'em a singsong and wake 'em
up.

His voice rang out across the sleeping barracks; rude and
powerful like the roaring of a bull in agony. The rest of us
joined in:

> *Im schwarzen Keller zu Askalon,*
> *da kneipt ein Mann drei Tag,*
> *bis dass er wie ein Besenstiel*
> *am Marmortische lag.*

> (In Askalon's dark cellar,
> a man tippled for three days
> until he like a broomstick
> stiff as a marble lay.)

"Christ almighty!" swore the Legionnaire, tossing his
equipment disdainfully into a corner. "This is one hell of a
stupid job for a man of my age to be doing!"

He was an instructor in the art of single combat, and he
had the chore of training all the recruits that came regularly
to us from prisons, barracks and camps.

Tiny shrugged his shoulders and tore off a mouthful of
ham from the tin he had stolen from 8th Company stores.
"Why do it if you don't like it?" he mumbled.

The little Legionnaire hunched his shoulders, lit one of
his perpetual cigarettes and filtered the smoke slowly and
reflectively through his nostrils. He leaned across the table
and thoughtfully applied the glowing tip of the cigarette to
the backside of a dying bee, watching its reactions. The bee

promptly expired, and the Legionnaire sighed. Straightening up, he looked at Tiny. "Why, might I ask, did you become a soldier?"

"Easy," rejoined Tiny, spitting food in all directions. "Didn't have no choice. It was either the fucking Army or starve on the fucking streets—so I joined the Army." He gnawed off another lump of ham. "I had a whack at the cavalry first, only they said I was too big—too big for the horses, they said—so they sent me off to the infantry—and was that a grind!" said Tiny reminiscently. "Nothing but marching your feet off day after day—and those stinking officers!" He spat, remembered too late that he was eating, and crawled about the floor in search of stray pieces of ham. "Thought they could treat you like dirt, just because you was a welfare kid—lived on public assistance, see, before I enlisted."

"Fair enough," the Legionnaire nodded. "I agree that you had no choice. It was a case of one evil stacked against another, and for my money that doesn't constitute a choice."

"Damn right it doesn't. Still," Tiny wiped the back of his hand across his mouth, "that's the way it goes, right? How about you?"

"Me?" The Legionnaire smiled grimly. "I didn't have any choice either. I was never on welfare and I was never in any real trouble with the cops—nothing like that. All I knew was being out of work and being hungry—my belly used to rumble for days on end. I used to chew paper when I could get hold of it; even that wasn't so easy to come by, but it did help relieve the pains. Until in 1932 I said the hell with Germany and headed for the sun of France—only when I got to Paris it was just as gray and wet and miserable as Berlin."

"So wha'd'ya do?" asked Tiny, chewing busily on his ham.

The Legionnaire gave him a mischievous wink. "Got myself picked up by a prostitute at a bus stop—I was very young in those days. Had a sort of wistful appeal for women—especially in bed." He grinned. "She taught me a thing or two, that old gal—including French, which came in quite useful, as it turned out."

"What made you join the Foreign Legion, then?" said Tiny. "Never did make sense to me."

"Like I said—no choice. The cops came around inquir-

ing after my old tart, and I decided it was time to piss off
It was either a spell in the pokey—I told you she taught me
a thing or two—or burning my boats in the Legion. So I
joined the Legion." He shrugged. "It could have been worse
There's always something worse . . ."

He walked across to the window and stood looking out a
moment.

"Hey, you!" He picked up a boot and hurled it at a passing
recruit as the quickest way of gaining his attention. "I've got
some equipment needs cleaning. Pronto. And make sure you
do a good job on it if you want to keep your head on your
shoulders!"

The recruit, a man in his early sixties, broken and bent
even beyond his years, turned his rheumy eyes in the
Legionnaire's direction. The Legionnaire jerked his head
and the old man shuffled over obediently. For the moment
he was destined to polish someone else's equipment until
it shone like silver. For the future his fate was more glorious,
though possibly just as futile; he was to die a so-called hero
on the banks of the Dnieper, to the north of Kiev.

The Legionnaire closed the window and stubbed out his
cigarette.

"There's always something worse," he murmured.

X

DEPARTURE FOR THE FRONT

The following day, a most regrettable incident occurred on the rifle range; Feldwebel Brandt was shot dead. Four times, straight through the forehead. The one comfort was, he could have known nothing about it. Death must have been instantaneous. Nevertheless we were all very properly shocked. The officer in charge was at once arrested and questioned nonstop for several hours, but they released him in the end.

Tiny and Porta volunteered for the grisly task of removing the body. They went out together and loaded it onto the back of a truck.

"How come it's so heavy?" grumbled Tiny. "You'd think he'd have lost a bit of weight, wouldn't you, giving up his soul the way he's just done?"

"Didn't have no soul," grunted Porta.

They climbed into the truck and pulled out a pack of cards, sitting one on either side of the late Feldwebel Brandt and using his corpse as a table. Porta put his hand into his back pocket and yanked out a bottle of schnaps. He offered it to Tiny.

"Thanks." Tiny took it and swallowed deeply. He wiped

the back of his hand across his mouth, snorted and spat. "We fired at the same moment, Julius and me. Exactly the same moment—I wouldn't like to say which of us got the bastard first."

Porta held out his hand for the schnaps and laughed as he recalled the scene. "Did you see how all the rest of the shits turned green? When it happened, they all looked sick to their queasy stomachs. They knew damn well we'd done it on purpose, only they can't prove nothing. What's the betting we get stood free drinks all round tonight?"

"Here's hoping," said Tiny, and he spat again on the card table. "Think the jerk's in hell by now?"

"Where else? Him up there wouldn't want the bastard."

"You've said it." Tiny snatched back the bottle and stared thoughtfully at it a while. "Wonder if He'll want us when our time comes. What's your guess?"

"I ain't guessing." Porta shuffled the cards and rapidly dealt out two hands. "Got more important things to think about. Pick your cards up and get on with it."

"Okay." Tiny set down the bottle, obediently scraped his cards off the Feldwebel's broad back and took a cursory glance at them. "His brains was splattered all over the place—did you see 'em there? When we picked him up? All over the place."

"So?"

"So nothing." Tiny hunched a shoulder. "I just wondered if you'd seen 'em, that's all." Another thought suddenly came to him and he closed up his hand and beamed across at Porta. "I know what, I'll go and visit his missus, that's what I'll do. Cheer her up, see? Tell her he was just a lousy mean bastard anyway, so she hasn't lost nothing by it—specially not if I get into bed with her. She won't know what's hit her. She won't know her luck. After all," he said reasonably, "it's only fair—I bump off her old man, it's only right I go and screw her. You could almost say I owe it to her."

"You do," agreed Porta solemnly. "That's a very beautiful idea. I like it. It takes a bighearted guy like you to think of it. Come to that, I'm not at all sure the whole company doesn't owe it to her."

Together they finished off the schnaps and threw the bottle overboard. Porta laid out his hand with a flourish across the Feldwebel's backside. "Full house," he said simply.

It was late when they arrived back at the barracks, so

they parked the truck and left the body in the back. It was
there for almost a week before anyone remarked on it.

A couple of days later, shortly after the regiment had received orders to prepare for departure, a small detachment
of new troops was marched across the courtyard. A group of
us were standing by the windows, watching them, when
quite suddenly the Old Man turned and shouted to the
Legionnaire, "Hey, Alfred! Come and have a look at this!"

The Legionnaire pushed his way to the front of the group
and stared in the direction of the Old Man's pointing
finger. "Well, I'll be damned!" He laughed and punched the
Old Man joyously in the ribs. "If it isn't our old friend the
Stabsfeldwebel! Let's say hallo to him."

They opened the window and hung out, waving and
shouting. Stabsfeldwebel Stahlschmidt looked up. He evidently recognized them at once, because even from that
distance I could see him turn pale. The man marching at his
side was Obergefreiter Stever. He took one quick look and
turned away again with eyes full of dread. He was a man
who has lived to see his nightmares come true.

Porta stuck his head out of the window, between the
Legionnaire and the Old Man, and gave a shout of derisive
welcome. "You just made it! We're pulling out of here soon
—another couple of days and you might have missed the
train!"

The column marched on. In the center was a man with
a trumpet. On the green collar of his tunic could still be
made out the marks of the black SS badge which had been
ripped off. He looked up as he passed the window, and his
eyes rested with brief hope on Porta and then turned down-
ward again.

"Who's that?" I said. "A friend of yours?"

Porta smiled. "Just a business acquaintance," he murmured.

Hauptfeldwebel Edel treated the newcomers to his usual
warm welcome with a speech full of threats, abuse, hatred
and withering scorn.

"Anyone will tell you," he roared, "that to them as I like,
I'm as mild as a newborn lamb and as sweet as sugar. Unfortunately, there aren't that many people I like."

The new troops were left in no doubt as to his feelings
toward them. He put them on ablutions for the rest of the
week, with a warning that if the latrine bowls were not

polished to a high gloss at least twice a day, he would see to it personally that someone suffered for it.

Colonel Hinka strolled up as Edel came to the end of his introductory speech. He smiled benevolently all around, and for a moment the hearts of the new men lightened.

Edel swung about, clicked his heels together and smartly saluted. "Sir! Hauptfeldwebel Edel, sir, 5th Company, with twenty new recruits."

Hinka cast his eye over them and laughed softly to himself. There seemed, on the face of it, no very good reason for him to laugh, and the twenty new recruits found their hearts automatically sinking again. Colonel Hinka raised his head and looked across at the members of the 5th Company who were hanging from the windows enjoying the scene. He smiled.

"Thank you, Hauptfeldwebel. Get them warmed up a bit, will you? Make them feel at home. I think we'll put—" He looked again at the windows, and his smile broadened, "I think we'll put Kalb in charge of them."

"Yes, sir."

Edel turned in search of the Legionnaire, but he had already left the room and was at the door. He walked across to the colonel and they exchanged salutes.

"Twenty new recruits—we'll need to make them feel at home, get them used to our ways and so on—haven't got much time, but do the best you can—think you'll be able to manage it?"

The Legionnaire ran his eyes calculatingly over the twenty anxiety-ridden men. "No doubt about it, sir."

"Good. Let us just introduce ourselves and then I'll leave them in your hands."

Slowly, graciously, the colonel moved through the ranks of the new troops. He was followed officiously by the Hauptfeldwebel, smoothly and silently by the Legionnaire. Hinka paused before Stahlschmidt. "Your name?"

"Stahlschmidt, sir. Stabsfeldwebel . . ."

Hinka glanced through the papers he was holding. "You're from the garrison prison? Never been to the front before."

"No, sir, I couldn't, I . . ."

The colonel held up a hand and silenced him.

"Don't bother yourself with excuses, they're no longer necessary. It won't be so very many hours now before you see some fighting. I'm afraid your palmy days are over, the time has come for you to make a real contribution to the war effort. We shall see how you take to it." He looked back at the papers and frowned. "So— The reason you were sent to us was that you were found guilty of ill-treating the prisoners in your charge."

"They've got it all wrong, sir." Stahlschmidt spoke in a hoarse undertone, very much aware of the little Legionnaire lurking like a beast of prey in the background. "It's all a mistake, sir, I never did anything like that, I wouldn't be capable of it."

"You don't have to explain, Stabsfeldwebel. Everyone who is ever sent to us claims to be here by mistake. It's quite the accepted thing, I assure you."

The colonel passed on. Edel passed on. The Legionnaire stood a moment, staring up coldly at Stahlschmidt. At last, rubbing a finger thoughtfully up and down the scar on his face, he gave a slow smile and walked on without a word.

Hinka had now paused in front of Stever. "Another one from the prison? They must have been having quite a purge down there."

Stever gave a sickly smile. "It was all very unfortunate, sir."

"I'm sure it was."

The colonel nodded and passed on. Edel passed on. The Legionnaire paused.

"Go and find Obergefreiter Porta. Tell him I sent you. He'll know what to do with you. I've already had a word with him. He knows all about you."

Stever was too terrified to move. He stood staring at the Legionnaire, mesmerized by the long, livid scar, by the deep-set eyes, the firm, hard mouth.

"Well?" The Legionnaire raised an eyebrow. "I gave you an order. I suggest you carry it out."

He moved on in the colonel's wake, not troubling to look back to check whether Stever had left the ranks.

Hinka had stopped now before the ex-SS driver. He gestured toward the trumpet. "You play that thing, do you?"

"Yes, sir. I used to be a bugler in a cavalry regiment, sir. SS Florian Geyer."

"Did you, indeed? And what brings you to the front line with us?"

Kleber swallowed painfully and dropped his eyes. "Theft, sir—and dealings on the black market."

"What did you steal?"

"Er—potatoes, sir." Kleber's face was by now flushed to a fiery red. "Potatoes and sugar."

"Potatoes and sugar—pretty silly of you, wasn't it?"

"Yes, sir."

"Hm. Well—it'll do you good to see some fighting. Take your mind off food perhaps."

One by one the newcomers were scrutinized. Each of them eyed the colonel with awe, Edel with apprehension, and the Legionnaire with something approaching naked terror. At last the colonel saluted and turned away, followed by Hauptfeldwebel Edel, and they were left alone with the Legionnaire.

He at once tipped his kepi over his left eye (in his imagination, it was still the white kepi of the Foreign Legion) and stuck an illicit cigarette in his mouth. He lit it and spoke without taking it from his lips.

"Listen to me, you bunch of lousy bastards. You're new here and you don't know the ropes, but there's one person I advise you not to cross—and that's me. I've served with the French Foreign Legion. I've done three years with a special battalion, at Torgau. And now I'm here, and so are you, and all I can say is God help the lot of you!"

The Old Man watched from the window as the Legionnaire marched his little band of unfortunates away in the direction of the farthest and most secluded exercise yard, where he could do with them as he wished. The Old Man grunted. "Well, that'll keep him happy for a bit—this is something in the nature of a personal revenge, as far as he's concerned. The Legionnaire doesn't forgive in a hurry . . ."

He worked hard with his new recruits. For over three hours he kept them at it, running barefoot up and down the hard stone of the courtyard, out into the mud, crawling on their hands and knees, half drowning in the thick, glutinous earth, jumping over the ditch, back into the mud all those who failed to make it, mud up to their ears, mud in their eyes, mud in their mouths. And the Legionnaire working as hard as any of them, encouraging them with oaths in French and German, sweating as he ran up and down behind them, the eternal cigarette drooping from the corner of his mouth.

"Don't think I've got anything against you!" he yelled at them. "Far from it, I'm only doing my duty, I'm only thinking of your own good—a few weeks with me and you'll be able to stand up to any amount of this sort of thing! Down on your knees, that man over there—down, I said, *down*. Never mind the mud! Swallow the stuff, eat the stuff, what's it matter? Get through it first and worry about breathing later!"

Colonel Hinka was standing nearby, leaning wearily against a Tiger and watching as the Legionnaire put his men through their paces. Alfred Kalb had come through a harsh school—starvation, the Legion, Torgau, the 27th Tank Regiment—he had fought the war on many fronts and he had survived. A man had to be tough to survive. The colonel laughed and shook his head. He did not envy the sweating, struggling men in the Legionnaire's capable hands.

"Right, let's get running again!"

The Legionnaire seated himself on an upturned packing case. He set them running up and down the courtyard, into the mud, back up the courtyard, back into the mud. His voice grew hoarse with shouting and he brought out his whistle and taught them how to respond to it.

"One blow—that means you run. Two blows—down on the ground on your bellies. Three blows—jumping with your feet together. Right? Right. Let's give it a try."

They gave it a try for another hour. The men began to wilt, but the whistle was as fresh as ever.

"Okay, that'll do." The Legionnaire looked them over with a critical eye. "God knows how you'll make out at the front, in that condition. You won't last five minutes. Look, I'll tell you what I'll do. For your own good, mind. I shouldn't really waste the time on you, but it breaks my heart to see you like this—so for your own good and to toughen you up, we'll have a final hour's marching."

The twenty new men were dispersed among various barrack rooms around the camp. Stahlschmidt was moved in with us. We gave him a locker and he began putting his belongings away. He was silent and sullen and his face was awash in a permanent sea of sweat. He was stretched out on his bed when the Legionnaire came in. The Legionnaire walked straight across to him.

"There's something I want to say to you, Stahlschmidt. That show I just put on out there, that was entirely for your benefit. And there'll be more to come. The rest of them, I don't know and don't care about, it's you I'm interested in. It's providence has brought you here to us, and I aim to take every advantage of it."

Stahlschmidt sat up, still sweating. He gnawed at his

lower lip. "Listen, Kalb, I know you've got it in for me because of what happened to your lieutenant, but it wasn't my fault they executed him, for God's sake!"

"It was your fault he'd been kicked around and ill-treated and half killed before they even got him up there!" The Legionnaire pushed Stahlschmidt back against the wall, one hand gripping his throat. "Unfortunately we haven't yet been able to lay hands on the bastard that runs the show. He was clever enough to get you sent here, out of harm's way, while he still sits smug on his backside twiddling his thumbs in his office—I refer to Bielert, in case you hadn't realized it. His turn will come, don't you worry, but right at this moment it's your turn, and I'm going to make the best of a bad job and work out my feelings on you. If you don't die at my hands, Stahlschmidt, it'll be the Russians that get you. Either way, you're going to be put through the hoop until you're screaming for mercy—and there isn't any mercy at the front, Stahlschmidt."

He suddenly crashed the Stabsfeldwebel's head hard against the wall. "Stand up when I speak to you! That's one of the first things you've got to learn!"

Stahlschmidt stood up. The Legionnaire stepped back a pace, looking at him through narrowed eyes, then grunted and walked off to his own bunk. As soon as he was safely out of the way, Stahlschmidt raised a foot and gave a mighty kick of defiance at a nearby pair of boots, then collapsed once again onto his bed. Unfortunately the boots he had chosen to kick belonged to Tiny, who was sitting up cross-legged on a bunk stuffing a sausage into his mouth.

As Stahlschmidt's head met the pillow, Tiny was upon him. With a loud shout of wrath, he grabbed Stahlschmidt by the shoulder, pulled him around to face him and sent a fist crashing into his jaw. A volley of blows was heard, a series of thuds and a scream of protest from Stahlschmidt, who presently rolled off the bed and lay twisting and groaning on the ground at Tiny's feet. Tiny rolled him over onto his stomach, jumped up and down a few times on his back, then kicked him disdainfully into a heap under the bed. He clambered back into his own bunk and picked up a couple of bottles of beer, which he opened with his teeth and from both of which he began to drink simultaneously—a feat of which no one but Tiny was capable. He tossed the empty bottles contemptuously onto the moaning Stahlschmidt, who was painfully pulling himself to his feet. Stahlschmidt promptly collapsed again.

A new era had begun for the Stabsfeldwebel; an era of hard work and danger, when it was he who received all the blows.

Late in the night, full of beer and goodwill toward each other, Porta and Rudolf Kleber walked together up the steep, winding path of Landungsbrücke toward the School of Navigation behind the Military Hospital. At the top of the hill was a bench. They sat down side by side and were silent a while, listening to the muted night sounds of the city.

"Well, all right, if you play as well as you say you do," remarked Porta at last, "you'll be okay. But I'm warning you, old Hinka's the very devil to please. You got to be really on the ball—get me?"

"Let me show you. Just let me show you!"

Kleber reverently brought out his silver trumpet from its case. He licked his lips a few times, put the instrument to his mouth and looked sideways at Porta, from the corner of his eyes.

"I was with one of the very best regiments," he said. "Real fancy. I played at Nuremberg for the grand parade. I played at one of Adolf's banquets. I played . . ."

"Shove the boasting, get on with the performance!" snarled Porta.

Kleber stood up. He took a deep breath and raised the trumpet to his lips.

A cavalry fanfare rang out over the dark town.

Porta sat picking his nose, determinedly unimpressed.

Kleber followed up with an infantry fanfare, then turned to Porta impatiently. "Well, all right, what do you want? What do *you* suggest I play?"

"Search me." Porta stifled a yawn. "Depends what you know, doesn't it?"

"I could play you a blues."

"Can't have that," said Porta. "Unpatriotic. The blues is a Yank thing. We'd go straight to the brig if anyone heard you."

"That scare you?" Kleber challenged him with a sneer.

"Certainly not," said Porta. "But don't crucify it, that's all I ask. I'm always meeting people say they can play the blues and don't have a notion."

"Just listen to me," said Kleber. "Just shut up and listen."

The silvery brass bray of the trumpet blared deep into the night. Kleber knew well the risk he was running, but he was at heart a musician and the moment was all that mattered. He arched his back, pointing the trumpet up at the sky, up at the stars, and the sound rose wailing into the darkness. Some clouds sailed apart and revealed the moon, and the moon was reflected in the silver trumpet.

"Not bad," Porta nodded. "You can give us some more of that."

The sound burst exultantly upon the sleeping town. It could not help but call attention to itself. It was not long before a policeman appeared, puffing as he toiled up the hill. Kleber advanced on him reproachfully, frowning, daring him to interrupt. The policeman stood a while, catching his breath. He held his head on one side, listening to the music.

"Memphis Blues," he said at last. He walked over to Porta. "Memphis Blues—well, it's a long time since I heard that." He took off his helmet, wiped a sweating bald head with his handkerchief and sat down on the bench.

Two girls came wandering up the hill, lured there by the magic of Kleber's trumpet. Kleber was playing as if his very life was at stake. His audience sat in silence.

Kleber cocked an eyebrow at Porta. "Well?"

"It's all right," said Porta. "How about this one?" He whistled a few bars.

"Ah, yes!" said the policeman. "Deep River—I know that one."

"Hang on," said Kleber. "Don't rush me." He was the artist now. He had them in his power and he knew it. He made them wait.

Then the old blues melody caught them all and held them, and they heard the compulsive rhythm of the slaves, the beat of a million marching feet, the pounding of horses' hooves across the hard ground, the throbbing advance of tanks and motorized vehicles on their way to meet the enemy . . .

Kleber stopped playing. He was out of breath. He turned again to Porta. "Now what do you say?"

"Heard worse," Porta admitted, but with a grin. "I have heard worse."

"I should think so!" said the policeman indignantly. "What more do you want?"

"You don't understand," Porta told him. "This guy wants to play officially, see? For the company. You got to have the touch of the gods to do that. Not like playing with a band. Anyone can do that. You play for us, out at the front," he looked hard at Kleber, "you're sending men off to their death, see? Last thing some of 'em will ever hear, that old tin trumpet of yours—know what I mean?"

There was a silence. Porta had touched upon a world to which the rest of them had never belonged. A world where death was the only familiar, dependable fact, and where grown men became as babies as they struggled out of this life and into another.

"Yeah, I see what you mean," said Kleber. "I never thought of it that way before."

"It's not like playing for a parade," said Porta.

"No, I guess you're right."

"It's not like playing at one of Adolf's lousy banquets."

"How about this one?" Kleber suggested, suddenly brightening. " 'The Death of a Musician'—'Viva la Muerte . . .' "

The trumpet's sweet-strident voice rose sobbing into the still night air. It rose and it fell, weeping, sighing, trembling, as it told of the musician who played himself to death. Kleber bent down to the earth beneath his feet and bent back to the sky above him. The air was full of sorrow.

Viva la muerte. Viva la muerte . . .

"All right," said Porta. "I'll see to it. You can play for the company, I guess you'll do."

They went off together, without a word to the policeman or the two girls.

Eight days later, the regiment received its marching orders and at once there were the usual scenes of feverish activity in the barracks. For ourselves, we still had not been sent a replacement for Lieutenant Ohlsen. Colonel Hinka was going to take over temporarily, until we reached the front. By then they would surely have sent us someone else. But meantime we were quite content to have the colonel. He was preferable to a stranger, he had commanded the 5th Company in the days before his promotion and he was known to all us old hands.

Before we left, our new musician showed us what he could do. He played the fanfare of farewell, while we all stood listening:

Adieu, vieille caserne,
Adieu, chambrées puantes . . .

(Farewell, old barracks,
Farewell, stinking barrack rooms . . .)

We were off again. Back to the front. It caught you un-prepared every time. We had known that it must be, we had known it for sure these last few days, but still it caught you unprepared, and Kleber's plaintive trumpet calls brought lumps to many hardened throats.

Slowly the train pulled out of the station. Out of Hamburg, out of Germany, on our way back to the front. On our way to Monte Cassino. We didn't know it then, of course, Colonel Hinka hadn't yet opened his sealed orders. But that was where we were going. To Monte Cassino.

ABOUT THE AUTHOR

At fourteen SVEN HASSEL traveled around the world as a cabin boy on a freighter. In 1930 the unemployment situation in Denmark caused him to emigrate to Germany, where one could still find work. He enlisted in the German army in 1937 and was wounded in a cavalry regiment while fighting on the Polish Front. He was then transferred to the Second Tank Regiment which took part in the invasion of Poland in 1939. In 1941 he was sent into a disciplinary army regiment that fought in Russia under the worst conditions. He took part in military operations on all except the North African Front.